C IS FOR CORRUPTION

The Horsemen Series

Zoe Dunn & C.M. Bowen

Ebook ISBN: 979-8-9924435-2-3
Print ISBN:

Cover image created by:
https://getcovers.com/

Shattered Sirens and the colophon are registered to Shattered Sirens.

Published by:
Shattered Sirens, LLC
www.shatteredsirens.com

TRIGGER WARNINGS

This book contains themes and content that may be distressing or triggering to some readers. Please proceed with care if you are sensitive to any of the following:

- Loss of a loved one & grief
- Violence and gore
- Murder and death
- Torture
- Kidnapping & abduction
- Dubious consent
- Non-consensual behavior
- Organized crime activities
- Betrayal and deception
- PTSD and mental health struggles
- BDSM and kink-related elements
- Explicit sexual content
- Strong language and profanity
- Revenge-driven plotlines

Reader discretion is advised. Your well-being matters—please take care of yourself while engaging with this story.

*A lot of people decided any spice in romance made it erotica,
and that they weren't cool with it.
We took that personally.
So if you're here for the same reasons we're all here, enjoy the
increased number of smut scenes and thank a complainer.
To the complainers: Go ahead, keep complaining. Chapters 5,
9, 13, 25, 27, 31, 33, and 36 are dedicated directly to you.
We can do this all day.*

P.S. from Zoe: I have my tear jars ready so CRY, REBECCA!

PROLOGUE

Craig

My blood roared in my ears, drowning out everything except for Victoria and Joey's pained screams. From the corner of my eye, I saw Joey lurch forward. Time seemed to slow as Az moved to pin him to the ground as another gunshot rang out. Pain rocketed through the back of my skull, and the world went dark.

Rough material caressed my face as I blinked my eyes to adjust to the darkness. A sense of vertigo settled into the pit of my stomach, telling me that I was in motion as soft whimpers filled my ears. The strain in my shoulders and legs hit me before the rough scrap of ropes registered against my wrists.

"Bunny," I managed to croak out. "I'm here, Bunny. We're going to be alright."

A sharp sob was the only response before a harsh male voice called out.

"Quiet back there. Don't make me shut you up!"

I clenched my teeth to bite back a snarl as I struggled to shift my body closer to where I'd heard Victoria's whimpers.

"We're good for the crash," I heard Candy murmur from nearby. "Less than a minute out from the extraction point."

Before I could piece together what that meant, something slammed into us. My body was suddenly weightless before it slammed against the hard metal roof of the vehicle. My head cracked against what could only be a window, and the world went dark again.

My shoulders ached with the sensation of being stretched too far with my arms above my head. My eyes fluttered open, and I immediately squinted against the light. Taking inventory of my body as my eyes adjusted to the lights, I noted the cold bite of chains against my wrists and the rough feel of concrete barely brushing the tips of my toes. Frigid air licked my bare torso, causing me to shiver. The harsh, cold glare of factory lights buzzed above me, casting an unforgiving light over the room. It flickered now and then, making the shadows jump and crawl.

"You're awake."

I knew that voice. "Fancy seeing you here, Mel." I replied, forcing a grin to my lips.

I raised my head the best I could and blinked away the blurriness in my vision. The basement reminded me of where we housed our prisoners. The air was damp, and a chemical floral scent was doing a poor job of masking the same metallic tang of blood and the acrid ting of fear that coated every place like this. The place was a tomb. No windows, no way out. The walls seemed to press in, and the air was heavy. Stale. The kind of room where screams didn't carry, where the world outside didn't exist. I couldn't hear anything but the hum of the bulb and the faint drip of water from somewhere behind me.

"Who's your friend?" I asked, noticing another woman standing beside a metal table holding all the usual tools of the trade—pliers, blades, clamps–some clean, some not. A car battery sat on a workbench in the corner, with cables coiled neatly beside it. Organized. I could respect that, even if I was about to be on the wrong end of it.

"None of your fucking business, horseman." The woman snarled.

"Ohh, someone woke up on the wrong side of the bed this morning." I laughed. The woman sneered, baring her teeth as she pushed her short black hair away from her face, revealing the shaved side of her head with the Golden Devils tattoo.

"Enough." Melissa barked. "This isn't a social visit, Craig. Though, I must say, I'm disappointed that of all people, one of you is chained to my ceiling."

"Sorry to be such a disappointment, sweetheart." I snorted.

Melissa looked at the other woman and jerked her head in my direction. My eyes narrowed as her apprentice grabbed a hunting knife from the table and stalked toward me.

"I'm going to ask once, before I let Anna here have a go at you. Why did the Horsemen take the Bristol girl?"

"What?" I asked, choking on a laugh of disbelief. "We didn't *take* anybody."

"Our information says differently, Craig. We have all the proof we need to know that your crew broke their protection contract and decided to take the girl." Mel paused, sliding a folded piece of paper from her back pocket before unfolding it to read from. "Posted by Voidphase: So, you all think you're hunters now, huh? A free-for-all on the girl is bold. Stupid, but bold. She's ours, and you know what that means? Come sniffing around here and you won't leave the way you came. I don't care who you are or your reputation. None of you make it out alive if you try to take what's ours. I've seen your kind before–desperate, greedy, willing to stab each other in the back for scraps. So, maybe some of you little rats are smarter than the others. The person who put this bounty on our head, who told you little shits you could take what belongs to us. Turn them over. If you can prove it's them, maybe we'll think about letting you enjoy the reward for helping us take this player off the board. The reward? It's her. Yeah, I'm offering you exactly what you're all out here tripping over yourselves for anyway. So, who's feeling brave? Or better yet–who's feeling smart? Clock's ticking."

I couldn't help the snort that left me. "That's your evidence? Seriously, Mel?"

"There's over three dozen messages on the boards offering her up for information from you, Craig. Each one more antagonistic and lewd than the last. It's clear your crew decided to throw out your code once shit got too deep. I didn't want to believe it considering I know the history of you boys, but the proof is irrefutable. Still, I can't help but wonder what made you break your code. So, tell me, Craig. Why was *this* the thing, and what else did you boys have planned for the Bristol girl when all was said and done."

"I already told you, Mel. We didn't take her. Those messages, that's us working to protect her."

"Wrong answer." Mel nodded to Anna and stepped back.

I hissed at the first slice of the blade against my flesh. The cut was shallow, for now, but just enough to make the pain burn up my chest. I gritted my teeth and sneered at the pair of women.

"I hope you cleaned that knife. Infection would really fuck up my tattoos." I said as casually as I could manage, raising a brow and giving Anna a patient expression. She scowled and took a hasty swipe at me with her knife, digging a deep cut into my stomach by my belly button.

I couldn't stop the yell that clawed out of my throat. *Fuck, that hurts...* The sticky feeling of blood down my stomach had the first thought of genuine concern flickering through my mind.

"Hey! Woah, there, new girl. Mel, you really need to have this girl read an anatomy book. A little further to the left, and you wouldn't get any answers out of me, even if there were any to get." I said through gritted teeth.

Mel seemed unperturbed as she continued to toss out the same questions over and over as her unskilled apprentice hacked away at my torso. It didn't take long before I couldn't offer any more witty banter as a cover. It took every ounce of control I had to keep from screaming as the blade bit into me time and time again.

I was back on my knees in the middle of the road surrounded by Jackals, except something wasn't right. There was a haziness to everything that made it seem far away. Candy's malicious smile was twisted into something more bizarre and inhuman as she pointed her gun toward Rich. Her finger tensed on the trigger, the bullet leaving the muzzle in slow motion. My eyes tracked it as it slowly closed the distance to Rich. It felt like hours ticked by before he collapsed backward on the pavement.

Leighton snarled something beside me. Turning my head to look at him, I barely had time to catch the pain that streaked across his features before they twisted into the monster he became whenever he worked. He moved at the same time as Az did, tackling the Jackal that stood behind him to the ground as Az forced Joey under him. The men who'd had them at gunpoint fired their weapons, the bullets barely missing my friends.

My eyes blinked open and landed on Mel leaning against the metal table with her arms crossed. The dried and flaking blood across my upper body left me with an all-consuming need to scratch, but my hands were still chained above my head.

"Welcome back." Mel spoke. "You ready to talk now?"

"Your girl needs more work. I could give her a few pointers, even though this wasn't usually my job. I pay attention." I huffed out, my voice raspier than I wanted it to be.

Mel sighed heavily. "We could have done this the easy way, you know. All you had to do was answer the questions."

"Mel. I *did* answer your questions. It's not my fault you don't believe the truth when it's dropped in your lap. You always were a stubborn woman." I said, trying to get her to understand I was sincerely telling her the truth.

"I'm going to give you some time to think about the situation you're in. Maybe a little time to reflect will leave you more willing to cooperate." Mel pushed away from the table and started to walk away.

"Wait, Mel!" I called out, causing her to pause, "Tell me something... Is Bunny okay? Did she make it out of the wreck?" My tone was almost pleading; I needed to know she was okay.

She didn't answer me. Instead, she flipped the lights off and left me in the dark. I don't know how long I hung there in the dark. My mind turned everything that had happened over, looking for any answers, though I wasn't even sure what questions I was asking beyond the one Mel refused to answer.

I felt the cold steel press against the back of my skull. The air was thick like it had been smothered with smoke. My heartbeat was so loud it threatened to drown out everything else, but nothing could drown out the sound of Rich's voice–heavy, pleading, and breaking as he begged Victoria to choose anyone but him. Telling her everything we'd all known far longer than he had. Candy raised her gun, Victoria spoke, but I couldn't make out the words.

The gun went off.

The sound split the world open, sharp and violent, and Rich's head snapped back as the bullet tore through him. Blood sprayed into the air, catching the light like some sick kind of halo. He crumpled, folding backward, and hit the ground with a sickening thud. Candy's calm and commanding voice cut through the static in my mind as I watched the scene unfold.

"Last chance," she said. "Choose, or I'll do it for you."

*I could hear Victoria, my Victoria–**our** Victoria–screaming. Screaming like I'd never heard her before, her voice raw with a pain that shook me to my core. I'd never get that sound out of my mind. She dropped to her knees, reaching for Rich's body like she could undo it. Her hands shook, desperate, but he was gone. There was nothing that could take this back.*

Joey roared, his mouth open in a furious scream, but it was a sound of loss, not rage. Az tackled Joey to the ground, trying to keep him from charging forward, trying to save what little he could from the chaos. They were struggling, Joey clawing to get away.

Two more gunshots. And they stopped fighting. Az lay on top of Joey's body, and both of them eerily still.

Leighton. The sound that tore out of him was inhuman, some feral animal taking over. His body shifted with rage so fast it was like the earth beneath him might crack open. He surged forward, hands outstretched, and tore through the Jackal behind him like a paper doll. A blur of violence. The crunch of bone. Nothing was going to stop him.

Until the thunderous sound of buckshot tore through the air, and Leighton's body blew backward, landing on Az and Joey like he was leaning back against them... with a hole in his chest and blank, lifeless eyes staring at me.

And here I was. Watching. Trapped. Still kneeling, the gun pressed into my skull, powerless.

I watched Victoria claw through the grime and blood on the ground, unsure where to go first. Her screams and cries broke something fundamental inside me. It was the symphony that marked the end of my family.

I woke with a start, jerking against my chains. My dreams were another form of torment. Taunting me with the deaths of all my brothers. Blowing out a harsh breath, I worked to reassure myself that Az, Leighton, and Joey were alive. They could have gotten away after I'd been knocked unconscious. I just needed to figure out how to get out of my current predicament, and I would find them alive and well.

"Ready to answer my questions now?" Mel's voice cut through the darkness just before the lights flicked on overhead, temporarily blinding me.

"I told you, Mel, I already gave you the truth."

"I wish this could have been different, Craig." She sighed, snapping her fingers in a signal that had Anna stepping forward.

Round and round, we went again. Mel peppered me with the same questions, and I gave the same answers. Her apprentice slicing me open, each cut sloppier and more deadly than the last. It felt like hours, maybe even days, had passed, my limbs growing heavier, my mind growing foggier, and a cold sensation settling into my bones. The blood loss was dizzying, and I knew it was only a matter of time before Mel's apprentice screwed up and killed me.

The heavy, familiar scent of coffee and wood wafted through the air. The dining room was bright and familiar. The table was cluttered with papers, some of Az's books, and coffee mugs. Like nothing had changed. But my mind itched. Everything had changed. It felt like a trick, the kind that didn't make sense no matter how long you stared at it.

I stood there in the doorway for a long moment, confused. Rich was sitting at the head of the table, his eyes flicking up from the paper he was reading. He looked... like he was just taking a break. Like it was any other morning.

I shook my head, feeling something deep in my chest tighten. I could feel the burn of tears in my eyes as I watched him raise his head. A wash of relief stole over me. He was here. He was whole. He was... alive.

"Morning Craig." His deep baritone almost had me crying, and I shook my head, trying to shake it off.

"I had the wildest dream last night," I said, entering the dining room. "Zero out of ten, would not recommend. Where's Bunny?"

"Honestly, I was surprised it wasn't her that you called up in your last moment. Didn't figure you'd want to hang out with ghosts." He said, tilting his head, his gaze softening just slightly. He looked tired now that I got closer.

"What?" I asked, brows furrowing. The need to back away and run from the room was creeping up my spine.

"Craig, you know what this is. You've been playing what happened in your head too much to really believe it was just a dream you had." He spoke slowly as if he were explaining it to a child.

*I took a step back, shaking my head. "No. That wasn't **real**. I refuse to accept that was real."*

Rich didn't answer right away. Instead, he stood slowly, his movements almost too careful as he approached me. When his hand landed on my shoulder, it was heavy but gentle, and the reality of the situation crashed into me. He gave me a sad smile, but it only made the inside of my chest worse.

"I'm gone, Craig." He said softly. "The others," one of his shoulders shrugged slightly, "I only know what you know. They could be alive."

"How are you here?"

"Craig..." he sighed softly and pinched the bridge of his nose. The move made me want to cry. "I'm dead. You're dreaming, man. And... you're not doing well. Pay attention to yourself for a second... that pain you're feeling? The shit they're putting your body through? It's killing you."

I felt the room spin, and my legs nearly buckled beneath me. Everything started to blur around the edges. I began to feel the pain in my torso, my arms, my legs. My whole body hurt. And I was cold. So fucking cold.

"That fucking amateur." I groaned.

"You're dying because of what they're doing to you, but you're letting it happen." Rich said, eyeing me expectantly.

"How the fuck am I supposed to get out of this?!" I snapped. Rich's grip on my shoulder tightened like he wanted to shake me at the same time he was trying to steady me.

"You've always been smarter than this, Craig. You can figure it out. I can't do it for you. But you have to wake up. Right now. Stop letting yourself fucking die. You're all Victoria has left right now, man. I can't be there, but you are. You know the game. You've played it most of your life. Now, **figure it out**. Don't let yourself die. Wake up."

"But–"

"No buts. You can't keep her safe if you're not alive to do it, Craig!"

"I don't–"

"Wake up, Craig!" Rich bellowed, his arm cocking back before his palm cracked against the side of my face.

My eyes popped open to find myself nearly nose-to-nose with Mel.

"There you are. I thought we lost you for a sec." She smiled, stepping back and revealing the Golden Devil's doc standing just behind her in a white coat. "It seems we've had quite the misunderstanding. Doc got you cleaned and patched up as best she could, but when you didn't wake up at first, we thought you were a goner."

I opened my mouth to retort, the pain in my body stopping me short. To my surprise, my arms moved when I shifted to wrap them around my now heavily bandaged torso.

"Yeah... I know. I'm supposed to take you to Helen now that you're awake. Do you think you can walk or do you need a wheelchair?" Mel asked.

"Fuck you. I'd rather crawl there on my own than take shit from you. I'll manage." I snarled before spitting at her feet to drive home my point.

CHAPTER ONE

Victoria

I rolled over with a groan, squeezing my eyes shut tighter against the brutal ache in my head. My head throbbed in time with my heartbeat until I forced my eyes open to search for something to dull the pain. They landed on a sleek, black nightstand that held a glass of water and two small pills. The world threatened to tilt as I eased myself upright. Hastily, I snatched the pills up and tossed them in my mouth, washing them down with water despite knowing it might not have been the wisest decision.

I allowed myself to take in my surroundings as I waited to see whether the pills would ease my headache or do something horrible to me. I was sitting on a king-sized bed, surrounded by pale blue blankets. There was a dresser against the far wall, the same sleek black as the nightstand, and the walls matched the comforter pooling around my waist. Sheer ivory curtains covered the lone window that let the light of the dying sun filter gently into the room.

Everything that had happened came flooding back, stealing my breath as I fought to get my bearings. Tears pricked my eyes, and a scream pressed against my throat, threatening to tear free, but if I'd learned anything from my men, I couldn't break down. Not yet. Not here. I needed to keep my wits about me if I had any chance of getting back to them.

My legs wobbled as I forced myself to stand. Steadying

myself against the nightstand, I took another look around the room. There were three doors. One of them had to be my way out. I carefully made my way to the closest door, opening it to find an ensuite bathroom. The second led to a large walk-in closet with clothing that looked suspiciously close to my size. The third was locked. The handle jiggled uselessly under my hand. Gently resting my forehead against the wooden door, I let out a frustrated groan before gathering my thoughts.

After a few moments, I straightened my spine and moved to the closet. From what I'd gathered in my time with the guys, I was most likely in the hands of the Jackals. I didn't know what they wanted me for, but I knew they wanted me alive. Whatever awaited me outside of this room, I was going to meet it in my version of armor. My nose scrunched as I noted the size was indeed mine on the tags of the black pencil skirt and emerald green silk blouse I'd snagged. I moved to the bathroom with purpose, having to pause to steady myself once, still determined that my captors wouldn't come in here to find a cowering, simpering victim.

As I entered the bathroom, I set the clothes on the counter and felt the world shift as I caught a glimpse of my hands for the first time. I hadn't let myself see it before, but now that I was standing there staring at my hands, it was all I could see. Dark, dried blood clung to the filth and dirt that coated my exposed skin. I felt bile rise in my throat.

"It's not his..." I whispered as images of Rich flashed in my mind like some kind of painful slide show.

"You're whatever we say you are." He'd tilted his head to the side as he appraised me. I could only imagine what I looked like through his eyes. But I'll never forget what he'd looked like to me... Tall, muscular, and undeniably handsome, he'd looked every inch like the man in charge. I could remember feeling like it was hard to breathe in his presence.

My head spun. And I had to lean against the counter.

Blood on my hands...

"It's not his..." I said again.

"No, Princess. We're... we're gonna work on that, okay? But you gotta come home, baby." His deep voice was comforting and soft as he brushed a lock of hair behind my ear. He'd looked like he was pleading with me. And I hadn't understood it then, but I couldn't have denied him anything if I'd tried.

Tears stung my eyes, my vision blurred, and I had to put my head on the cool granite of the counter, sucking in deep breaths of air.

"It's not... his..." My voice cracked.

"It absolutely does make my life easier knowing that you're safe, Baby girl. Look..." I could remember how his hands had felt, his thumbs brushing away tears on my cheeks even as an unknown infection was eating him up from the inside. He'd been in pain, but he was always looking out for me. "I'm sorry, I was too harsh. I know this hasn't been easy on you, this isn't the world you belong to but it's found its way to you anyway. They–we have to know that you're okay..."

My stomach rolled, and my legs were threatening to give out from under me. Rich's face flashing through my mind wouldn't stop. Replaying every moment we'd had together like a sick reel.

"It's.. it's not... his..." the words were a barely audible whimper as they left my lips.

"Don't you pick me, Babygirl. I... I don't deserve it for how I hurt you. Pick someone who was honest with how they loved you. If I could have, I would have spent the rest of my life making it up to you. I'm so fucking sorry for being too stubborn. Too stupid to just... I love you, Victoria. And if I could go back, I'd have told you so much sooner... I was so caught up in my own bullshit, I couldn't see the forest for the trees. I wish more than anything I could take it all back. That we could start over at the beginning and I could do

it right. I need you to know that. I might have been a better man with you, if we'd had the chance. If I'd given us the chance. But I'm serious, don't you pick me, Baby." His dark eyes had looked up at me with such pain and tenderness as he begged me to save anyone but him. This larger-than-life man that had given everything to keep me safe...

"It's not his," I sobbed, knowing it to be true but unable to believe it.

It was all my fault...

My stomach roiled, and I lurched toward the toilet, barely making it in time before my empty stomach violently revolted. My shoulders heaved as I vomited bile. My fingers gripped the porcelain tightly as if it could somehow be the liferaft to save me from everything that had happened. Everything I had lost. Rich was gone. I'd lost him before I ever got to love him the way he deserved—the way I'd wanted to, even when I refused to acknowledge it to myself.

"What is it going to take for you four to screw your heads back on straight?! Is one of us going to have to fucking die keeping her alive before you realize this whole thing is a fucking MISTAKE!?" The thunderous sound of the wooden dining table splintering had me rushing down the stairs for fear they'd killed each other. He'd known somehow...

I froze, remembering what Rich had said to Joey. It felt like someone had injected ice water into my veins. If I had listened to Rich if I had acted the way he'd told me to. If I'd understood that he wasn't just on a power trip to cage the little rich girl. He was trying his damndest to keep me safe, to keep them all safe. The responsibility he shouldered over all of us...

"And all I could do was fight him about it..." I murmured to myself as I stood from where I'd hugged the toilet and lost the non-existent contents of my stomach.

I had protested I wasn't a spoiled brat, and while I hadn't been anything like most of the people in my social circle, I had absolutely been the spoiled rich girl with no idea how the real world worked. That wasn't even entirely true. My *home* had been blown up; I *should* have known better. But I was too stupid to see that the attack on the manor wasn't just a fluke, that the danger was truly something my status couldn't protect me from like it had always done before. I *had* to be smarter if I didn't want his death to be in vain.

"Get up, Bitch," I hissed to myself. "Clean yourself off, put your fucking game face on, and be the smart woman he thought you could be."

Forcing every painful thought that kept trying to creep in aside, I quickly discarded my filthy clothing, turned on the shower, and climbed in. The initial shock of cold before the water warmed helped me steel myself against whatever might be coming next. With each swirl of blood and filth washing down the drain, I hardened myself, preparing for battle. The severe bun I twisted my wet hair into once I'd climbed from the tub and toweled off, the makeup I'd found in the drawer, each layer sharp and dark, the outfit I'd selected. Each was a piece of my armor, preparing me to step into a role I wasn't born to play.

Padding barefoot back through the spacious bedroom, I found a pair of black, red-bottomed heels. I briefly considered whether they were the right choice with how my head still throbbed and spun, but I knew they were the *only* choice to complete my armor. Slipping them onto my bare feet, I settled onto the end of the bed, my spine straight, hands in my lap the way finishing school taught me, and stared at the locked door, waiting for God only knew what.

Darkness had fully claimed the room by the time the handle jiggled. I hadn't moved from my place, letting the darkness blanket me like a cloak. The door swung inward, the light outside silhouetting a petite figure, before the bedroom light was flipped on. I kept my face blank as I watched the round-faced woman with long black hair fly toward me in a rage. She had thick lips and perfectly feminine features that, had she not been in a rage, would have been almost doll-like in her beauty.

"You could have saved him." She hissed, inches from my face, causing me to rear back slightly. For a moment, I thought she meant Rich. "Why didn't you pick Joey? You stupid bitch."

Confusion clouded my mind and tied my tongue.

"You may be protected, but I will find a way to pay you back for this." she snarled as she grabbed my upper arm in an iron grip and yanked me to my feet.

I allowed her to drag me from the bedroom and down the long hallway. Whoever this woman was, she radiated hatred for me with each step. I could only imagine how badly things would go if I said a word to her.

"That will be all, Ciara." A familiar woman's voice called out as I was jerked into a dimly lit sitting room.

"Helen?" I spoke, my eyes taking in Reginald Humphreys' first wife before shifting to her right, where her daughter sat. "Sophia?" My eyes slid left, and I gasped. "Tiffany?"

Tiffany rose from her seat and raced to throw her arms around me. "You're safe. I promise, you're finally safe."

I pulled back slightly, confusion plain on my face. "What are you talking about? How am I here? What is going on?"

"Tiffany, why don't you allow Victoria to take a seat so we can discuss everything." Helen said, raising one brow at my friend.

Tiffany nodded before leading me to an empty high-backed chair and then returning to her place on Helen's left.

"Victoria," Helen smiled softly, "I'm glad that we were able to get you out safely, though our physician says you have a mild concussion and some minor bruising from the car accident. Unfortunately, that couldn't be avoided if we wanted it to be believable."

"I– Ms. Arnoult, I don't understand."

"Please, Victoria, call me Helen. You know I think of Tiffany as my own, and you are as close as she is with her own sister, Sophia, there's no need for formalities between family."

"Helen," I said, testing the feel of her name. "I don't understand what's happening. I thought... Wait... Please tell me I am losing my mind and you're not the leader of the fucking Jackals!" I shrieked.

Helen's lip curled in disgust. "Absolutely not. I am the head of the Golden Devils, darling. Sophia is my heir, and Tiffany is learning the ropes. Though, I will deny all of that vehemently should you think turning me over to the police is the play here."

I raised my hands to rub my temples. "This doesn't make any sense," I mumbled. "The Jackals are the ones that killed Rich and took me captive."

"Yes, and no. Candy is one of ours. She's been working as a double agent for years. When Tiffany brought your situation to my attention, well, it was time to extract Candy and go over her intel so we could clean this city up once and for all."

My eyes snapped to my best friend. "You? You did this?" Shock and anger warred under my skin. "Do you know what you've done?"

"I know you thought you were safe with the Horsemen, Tory, but they were planning to trade you for intel." She said softly.

"You fucking bitch!" I screamed, bolting out of my seat so fast it fell behind me. "It's your fault he's dead."

My body seemed to move on its own toward Tiffany. Every ounce of pain and grief within me twisted into an inferno of rage and a desire to *kill*, no—*destroy*. In a blink, I was in front of my former best friend, my fist connecting with her face the way my men had taught me. Animalistic sounds ripped from my mouth as I used every bit of training they'd given me. My vision darkened with the destructive need boiling over inside me. I didn't even realize I'd managed to take Tiffany to the floor until I felt arms looping through my own and locking behind me as I was pulled away.

"Victoria," Helen tsk'd, a look of disappointment on her face. "What has gotten into you? This behavior is not acceptable for someone of your breeding."

"My... my behavior?" I shouted in outrage. "My behavior seems pretty fucking acceptable when I find out my so-called best friend is the reason one of the men I love is dead." I let my gaze fall to where Tiffany sat on the floor, being tended to by someone I didn't recognize. "I will never forgive you for this. If I see you again, I will do what I should have been allowed to do here, and fucking kill you. Do you understand?"

Tiffany's eyes widened in alarm. "You don't understand, Tory. The Horsemen broke their own creed. They were planning to give you to anyone who could bring them information on the head of the Jackals. They were offering to pimp you out among other horrible shit. I couldn't let that happen."

I rolled my eyes and scoffed. "You think I didn't know about the message board posts?"

Tiffany's mouth fell open in shock.

"My men *love* me, they would have never actually done any of those things to me. I told Craig I didn't want the specific details, but he talked to me about what he wanted to do to try and flush out information."

"I couldn't know that," Tiffany said, her voice barely above a whisper. "I looked for you after news broke about the manor. I tried every contact I had and *nobody* could find you. None of my calls went answered, nothing. And then the posts started on the message board. What else was I supposed to think, Tory? Everything.. *Everything* pointed to you being in danger with them."

"You could have trusted that I would have found a way to reach you if I were in danger!" I bellowed.

"This isn't your world, Victoria." Tiffany retorted. "You don't know how this shit works. They never would have given you the opportunity to call for help."

"That's rich, coming from some boozed out party girl who—" I started.

"I think that is quite enough, girls." Helen interjected. "It appears we have acted on a misunderstanding that we must now rectify. Tiffany, find Melissa and let her know to bring Craig here, have yourself tended by the physician when you're done."

Helen motioned for me to sit as Tiffany slipped from the room, her shoulders hunched forward. Righting my chair, I let myself collapse into it. Time ticked by slowly as I seethed, my anger toward Tiffany growing with each passing minute. Sophia attempted to make small talk with me while we waited, but I couldn't be bothered to respond. I felt like I'd aged a decade when I finally heard two sets of footsteps nearing the room. Turning toward the doorway, I caught sight of a woman leading Craig into the room.

I lurched out of my chair and hurried to close the distance between us. My eyes roamed over Craig's body, taking in the sheer number of gauze bandages covering his torso. A number of them were stained with fresh blood as if the wound they covered still bled.

"I'm okay, Bunny." He whispered, taking my face in his hands and pressing his forehead to mine.

"This is far from okay," my voice was thick with tears I struggled to hold back. "What did they do to you?"

"Nothing I wouldn't have done if I were in their shoes." He shrugged, wincing.

"You are far too patient with people, Craig." I said softly, pulling back and tracing my fingers over his face like I was trying to convince myself that he was real. "I don't know what I'd have done if I lost you too."

"You'd have survived, Bunny. And then you would have found the others so they could enact your vengeance." He smirked. "But don't go thinking I was going to make it easy for them to take me from you, Bunny."

Before I could stop myself, I slipped my arms around his waist to hug him. Craig hissed in pain before his arms settled around me.

"I am going to murder Tiffany the next time I see her and

I don't mean that as a turn of phrase. I mean I am literally going to gut that vapid bitch alive."

Craig's eyes widened in shock for a moment before a grin split his face, and pained laughter bubbled out from him. "Don't... don't make me laugh, Bunny. It hurts to laugh. I know you're not being funny; I was just surprised."

I opened my mouth to respond, but the sound of Helen clearing her throat behind me pulled our attention to her.

"Mr. Dougherty, I would like to apologize for the misunderstanding that has led us here. It is clear from this little display that you are very much in love with Victoria, and from the way she reacted that she is with you, and the intel we had that led us to believe otherwise was pure misdirection."

I helped move Craig over to sit in a chair, even though every part of my body was loathe to let him out of my arms. I settled for standing behind him. I fought the urge to fuss over his injuries while waiting for him to address Helen.

"Ms. Arnoult, while your apology is acknowledged, I think I can speak for everyone when I say it's far from accepted. Your hastiness in not seeking us out cost Rich his life, nearly cost me mine, and our organization suffers from the losses you've caused." Craig said, his voice still pained as he sat up straighter in his chair.

"To be fair, Mr. Doughtery, the attack from the Jackals against your organization was in motion already. Our mole simply capitalized on it to extract Victoria from what we thought was a dangerous situation. She was not authorized to eliminate any of your men, only to show as much force as required to retrieve Victoria, and one of you for questioning, while maintaining her cover."

"Well then you need to get a leash on your little psycho–" I snapped, reeling as Helen offered us technicalities to answer for what had happened because of her people.

"Bunny. I know," Craig said, patting my hand on his shoulder. His eyebrow twitched, and I could see the tightening in his jaw. "Ms. Arnoult, I respect that you weren't the orchestrator of the entire situation. However, that doesn't change the fact that your involvement led to losses that we wouldn't have otherwise taken. Your mole murdered Rich in cold blood in what seemed to be a game for her. This, I'm going to hope, was well beyond anything you would have been aware of when it happened." His voice was steel as he leaned forward, resting his arms on his knees. I cringed internally at the pain he was putting himself in to look strong. "You *knew* Richard Innocenti, Helen. You should have gone to him directly about this before acting on information so inconsistent with the way we do things that it should have given you pause."

"I will not deny that Candy wildly overstepped the bounds of her orders. For that, we will make amends. But it has been a long time since we worked with your crew. You and I both know how doing the things to make it in this world can change you. I am willing to hand over my best hitwoman and intelligencer by giving you Candy in reparation for her overstep."

"I want Tiffany." I spat out before Craig could respond. "She deserves to pay for this too." Craig looked at me briefly, his brows furrowed as he searched my face.

"Bunny... You can be angry with me for this later. But no, we're not going to take Tiffany as reparations. That's a road you don't want to go down. And besides, the reparations are owed to the Horsemen, which you are not."

I bit my tongue to avoid arguing with him. As much as I wanted to rail against his assertions and demand my due, I knew it wasn't the place for that. Instead, I swung sharply between relief that he was alive and stewing in silent anger as I tuned out the rest of his negotiations with Helen.

CHAPTER TWO

Az

Victoria's screams rent the air as Rich crumpled backward. Time seemed to speed up around me as my body moved without thought to pin Joey beneath me. His anguished bellows mingled with Victoria's screams to form a sickening crescendo as he fought against my hold.

"Stay down." I barked, struggling to maintain my grip as his elbows slammed into my gut.

My legs wound around Joey's in a desperate bid to stop his flailing attempts to free himself and reach Rich's lifeless body. I barely noted the gunshots ringing in my ears, too focused on subduing the wild thing my friend had become. From the corner of my eye, I saw Leighton's hand fist on the ground in front of him before he twisted to face the man holding him at gunpoint, nearly too fast for me to track. My attention was snapped back to Joey as his elbow connected with my ribs.

"Damn it, Joey. Stop fighting me." I snarled, balling one hand into a fist before slamming it into the side of his head. "You're going to get us all fucking killed."

"Az, let me go! Rich!" Joey screamed again, still struggling even as I pulled his arms behind his back. "*Rich!*"

"He's gone, Little Brother! And I'm not letting you get shot trying to do something fucking stupid!"

"I could use a little help here!" Leighton called out. "Fuck.

Az, they're taking them!"

I risked a glance away from Joey to see Leighton struggling to keep our attackers at bay. The feral grin he gave them revealed his bloody teeth, and I had to fight back a gag as I noted the body by his feet, neck torn away in a macabre display.

"I can't keep ripping necks with my teeth here, fellas," Leighton cackled before turning serious. "And I can't go after our girl and Craig while managing these fuckers."

It was then I noticed the stark absence of Victoria's screams. My entire body tensed the need to find and protect thrumming through every cell of my being as my eyes scanned the area. Joey seemed to sense the shift in me, breaking free of my hold and scrambling to Rich's body.

"Where?" I barked.

"That way," Leighton replied, firing shots from his stolen weapon into the advancing group of men before pointing in the direction behind our SUV.

"Can you hold them off?" I asked.

"*Can you hold them off?*" Leighton mimicked. "If Joey could snap the fuck out of it, *maybe* we get out of this alive."

I turned my gaze back to where Joey had fallen next to Rich's body, seeming to stare down at him without really seeing anything. His hands hovered close but not touching him either.

"Fuck." I grumbled, grabbing the gun off one of the dead Jackals. I scrambled over to Joey, grabbed him by his shoulders, and hauled him to his feet. Turning him to face me, I drew back and slapped him. That did it. Joey blinked a few times in a daze before his gaze shifted to a dark rage I'd never seen before. "He's already gone, and he wouldn't want you to stand here and let yourself get killed too." I snapped, putting the gun in his hands. "Get your shit together and help Leighton, or *none* of us make it out of this alive."

Joey had barely wrapped his hand around the gun when a sharp whistle tore through the air. My head snapped toward the sound, and it was all I could do to keep my mouth from dropping open in shock. The men who'd been advancing on us were now retreating. Piling into their vehicles as quickly as they could while trying to dodge Leighton's shots.

"What they fuck is happening?" Leighton asked, as confused as I was. "They have us. They fucking have us, and they're just.... Running away?"

"I don't have a fucking clue, but we need to get Rich's body and move before they change their minds."

"What about *Ma Petit* and Craig?"

My bloodied hands tore through my hair as I tried to think, coming up with nothing of use. "I don't know. I don't *fucking know.*"

"We can't just do nothing." Leighton balked.

"Don't you think I know that? Fuck, Leighton. We should be dead. All of us. Not just..." my voice cracked. "Not just Rich. This isn't... He's supposed to be here to tell us what the fuck to do." My words grew more frantic as I began to pace. "This isn't like our other skirmishes, this is... this... Fuck!"

My head rocked to the side as Leighton's palm cracked across my cheek. "Snap out of it. Fuck, you're supposed to be the more levelheaded one here. Psycho," he pointed at himself before pointing at Joey, "Kid brother," then pointing at me, "Az-hole."

"What... the fuck does that even mean!?" I snapped.

"It *means* fuckface, that you've had to step into Rich's shoes before. So fucking do it." Leighton hissed, slapping me a second time before bellowing. "Catharsis!"

I don't know why it worked, but it did. When my ears stopped ringing, I looked around the scene again, and I could feel the panic ebbing away. We needed to get the fuck out of dodge, and we sure as fuck weren't leaving Rich behind.

"Body or brother?" I asked Leighton, using the term to compartmentalize what was happening.

Leighton studied me momentarily just as police sirens sounded through the night. "Brother."

As quickly and carefully as I could, I loaded Rich's body

into the back of the SUV while Leighton handled Joey. None of us spoke as the vehicle doors shut around us, and we tore away from the scene. With nowhere else to go, I turned us toward the Spotted Cobra. We couldn't be touched there, assuming Harrison didn't toss us out on our asses.

I knew we looked like hell when we finally pulled into the gravel lot of the Cobra and unloaded from the vehicle. Joey let out a pained sound, his hand lingering on the door a moment longer than necessary before he straightened to his full height and turned toward the bar entrance. We pushed through the doors, nearly shoulder to shoulder, catching Mags and Harrison's attention immediately. I swept my gaze around the room, thankful the place was basically empty aside from the father-daughter duo.

"What the fuck happened to you boys?" They said almost in unison. Mags' eyes widened, and she gathered a few bar towels, handing them to her father, who stood and strode over to us.

"Every thug in the city came for us at once," I grunted.

"Yeah, but you should see 'em." Leighton chuckled. "Splat." He waved his hands down and to the side in a flattening motion.

"And the rest of you?" Mags asked cautiously, raising a brow.

"Victoria and Craig were taken during the shit show and–" I started.

"Rich is… in the car. He… won't be coming in," Joey said, his voice sounding almost automatic. Harrison and Mags exchanged a heavy glance, catching his meaning.

Joey's words flipped a switch in Leighton. All traces of humor wiped from his face as he grabbed the nearest barstool and slammed it into the bar with enough force to break it apart. Mags' reaction was instant. She launched over the counter, grabbing Leighton's arm before twisting it violently behind him. In the time it took me to blink, she had him slammed face-first onto the sticky bar floor, her knee pressed between his shoulder blades.

"That's enough, Gatlin Magazine. Let the boy up. He didn't mean no harm." Harrison's droll voice echoed through the bar. "Though, you boys will be replacing that stool, with interest."

"Gatlin... Magazine?" Joey murmured, blinking at us.

Leighton burst into laughter. "Is that... is that your real name, Mags?" he wheezed. "How did we not know this?"

"Because of this reaction right here, L," she hissed. "You gonna keep laughing, or am I breaking your arm for giving me shit?" She leaned forward, pressing her knee harder into his back.

"Oh, come on now, Gatlin Magazine!" Leighton said before wincing in pain as Mags increased the pressure on his arm. "Alright, *alright!* Fuck, Mags!"

"Let him up girl. These boys need tending, and it ain't their fault I panicked with naming ya." Harrison chuckled. "Take 'em upstairs and see to their injuries. I'm going to make a few calls about... the body. See if we can't get it out of my parking lot and on ice for now." he paused a moment before narrowing his eyes at me. "As soon as you boys are patched up, you'll need to sort it out on your own, mind."

"Understood," I replied with a terse nod.

Mags warily stood from where she had Leighton pinned, watching him for any sign of, I could only guess at what. Leighton clambered to his feet, rubbing the arm she'd twisted before grabbing Joey by the shoulder and pushing him toward the back stairs that led to the apartment above the bar.

"Just in case you boys forgot. This here is neutral ground." Harrison spoke just as Joey and Leighton disappeared into the back. "Leaving your friend in my parking lot would put me in a bad spot, one you boys don't want me to be put in. Now, I like you boys, but you *will* owe me for this when all is said and done."

"Pops," Mags started. "I thought you said we don't take

favors."

Harrison leaned back against the liquor shelf, one arm across his chest as he stroked his beard with the other hand. "*You* don't take favors, girly. But I smell war coming, and I'm willing to hedge my bets to keep us safe." He motioned toward Mags and me, pulling his phone out of his pocket. "Go on, now. Patch them up while I tend to this, call me if there's anything you need help with."

CHAPTER THREE

Joey

My mind was a riot of emotions, so loud they drowned everything else out. I was in a haze as Mags sat me in a high-backed wooden chair at her and Harrison's kitchen table. Withdrawn so deep within myself that neither the sting of antiseptic nor the bite of the sewing needle that pulled my wounds closed earned so much as a hiss from me. I was entirely on autopilot by the time I climbed under the shower spray, retreating deeper and deeper into myself as blood and grime washed down the drain.

"I'm going home," I mumbled, barely audible, as Az collapsed onto the couch beside me. "I have to figure out how to tell my folks."

"We'll go with you. You don't have to do this alone, Joey." Az replied softly.

I didn't bother with a response. I didn't have it in me. Travel plans were made around me, Az and Leighton occasionally asking for input I couldn't find the energy to give. I was vaguely aware of Harrison arriving at some point to speak with Az, their voices a low murmur against the background of my mind. It felt like I had only blinked, and then I was standing in the living room of the home we'd bought our parents after our first big score.

"Hey, Little Brother." Rich's voice felt like a slap to the face, and I turned so sharply it nearly threw me off balance.

My heart sank back into my stomach when Az, not my brother, entered my view. "You need to eat something, even if you don't feel like it." He said as he held out a sandwich for me.

I took it, biting into it before baring my teeth in a grimace meant to be a smile. My movements felt mechanical; each forced bite felt like chewing cardboard. Not even Az's worried expression could break through the heaviness that had settled inside me, weighing me down and making everything feel pointless.

Time seemed to pass in another series of blinks. I closed my eyes to Az and opened them to my mother, pulling me against her as she sobbed. Another blink, my father was in the recliner across from where I sat on the couch; his head hung low as he stared at the floor. Yet another, my parents sat on either side of me while they addressed their pastor.

"Hey bro," Leighton said, "I brought your suit. Your mom said you need to change. It's almost time."

Another blink, and I was staring at a closed, dark mahogany casket, a pall with a death's head moth laid across it. I could almost reach out and brush my fingers across the casket pedestal. Tilting my head, I studied it in confusion before turning to speak to Rich.

"Wh–" The whispered word never fully left my mouth as pain crashed over me. My hands clenched into fists, my nails biting into the skin as awareness sank in for the first time in days.

A ragged breath left me, my whole body shuddering with it, before I clawed my way back to the numbness. To the place where none of this was real, and I'd eventually wake to find it was all a horrible nightmare. The pastor's words helped lull me back to that place, the soft tenor of his voice a lullaby in a sea of grief and anger. Not even the cold bite of late winter air could snap me back from that place as we strolled from the funeral home.

It wasn't until the car had fully stopped and *she* emerged that I felt anything. My eyes narrowed on her then, in her sleek black dress, smoothing the non-existent wrinkles while Craig stood at her side. A quick once over of Craig was enough to tell me that his smart suit hid extensive injuries, and yet, the fucking *princess* was wholly untouched.

"What is it going to take for you four to screw your heads back on straight?! Is one of us going to have to fucking die keeping her alive before you realize this whole thing is a fucking MISTAKE!?" He roared, slamming me into the dining table. *The wood buckled and split in half under the impact of my body.*

Bile bit at the back of my throat, and I had to fight my initial instinct to tell her to get back in the car and go back to wherever she came from. Some small voice told me there was a better way to make that point, so I swallowed the sneer that threatened to split my face as I watched them approach.

She strolled next to Craig for a moment, seeming to fret over him, until her eyes swung up, and she saw the three of us standing outside the funeral home. Once upon a time, the smile that lit up her face would have melted my insides as she broke into a run. Leighton was the first to reach her, sprinting across the distance to sweep her up in his arms in a spin. Az was hot on his heels, if a bit more controlled.

Awe, look, she's crying. How convincing. I thought to myself as I strolled along after my remaining brothers with my parents. It took several breaths to steady myself when the attention turned toward us, and I was glad I'd had my parents to duck behind to avoid being pulled into one of her performative hugs.

"Love, these are Dawn and Ian—Rich and Joey's parents," Az said, making a gesture between *her* and my parents. "Dawn, Ian. This is Victoria Bristol."

"I know who she is," my mother scolded Az, and for a moment, I hoped it was disdain I heard in her voice. "My boys told me so much about you, Victoria. I wish this were a happier occasion, but I'm glad to lay eyes on the woman my boys love."

Mom sniffled, wiping her eyes with a tissue before embracing the viper in our midst.

I wanted to puke when her eyes widened in surprise before she recovered herself and smiled sympathetically at my mother.

"Mrs. Innocenti–" She started.

"None of that, honey. Call me Dawn. And you call this ol' lug here Ian." Mom interjected, patting my father's chest, my father wrapping his arm around her shoulders.

I stood away from the group just a bit, watching them welcome her back into our family like she belonged there. I wasn't sure how much longer I could stand it. None of them seemed to care that everything we'd lost and been through was Victoria Bristol's fault. If Az had just let the crowd trample her during the gala fire, Rich would still be alive. She wouldn't have been around to spread her poison through our family so thoroughly. To think I'd nearly fallen for it completely was enough to set my teeth on edge.

I wanted to recoil when Victoria's eyes finally landed on me. That warm brown had once been comforting and drawn me in. But now I knew better. All of her "misunderstandings" and "mistakes" when it came to the rules we'd put in place for her, that *he'd* put in place for her, were coming under a whole new light. She was more like a siren tempting sailors to their deaths rather than a princess we needed to save.

I forced myself to stand still as she approached, but I couldn't bring warmth or receptiveness to my face. It was all I could do not to push her away.

"Joey..." She said softly, holding her arms out as she got close.

"Don't." I hissed.

"Joey," Az's voice was a warning. My eyes narrowed on his hand gently taking her arm to pull her back. "He needs time, Love. He's not in a good place right now, and I don't want you taking the brunt of it. Why don't you go with Dawn and Ian, get Craig settled in? I'll bring you to him when he's ready."

"It's fine, Az, I'll be okay. It wasn't all that long ago that I lost my mom. And we're all grieving right now. I know what it's like to be where he's at, I understand that dark place." She said, her voice softening as she got almost close enough to wrap her arms around me. Her words felt like a slap to the face, and I jumped back, unable to help myself, as I pushed her away from me hard enough to make her fall off her heels.

"The *fuck* do you think you understand, *Princess*?" I spat at her, finally letting go of the iron fist I'd kept around my emotions since she'd stepped out of the car that had dropped them off. "It's *your* fucking fault that my brother is in a casket in there right now, a bullet between his fucking eyes!" My voice started rising until I was shouting, and I couldn't bring myself to care about the scene I knew I was making. "And everyone here is a fucking idiot for letting you back into the fold like it's anything other than your own machinations and plans that got us here in the first fucking place! It's like Rich said, when I was stupidly fighting for what I thought was your fucking honor, how many of us have to fucking die for everyone to get the fucking point?! You're a fucking *poison*, Victoria." I curled my lip into a vicious sneer as I stepped toward her. "Stay away from my family. Stay away from my brothers. Stay the fuck away from me!"

"Joseph Dario Innocenti!" My mother screeched, making my attention instinctively snap to her.

Leighton shoved past Az, planting himself between me and Victoria, his face twisted into a snarl as he jabbed his finger into my shoulder. "I'm not going to do what you deserve in front of your mother because I fucking love Dawn, but that's one mother fucker."

"What the fuck, Joey?!" Craig said, trying his best to help Victoria up in his injured state.

"This wasn't her fault, Little Brother," Az said, his brows furrowed as he stood beside Leighton. "We could have walked at any time. We *chose* to be there."

I felt my collar pulled sharply as my father stepped

into view, his soft baritone carrying a note of finality as he spoke. "That's enough, boy. Not here. Not now. To the car." He shoved me forward, not hard enough to make me stumble but sufficient to get the point. "I'm taking him home. Get Dawn to the cemetery; I'll meet you there."

I shoved my hands in my pockets and started heading for the car, my father on my heels. For a moment, I almost felt bad for my display, not because of the snake everyone was protecting but because of my parents. I knew they were going through it, and none of it was fair to them. I just wished they could see I was *trying* to protect them from a similar fate. Because I wholeheartedly believed that if Victoria Bristol had her way, we'd all be joining Rich sooner or later.

CHAPTER FOUR

Craig

Somehow, I made it through the graveside service without leaking through my bandages or passing out. The Devils' doc had done a hell of a patch job on me, but the damage inflicted by Melissa's little protege was extensive. By the time Az pulled the SUV into the Innocenti's driveway, I regretted not adding that amateur to the deal I'd sealed with the Devils. I almost felt bad that I couldn't be as emotionally present as I would have liked for Victoria and my brothers during the service, but I was focusing every ounce of will I had into just getting around upright. I was in far too much pain to have room for anything else. I would grieve on my own time.

The Innocenti home was large but not lavish. Every room had a touch of Dawn, and the warmth the woman exuded filled the space and made coming here always feel like coming home. Even though the air was thick and the mood was somber, it hadn't lost that feeling. I let Victoria' help' me to my room; arguing with her would have only distressed her more, and if this was the comfort I could give her, then I was happy to let her fret for a moment.

My room lacked some of my creature comforts, but like all of our rooms, it stayed made up for us if we ever needed them. A large, mostly empty, desk took up one wall, a bookshelf stood by an overstuffed armchair, and several frames with preserved butterflies and moths hung on the walls to distinguish my room from the others. I would have to rebuild my entire setup in the coming days; the spare laptop that Leighton grabbed for me on our way back wasn't going to suffice for long. I situated it on the desk and sighed heavily, still feeling Victoria hovering over my shoulder.

"Bunny?" I asked, turning to face her.

"Do you need anything else? I'm sure your bandages probably need to be changed, or at least looked at. If you want anything for pain, we can probably get something from Dawn... or have someone bring something by if you need something stronger. I—" She was wringing her hands as she spoke, and I could see her desperately looking for something that would keep her from being left alone with her thoughts.

"I'm fine, Bunny. I have to gather the guys for a debrief, they need to know what happened." I said gently. "Maybe you can go check on Dawn. I'm sure she could use the company."

"But, you're injured! You need—"

"I *need* to do my job, Victoria." I cut her off again, grabbing her by the shoulders and moving her toward the door to my room. "I understand what you're trying to do, and I appreciate it. But right now, I don't have time for comfort or care. Don't forget you attached yourself to gangsters; this is part of the job. Now, go check on Dawn." I sat her outside my room and cupped her cheek for a second to let her know I wasn't angry with her before jerking my head to the side, silently telling her to get going.

"I just want to help." She said lamely.

"Then call Harrison while you're down there. This patch job is almost as bad as the torture itself." I offered, looking past her to spot Az in the hall. He nodded to me as he headed down the stairs. "I love you, Bunny. But for right now, for the love of god, just stay out of our way and let us do our jobs." I kissed her cheek and moved past her, slowly making my way back down the stairs.

Ian was sitting back in his chair in the large living room, looking toward the television's black screen. He seemed to be staring into the middle distance and not seeing anything, and my heart ached for him. I couldn't imagine what he must have been feeling.

"Ian," I said by way of greeting. He didn't answer, simply motioning toward his 'man cave' set up off the living room in what was supposed to have been a study. I nodded my thanks.

The guys were already gathered in the room when I entered and shut the door behind me. The room was like an explosion of all things Texas and rodeo cowboy, calling back to Ian's younger days as a rodeo rider. It was like an assault on the senses, with the cowhides, cowboy hats, spurs, and taxidermy bull head on the far wall. It hurt my eyes, but I'd never say that out loud.

Az was standing by an end table, looking at a glass decanter with a crestfallen expression as he examined the clear liquid inside it.

"You don't know what I'd give for this to be vodka..." He said with a huff before pouring himself a glass.

"I hope it doesn't end up being vodka after all this; there's only been water in that thing for as long as any of us have even been alive," I said sadly, knowing that if there were ever anything that could make a recovered alcoholic fall off the wagon, it would be something like this. Ian was a strong man, so I hoped for the best.

"Dad will be fine," Joey said, his voice still clipped, causing us to look at him. "Let's get to it. What happened, Craig?"

"We'll get to that. First, I want to know how you three got away from the Jackals. Ya'll were literally in the frying pan, so why aren't you cooked?" I asked, sinking painfully into a chair, my gaze flicking between them.

"Well, after I ripped out a few throats with my teeth," he paused, baring his teeth and pointing at them. "My fucking teeth! They just up and took off. No rhyme, no reason. Musta scared 'em off."

"That's decidedly *not* why they left." Az snorted, rolling

his eyes as he sipped his water. "But, the fact remains that once they were clear with you and Victoria, we don't know why they left. We *shouldn't* be having this conversation, but here we are."

"Shit... called them off. Things are still a little fuzzy, but now I'm sure I didn't dream her calling them off and then calling in for someone to wreck our transport."

"Your ex is a fucking psycho. I should know." Leighton interjected.

"Beside the point." Az barked at Leighton before motioning toward me. "Continue."

"Tiffany fucking happened," I replied bitterly.

"I knew it! I fucking knew it! I told you, I told all of you that bitch barbie was a gangster." Leighton hooted, hopping up from his seat and doing some strange celebration dance.

"Well, before you celebrate your premonition too hard, she's the whole reason Candy was there and why we just left a funeral. Apparently, Victoria's lack of contact sent the socialite-turned-mobster on a spiral of thinking we were getting ready to traffic her because of partial information that she was gathering from the forum posts we used to try and draw out the mastermind behind the free-for-all." I sneered with a shake of my head. It would have pissed me off no matter *who* had been behind the attack on us, but the fact that we missed so many key details. We closed ranks and reacted to the whole situation without thinking beyond protecting Victoria. "Woah," Leighton breathed, flopping down into an empty armchair. "She pulled a *me*. I'm pissed and want to kill her, but also, props to Barbie."

"What the fuck did you just say, L?" Joey snarled, his expression darkening as he snapped his gaze to Leighton. "Are... Are you really congratulating the woman who got not only my brother but your friend, and our boss fucking *killed*?! What the fuck is wrong with you?!" He stood sharply, moving as if he was going to approach Leighton. Az intercepted him, casually stepping between the two.

"You know he didn't mean it like that, Joey." Az said. "If

he did, he wouldn't still want to kill the woman."

Joey let out a derisive snort and moved to retake his seat. After a moment of sitting in silence, waiting for him to get himself somewhat together, Az motioned for me to continue.

"The long and short of it after that is that Mel let her little protege play amateur night on me in their basement while Bunny must have been clearing up the misunderstanding." Joey snorted again, and I turned my head toward him just in time to catch the eye roll that went with it. "Helen offered us reparations, and I accepted Candy and her second on our behalf. They will deliver in two weeks."

"I don't care who does the second, but Candy is mine." Joey clipped. No one argued; we understood. "But you mean to tell me that you had a chance to get Tiffany, and you just... *didn't*? What, did the viper talk you out of it?" He sneered.

Leighton stood and got in Joey's face before I could open my mouth to respond. "You may be my chosen family," he hissed, gripping Joey's collar, "but you're not going to keep talking about Victoria like that. I'll let it slide this time, along with that shit earlier, because you're a fucking mess, but keep going and you're not going to like where it leads."

"You don't get to decide what I choose to call her. I—" Joey started.

"Actually," I said hastily, interrupting what would turn into another pointless argument. "Victoria wanted Tiffany, and I had to tell her no. From the look of her when she came to tell Mel to bring me to Helen, someone, who I can only assume was Victoria, had beat the shit out of her too." I didn't miss the prideful look Az and Leighton exchanged. "All of us need to accept that Victoria gave Tiffany her licks and leave it there. If one of us had gone missing, with no other information besides concerning forum posts to go on, the rest of us would have done the same thing. We would mobilize every asset and ally we could. We've *killed* for less. And I believe Helen when she told me Candy was acting outside of orders when she pulled that trigger."

"Helen has always owned her orders. If she'd told Candy to kill one or all of us, she would have said so." Az added. "If she told you she didn't give that order, she didn't."

"Of course she would say she wanted Tiffany," Joey scoffed. "The vip– *she*, would know damned well you wouldn't agree to that. You got played. Fuck sakes, it took my brother being murdered for me to realize it, who else do we have to lose before the rest of you wake the fuck up?"

"Joey!" I snapped, turning to face him. "I understand you're, like Leighton said, a fucking mess right now. Shit, on some level, we all are. You're not the only one who buried someone today! This wasn't any of our fault, were you not fucking listening? This was a rogue operative, working outside the scope of her orders to indulge her own brand of sadism. That's who Candy is. She didn't *need* any help to create that carnage." I could completely understand Joey's mental state; Rich was important to all of us. We were family, and we'd been through hell together. But we had to get his head back on straight if we were going to make it out the other side intact.

Joey chuckled darkly, "You know, we had shit right the first go round. The one thing that should have given it away, even with all the misdirects she managed, was how easily she fell into all of our beds. Nobody, and I mean *nobody*, wants all five of us unless they're a conniving slut."

The air in the room stilled, and I could see Az moving toward Leighton to stop a fight before it started. That was all I needed. I stood, my body screaming from the sudden movement. There wasn't any thought; all I could see was red. I was in pain, physically and emotionally, and I didn't have the patience or energy to sort Joey's shit out for him.

I didn't even realize it had happened until the sound of my fist connecting with Joey's jaw reached my ears. His head snapped back, and he snarled at me as he jumped to his feet. I was vaguely aware of Az and Leighton freezing in my periphery.

"This. Is. *Not.* Her. Fault. You. Fucking. Idiot." I clipped between gritted teeth.

Joey spat a glob of blood by my feet before wiping his mouth with the back of his hand and shooting me a feral grin. "You're lucky you're injured, or else I wouldn't let that cheap shot slide. All of you are going to be singing a different tune when you realize just how wrong you are." He slammed his shoulder against mine as he strolled past and left the room.

CHAPTER FIVE

Victoria

We hadn't talked about what happened when he debriefed the others, but I'd noticed Joey's blossoming bruise and split lip and how Craig had nursed the knuckles of his right hand as we sat down for dinner with the Innocenti's. There was a tension in the air that crackled with the threat of violence. Not even the cloud of grief hanging over all of us could suffocate it out. I excused myself as soon as was socially acceptable and made my way to the room Craig had claimed for his own.

Night had fully set in, and moonlight was filtering through the curtains when Craig entered the room. I watched him as he carefully moved around the space, hissing slightly in pain as he peeled off his suit and underwear. My brows furrowed as he paused, standing naked near the dresser, considering a pair of pajama pants he'd dug out of a drawer. He let out another low hiss of pain, his free hand pressing against his abdomen before he tossed the pants aside and turned toward the bed.

"I wondered where you disappeared to, Bunny." He murmured as he eased himself into the bed next to me. "How are you holding up?"

"Don't worry about me," I replied, reaching up to smooth the pained crease above his eyes. "You should be focused on you. You're injured and I could tell at dinner the debrief or whatever didn't go well. Tell me how I can help, what do you need? Name anything and I'll find a way to make it happen."

"Would it be wrong if I said all I want is to bury myself in you and forget everything else for a while?"

"I–" I started to protest.

Craig propped himself up on his elbow and leaned over me, his voice a whisper. "Bunny, I need to know that there's still something to feel besides pain. I *need* to feel something good. You offered to do whatever I needed, and that *is* what I need."

With speed he shouldn't have had in his current state, he wrapped an arm around me and rolled us so that I was straddling his thighs. My eyes frantically moved to take him in, searching for any sign he'd hurt himself further.

"Craig, you're hurt. We shouldn't, not until you're healed."

"Do you trust me, Bunny?" He asked, lifting his hands to sweep my hair behind my shoulders.

"You know I do." I replied with a frown.

"Then trust me now. I know what I need, and I won't push past my limits." He said. "What I need right now is for you to ride me until we're both too sated and exhausted to move."

Craig slid his hands up my sides, my shirt lifting slightly with the movement, and I started to open my mouth to protest. To tell him again that he was too injured for what he wanted.

"Now, Bunny." The tone of his voice sent a shiver up my spine. "You can play my nursemaid tomorrow. Right now, you're going to strip off those pajamas and impale yourself on my cock before I do it for you."

His words were punctuated with a thrust of his hips that had need coiling in my core. I carefully moved off of him and gripped the hem of my sleep shirt.

"Promise me you'll tell me if it's too much. I don't want to hurt you anymore than you are." I said, my hands hesitating.

"If it makes you more comfortable, I promise I will safeword if it gets to be too much." He smirked, causing me to arch a brow in a scolding manner. "Yellow to slow down, red to stop. Promise. If you're really worried about my injuries, my face is perfectly fine."

"Oh yes, because I'm sure being suffocated on top of being injured is just what you need," I said with a roll of my eyes.

"I'd die a happy man, Bunny. Now strip and sit on my fucking face." He growled, shifting upright before reaching for my pajama shirt.

I let out a squeak of alarm, swatted his hands away, and then jerked my shirt over my head.

"That's better," he smirked again, laying back down with his eyes still pinned on me. "Pants, too."

I shimmied my soft sleep bottoms down, taking my panties with them before tossing them somewhere on the floor. I settled back on the bed beside Craig, my legs under me as I considered the safest way to give him what he wanted without causing further harm.

As if sensing my thoughts, he forcefully pointed a finger at me and then his face. "I'm not going to ask again, Bunny."

Something in his tone sent a shudder skittering up my spine, and I couldn't help but respond. I was scrambling up the bed, using the headboard to help me straddle over his head. I hesitated, feeling awkward about how to position myself best so I wasn't cutting off all of his air. The last thing I wanted was to hurt him somehow. I supported most of my weight on my knees and hovered over him.

Craig's hands moved to my hips, his fingers digging into the soft flesh hard enough to bruise. "I said *sit*, not hover." he all but snarled before forcing my full weight onto his face.

The first swipe of his tongue through my folds caused me to lurch forward and grip the headboard. I felt the vibrations of his chuckle against my sex before he set upon me like a man starved. Any concerns I had about suffocation fled in the wake of his skilled tongue working my clit. My eyes rolled back and fluttered closed as he feasted, his tongue curling and rolling around my clit in a way that had sparks streaking through my nerves.

"Oh... Fuck..." I gasped, back arching. I tried to roll my hips against his mouth, grinding against him as he worked me, but his grip holding me in place prevented me from doing anything but taking what he gave me.

I bit my lip, trying to hold back my moans as he growled against me with each pass of his tongue. I couldn't help but cry out as his tongue swirled around my clit. He grunted as he shifted my hips, and I moved to help him, groaning deeply as his tongue slipped inside me. My back arched as he worked me with the same masterful skill he used in the kitchen. His tongue flicked in and out of me, and it was everything I could do not to give into the instinct to bounce on his tongue like I was riding his dick.

"Fuck... Craig..." I pleaded as he ate me out with a fervor that was driving me mad. My legs instinctively tried to close against his head as my impending release barreled toward me. I was on the precipice when Craig suddenly stopped, and I felt myself lifted from his face. A whimper of protest left my lips, and I looked down at him, pleading with my eyes for him to continue.

He stared at my pussy, fully bared to him, with a smug grin. "Look at you, soaked and needy."

"Craig," my voice came out on a whine. "Please."

His fingers gripped my hips tighter, and he shifted me down his body. "Get on my cock, Bunny. I wanna be so deep inside you when you cum that you can't ever get me out."

My hand wrapped around his base, and I positioned him at my entrance, letting his hold keep me steady. In a single motion, I impaled myself, taking him fully as we both groaned in relief.

"Ride me like your life depends on it, Bunny, because right now, mine does." Craig bit out through gritted teeth.

I paused at his expression, uncertain if it was ecstasy or agony. "Craig.."

"Bunny... I'm fine. Now, move." He punctuated his command with a light swat across my ass while his other hand forced me into motion.

My hands fell against his chest as I ground into him in response. Realizing what I'd done, I shifted to pull away, only for Craig to quickly cover my hands with his, a warning written on his face. I didn't protest on his behalf this time, shifting slightly so that I could give him what he needed.

I moaned as I lifted my hips before sinking back down onto him. I set a slow, languid pace as I rode him, feeling every inch of him filling and stretching me, sending sparks of pleasure through my body. My pace picked up as I chased my release, each movement driving me closer to the edge. The knowledge of where we were flashed through my mind, and I bit my bottom lip to hold back my moans.

"None of that," Craig groaned, "I want to hear you." He gripped my hips, encouraging me to gather speed, his head rolled back against the pillows. I rotated my hips and took the hint about what he needed, rocking harder and faster, letting moans fall from my lips. "That's it, Bunny. Fucking hell, you're perfect. Don't you fucking stop."

He tilted my hips with a push on my lower back, and the friction against my clit was all I needed to push me over the edge as I rode him. My climax slammed into me, stealing my breath and made all the more intense by his earlier teasing. It made my head spin and whited out my vision. My back bowed, and I clapped my hand over my mouth to stop the scream that tore up my throat, attempting to muffle it so that we didn't wake the entire house. Craig thrust into me as he ripped my hand away from my mouth, chasing his own release.

"I told you... I wanna hear you." He growled out, his hips stuttering as my scream filled the room. "Fuuuuck..." He groaned out as he shattered beneath me. His back bowed, and his eyes rolled back, and god damn if it weren't the hottest thing I'd ever seen. I didn't stop moving, riding out his orgasm as he writhed beneath me, riding the powerful high of watching my man lose his mind.

After a few moments, Craig shifted his hips to roll us over. I let out a yelp as gravity helped pull me under him before sense caught up with me.

"Craig! Your–"

"I know, Bunny," he huffed with a little laugh before shifting to collapse beside me. "I'll take something later if I'm hurting. Right now, I'm not feeling anything but good."

He stretched out his arm in my direction, and I took the unspoken cue to curl into him, placing my head on his shoulder and carefully avoiding any bandages. I'd barely gotten situated when I felt him trembling.

"Craig?" I asked, shifting to look at him.

A loud sob tore from his mouth, and his entire body shuddered. "Fuck. I hit him, Bunny. He's grieving and I slugged him right in the face while he sat there and took it. I swore–" his voice cracked as tears streamed down his face. "I swore I wouldn't ever be like my old man. But here I am, sucker punching someone I consider my brother."

I leaned up on instinct, shifting around him so that I was cradling his head against my chest, his arms tightening around my middle. "Craig! Baby, you're not anything like your father. You're grieving too, and you've been pushed too far. You're only human, and it's okay to be reactive sometimes." I hushed him and rocked him against me, stroking down his back.

He swiped the tears from his face with the back of his hand, sniffling, and I could tell he was trying to get them to stop. "I'm sorry, Bunny. Fuck. It's not fair for me to dump my shit on you. I know you're grieving too and I—"

"Craig Dougherty. You don't do that." I snapped, harsher than I'd intended. I tilted his face up to look at me. "We're in this *together*. I'm sure I'm going to fall apart any time now and you'll be right there to pick me up and piece me back together. But right now, it's my turn to pick you up. Don't take that from me. Let me be strong for *you*."

His arms tightened around me again, and he buried his face into my shoulder. I made soothing shush noises as I held him, feeling his shoulders shake as he permitted himself to grieve. I rocked and rubbed my hand across the back of his head, shoulders, and back.

"It's okay, let it all out. I've got you." I murmured.

"We don't deserve you, Bunny." His words were soft, muffled against my skin as he cried.

"I decide who deserves me." I replied. "And I say you do."

I held him as he cried, letting him release everything he'd kept bottled inside for far too long. Eventually, he stopped trembling, his breathing evened out, and he fell asleep against me. I carefully shifted us so he was more comfortable against me, but I was still holding him. I watched him, the peace on his face making him look younger and softer despite his tattoos and piercings. It struck me that he'd been through so much, just as much as the rest of us, and he'd never complained or asked us to hold space for him the entire time. He was always the rock for us. I kissed his forehead and snuggled closer, latching onto the moment's peace while I could.

CHAPTER SIX

Craig

"Come on, we're meeting in Ian's office," Az said as he poked his head into the room I'd claimed.

"Mmmm, five more minutes," Victoria mumbled, snuggling deeper into my side.

"You can stay in bed if you like, Love. I just need Craig." Az's voice was soft in a way I don't think I'd ever heard as he addressed her before turning his attention back to me. "Five minutes."

He ducked back out of the room and quietly shut the door before I could respond, leaving me to disentangle myself from Victoria gently. I moved to the dresser, snagged the black sweatpants I'd tossed aside the night before, and pulled them on along with a shirt I pulled from the drawer. I didn't bother looking for socks or shoes as I padded out of the room and headed to Ian's office.

Az nodded from where he sat at Ian's mahogany desk, gesturing toward a cup of coffee near the edge. Noting the dark circles beneath his eyes, I grabbed it and took a sip before settling into one of the empty armchairs. Leighton followed not long after with a scowling Joey in tow. I couldn't help grimacing at the bruise that had fully set in along his jaw, but the way Leighton, of all people, gripped Joey's collar and steered him to a seat was enough for me to know it wasn't the time for apologies just yet.

"I've been fielding calls all night," Az started with a tired sigh. "Our people are scattered to kingdom fucking come, and nobody has any idea of what's left standing. I can't even get an accurate tally of who's left alive. Leighton, I need you out there. If you're up for it, you too, Joey."

"Who the fuck left you in charge?" Joey sneered. "Pretty sure if *my* brother had an heir it would be me. I should be the one making these calls."

Az rubbed a hand over his face and pinched the bridge of his nose in a move startlingly similar to Rich's. "It's not about heirs or being in charge, Joey. If we don't sort out who's left and what territory is still intact so we can shore up before the vultures descend, there won't be anything left."

"Az is right, Joey. Right now it doesn't matter who's giving the orders." I added. "You and Leighton are the most familiar with our boots on the ground, you know where they'd hole up, and have the connections to mark them off the dead rolls if they're alive."

"Oh, fuck off, Craig. What are you even doing here? We don't need a fucking hacker for this. Your precious computers are useless here." Joey snapped.

"Woah, woah, woah. He does more than that, besides, he can check the camera feeds and narrow some shit down for us." Leighton said my brows arching in alarm that somehow *he* was acting as a voice of reason.

Joey narrowed his eyes at Leighton and scoffed. "Figured he had better shit to do," he said before turning to look at me with a malicious smirk. "Ran right up in that poisonous pussy as fast as you could last night, huh?"

My eyes widened at the vitriol in his voice before narrowing in anger. Before I could open my mouth to put Joey in his place again, Leighton reared back his hand and slapped him across the face.

"Two, god damn it." Leighton said in an exasperated tone. "You're my hetero-life partner dude, but I *will* fuck you up if you keep going on about *our* girl this way."

"And you three can share her 'til you come to your senses." Joey started, sneering at Leighton. "And—"

Az sighed heavily. "Enough!" he bellowed. "He did warn you. Now, if you don't mind, we have actual business to deal with and not whatever this childish bullshit is."

"I will need a laptop, at minimum. Unless you three have secured the house?" I posed my question to Az.

"We haven't. Nothing is secure at the moment. We have been here, looking for you and Victoria for the last few days while Ian and Dawn managed the arrangements for the funeral. You weren't with us, so I don't know if your lockdown protocol was enabled when we left."

I heaved a little sigh, looking around as I considered the property we were on. "Any digital footprints or fingerprints we might have left at our place, safehouses, or warehouses are gone. We won't have to worry about anyone getting anything they shouldn't from those access points. If the computers aren't completely destroyed already, they're no better than empty personal PCs." I instinctively reached for my phone and huffed when I remembered it wasn't there. "I'll need to make some stops, but I can get us set up here. I need a phone, and more computing power than the dinky back-up I have up there right now..." I was mostly talking to myself when I registered Az speaking to me.

"Make a list, we'll make sure you get what you need. Phil, thank fuck, is still alive and kicking. He can make the run." Az said, his tone bordering on being an order.

"I'm perfectly capable of going to an electronics store." I deadpanned.

"The city is still gunning for us, and you're barely in the condition to walk from here to your fucking room. I'm not risking your safety for your pride. Make the damned list." Az barked.

"Yeah, you need to just sit tight and look pretty until your Frankenstein scars heal up." Leighton cackled. "Let ma petit kiss all your boo-boos." he paused, a dreamy look crossing his face. "I need to get stabbed real quick."

Az pinched his nose again with a groan. "Can you not? We have enough shit to deal with as it is. We don't need another one of us out of commission."

"Yeah, besides, who knows what sort of infection you'd get from *that*." Joey snarked. He didn't say her name, but something in his tone made it obvious Victoria was the 'that' he meant, not the stabbing.

"Leighton, while you're out, secure a location to stash two guests securely. Per the deal Craig made, we only have two weeks until they arrive."

"It needs to be *extra* secure," I added. "Candy will do anything, including self-inflicting bodily harm, if it means she lives. I can only imagine what sort of person she has as a second."

Joey huffed, and Az snapped his head in his direction. "Something you'd like to add?"

"Yeah," Joey said, standing from his seat. "That deal is bullshit and we all know it. Nobody gives a fuck about her second. I want Tiffany. Candy and Tiffany. The bitch who set shit into motion and the bitch who pulled the trigger. Nothing else makes us square with the Devils."

"The deals made, we're not going back on it." Az replied.

"Fuck your fucking deal!" Joey shouted, stalking forward and slamming his fists on the desk. "It wasn't Craig's to fucking make. It was *mine*, and I say it's not fucking good enough."

Az pushed his seat back from the desk and stood slowly, a thunderous look on his face. "That is enough. We may generally make decisions together, but *I* was the second in command. That means that *I* am in charge with Rich gone, whether you like it or not." his voice was like steel as he continued to speak. "Furthermore, Joseph, Rich didn't even want you in this life in the first fucking place. You forced your way in against that better judgement, and now here you sit. But do not forget, Craig was here first and *even* Leighton outranks you. You have one of two choices. You hit the streets with Leighton or you stay. Either way, one more outburst from you and you *will* be taking licks as punishment like the petulant child you're behaving as."

I looked at Az momentarily, unsure when the last time I saw him like this, if ever. It was like looking at Rich reincarnated, right down to the hard stare and how he pinched his nose to ward off the headache in his eyes. My mouth opened as if I was going to tease him about it the same way I'd done Rich so often before I caught myself and snapped it shut.

Joey bared his teeth at Az, his fists curling tighter until his knuckles were white. "Fine." he gritted out. "I'll hit the streets, I need some fresh air anyway."

"Good," Az replied, holding Joey's gaze until Joey finally stepped back. "I expect regular reports and check-ins. We need to know exactly what we're working with so we can right this ship." He paused and flicked his eyes to me. "I don't like the idea of sending anyone in blind, so get your list together. Phil will get what you need and bring it to me at our drop point. Once you've had a chance to scope out what you can, Leighton and Joey can head out."

Leighton moved first, grabbing Joey by the arm and pulling him further away from the desk. "Come on, Pookie, let's go to work." Leighton's words were light, but the look he gave was hard. He didn't give Joey a chance to respond before pulling him from the room.

Once they were clear of the door, I turned to study Az. He had settled back into his chair and had his elbows propped on the desk, head in his hands. Exhaustion deeper than any I'd seen on him was evident in how he held himself.

"How are you holding up?" I asked, causing him to startle and jerk his head up.

"Figuring out why Rich was always so goddamn tired..." He said softly, "That man had stronger shoulders than we realized."

"I think we knew, we were just grateful he carried that weight for us. He didn't have to deal with this infighting going on either. We fought, but.. Not like this. We always knew we had each other's backs at the end of the day." I trailed off, considering my next words. "Was he like that the whole time we were gone?"

Az was quiet for a moment, looking like he was sorting through memories he could barely recall. "No. He was mostly just... quiet. This started the moment he laid eyes on Victoria again."

"He's just looking for someone to blame. Something to do with the shit he's not working out." I offered, though it didn't mean the hatefulness was any less grating.

"Fuck, I hope you're right." Az puffed out a breath. "He's trying damned hard to force us to choose, and I'm not sure I can stop Leighton if Joey keeps pushing." Az raked a hand over his face and into his hair, tugging at the blond strands. "I don't know how to stop it. Rich would have known exactly what to say to make him see sense, but I'm completely at a loss here. I'm afraid *none* of us will be able to make him see sense before it's too late and he's done damage to our family he can't undo."

CHAPTER SEVEN

Leighton

Joey shrugged off my hold and stomped to his room to sulk the moment I pulled him out of the office. We had time to kill before we could hit the streets, and I spent a good chunk of it wandering the house until I ended up in the garage with Ian. He was under the hood of a '57 Chevy Bel Air, an array of tools and greasy rags spread out on a rolling cart beside him. At the sound of my approach, he grabbed a wrench, holding it out to me.

An unsettling sense of relief washed over me as I accepted the tool and settled beside him. Ian had been a quiet man as long as I'd known him, but it never ceased to catch me off guard just how well he seemed to know when I needed something to do. It used to have me preparing for an attack, but now I was grateful for it. Ian knew I didn't have feelings I needed to talk out; so we tinkered silently for hours before Dawn appeared in the garage doorway.

"Lunch is ready. You boys clean up." She said softly before turning back into the house.

I washed up quickly in the downstairs bathroom before making quick work of the sandwich left on the kitchen island for me. It was weird that Dawn hadn't wrangled everyone around the dining room table for the simple meal, but I barely had a chance to ponder it. Az strolled into the kitchen looking haggard as I swallowed down the last bite of my food.

"Craig has pulled what he could. We already knew the Tenth, Lotus, and Union were gone, but we've lost the safehouses on Vermillion and Parkside. There are cars that aren't ours patrolling our neighborhood, Temptat!on, the warehouse on Cathedral, my office on Third, and the entire area around our drop site on North Twenty-Fifth. It doesn't look like they know where that drop site is and are hoping to catch one of ours out."

"So we start east and work our way through," I replied, mentally mapping out the locations he'd mentioned.

"Maybe... West," Az hesitated. "We've completely lost eyes to the east. Craig hasn't been able to access the city's systems yet, but the coverage on the east side of the city has always been shit."

"West..." I replied slowly, "That's awful close to Jackal territory, you sure it's a good call?"

Az raked his hands through his hair and tugged at the strands in frustration. "I don't know. From what Craig can gather, the criminal underground is crawling damn near all over the city like cockroaches looking for us. I don't like the idea of you and Joey being so close to enemy territory, but it seems like the only fucking place nobody is actually looking right now."

"Sounds like a solid plan to me." I shrugged. I wasn't against the idea of a run-in with some Jackals. If anything, taking some of them out would give me something useful to do.

Az frowned at me, digging into his jeans pocket to pull out a set of keys. "Don't do anything stupid, Leighton." he drawled as he handed me the keys. "These are for a silver minivan, the best Phil could do on short notice, but I looked it over, and it won't draw attention."

"Me, do something stupid?" I gasped in mock offense as I snagged the keys. "I would *never*."

He sighed heavily, rolling his eyes and pinching the bridge of his nose. I smirked at him as he shook his head and muttered something unintelligible. Snagging my paper plate from the counter, I tossed it in the trash and clapped him on the shoulder.

"I'll grab Joey and we can go do some Danger Duck bullshit." I grinned as I strolled away. I couldn't suppress the chuckle as I heard Az silently curse under his breath.

Joey was where I left him—holed up in his bedroom, reliving his emo phase. "Yo. My chemical imbalance, it's time to roll." I almost had to yell to be heard over the sappy ass music he was listening to.

"Fuck you, L." Joey clipped, rolling his eyes as he stood from his bed.

"We're bromo, not *homo* my dude. Now get your ass up so we can go to work. We might even get to stab some fucking Jackals today."

"I *am* up, shithead," he said, motioning to himself standing, stepping into his shoes, and hastily putting on a hoodie as he stalked toward me standing in the door.

Spotting a conveniently laid-out pair of scissors, I pushed past him and lifted them up. "Don't forget your thumb holes. Gotta have the thumb holes."

"Let's go before I stab you with those scissors. I'm not in the mood," Joey said over his shoulder.

"Fine, but you're driving the mom-mobile. I'm not cut out for this parent of a moody teenager shit." I replied, tossing him the keys Az had given me.

I was practically bouncing in the passenger seat as we navigated closer to where our territory bordered the Jackals. Joey had kept up the sad sap routine the entire drive, but I wasn't letting his shitty attitude ruin what I knew was about to be one hell of a good time. Aside from a few angry glances in my direction, he'd moped right up until he pulled into an empty parking lot a couple blocks south of our first stop.

"You sure you didn't want to stop for eyeliner on the way?" I grinned. "We still can; there's a shop just a block up."

"What the fuck is wrong with you, man?" Joey snapped.

Shaking my head at him, I climbed out of the van and moved to the back, opening the trunk to arm up before responding. "I mean... What *isn't* wrong with me? You've met my parents, they're not the type to have me tested so we may never know." I shrugged as I inspected a particularly interesting blade.

"I get everything is a fucking joke to you, L, but we just buried my brother. Give me the space to have it hurt." He said, slamming the van door as he climbed out. "And you could at least *act* like it fucking bothered you."

"What do you think I brought your ass along for?" I snapped. "Stabbing Jackals is helpful. It's downright fucking cathartic, I'd assume. You shouldn't be out here in your current headspace. Even *I* know that. But I also know how fucking good it feels to get your hands on the enemy and tear them to fucking shreds. So, if you're quite fucking done, we have a job to do and people to kill."

I mentally patted myself on the back for the mature way I'd handled my response to Joey's outburst. It was almost *parental. Ha.*

Joey huffed a response but didn't continue his little tantrum. He just moved up to the back of the van and held out his hand. "Fine, if we're stabbing, then I want *my* knife."

We spent the next several minutes arming up as best as possible while I continued to mentally congratulate myself on being a responsible parent. I was full-on beaming when we shut the trunk and started toward the first spot on our list. It wasn't a safe house, per se, more of a guardhouse to keep eyes on our border, but if Az was right, we might find some of our people still there. By the third stop, we still hadn't found any of our people, and I was growing antsy from not having stabbed anyone yet.

"You see that?" Joey asked, nodding to the odd colored lighting coming from the window of the house we were heading to check.

I followed his gaze and noticed what looked like some weird failed attempt to have lights without them shining through the window. "Yep. Looks like we get to stab someone finally."

We crept closer, sticking close to the other houses' shadows until we were close enough to peek in one of the windows. Two of my street guys were tied down to wooden dining chairs, beaten and bloodied. A third was on the floor at their feet with a bullet hole in his head. My eyes scanned the room more closely; I spotted three injured men I didn't recognize and another five who appeared uninjured, sporting clear Jackal tattoos.

"Eight. Three injured, but I can't see any identifiers from here. Could be Jackals, could be run of the mill thugs helping with the dirty work. Three of ours, one dead." I rattled off to Joey in a hushed tone. "We should check–"

The words died on my lips, my mouth falling open in shock as Joey stalked to the front door and kicked it in. Under normal circumstances, I would have reveled in the chaos he'd just unleashed, but Ian and Dawn would murder me if I let the dumbass get himself killed.

"Mother *fucker*," I huffed before pulling knives into my hands and chasing after him. "I'm supposed to be the chaotic stupid one!" I bellowed as I charged through the busted door, shouldering one of the Jackals Joey had taken by surprise out of my way.

"Shut up and start stabbing!" Joey hollered back.

"Wait a fucking minute!" I shouted as I turned back and thrust my blade into the Jackal's gut and jerked it to the side, spilling his entrails. "That's my line, damn it!"

I looked over as Joey dropped the body of his first Jackal, something feral on his face as he faced one of the unmarked thugs. The two unmarked men paled, and a wet spot started spreading on the nearest one's pants as he pissed himself in the face of Joey's rage. Barking out a laugh, I sent a blade flying toward them, only missing because they seemed to wise up enough to make a break for the back exit of the house. I moved toward our bound men as Joey continued to rampage. The little *alpha* could use the release, so I'd let him keep the other four Jackals busy while I untied our guys.

"Sit still. When you're out, go straight to the Spotted Cobra, get patched up, and then I want check-ins." I ordered as I cut through their bonds. They froze up, and the looks on their faces warred between shock and fear. I furrowed my brows as I worked my blade through the ropes. "I told ya'll to go to the Spotted Cobra; I'm not going to hurt ya'll. Unless... is there a reason you'd think I might?"

"No... No, Sir. It's just.." One of our men rattled off before jerking his head to indicate behind me.

"Joey's just keeping them busy." I rolled my eyes as my blade sliced through the last bit of rope, freeing our second man. "Don't tell me you fucks are getting soft."

The pair exchanged a glance before shaking their heads. Clapping them on the shoulders, I gave them a subtle push to get them moving and turned back to dive into the fray. Except... where the fuck was the fray?

"What the fuck, dude?" I shouted, taking in the sight of Joey standing in the center of a pile of bodies, covered head to toe in blood like Carrie on prom night. "You asshole, I wanted to stab some fuckers."

Joey didn't answer me; instead, he lunged down with his blade ready. My eyes tracked him, and I realized one of the men in the pile wasn't totally dead after all. I struggled with the urge to rip Joey off his last victim so that I could add to my own kill count, but something in his demeanor kept me rooted in place. I wasn't watching Joey take a life; I was watching a feral animal eviscerate its prey. I shuddered, wondering briefly if the tickle up my spine was what fear felt like, before snapping back to myself.

"Bro, there's nothing left," I called out finally after Joey had gone far beyond brutalizing the body. My words didn't stop him, causing me to step forward and grab his hoodie, giving it a firm jerk. "He's way past dead, man. Now you're just beating a dead horse, and we got shit to do."

He didn't respond so much as snarl, struggling to escape me. I had to pull him further away, feeling like I was holding onto a feral cat and trying to avoid getting scratched.

"Joey! Stop!" I yelled, pushing him hard away from the pile of corpses, causing him to trip and fall, landing against a wall. For a moment, he just stayed there blinking before standing again and turning to face me. The wild look was gone from his eyes, but the cold anger had taken its place.

"Since when did you have a problem with carnage?" He sneered. "I was just doing what needed done."

"Since when has overkill been your thing?" I snarked back. "And you didn't even leave any for me, which, come on. Party fucking foul dude."

"Don't be childish. You did your job, I did mine. So what if a cockroach ends up a little more smashed than the others. No one cares." He rolled his eyes, brushing past me.

"Me? *ME being childish?* Have you listened to half the shit coming out of your mouth the last couple of days? All you've done is be fucking childish about our damned woman, but *I'm* being childish. Be fucking for real." I shouted, moving into his space.

"It's not childish to recognize a fucking snake in the grass after it's already bitten you. It already took us too long to figure it out, and I can't get you chucklefucks to see it!" He yelled back, crowding toward me.

I shoved him back, intentionally slamming him into the wall this time. "I warned you. I fucking warned you. What happens next is on you, I just want to make that cl–" My words cut off as I felt a sharp prick in the back of my neck. Joey grunted and reached toward his shoulder, drawing my eyes to see where a dart was sticking out of him. I reached my hand back and pulled out a dart from the back of my neck, squinting at it as it came into my line of sight. "What the f–"

CHAPTER EIGHT

Victoria

Being alone wasn't something I'd had to deal with in so long that now that I'd found myself alone in Dawn and Ian's house, I wasn't sure what to do. I hated the feeling of being in a new place; even though the house was warm and comfortable, I just couldn't get myself to relax. So I found myself doing what anyone restless in a new place did: snoop. I wasn't going through anyone's things, but wandering through the house, seeing what doors led to where because curiosity was all I had to indulge in. Or rather, was safer to indulge in. I opened a door, looked around a small bathroom, and closed it again.

As I wandered down a hallway, looking at the pictures on the walls of the boys, Dawn and Ian, and other people from their lives I'd never met, I stopped to look at a picture of Joey. The walls of this house weren't as thick as the boys would have liked, and even though they didn't say anything after their talks or meetings, I knew fractures were starting between them. It was hard to reconcile the man who was so angry and hateful toward me with the Joey I'd gotten to know. It made the others act like they had to handle me with kid gloves.

I sighed softly, continuing my exploration. It felt like we were all waiting for something, and none of us knew what it was. I opened another door to a bedroom that had me drawing up short. It was one of the only unused bedrooms I'd seen, and as I stepped inside, a scent washed over me that nearly buckled my knees.

This was Rich's room.

It smelled just like him, and I could almost see him in it after a second look around. There were books on gardening stacked up on a small desk and a neatly made bed, and there was a straightforward and logical order in his room. Tears pricked in my eyes as I realized the room was largely dust-free, even still. Dawn must have cleaned it, and the idea of the woman cleaning her son's room, knowing he would never use it again, was enough to nearly steal my breath from my chest. I couldn't imagine.

I sat on the edge of his bed. It occurred to me that someone would have to do the same thing at our house if we ever managed to make it back there. We'd have to pack his things... or keep the room clean. Who would take care of his flowers? I didn't know anything about gardening, and I could only imagine how angry he'd be if they wilted because they'd been poorly cared for.

I grabbed his pillow, pulled it into my lap, took a deep breath, closed my eyes, and let the familiar presence surround me.

"I wondered how long it would be before I found you in here." Dawn's voice made me jump, and I jerked my head toward the door. She smiled softly, an understanding look on her face as she stepped into the room.

"Dawn! I—" I stood quickly, putting his pillow back.

"It's alright, honey. You have just as much right to come in here as anyone else does." She moved to his desk, letting her fingers trail along the books and the surface. "You meant a great deal to him."

"I... wish I had known. I spent most of the time I knew him fighting with him." I said sadly, looking at my feet.

"That was one of the things he liked about you." Dawn chuckled. "He wasn't used to that, and you came as a surprise."

I didn't know what to do with that, so I said nothing. My eyes burned, and I blinked rapidly in an attempt to keep myself from crying in front of this woman who'd lost more than I would ever know. I shuffled my feet together, picking at the hem of my shirt as I looked back up at her. She'd handled everything with more grace than anyone, and it hadn't taken long for me to understand why all the guys treated her as a mother.

"Dawn, how… How are you okay?" I asked softly.

Dawn pressed her lips together momentarily before letting out a soft sigh. "I'm not. I'm only still standing because the rest of my boys need me. They won't make it through this without someone to hold them steady, and *you* still need a moment to grieve before you can be that for them. When you're ready, then… then I'll fall apart." She looked at me, and it felt like she was looking into my soul. I could see the weight of Dawn's grief then, like the crushing pressure of an ocean on her shoulders. It amazed me that she was still upright. Then she let out a long breath, and it was gone. "And I have Ian. We have each other. He holds me up when I need it. He's…" She trailed off, and even though I had seen how badly she was hurting, the light of love was still written all over her face as she thought about her husband. "He's more than a rock after all this time. He's my bullfighter. He has been since the first time we met at the rodeo."

I'd seen the pictures in his study—a young Ian and Dawn at the rodeo. Dawn was beaming with pride as a smiling Ian held up a first-place buckle and a trophy with a bucking horse on it. I couldn't picture Ian as a rowdy cowboy, but I imagine married life and children would settle a man down.

A hand on my shoulder pulled me from my reverie, and I blinked to bring Dawn back into focus.

"Come with me. I have something to show you, " she said with a small smile, leading me from the room. When she shut the door behind us, she did it so gently that it was like she was closing up a shrine as we left the room. I followed along beside her, listening to her talk because I wasn't sure what else to do.

Dawn filled every second of silence with idle chatter, and

by the time we reached the greenhouse doors, I understood why Ian was so quiet. He didn't have to do much talking when she did it all for both of them. It wasn't until we stepped inside that her words started to paint a picture of how things used to be for the Innocenti family.

"When the boys were coming up, Rich and I always spent our time in the garden. We didn't have near the space of this place back in south side, but we were proud of it." She closed the door behind us and ushered me toward a small table off to the side. There were pictures of Rich and Joey as little boys at varying ages, and it made my heart clench. "I took up gardening before the boys came along. Ian and I struggled to have children, and after my first miscarriage I needed something to do with myself. And this was what just clicked for me. Making things grow was comforting."

She picked up a picture of a teenage Rich, Joey looked to be just older than a toddler. I couldn't help but giggle at the image. Rich was dirty, with smudges on his face, soil-stained jeans, and wearing gloves with a smile on his face. Joey, conversely, looked like he'd rather be anywhere but there. "When we were finally blessed with Rich, he was always out in the dirt with me; it was what we shared. I taught him everything I'd learned until he started teaching me new things. He had a way with plants."

"Yes, he did. Everything in my mom's old greenhouse was immaculate after he started working there. I was surprised that someone like him was even interested in gardening, or flowers of all things." I set the picture back down, letting my fingers trail over a couple of others on the table that made me smile. A five- or six-year-old Rich was in muddy clothes with a potted flower that looked like it was drowning in all the water in the pot. Another of a toddler Rich, with Dawn, playing in the dirt while she was kneeling in the garden next to him.

"People had all kinds of assumptions about him. Well, no... assumptions is the wrong word. They weren't necessarily wrong, but they would have been surprised by how much more he was than the image he presented to the world. He could be hard, gruff, serious, even ruthless. But..." She trailed off, turning to idly tend to a shelf of sprouts nearby. "He always enjoyed being part of making things grow, breathing life into his plants. We knew what he had to be to do the job he'd made for himself, but I know my boys. He stuck to his morals as best he could, and we were always proud of him."

My eyes burned again, and my gut twisted, listening to Dawn talk about her son. The affection in her voice was unmistakable, and I felt like I wanted to be sick. I knew if it weren't for me, she wouldn't have had to bury one of her children. It took an immense effort to stay in my spot and not back out of the greenhouse.

"I always regretted that he couldn't, or wouldn't, let people close enough to him to know how deeply he did feel, how much he cared... about all of you. About everything. He would have traded his life for..." Her voice cracked, and I felt something in me do the same thing. Fresh tears started spilling from my eyes. "For any one of the people he loved."

I gripped the table to keep myself standing, breathing heavily as a wave of grief crashed over me. Rich *did* trade his life for us. Dawn and Ian had lost a son. Joey lost his brother. Az, Craig, and Leighton had lost one of their closest friends. I was never going to be able to forgive myself for costing them that.

"I'm so... so fucking sorry..." I choked out as a sob shook my chest. Dawn turned to face me, her eyes wide. She stepped toward me, reaching me just as my knees gave out, and knelt with me when I sank to the ground. She gathered me to her chest as I cried and apologized.

"Shhhh honey. I know." Dawn crooned, petting my hair and rocking me slightly. I wanted to pull away, but I didn't have the strength.

She didn't know. Her and Ian's grief, Joey's anger, the weight on Az's shoulders, Craig's tears, and even Leighton's refusal to acknowledge what was happening... The voice in my head wouldn't stop screaming that it was all my fault.

"None of this is your fault," She said as she continued to soothe me. "The boys may not have liked me and Ian in their business, but Rich told me about your situation. Sometimes, even mob bosses need advice from their mothers." She chuckled lightly before continuing. "From everything he told me, this mess has been about our boys all along. You just happened to be the carrot that got dangled from the stick. If it hadn't been you, it would've been *something*, but this way, we can know he was truly loved for everything he was before he left this world."

"But, if I–." I started to protest.

Dawn pulled back enough to look me in the eyes, her hands gently squeezing my shoulders. "When he decided on his line of work, I knew there was likely going to be a day I put one or all of my boys to rest. It's why we fought him so hard on it for so long. Even long after they'd established themselves in their world. None of it is what a mother ever wants for her child, but Rich... he's always been stubborn. Stubbornness and a mother's prayers don't change what the life they lead costs. And neither does blaming yourself for something that was always a possibility for them long before you were in the picture. There will be a day when you have to decide if their life is the life for you, or if you're going to walk away. But I'm gonna tell you now, if you stay, you need to start preparing yourself now for this sort of funeral being a given for your future. Whether it's one of them or another in their ranks. Only you know if that's something you're strong enough to endure."

The tears had stopped while she talked, and I was just sitting curled against her, considering her words. Before this, I hadn't really thought that any of my men would die despite everything I'd seen. Could I go through this again?

"And honey, you're entitled to make whatever choice is best for you, but I hope for their sake that you choose them. Because I know my boys well enough to know that if you walk away, you're going to take part of them with you."

CHAPTER NINE

Victoria

After I chatted with Dawn in the greenhouse, I went back to exploring the house. It didn't take long for me to fully explore, and I found myself outside the home office. Az was seated behind the desk, his hands tugging at his hair in frustration as he studied something on the laptop in front of him. Clearly, he was stressed, and if the dark circles under his eyes were any indication, he wasn't sleeping well either.

Before I could second-guess myself, I strolled into the room. "You remind me of my mother right now," I said with a soft smile, causing Az's gaze to snap to mine.

"I'm not sure how I should take that, Love." He replied, the corners of his lips tugging down.

"She used to work herself into the ground too. Just like you appear to be doing right now. Come to think of it, my father is also a workaholic. I suppose that means I was destined to follow her footsteps and find my own."

"Yeah, I'm sure Prudence would have loved the idea of you ending up with guys like us." Az snorted. "Her ideal workaholic for you was probably a doctor or a lawyer. Not four mobsters."

Shrugging, I let my fingers trail along the desk as I moved around it to step into his space. "She wouldn't have cared about the things you think. She'd have only cared that you make me happy and that you're all good men."

Az studied my face as if searching for something. "I'm glad you're happy, Love, but... We're not good men."

"Yeah, yeah, you're the boogeymen," I rolled my eyes and pushed on his shoulder, making him scoot the chair back so I could slide into his lap. "I'm going to find you under my bed one day just waiting to gobble me up."

His hands settled around my waist as he chuckled. "Yes, exactly. We're going to eat you up. But, that's not what I meant and you know it. Good men, they do the 'right thing' all the time. They're selfless. We're the farthest thing you can get from that."

"You're—"

"If we ever lost you," his arms tightened around my waist, "it'd be everyone's fucking problem until we got you back. I'd step on every neck, and burn every bridge until the whole city was on fire if that's what it took to have you returned to me... to us."

"That's probably true," I replied, Leighton's tendency to create chaos coming to mind. "But you'd never hurt me, and if I wanted to go..."

"That's the only way I *could* let you go," Az interjected, finishing my thought. "If you wanted to leave, of your own accord, Love, I *would* let you. It would be the hardest fucking thing I'd ever do, but I would."

I tapped his nose with my finger and smiled. "And *that* is what makes you a good man." I leaned forward and kissed the corners of his lips. "The four of you are perfectly good men... aside from all the mafia stuff, y'know, little shit like that."

Az threw his head back, letting out an infectious, deep belly laugh. Before I knew it, we were both chuckling as he cuddled me in his lap. It felt good and *needed*. Once we'd caught our breath, he touched his forehead to mine with a soft smile.

"Well, you know, nobody's perfect."

His words only made me want to feel closer to him, to remove everything that was separating us until there was nothing but pure pleasure left. "I know how you can make it a *little* more perfect and prove just how good a man you are," I smirked.

"Oh, do you now, Love?" He replied, arching a brow. "And how is that?"

"I'm going to go close that door and when I get back over here, you can bend me over this desk and fuck me to within an inch of my life."

"That might be what you think you want, but it's not what you need. It's not what *we* need."

My lower lip jutted out before I could stop it. "Are you turning me down Az Casadei?"

"Love, if I ever do that, it's a case of the body snatchers, and you should run," he said, his face completely serious, which made me bust out laughing again.

"You're adorkable. I'm trying to get in your pants and you're making jokes!" I giggled.

"There's nothing wrong with laughing with your partner, even when things are heating up." He smirked, running his hands under my borrowed shirt, tracing his fingers along my spine. "It's a good thing to be able to find joy even during intimacy; it doesn't have to be taken so seriously every time to still be *perfectly* pleasurable."

I arched a brow at him and tapped a finger to my chin as if considering his words. "I think I need a demonstration," I said finally, my voice breathier than I'd meant it to be.

The grin that spread across his face was positively sinful as he pushed aside his laptop and sat me on his desk. He stood and crossed the room in long strides to shut and lock the office door. All at once, my skin was tingling with the anticipation of his touch as he came to stand between my legs and pulled me toward him, so I was sitting on the edge and pressed against him.

"Like I said, I'm always happy to oblige, Love." He said, his voice dropping low as he ran his hands up my shirt again, sliding it up and off me and tossing it away. "And it can double as evidence you can use if you ever suspect a body snatcher."

He snickered at his joke, making me roll my eyes even as his hands trailed down my body to the waistband of the borrowed sweats, shimmying them off and letting them fall to the floor.

"I still stand by the fact that you're adork—" My words died in my throat as his lips closed around one of my nipples, his tongue flicking across it and making me groan.

I threaded my fingers through his hair, arching my back. He didn't neglect my other breast, his fingers pinching and rolling my nipple until they were both tight and stiff with his ministrations. He worked me with such skill I found myself wondering if I could cum from him playing with my tits alone.

He released my nipple with a pop, his hand falling away from the other, before planting a trail of kisses across my chest. His lips wrapped around my other nipple as his hand slid between my legs. His fingers slipped through my folds, and his lips released me. Tilting his head back, he looked at the flush starting to spread across my chest and face with a wicked smile.

"So fucking wet and needy aren't you, Love." He smirked. "Tell me, is this all for me? Or are you imagining someone walking in on us? You never know who has a key to this room. Or is it the memory of the last time we were in an office like this?" His thumb brushed across my clit as he slid two fingers inside me, and any response I had became just noise in my head. He tilted his head, that self-satisfied smirk still painted across his face. "I asked you a question, Love. If you don't answer, I'll stop."

"If you stop, Az, I might slap you." I huffed out, letting my head roll back as my hips rocked against his hand. I heard him chuckle low, and then he redoubled his efforts.

"Wouldn't want that, now would we?" He replied, leaning forward and nipping at my lower lip. "Look at me, Love. I love to watch you." His fingers curled inside me as he thrust them into me, his thumb circling slowly around my clit in a way that had me trembling against him, mewling and gasping for breath.

His pace was languid, slow, and torturous. I squirmed and rocked my hips as he took me higher, but I desperately needed *more*. The devilish smirk on Az's face told me he knew that, too, and he was purposely holding back from what I needed.

"Az..." I panted.

"Yes, Love?" His voice was deceptively sweet as he tortured me. God, he was infuriating.

"If you don't fucking make me cum." My attempt at a snarl was too breathless to hold any actual weight. He curled his fingers inside me in a way that had my back arching.

"You'll what? Beg harder?" He chuckled. "You're in this position because you already threatened me once. Are you sure you want to go for twice?"

Fuck, he wasn't wrong. I knew him well enough now to know he would meet my demands with more orgasm denial.

"Please, *Sir*, make me cum," I asked, injecting as much sweetness as I could into my voice in my current state.

Az narrowed his eyes, picking up on the tiny bit of sass I'd thrown in. "I think you can do better than giving me attitude, Love." He pulled his hand away and slapped my aching sex before thrusting his fingers back inside me; their pace slowed to the point where I could feel myself winding down. Internally, I started screaming in frustration. He could get under my skin like no one else, and it was infuriating and sexy.

"*Please.* I'm sorry, Sir. I take it back," I whimpered, "Please, *please* don't stop. I need to cum. I'll be so good, I promise." I grew increasingly desperate with every slow stroke of his fingers. "Fuck, Az... Sir, please..." my final plea came out on a fraught whine.

"*Much* better, Love. You can be so sweet when you want to be," Az crooned. His pace picked up, his fingers stroking the place inside me that drove me wild, making my body sing for him in just the tune he wanted. It didn't take long before I felt the familiar tension coiling inside me, my moans filling the room as I gripped his shoulders, riding his hand to push myself closer to the edge.

"That's it... Right there..." I pleaded for him to continue, feeling myself about to fall over the edge.

His hand abruptly stopped, leaving me bereft and empty. My mouth opened to protest, but the words came out a strangled sound as he slowly thrust his length into me. I'd completely missed him freeing himself from his jeans because his fingers had held my rapt attention.

"Shh, shhh, Love. You've been such a good girl. I'm going to let you cum, but it's going to be all over my cock." He ground out as he filled me, his arms wrapping around me and holding me close.

I started on his buttons, wanting to feel his skin against mine, but I couldn't focus. I sneered as I fumbled with them before gripping the fabric and yanking sharply, sending buttons flying as his shirt fell open. I sighed happily, sliding my hands across his skin, letting my head drop forward onto his chest. I breathed deeply, reveling in the sharp, masculine scent surrounding me. The combination of his smell and measured thrusts was heady. I shuddered, moaning, letting him hold me close and take me so slowly that it left me feeling drunk on pleasure. I panted and heaved, groaning deeply as I moved with him, our bodies rocking in sync. He took me higher with every slow, deep stroke so that the low inferno of my release was gently being stoked to raging flames under his patient ministrations.

"Don't... stop..." I breathed.

"That's it, Love. I got you." He murmured, pressing gentle kisses to my face, "Let go for me, drown my cock in your release." He pulled almost all the way out, his hips rolling slowly as he pushed back in—the slow, deep motion setting my nerves on fire. His words threw me over the edge, my orgasm washed over me like a tidal wave. It swept away everything that wasn't pleasure, and my entire existence narrowed down to where our bodies were connected. My vision whited out, and my teeth sank into my lower lip, drawing blood as I attempted to keep from screaming down the entire house.

"That's right, let me feel you, as close to heaven as someone like me is ever going to get." He groaned, kissing me deeply the moment my teeth released my lip.

He swallowed my sounds as he picked up the pace, prolonging my climax. My nails dug into his skin as I felt myself crest again. His rhythm faltered, his hips stuttering as a second orgasm rolled through me. Our moans mingled in the space between our lips as I felt him tense. A low, almost tortured groan rumbled up from his chest, and I felt his cock swell and pulse inside me just as he let go, filling me with his hot cum.

"Fucking hell," he breathed, placing his forehead against mine. "You're perfect. My perfect girl."

Giggles bubbled up my throat, my hands flying to my mouth to hold them in. Az pulled back enough to give me a confused look, and I lost it completely.

"We should probably get the fuck out of Ian's office." I laughed.

Az barked out a surprised laugh and shook his head. "Yeah, you're probably right."

CHAPTER TEN

Leighton

My head throbbed and even lying on my back, I felt dizzy. Keeping my eyes closed to stave off a wave of nausea; I mentally took inventory of my body and senses. I felt wholly uninjured, and the surface beneath me felt surprisingly soft. Inhaling deeply, I caught a whiff of a familiar scent and cracked my eyes open in curiosity.

"Mother fucker." I muttered as my surroundings came into focus.

"Good, you're finally awake." My mother drawled, drawing my attention to where she stood at the foot of my childhood bed.

"What the fuck, *Cicely*?" I demanded. She didn't deserve the respect of being called 'Mother.' "You better hope like hell that Joey is still breathing or we're going to have a big fucking problem."

"Leighton! Language," She scolded, clicking her tongue as her face twisted in disgust. "Really that garbage you've lowered yourself to associating with has done a number on your manners."

I carefully eased myself upright, placing my feet on the hardwood floor. "Right, and pulling a snatch and grab of your own son is such *good* manners." I snarked. "What is this even about? What do you want?"

Her lips pursed briefly before her face settled back into

a smooth mask. "I told you when we came to that *hovel* you called a home. You're to be married. Unfortunately, word of your... situation, reached the family of your original intended and we've had to make different arrangements. You will wed Ksenia Sidorov in a few days' time."

"Sidorov," I replied slowly. "You're marrying me to a Bratva Princess? Wasn't your whole issue with my *actual* girlfriend that her mother wasn't up to your standards? How is her bloodline less desirable than the fucking *Bratva?*" My voice rose with each word until I was yelling.

My mother let out an exasperated sigh and pretended to wipe lint from her shoulder. "The Sidorov's are established, they come from old money. Their illegitimate dealings aren't quite what we desired in a match for the Laurent heir, but they are wellbred and understand our world in ways someone from the slums could never. The darker parts of their business may even suit you well, given your... disposition."

"And what do you and *Daddy Dearest* get out of this deal?"

"It's not what we get, darling. It's about our legacy. Once you and the Sidorov girl produce your own heir, our line will be forever tied to one of the most powerful families in the country."

"I'm pretty sure you need me to agree for any of this to happen." I said. "I told both of you when you showed up in *my* home unwelcome and unannounced that I was with Victoria. *When* I decide to get married it will be to her. I'm not your little puppet anymore, you can't control me like you used to when I was a child."

"Is that so," my mother replied with a sly smirk. "The chain around your ankle and the fact that I have a gunman keeping your precious sweetheart in his sights around the clock would say otherwise. You really didn't think your father or I would be so stupid as to not have leverage now did you?"

I kicked my leg out, taking note of the shackle around my right ankle for the first time. The material was lightweight enough I hadn't noticed it over the material of my jeans, but knowing my mother, it was sturdier than anything you'd find in a hardware store. She may have caged me, but I was calling bullshit on the rest of her threats. If she had someone on *Ma Petit*, we'd have known it.

"I can see the gears in that little brain of yours turning. You don't believe me about the girl," she stated matter-of-factly before moving to the doorway. "Alfred, the pictures, if you would please," she called out to the family butler, who must have been waiting in the hallway.

The elderly man who had been our family butler my entire life strode into my room wearing his usual black suit and tie. His white-gloved hands held out a silver tray with an envelope to my mother. She barely acknowledged the man as she took the proffered item and pulled out several photographs. I bit back a snarl as she turned them so that I could see. One of the photographs showed Victoria and Dawn Innocenti embracing in Dawn's greenhouse.

"How did you get that close?" I demanded, surging to my feet and stalking toward my mother.

"I told you, darling. We made sure we had leverage." My mother replied dryly. "Now, if you're quite done with your tantrum, I wanted to tell you the tailor will be here in the morning to measure you for any necessary adjustments to your tux. Your father and I will be busy handling the other arrangements, so we won't see you again until it's time to escort you to the chapel." She turned her back to me, stepped toward the door, and paused. "Don't think about it, Leighton. If you attack me now, there's nobody to ensure your sweet Victoria's head remains intact."

I clenched my teeth and fisted my hands at my side. My mother clearly still knew precisely how to control me, to keep me from lunging forward and murdering her in the middle of my old bedroom. It took every scrap of willpower to stay rooted in place as I watched her stride confidently out the door. She let the photos drop from her hand to the end table as if they were a parting gift, and then she was gone.

My entire body trembled with the need to commit violence as I stalked over and snatched the pictures. Several seemed to chronicle the days between Rich's funeral and Joey and I leaving together to check out our territory. Part of me knew they were all taken *before* Craig had a chance to set up any sort of surveillance system. The rest of me wasn't willing to take the risk with Victoria's life that whoever my parents had hired couldn't access her any longer.

"Fuck it. Being a widower wasn't on this year's bingo card, but here we are." I muttered to myself.

Saying the words out loud seemed to cause a plan to settle in my mind. I'd go through with the sham of a wedding. Killing my bride-to-be in front of her Bratva family would only end with me dead, too. I'd have to wait until we were alone for the wedding night. If I timed things just right, I could off the girl and slip away before anyone knew I was gone. My parents would be left to deal with the fallout of a dead Bratva Princess. Shit, the Russians might even do me a favor and off Alistair and Cicely for me. I couldn't help the grin that spread across my face. The boys would be proud. I was actually *planning* for once.

Planting a sloppy kiss on one of the closer-up photos of Victoria's face, I strolled back to my bed and plopped down. My stomach rumbled just as I considered how I would entertain myself until I could put my plan into motion.

"Yo, Jeeves!" I called out. "You still in the hall?"

I snorted as the butler moved to stand in my doorway. "Yes, young master. Your mother ordered me to stay nearby in case you needed anything."

"Don't call me 'master',"

"Of course, young master."

"Dude, what did I just say?"

The elderly butler jerked back as if I'd slapped him before quickly regaining his composure. "My apologies, Sir. How may I be of assistance?"

"I'm hungry. Go make me a sandwich or something." I

adopted my haughtiest tone and flapped my hand at him in dismissal.

"Yes, Sir. Very good, Sir." he simpered as he retreated from my room.

His statement that my mother had ordered him to stay nearby was a threat as much as a warning. The man had reported every little thing I'd done to my mother starting the day after she'd murdered Angelica. I couldn't even take a piss without her knowing how strong and steady the stream was. His reports to her had been directly responsible for a few of my more intense punishments. I wouldn't be surprised if it were something he said that led to my parents putting me out in some twisted attempt to teach me to control my urges. It would be fun making his life hell for the next few days.

I strolled around the perimeter of my room and then into the ensuite bathroom, determining just how much chain my mother had left me. I could easily access both spaces, which meant I could step into the hallway, though I wouldn't get far doing so. The sound of metal on metal as I moved had me searching for the anchor point next. Several steps and a few kicks later, I'd pushed my bed aside and stared at a narrow grate bolted to the floor. As I moved closer, the chain slid between the slats, a step away, and links slid out. I was about to start pulling the chain out as I stood over the grate to figure out how far below the chain was secured when I heard footsteps coming down the hall. I shoved my bed back haphazardly and flopped onto my back on the soft mattress just as Alfred appeared in the open doorway.

"I can tell from all the way over here, that sandwich is a travesty." I snipped, snatching a pillow from the top of my bed and throwing it in his direction. "Make it again, Tweedlepot!"

Alfred bowed, the muscles in his face twitching as if he were fighting the urge to sneer at me. "As you wish, sir."

The moment the sound of his footsteps disappeared, I started searching my old hiding spots for anything that might work to remove the bolts, keeping the grate under my bed in place. I tore the room apart, tossing old knick-knacks and mementos to the floor, pulling open drawers, and dumping the contents into the ever-growing mess, finding absolutely nothing. My mother must have swept the room and found everything before she had me brought home. Growling in frustration, I slammed the last empty drawer shut as Alfred reappeared in the doorway, startling me.

"Fucking hell, Waddlesby. Warn a man when you're about to sneak up on him!" I snapped. I looked at the silver serving platter where he'd plated a new sandwich. "And seriously, *generic white bread?* What do I look like? A fucking soccer mom? Make that shit again, and make it *right* this time!"

"Yes, sir." he replied tersely, backing out of the room.

I waited until he was out of earshot and moved my bed again. Testing the bolts with my hands was futile, but I had to try anyway. A few attempted twists and tugs, and I was satisfied that my mother had covered all her bases—an unfortunate obstacle to any plans I might have made to escape before the wedding. Putting the bed back, I laid down to think. I could practically hear Joey teasing me about it hurting my head as I worked through a real plan to become a widower and get back to *Ma Petit* on my wedding night. All before the consummation, because I may have been a lot of things, but I was *not* a fucking cheat.

Alfred returned with a third sandwich, and I took it without a word. An idea popped into my head as he strode toward the open door.

"Yo, Bibblesworth. Pick up this fucking mess." I demanded, gesturing to the disaster I'd created in my room.

Under normal circumstances, Alfred would have sought out the maids to pick up after me. The fact that he instead bent down and began picking up items off the floor told me I had been correct about him spying on me for my mother. A sinister smile split my face as I watched the older man work. I would make his life hell for the next few days, and I knew just where to start.

"For fuck's sake, Wrinklebottom! If you're going to clean, make sure you do it properly. You can't just put things away all willy-nilly! *Fix it, **now.***"

CHAPTER ELEVEN

Craig

After I'd passed off what little information I could pull with my hasty setup, I made my way to the garage to find a ladder. Ian was leaning against the hood of his '57 Chevy, finishing the last few bites of a sandwich. His eyes tracked me as I moved to the back wall where his ladder was hung. His footsteps echoed on the concrete floor until he stood beside me. Swatting my hand away with a grunt, he grabbed the ladder and carefully turned to face me. It was clear from his stance that he was waiting for me to tell him where to put it.

"I have cameras that need installed. I need to go grab them from my room, if you want to set that up by the front door, I can start there." I said.

Ian nodded and moved toward the garage door, hitting the switch on the wall to open it as he did. Not sure what to make of his behavior, I quickly went to my room and grabbed the cameras before meeting him on the front porch.

"Thanks," I said when I got there, noticing the ladder was already in position. "I'll just get started."

I started to step around him, intending to climb the ladder and install the first camera. Ian sighed, the sound making his annoyance clear, and gave me a look I could only describe as *the* 'dad look.' Putting one hand on my chest to stop me, he reached the other out and curled his fingers in a 'gimmie' motion.

"I can handle installing some cameras," I attempted to argue, only to have him gently push me back and make the motion again. "Do you know how to wire these up?"

His response was an exasperated look as he snatched one of the camera boxes free from the bags in my hands. Shaking his head, he turned and started up the ladder. Ian didn't say a word as he worked, only pointing when he needed a tool or turning to stare at me if he needed some instructions. It was comforting in his own strange way, and with each new camera we installed, my mind slipped deeper into memories of the man when I was a child.

As I replayed the memories of growing up with the Innocenti's down the street in Southside, it didn't take long for my mind to return to the night I murdered my father. Most of what happened after my mother found me standing over his body, covered in blood spatter, was a blur. But the memory of walking into the Innocenti's home was still crystal clear.

Dawn and Ian had been waiting for me, opening the door before I could knock and ushering me inside. Dawn had fretted over me with a washcloth for a few minutes before Ian gently grabbed my shoulder, led me into their small living room, and motioned for me to sit. I'd been utterly numb as I settled into their worn-out sofa, not even noticing the large man taking a knee in front of me.

"You did the right thing, son," Ian said, his deep baritone carrying a hint of gravel in his heavy Southern accent. The sound was shocking enough to startle me out of whatever place I'd gone to in my mind. Ian never spoke. Ever. "We tried everything we could to get him away from the pair of ya, but nothing worked. I'm sorry you had to do what you did, but you did the right thing. A good man protects his family, and that's what you did."

My mouth fell open in shock, and I could only nod. Ian pinched his mouth closed and studied me briefly before nodding and stepping back like he'd never spoken.

"Craig," that same rough baritone jerked me out of my memories. It was probably the fourth time I'd heard him speak in my entire life.

I looked up to find Ian on the ladder, staring at me in irritation with a hand out. He almost looked pained to have needed to say my name to draw my attention back to our task. Muttering an apology, I handed him the next camera box.

Ian looked past me as he reached for the box. He startled me as he jumped down from his perch atop the ladder to the ground. He brushed past me with surprising speed for his broad body, and when I turned around, he was sprinting across his property. I followed him as quickly as I could comfortably move, drawing up short when Joey came into view.

"What the fuck happened to you?" I hollered, taking in his blood-soaked appearance. Joey didn't have a chance to respond before Ian started silently checking him over. Turning and handling him like he might a small child as he looked for wounds. He got as far as pulling Joey's shirt off him while we stood in the front yard before his son stepped back with his hands up.

"Dad... Dad! Stop it, I'm fine! It's not my blood." Joey clipped, snatching his shirt back from his father. I could see the tension visibly leaving Ian's body, and the heavy sigh of relief sounded like it was heaved from his whole body. There was a pause as Joey put his shirt back on, rolling his eyes when he looked at his dad.

Ian's hand snapped out, and he slapped the back of Joey's head before settling his hands on his hips and staring Joey down.

"I'm a mobster, Dad. What did you expect?" Joey snarked, rubbing where his father had slapped him.

"Yeah, and so am I. I've never come home looking like Carrie on prom night." I responded with a raised eyebrow. "That's outside the norm even for our line of work, unless you're Leighton and it's fight night."

Joey shot me a dirty look as Ian shifted his weight and then looked back at his father. It was clear there was some unspoken conversation happening between them that I couldn't follow without seeing Ian's face. I wasn't even sure I *wanted* to see his face, having been on the receiving end of his looks once or twice growing up. After a few more moments of silent standoff, Ian jerked his arm out and pointed to where their hose was stored. Joey hung his head and stomped in that direction, reminding me of how he'd react to a scolding as a teen.

Ian sighed again, momentarily tilted his head toward the sky, and then marched toward his son. Without a word, he pulled the hose free and turned the knob on the spigot. He didn't bother giving Joey so much as a warning look before he pressed the handle and started spraying him down.

"Fuck! Dad, that's cold!" Joey yelped, jumping back. "A heads up would have been nice!"

Ian groaned, pinching the bridge of his nose, and then twisted the nozzle to the jet stream. Joey practically danced as bloody water streamed below his feet, and Ian continued to spray him with cold water. I stood there, fighting the urge to laugh, as it became increasingly apparent that Ian was prolonging things by focusing the stream on Joey's shirt. When Joey opened his mouth to say something, Ian raised the nozzle and sprayed him in the face, causing me to lose hold of my laughter.

I regretted it immediately as freezing cold water blasted me in the face in response to my laughing at Joey's predicament. I raised my hands in surrender and stepped back a few paces. Ian turned the hose back on Joey, motioning for him to lean down, and began to spray Joey's hair down. Joey scrubbed his hands through his hair until the water was as clear as he could get it without soap.

He turned the nozzle back to regular stream before shutting off the hose and hanging it back on the storage. He jerked his head toward the garage.

"Where's Leighton?" I asked as we followed behind Ian.

"Don't fucking know." Joey replied through clenched teeth. "We got tranq'd and the next thing I knew I was being shaken awake by one of our street guys that Leighton had ordered to head to Harrison's."

"You're lucky our man disobeyed an order," I murmured. "But tranq'd? That makes no sense."

Joey jerked his head toward Ian, who was closing the garage door, as we entered. "We'll talk about it later, with Az."

I nodded. None of us wanted to get into our work around the parents, and they were happy not to know more than they needed to. Joey reached for the door to the house and froze when Ian cleared his throat behind us. We both turned to Ian, standing there with his arms crossed over his chest and his eyebrow raised. He motioned toward Joey's blood-soaked and now dripping-wet clothes. His meaning was obvious, and he was right. Dawn would flip if Joey tracked any of that into the house.

"Seriously?" Joey said. Ian gave him a look as if to say, 'Do I look like I'm joking?' It took everything in me not to chuckle, lest I be punished as well for acting out of turn. Joey huffed and took his shoes off. He looked at his dad, who motioned to the rest of him. "It's freezing out here!" Ian shrugged.

"I mean, do you want to deal with your mom if you leave blood drops on her carpet trying to get to the bathroom?" I offered. Joey considered it for a second before he undressed himself in the garage until he was standing there in soaked boxers. He gave a cold shiver before looking back at Ian, who shook his head.

Joey clenched his jaw, removed his boxers, and threw his hands up. "Happy now? There's nothing left that can drip on Mom's carpet!" Ian looked him over for a second before going back out the garage side door. We heard the sound of running water a moment before he came back into the garage with the hose again, motioning for Joey to step away from the door. "This is starting to be cruel and unusual punishment, Dad."

Ian chuckled with an almost innocent shrug before he turned the nozzle on Joey again and sprayed him down until the water ran satisfactorily clear. He turned the nozzle off and gave Joey another once-over before nodding in approval. Joey rolled his eyes and gave him a thumbs-up with a sarcastic grin. His thumbs-up became the middle finger when Ian turned his back to take the hose back outside.

"I'm gonna tell him you did that." I quipped with a smirk.

"Do it and see what happens." Joey grumbled, turning back to the door to go inside.

I shook my head and chuckled. "I'll grab Az and we'll meet you in your dad's office after you're showered and dressed."

Twenty or so minutes later, the three of us were sequestered in Ian's office. Joey relayed everything that had happened while he and Leighton had been checking our territory, though he conveniently glossed over how he'd ended up so thoroughly soaked in blood.

"Shit," Az hissed. "While it's still a possibility, it's highly unlikely someone who was gunning for us would have tranq'd you and left you alive." He paused, and I could see his mind working. "Did you notice if you two were being followed at any point?"

Joey pursed his lips as if holding back a snarky response before answering. "No," he said on an exhale. "If we *were* spotted and followed, they covered their tracks with serious skill."

"Fuck. So we have nothing to go on." Az replied, running a hand through his hair before tugging on the strands. He'd done that so often lately it was starting to seem like a compulsion.

"We have to consider that someone knew we were here and that the house could be bugged," I spoke, my mind working over the severe lack of security at the Innocenti house.

Joey's eyes slid to me and narrowed. "The house is owned by a shell corp, you took care of all of that yourself so that it would be impossible to find any connection to us through this house."

"Dawn and Ian took my advice and avoided having any sort of wake or gathering here before Rich's funeral, too. And you've been here ever since to see for yourself that they haven't had any guests." Az added.

"What about deliveries? Food, flowers? Condolence gifts?" I asked.

Joey just shrugged and shook his head as if to say he didn't know. Az, on the other hand, let out a muttered curse.

"We didn't think to tell them not to." He said, clenching his teeth. "Fucking hell. I may have compromised all of our safety by missing something so fucking stupid."

"I'm going to need Phil to make another run. Let's not panic until we're sure." I replied, unsure how to stop Az from beating himself up over something anyone could have missed.

"I'll make the call, what do you need?"

It was nearly midnight when Az returned from meeting Phil at the drop point. I'd laid down with Victoria while I waited, not wanting to cause her to panic if I was wrong. Az didn't bother knocking on my door. Instead, he walked straight into the room and waved the radio frequency detector in the air. Carefully untangling myself from Victoria, I moved to take it from his hand and motioned for him to lead me to where Dawn had stashed any deliveries they'd received in the last week. I'd scanned a casserole dish, a plate of cookies, and two condolence cards before the detector went off on an ornate vase of white lilies and roses.

"Fuck," Az spat, slamming the side of his fist on the end of the counter the vase sat on.

"We found it," I said, trying to reassure him. "That means I can disable and track it. And I've already started beefing up security around here. We will be fine. We will *make sure* we're fine."

"I really need that fucking head count and names of

who's left." Az growled softly. "I'm not going to bring them here, but I can station them at the drop point in case we need back up. It's not too far for that."

"Until we find Leighton, Joey is all we got to check things out. I'm not sure it's such a smart idea to send him out alone. He turned up here covered in so much blood it had even saturated his boxers. Ian had to spray him off with the hose... twice."

Az lifted his hand toward his hair before stopping midair and scowling at it like it had offended him. "I'll sync up with Phil and we'll do the sweeps. You figure out who the hell that bug belongs to."

CHAPTER TWELVE

Leighton

I was starting to grow bored of tormenting Alfred, though it had been pretty amusing when the man nearly broke. Still, I was ready for this sham of a wedding to be over so I could get back to *Ma Petit*. I hadn't seen anyone other than the butler, so I wasn't too surprised when Waddlesworth walked into my room while I stood in the middle of it butt-ass naked.

"Like what you see, Bixby?" I asked, shaking my hips to make my dick swing back and forth.

"Leighton," My mother's voice called from the doorway, interrupting my fun. "Put on pants, we need to go over your schedule for today and I'd prefer to do so without your genitals exposed."

Alfred moved to my dresser and retrieved a pair of Versace cashmere joggers before turning toward me like he was going to put them on me himself.

"Woah there, Woodworth, I can put on my own pants. Don't need you copping a feel of my junk, you filthy dog, you." I snarked, snatching them from his hands and pulling them on.

My mother glared at me until I settled onto the edge of my bed and motioned for her to proceed.

"The tailor will be here in an hour with your tux. You will be showered and shaved before he arrives. We have a hairstylist and makeup artists scheduled to arrive shortly after. You need to be in your tux before they arrive so they can get to work covering those unsavory tattoos of yours. Your father and I will escort you to the chapel at noon. We will have a full guard detail so I expect you to be on your best behavior. I'd hate to see you injured on your wedding day."

"Wait, wait, wait. Shouldn't there be a photographer taking photos of me getting ready? It is my day after all, what if I want to save these *precious* memories? And where are my groomsmen, you don't really expect me to get all dressed up and pretty without my fellas?" I snarked.

"Given your attitude concerning this wedding, we decided it was for the best to have a small ceremony." My mother continued, ignoring my outburst. "The Sidorov's are aware of your disposition and have agreed to our recommendation of chaining you to the altar until *after* the ceremony. The guest list has been limited to myself, your father, your sister and her husband, the parents of the bride, and your precious Bristol girl."

"You didn't." I snarled.

My mother shot an irritated look in my direction and then smiled with false sweetness. "It's only appropriate that you and Victoria Bristol *both* be made aware of the change in your circumstances. The simplest way to do that was to invite the poor girl so you couldn't drag her along with false promises of a life with the Laurent heir. I expect that once the marriage is final, she will see sense and accept that she can no longer sink her claws into you. Honestly, it's rather distasteful the way you passed her around that little group of thugs."

My hands curled into fists in my lap. As much as I wanted to jump to my feet and strangle Cicely until the life bled out of her eyes, I knew that was the reaction she was after. She made it clear that she had safety measures in place if I tried to harm her, and I couldn't be entirely certain that the guys had had time to secure the Innocenti's property to prevent them fully. I just hoped they would keep Victoria from falling into my mother's trap by attending this farce of a wedding.

"I hope you covered your tracks well, *mother*, because

Hugo Bristol can't be bought. Not when it comes to his daughter." I replied through gritted teeth. "Though, I suppose if your intent is just to show her I'm off the market.." I trailed off with a slight shrug of my shoulder.

My mother's face flushed an angry red, and she clenched her jaw. It always got under her skin when she found herself outplayed. Cicely thought she was the smartest person in any room she walked into, but she never accounted for the fact her fucking ego left her half-blind.

"I suppose what happens is up to you, darling." She replied, trying to regain the upper hand. "I only invited the girl. I can't control how the Sidorov's respond if you do something foolish, like attempt to run away with her. Now, if you are done with the interruptions, we need to review the rest of today's schedule.The ceremony will commence at one and it will move quickly. You will simply need to say 'I do' and then sign the marriage license. From there, the Sidorov's will escort you and your new bride to their hotel for consummation. Ivan Sidorov has informed me that once you have done your duty and put an heir in Ksenia, he has work for you so that you may keep your wife in the lifestyle to which she has become accustomed."

"What?" I shouted. "No cake?! Who has a wedding with no fucking CAKE!? I demand a cake mother, or I will *not* be getting married today."

Alfred scowled in my peripheral, and I almost lost it. The butler had had enough of my shit. However, my mother only sighed and slipped her hand into the pocket of her white designer slacks. Somehow, I wasn't surprised to see a valium in her hand.

"You *will* behave today, Leighton. Or I will ensure that you are too drugged to cause any sort of scene."

"But that might make my dick not work, Cicely! How am I supposed to make a baby without my dick?"

The look on my mother's face told me I'd taken my antics just a little too far. The sensation of being hit in the back by a couple of paintballs shot through me, and then my entire body seized. Burning pain tore through every muscle, and wetness spread down the front of my leg and joggers as my bladder released. That fucking Belvedere had gotten brave in my mother's presence and tased me.

"*Must* you be so crass?" Alfred asked in a haughty tone as my body fell back onto my mattress.

I was going to murder that asshole the first chance I got.

After being tased by the fucking butler of all people, I spent the rest of the day too exhausted to care about what was happening to or around me. Someone had put me in my tux and shoes, styled my hair, and covered my tattoos with about three pounds of makeup by the time both of my parents appeared to escort me to the chapel. When we arrived, I did a cursory glance of the place while the chain that held me was attached to a plate bolted to the floor and looked suspiciously like Az's 'parking spot'. I scowled at the square of steel and briefly considered how long it would take to chew through my leg, but I reminded myself I had a plan. I just had to get through this sham, and I could make my way back home.

The place was all but empty. A priest was standing next to me, my mother and father were sitting in the front row, and my sister and her husband were behind them. They both looked bored out of their mind. On the other side of the aisle sat what could only be soon-to-be former in-laws. I couldn't help myself as I shot them a cheeky wave. I'd considered adding finger guns, but they might take that as a threat. Before I could do anything else that would embarrass my parents, the wedding march sounded through the small chapel.

The doors near the back row opened, and what could only be described as miles and miles of tulle piled together stepped onto the aisle. I couldn't make out the shape or face of my soon-to-be-dead bride for all the fabric covering her body from head to toe. That didn't mean I missed the moment she hesitated and started trembling. Her father barked something in Russian, and she resumed her walk down the aisle. The air of dread around her was so heavy that I could not even sense it.

I started taking mental notes of the *choices* made with the woman's dress as I watched her walk toward me. There was no way she'd picked it out, and I would definitely be dissecting the decision with *Ma Petit* later because I was starting to wonder if killing this woman was the right call. Not because I wanted to be married, but because that dress was such a fucking tragedy; I felt terrible that it was going to be the last thing she ever wore. I'd make time to let her change before I killed her later on. I would at least do that final service for her.

Ksenia finally reached her place beside me at some point during my musings and lifted her veil away. My eyes widened to the size of saucers as I took in her pretty face. Given the amount of fabric they'd buried her under, I'd expected her to be hideous, but she was fairly attractive with her golden blond hair, big, bright blue eyes, and cupid bow lips. Before *Ma Petit*, I'd have been into it, but nobody could hold a candle to my girlfriend.

I leaned forward to whisper in her ear, not missing how her eyes widened in fear. "I'm really sorry about that dress." Her entire body tensed as if preparing for me to rip the fabric from it and attack her. The reaction caused something to shift inside me. "I'm really and truly sorry about everything that's going to happen to you after this is over. If there was another way for me to get home to my girlfriend..."

Ksenia's blue eyes widened as she started blinking at me in stunned silence.

"Huh, that's new," I mused, still leaning close and whispering in her ear. "I've never apologized to anyone except my girlfriend. Another one for the bingo card." I shrugged.

The priest cleared his throat, and I straightened up, pulling away from Ksenia. A strange, bothersome sensation started to grow in my chest as the priest spoke the opening lines of the ceremony. For a second, I wondered if it was what guilt felt like.

"If anyone knows of any reason these two should not be joined in holy matrimony, speak now or–"

Five pops sounded off in quick succession, and blood splattered from the priest's head against my cheek. Turning toward the pews, I spotted Lacey standing with a gun in hand, smoke curling out of the silencer, her husband still tapping away on his phone with a bored expression on his face. Our parents and Ksenia's were all slumped over in their seats, perfectly placed bullet holes in each of their heads. My almost-bride screamed as my sister turned the gun on her, and I did something that surprised even me.

"Hey, not her!" I called out, stepping in front of Ksenia. "She didn't even want to be here."

Lacey rolled her eyes and lowered her weapon as she moved toward me. "You owe me two."

"Wait a minute now, damn it. I didn't *ask* for you to ruin my wedding. No way I owe you for this one."

"Let me guess, you were going to murder her tonight and then what? Escape unseen from a Bratva owned hotel?" Lacey drawled. "I did you a favor putting an end to this ridiculous farce before you got yourself killed with whatever nonsense you had planned."

"Okay, fine." I scowled. "You might have a point. So what do you want?"

"For the van, you sign over your claim to be the head of our family to me."

"Done, I wasn't interested in 'taking my place' anyway." I said, finger-quoting to express my annoyance at her insinuation I would even *want* to be the family heir.

"I haven't quite decided what I want for this one. I will let you know when I've decided." Lacey continued.

"Wait... hear me out. Wouldn't it be in your better interest to have that favor owed to you by the new head of the Sidorov Bratva?" I jerked my head to the woman behind me, shaking in fear. "The horsemen aren't in a position to grant favors right now, but–"

"Leighton–" Lacey attempted to interrupt.

"Just hear me out, Lacey, damn. Ksenia here doesn't even know how to *run* a family, let alone the entire organization you so kindly just dropped in her lap. She's gonna need someone to be her second and train her up. Who's better to do that and help take control of a Russian mob than you? Just think about it. The Laurent name and wealth combined with the full power of the Sidorov's behind you."

Lacey pursed her lips, her eyes boring into me as she considered my words. "While I am well aware you're just trying to flatter me out of holding you to a second favor, I can't argue with your logic. I'll accept what you've offered, *this* time."

"Fantastic," I grinned, clapping my hands together. "Now unchain me and take me to my motorcycle so I can get home to my girl."

CHAPTER THIRTEEN

Victoria

I sat drumming my fingers impatiently on the dining table, staring into space as I turned over what limited information I had about what happened to Leighton for what felt like the millionth time. It had taken a while to get anything out of the guys, especially with Joey now only speaking to me long enough to insult me, which always started an argument between him and the other two. Az did eventually tell me what they knew, and it sent alarm bells off in my head.

From what I understood, what happened wasn't in the playbook for anyone on the board right now that they could think of. But something was itching in my mind and driving me crazy, like a puzzle I was putting together without all the pieces.

"Victoria, honey," Dawn's voice broke through my thoughts and made me nearly jump out of my skin with a yelp. I turned to her, my hand to my chest as if I could keep my heart from leaping out of my chest. "I'm so sorry! I didn't mean to scare you, dear." She smiled at me sheepishly.

"It's alright, I was just... lost in thought." I said with a shake of my head. "Did you need me?"

Dawn held out a cream envelope with delicate calligraphy addressed to me, a puzzled look on her face. "This was in our mail, and there's no return address or anything. It didn't feel right for me to open it but... well, here."

I raised a brow and took the envelope from her, turning it over as if I'd find some clue on the outside. "I don't know who would have sent it either…" I said absently, opening it slowly. I pulled out the elegant six-by-nine card, and my jaw hit the floor.

I stood from my seat so fast that the chair toppled over. I barely had time to register Dawn's shocked expression before I was running through the house toward Ian's office. The guys had been holed up in there since breakfast, but I didn't hesitate to barge in without knocking. The door slammed against the wall as it flew open causing all three of their heads jerked up to look at me.

"I know where Leighton is!" I said breathlessly, waving the wedding invitation in the air. "We have to go…*Now.*"

"Whatever it is, no." Az replied without hesitation. "One, we aren't going in *anywhere* blind, and two, *you* aren't equipped or trained to handle a rescue mission. You'll stay here, period."

"It's a fucking *wedding*, Az-hole. His fucking parent's are marrying him off and we *have* to stop it." I shouted, throwing the card at his head.

The weight of the cardstock wasn't heavy enough for it to do much beyond twist and flutter in the air before landing on the floor a few inches in front of me. I bent over and snatched it up before storming to the desk and shoving it in his face.

"How did you get this?" Az asked, studying the delicate calligraphy outlining Leighton's wedding details.

"Dawn said it was in the mail for me." I snipped. "Now can we fucking go? The wedding is in less than an hour, we have to leave now or we won't make it in time."

"There's no way this isn't a trap." Az said, moving to pass the invitation off to Craig. "Clearly, the Laurent's are the ones who found us here, but given Alistair and Cicely's opinions of the three of us, I doubt they sent this with good intentions."

Craig studied the invitation, turning it over in his hands much like I had done when I first opened it. "Even if there was the remotest chance it *wasn't* a trap, if we let you just walk into a wedding with Russian Bratva in attendance, as well as his parents... Leighton would be so pissed he'd beat us to hospitalization just on principle." He said, passing the card to Joey.

"But it is *absolutely* a trap. So the answer is still no." Az said, deadpan.

"Fuck it. Let her go," Joey interjected with a shrug. "If she gets her ass killed , then it's just that much easier for us."

My mouth fell open in shock. Sure, Joey had been making snide and downright mean comments toward me lately, but this felt different somehow. My hands clasped against my chest against the jolt of pain they caused me as Az stood from behind the desk and strolled over to where Joey sat. His body language didn't give anything away until his fist connected with Joey's face in a sickening thud.

"I am so fucking sick of the shit spewing out of your fucking mouth." Az snapped, rubbing the knuckles of the hand he'd hit Joey with.

"Fuck you," Joey spat, leaning forward and pinching his nose to stop the bleeding. "I'm sick of all of you being so deep in her fucking pussy you can't think straight. Maybe put your dicks back in your pants for a fucking minute and stop playing nice with the whore long enough to see what's right in front of all our faces."

My feet moved before I was aware of them. In seconds I was standing in front of Joey as he looked up at me in disgust. Cocking my arm back, I let my hand fly, my palm cracking across his cheek hard enough to cause his head to whip sideways. He turned his head back toward me and stared me down, a clear challenge on his face.

"Enough." Az boomed. "If you can't get yourself together enough to not being a piece of shit, then get the fuck out, Joey. Whatever sick little games you think you're playing right now, they're done. We get it, you're fucking grieving and looking for somewhere to place the blame, but you're crossing lines you damned well know you shouldn't."

I stepped back as Joey pushed up from his chair; he gave me a twisted little grin as he briefly moved into my space and then stepped around me. "You'll figure it out eventually." he shrugged, moving toward the door. "Play house all you want, I was just trying to save us some fucking trouble."

Two hours later, Az, Craig, and I were *still* arguing about me coming along to rescue Leighton. They'd stressed the dangers and made sure I understood them, and I did. But I was also getting sick and tired of them relegating me to the sidelines of my life, as if I wouldn't put it all on the line for any of them the same way they would for me.

"I'm fucking going. We've missed the god damned wedding by now, but no fucking way am I leaving one of **my** men in a fucked up situation. And make no bones about it, you're *all* my men." I snarled, standing on my tiptoes so I was practically nose to nose with Az.

"I will have Craig tie you up if that's what it fucking takes, Victoria!" He bellowed back.

"I–" Craig started.

"Awww, that is so fucking sweet!" Leighton's voice rang out, causing me to whip around toward the door. "I knew I was your favorite. That's why I'm the only boyfriend." He smirked as he stalked across the room toward me, his expression changing into something I'd never really seen on him when he drew close enough to grab me. "I did *not* cheat. I saved myself for your eyes and hands, and lips, and—"

My palm connected with his cheek, wiping the serious expression from his face before I knew what happened. "If you *ever* scare me like that again, I swear to god, Leighton!" I shrieked.

"I was kidnapped, it's not my fault," He whined, poking out his bottom lip. "You know I wouldn't have had a wedding without you."

"How did you escape?" Craig asked.

Leighton looked at him, then to Az, then back to me. "I'm an orphan now. *Ma petit,* I need to be comforted!" He ducked down, putting his shoulder against my abdomen before lifting me up and over his shoulder.

"Leighton!" I squeaked as he started for the door.

"We need to talk about this, Leighton." Az said.

"Not now! Orphan, big sad about it." Leighton replied with a laugh and continued out of the office, carrying me toward his room as the other two called after him.

"You're not fooling anyone, L! Be back in an hour for debriefing!" Craig called out the door with a laugh before he shut the door again.

Leighton carried me into his room, kicking the door closed behind him before dumping me onto his bed. "I don't know, *Ma Petit,* I'm real, real sad right now. It might take more than an hour to make me feel better about being away for three days, what do you think?"

"I missed you, too, you big idiot." I giggled. "But we really should try to keep it to an hour or else they might break down your door."

Leighton paused in the process of pulling his shirt off and shrugged. "They do that then they can watch or join, don't care."

"I am *not* having a group session in Dawn and Ian's house in the middle of the afternoon!" I quipped.

"So you're saying that's a night time only activity. Got it." He grinned. "I'll let the guys know during debrief."

"Oh my god," I said, rolling my eyes.

"No, babe, I'm Leighton." He smirked, quickly stripping out of his clothing and stalking toward the bed. "I didn't push my motorcycle to the limit to get back to you so that you could confuse me with another man."

"Shut up and come here," I motioned at him to join me in the bed, shaking my head.

"Strip for me first." He replied, wrapping his hand around his cock as his eyes darkened. "I want to see you naked in my bed and as desperate for me as I am for you."

I sucked in a breath from the way he looked at me, the dark need in his voice. Somehow, Leighton could take me from laughing to breathlessly wet in no time. I moved slowly, letting his gaze follow my hands as I reached for the hem of my shirt, shimmying as I pulled it up and over my head.

"Good girl. Keep going." He said, his voice deep and husky as he pumped his length slowly with his hand.

I bit my lip, hooking my thumbs under the waistband of my jogging pants, lifted my hips, and slowly slid them down my thighs. Leighton growled in frustration when I laid back in nothing but my panties, and I smirked at him before I started to slide my hands down my stomach. My fingers played with the elastic band, taunting him as his eyes focused on my hands.

"Get them off, *Ma petit*." He growled, releasing himself before he moved to the nightstand and pulled out a pocket knife. "If I have to do it, they won't be left in one piece."

The need lacing his tone was intoxicating, and I was helpless to his command. I shimmied out of my panties, tossing them on the floor beside the bed, and then looked up at him through hooded eyes. He fisted his cock again, his forearm flexing as he stroked himself.

"Spread your legs," He ordered. "I want to see you touch yourself."

"Fuck," I breathed, letting my legs fall open as I laid back and obeyed.

I slid one hand between my legs, gently circling my clit with my fingers and drawing out a soft moan as my other hand slid up my body to squeeze my breast. My hips jerked as I worked myself over, my fingers gliding through the gathering wetness. Leighton groaned as my eyes closed, my legs trembling with my growing pleasure. I felt the bed shift under him, and then his hands were on me, pulling my hands away as he positioned us so that I was straddling his hips. The head of his cock slid through my folds and notched at my entrance just before he pulled me down, filling me in a single thrust as I cried out.

My eyes flew open as he rocked into me, his pants mingling with my soft moans.

"Mark me," He barked, opening the pocket knife and placing the handle in my hand. "I want you to carve yourself so deep into my skin that nobody will ever question who I belong to." He wrapped one hand around mine, the other on my hip, as he positioned the tip of the blade against his chest. "Make me fucking *bleed*."

I stilled, looking down at him and taking in his face. "I–"

"Do it. *Please*." The hint of desperation in his voice sent my objections scattering to the wind, and I carefully drew the blade across his chest in a 'V.' "Deeper. I need... Fuck, I need you to make sure it's permanent. Scar me. Fucking, *please*."

He didn't give me a chance to respond, his hand wrapping tighter around mine and forcing me to press the blade deeper into his skin. Blood tailed behind it, bubbling up as he guided me to carve the letter deeper. The look of sheer, unadulterated pleasure and soft sigh that left his lips was unexpected.

"Yes, fuck. *Yes*." He groaned, stilling my hand and flipping us so that I was beneath him, the blade still piercing his chest as he rolled his hips.

Blood dripped down my hand and wrist as he drove into me. The wild look in his eye left me yearning to feel the same. Jerking our hands from his chest, I turned the blade to mine as I wrapped my legs around his waist and used my heels to drive him deeper into me.

"Wha–" he started

"Mark me," I panted, rolling my hips to meet his. "I want... I want to feel what you feel." my moans punctuated my words.

Leighton blinked, his hips stuttering to a stop. "Fuck... Fucking *red*."

My heels pressed into his ass, and I rolled my hips as I

whined.

"Pumpernickel! Red! God fucking damn it! STOP!" His voice raised with each word until he finally raised up and pulled out of me, sitting back on his heels as he all but yelled the last word. Shock and confusion painted his expression, but I couldn't understand why.

"Don't you... want to mark me too?" I said, confusion furrowing my brow as I spoke.

Leighton sighed, his shoulders slumping forward and his head hanging down. "Fuck, more than anything, but..." his hands moved to his thighs and curled into fists. "Victoria, you will never feel what I feel. I wouldn't *want* you to. It's... Ugh, shit. It's just not good things, okay?"

I sat up on my elbows, searching his face. He had pain written all over his face and tension set in his jaw. It was like someone dumped cold water on the way I'd been feeling moments ago. I sighed heavily, sitting up the rest of the way and smoothing the worry lines from his forehead.

"If anyone else said that to me, I'd probably take it some kind of way." I said softly, running my fingers up through his hair.

His gaze snapped to mine. "What? No, I didn't mean it like that." his fingers moved to his chest, running through the still bleeding mark he'd helped me make. "I fucking *loved* this, but–"

"I *know*, I was there. I saw how you reacted to it. I'm not taking you wrong, I know you're trying to tell me that what I asked for wasn't me, and you don't want me to do something I would have regretted." I said softly, pulling him toward me so I could touch his forehead to mine.

"I don't know how to do this. I'm usually the one doing the cutting. That's my thing. I've never let anyone cut me before, and I've never said no to someone asking for it. I'd love to see you bleed, fuck, I *dream* about it. It makes my dick weep just at the fucking thought, but... Fuck, I don't know. Maybe I should get Craig, he's better at this talking shit than me."

"You're doing just fine, Leighton. I get it. This," I made a motion between myself and him, "is a good thing. You don't have to talk to me like Craig, you'll learn to talk to me like *you*."

His sad expression was heartbreaking. He looked so lost. "What if I can't?" he whispered. "What if one day, holding myself back like I did just now becomes too much, and I just..."

"Leighton, you aren't giving yourself enough credit. What if you can't? You are. Right now, you are. And it'll only get easier for you, if not with everyone, then with me." I kissed the corner of his mouth and smirked when I pulled back to look at him again. "Besides, I've learned quite a few things from you and Az, I'm pretty sure I could kick your ass if I needed to."

He barked out a surprised laugh and wrapped his arms around me. "Yeah, okay. If you say so *Ma Petit.* If you're ever able to kick my ass, I will let you walk my ass naked through our home on a fucking leash."

"Deal." I giggled as he pushed me back down into the mattress. "We'll make sure it's a really nice leash."

"Alright, *Ma Petit*, but first... I'm going to finish what we started."

CHAPTER FOURTEEN

Joey

Leighton's debrief was a nothing-burger. His psycho parents were behind his abduction, and his psycho sister saved his ass. Given our current situation, he'd have been better off as a married man. At least *then*, one of my so-called brothers wouldn't have the viper's fangs in them anymore.

"Anyway, I'd just like to reiterate that I am the only boyfriend, and I earned that place by *not* getting married." Leighton continued on from whatever he'd been saying while I was lost in thought. "None of you can use that as an in, either. I'm Virgin Mary-ing it. One time only deal."

Az shook his head, a slight smirk on his face, and Craig just stared at him like he was trying to figure out why Leighton was the way he was. I... wanted to puke.

"That's... not how that works at all, Leighton." Az said with a chuckle.

"That's not how any of this works." Craig followed up.

Leighton crossed his arms in front of his chest and frowned. "Yes huh. It's like dibs, I got the title first so it's mine. But I promise, I'm still happy to share." He paused and pointed at Az, "You can be the sassy booty call, and Craig is clearly the mistress. Joey is... I don't know what Joey is, he's confused right now and he doesn't even have the spirit. Maybe he can be the pity fuck until he gets his head on straight, I don't fucking know."

It took every ounce of willpower to keep my mouth shut during Leighton's diatribe, but I wasn't in the mood to be hit again. My nose still hurt enough from Az's blow to make me think twice. At this point, they'd all taken shots at me for trying to tell them what was right in front of their face. As much as I loved seeing them laughing and having a reason to smile, considering our circumstances, I just wished it was something that wasn't going to get them killed in the end. And they were all too close to her to see it coming.

"If that's all, I've got shit to do." I said finally, standing from my seat.

"Aww, you don't wanna see my new addition? I was just about to show everyone." Leighton grinned, wiggling his brows at me.

"Pass," I replied, knowing I didn't want to know whatever it was.

I didn't bother waiting to see how he responded, walking out of the office and heading straight for my room. As soon as I stepped inside, I locked the door behind me and booted up the laptop I'd added to Phil's supply run. Craig may have been the tech guy, but I knew how to access the backups of everything we kept stored, and I was currently combing through every piece of evidence we'd gathered while Az was locked up. I let out an annoyed huff. His six months in jail because of the fucking princess was something else he seemed to have forgotten about.

While I waited for everything to load up on the laptop, I turned to study the wall opposite me. I didn't have much on it at this point, but it was a start. I'd managed to get the original pictures Gary had collected for us, which felt like a lifetime ago. I'd circled the one of her with Rinaldo Marino because it felt significant that she'd managed to convince even the Jackals' consigliere that she wasn't the one who orchestrated his entire downfall and demise. I'd printed out the articles from Az's arrest and added them to the wall. A picture of Az and my brother were up there too, both victims of her machinations in some way. Though, really, we all were. I'd also grabbed the picture of the box Rinaldo had sent her, which had contained the heart and Tiffany's picture as an obvious threat. And Tiffany… her picture was next to the viper's. There was no way that *she* could have pulled it off alone, and Tiffany was clearly helping her.

Could I prove any of this? No, not with what we currently have. But I knew. I knew we were right in the beginning, and Rich's death was just the latest of her moves to somehow take us out from the inside. I just had to figure out how the pieces fit together, and then I'd show my brothers how much danger they were in. She wasn't worth all of our lives.

Shaking my head, I turned back to my desk and settled into the chair, my fingers tapping on my desk for a moment before I started on the next batch of files in the backup. Craig had neatly organized everything, including the police report and court filings, that I was working my way through. Victoria's initial report had been circumstantial at best. According to the report, someone had attempted to take her *during* the gala fire, and she magically managed to escape their clutches with her wholly nonexistent self-defense skills. That was when Az's dumbass tried to help keep her from getting trampled. Except, the way she told it to the police, he was the man trying to take her all because of his moth tattoo.

"Should have fucking let her be trampled." I muttered to myself, moving to the next document in the file.

It was mainly legalese I'd need more time to decipher, but instead of seeing Hugo's name on the court filing as I'd expected, it was Theodore Abrams. My brows shot to my hairline as I continued to skim the filing and moved into the court transcripts for the arraignment. For all intents and purposes, Az had been an upstanding pillar of the community until that fucking fire, but reading the transcript, you'd have thought he was a common criminal. I mean, he was, but they should *not* have known that. We'd always been exceptionally careful at ensuring he wasn't involved in *anything* that could have one of us getting caught doing. Clearly, dear old Uncle Theo was helping her, too. I made a mental note to look closer at the emails he'd sent Rinaldo when I got to them.

I pulled out the cheap cell phone Phil had managed to grab for me on his first run and dialed his cell. My leg jiggled impatiently as I listened to it ring.

"Pick up, pick up," I muttered just before the call went to voicemail. "Fucking hell man, come on!"

I hung up without leaving a message and immediately called him again. He still didn't answer. I tried several more times to no avail and was about to redial him when my phone rang.

"What?!" Phil shouted before I could say a word.

"*Excuse me*? You wanna remember who the fuck you're talking to and try that again?" I snarled back.

"I know who the fuck you are, Joseph, but I'm kind of fucking busy trying to put out every god damned fire in *your* organization so you still have something left when you decide you're done acting like a fucking child because I shouted at you. Pardon the fuck out of me for being a little stressed and losing my shit." He shot back. "Now, what the fuck do you need so I can get back to fucking work you little shit."

"If you were anyone else, you'd be ending the night with a bullet in your head."

"Well the fuck aware. As it is, I'll be spending the night between my therapist's thighs if you'll hurry the fuck up and tell me what you want? A man needs a god damned break now and then, ya know."

I gritted my teeth for a minute before blowing out a calming breath. "I need someone on Theodore Abrams."

"On him, or *on* him?"

"*On* him. Any information we can find, and around the clock tail if we can swing it."

"What are we looking for?" Phil asked.

"I'll know it when I see it. Just… figure out how to get the shit done and have whoever you put on it report directly to me.

Nobody else. And I want to know everything, even when he takes a shit. Got it?"

"Az ain't gonna like me putting one of ours on a detail like that right now."

"Did I ask what Az was going to think about it?" I snapped. "If I wanted Az's opinion on this I'd ask him to take his dick out of your mouth long enough to have a chat. Now get it done. And remember, they *only report to me.*"

"Jesus, Joey, I think you need to talk to my therapist. You got some real anger issues going on right now and I gotta say, they aren't the vibe." Phil said in a snarky tone. "Besides, we *all* know it's Craig's dick in my mouth. But if you want any pointers to help you keep Az–"

I ended the call without waiting for him to finish his ridiculous statement. He was a good man and a damn good soldier, but he sometimes forgot his place. Receiving direct orders wasn't the fucking time for his poor attempts at humor.

"As long as he does what he's told..." I muttered to myself, turning back to the laptop and where I'd left off in the court transcript, glad it was easier to read than the filing. Either way, it was going to be a long fucking night.

CHAPTER FIFTEEN

Az

After days of hitting the streets with Phil after the others had gone to bed, we finally had a semi-accurate headcount and a secure warehouse to gather everyone. Word went out for all remaining crew members to meet there at midnight. We told anyone who thought they might have a tail to phone it in if they could find a secure place to make the call. Craig had talked Phil through his tech wizardry to ensure we could have a conference call in a deserted warehouse.

"Dawn wants everyone at the table in five for dinner," Victoria's voice called from the doorway of Ian's office as I skimmed over what little information I'd gathered on the streets. She moved from the doorway toward where I sat at the desk. "You look tired, have you been sleeping at all? Don't lie to me either. I've heard you sneaking out the past few nights."

"I sleep when I can. There's too much to do and not enough bodies to get it done." I replied with a slight shrug. "I'm finished up for now, though. Let me just wash up and I'll join everyone at the dinner table."

"If you're not down in ten, I'm coming back, and I'll drag you to the table if I have to." She said with a smirk. I raised a brow and shook my head in amusement.

As promised, I joined everyone at the table five minutes later. Sliding into the only empty seat left between Craig and Leighton, I made a show of settling in for Victoria. She smiled and rolled her eyes before turning to ask Dawn if she needed any help.

"I'm glad everyone made it to dinner," Dawn said, waving away Victoria's offer to help. "We've all been under the same roof for a week or so, but I feel like we haven't spent any real time together as a family. We need it. We can grieve alone all we like, but there's nothing as healing as coming together as family."

I cast a sidelong glance at Joey, waiting for his response to Dawn's statement. Surprisingly, even Joey stayed quiet, looking down at his plate. I moved my gaze toward Ian, who reached out from where he sat beside her and gently squeezed her hand. He wore the same soft expression I'd always remembered him having whenever he looked at his wife. Dawn smiled back at him and then flapped her free hand at the rest of us.

"I didn't put in all that work in the kitchen for nothing, eat up before it gets cold."

Ian made Dawn's plate, then his own, before the rest of us dug in. Dawn talked around the table as she ate, taking time to speak to each of us as if this were a regular catch-up. Joey mumbled his responses, barely able to look at his mother before she moved on to Craig. She fretted over the state of his injuries with motherly concern. Craig must have answered a few dozen questions and offered just as many reassurances before she moved her attention to me.

"And how are you, Az? You're the one carrying the weight of things now. I know you boys never liked me in your business, but Rich would call me when things got too heavy. He would tell me enough that I could give him my thoughts and advice." Her voice was steady, but nobody could miss the hint of sadness that tinged her words. "You know, if you ever need the same, you can come to me."

I saw Joey stiffen, looking at his mother with an open look of betrayal before he turned inward, scowling at his plate. The deep frown that etched Ian's face as he studied his son didn't escape my notice.

"I appreciate that, Dawn, truly I do. I've got the other three to lean on, but I'll keep your offer in mind should I ever find myself in need of it."

Dawn gave me an approving smile before chuckling. "In that case, the rest of you boys, and you Victoria, any of you up for a bet on what the tick will be? Rich took after his father and always pinched the bridge of his nose when he was at his limit."

"I'll take that action!" Leighton said enthusiastically.

"I'm pretty sure that's cheating, Leighton. You can't do Dawn like that!" Victoria chastised him.

"What? He hasn't settled into it being a tick yet!" Leighton pouted.

Craig leaned forward and raised his voice to be heard over Leighton continuing to argue with Victoria. "Az has been tugging at his hair constantly lately," he explained to Dawn. "That's most definitely settling in to be his tick."

"It is *not* a tick. It just eases the headache you three cause!" I retorted.

"See!" Leighton shouted.

"You little scoundrel!" Dawn laughed, turning her attention to Leighton. "Well, aside from attempting to make a fixed bet with little ol' me, what have *you* been into? You disappeared there for a few days and nobody would tell me anything at all."

Her continued conversation with the others faded to background noise as I finished my meal. My mind was busy reviewing what needed to happen at the meeting later, and nothing else registered. It wasn't until I insisted on doing the cleanup that I zoned back into the present.

I gathered the plates from the table and walked into the kitchen, where Victoria was shooing Dawn away from the sink, insisting that she take care of the dishes since Dawn had cooked for all of us.

"Let us take care of it," I interjected, putting the plates

in the sink and a hand on Victoria's shoulder. "The meal was delicious as always." Victoria made another shooing motion and Dawn smiled despite narrowing her eyes before she huffed and left us to clean up.

"Thanks for the assist, I didn't think she was going to let me do anything," Victoria said.

"She probably wouldn't have. You'll have to come around a little more before she stops treating you like a guest." I chuckled, scraping off food into the garbage disposal and rinsing dishes before handing them to Victoria to put into the dishwasher. "It took her ages to even start using the dishwasher."

"You'd think with me hopping between Craig and Leighton's bed, she'd have either dropped the politeness or ratched it up to an uncomfortable level." Victoria chuckled.

"Nah, Dawn's not judgemental like that. She's seen it all living in the southside and has always made it clear to us that she just wanted us happy and healthy." I chuckled, my memories of Dawn through the years playing like a flip book in my mind. "And I've heard a few stories growing up. She was quite the character herself before she settled down."

"So, no weird politeness politics if she catches me slipping into your room tonight then?" Victoria grinned, taking the next dish from my hand, before turning serious. "Just to sleep though. I miss you, you're so busy lately that I feel like the only time I could possibly get with you is cuddled up asleep."

I grimaced, not only at her words but at the knowledge I was about to reject her offer. "As much as I wish we could, Love, tonight isn't a good night. Me, Leighton, and Joey are meeting our people and I'm not sure how long that's going to take."

"I could come." She said, not an ounce of hesitation in her voice.

"No," I replied quickly, then sighed, realizing how that probably sounded. "Not because I think you need to stay put, but because this is Horsemen business."

"Okay, and?" Victoria huffed, putting her hands on her hips and turning to face me fully.

I turned to face her fully, fighting the urge to tug my hair after the conversation at the dinner table. "You're not a Horsemen, Victoria. A partner, yes, but you don't have the training or experience to weigh in on our business."

"I realize that I'm not officially a member of your boy's club," she spat, "But I've been through enough both *with* and *for* the Horsemen. When is it going to be enough to have some kind of voice or stakes here?"

"Don't make me the asshole here, damn it. Yes, you've been through a lot with us, and yes, whoever mixed you up in our business was using you to target us, but don't forget *Princess*, that every damned time, it's been our skill that's saved your ass. Let's say I let you come, one, you aren't part of the organization, your mere presence will cause people to question *our* authority. But let's say for argument's sake, they accept the bullshit reasoning that you're there for your protection. You are safer here. You had, what, a few weeks of self defense training while everything has been going to shit? You don't have the skills to protect yourself if shit goes sideways at the meeting place. And the odds aren't in our fucking favor right now, Victoria. So much so that Craig is staying behind because *he* understands that his injuries currently make him a liability."

The entire time I was speaking, Victoria merely stood there with her arms crossed over her chest. She weighed my words for a moment, and I could see the wheels in her head turning. "I... see your point. I don't want to, everything in me says you're being an Az-hole." She sighed heavily, letting her arms fall to her sides. "I'm tired of being left behind, and I'm tired of being *reactive* rather than *proactive* to keep not only myself safe, but you four as well." I opened my mouth to speak, and she made a 'shut' motion with her hand.

"Shut it. I'm talking, you got your monologue," she snapped, "I know I don't have the skills to be useful, I'm aware that my presence will be a distraction if something goes sideways and you have to worry about getting me out alive on top of yourselves. Do you think that I don't fucking *know* how useless I've been to you all this entire time? Sure, Joey trained me enough with a gun that I can aim and fire, and stand a decent chance of hitting what I meant to, most of the time. I'm reasonably sure I can keep myself from getting dragged off. But if you think I'm fucking going anywhere, Az-hole, you've got another thing coming. I've been through hell with you four! And back! So if your reasoning for me not contributing is because I've not got the skills, fine, help me develop them. If not directly, then give me something to work toward!"

"Fucking hell, woman, why can't you just be our peace?!" I bellowed. Victoria drew back like I'd slapped her, and I could see the wind leave her sails. "Christ, I didn't mean to scream that at you, but fuck's sake, Victoria. There's nothing wrong with just being the calm in our storm. We *need* that."

"I..." She faltered, looking away from me. "I'm not trying to... be a problem. I..." I reached for her, seeing the struggle on her face so clearly. But she pulled away from me. "I want to be your peace, but what's wrong with me also wanting to be a shield for the men I love? So I don't... have to lose any more of you?"

I cupped her face in my hands, my thumbs stroking her cheeks as I held her gaze. "You're not a problem, Love. That's not at all what I meant by that. You're just so busy trying to dive on the sword for us you haven't stopped to consider that you've picked the wrong battle. One day, you will have the skills to be our shield; I promise you that. But right now, the best way to be that shield is to be the softness we come home to." I slid a hand down and grabbed one of hers before bringing them to rest just over my heart. "This is what we need you to protect, Love. Not our bodies."

"Hey guys—" Craig's sudden interruption caused us both to jump away from each other. I turned to look at him, where he leaned against the doorframe to the kitchen with a smirk on his face. "Didn't mean to scare you. I wanted to go over a few things before it got much later. I'm tired, and I'd like to catch a little sleep. I'm starting to get too damn old for this middle of the night shit."

I nodded, turning back to Victoria with a questioning look. She raised up on her tiptoes and kissed my cheek, her expression soft. She brushed past me and kissed Craig's cheek similarly before leaving the kitchen.

"Alright, what did you want to go over?" I asked, motioning in the direction of Ian's office.

"First, I..." Craig trailed off, his expression thoughtful. "Neither of you were wrong there, you know? She wasn't made for this life, but she's found herself in it nonetheless. And no one in this life gets to *just* be a shield." His voice was soft as we fell in step with each other toward Ian's office. "None of us want her in this, but she *is* in it. And, Az, we've made members of people who've been through less... There are—"

"We're not having this conversation. If the time comes that I have to reconcile with it, I will, but we're not discussing it. And I swear to God, if you tell her we've brought in people for less..."

"I'm not planning on giving her *more* ammo. I'm injured, not brain dead." Craig snarked.

I glanced at my wristwatch and saw that it was closing in on three in the morning. Craig wasn't the only one getting too damned old for these late nights, and I still had at least another hour of reports to work through when we got back to the Innocenti's.

"Alright, so that just leaves Todd." I said to Phil before muttering under my breath. "What sort of mobster is named Todd?"

I must not have spoken as quietly as I thought because Phil chuckled before calling the man to stand before us. He had a similar build to Joey, but his face was forgettable, and I couldn't help wondering why Phil hadn't suggested him for the recon jobs I'd assigned already. I briefly considered calling back one of the others and swapping them out as Todd studied me, Joey, and Leighton, waiting for our orders. Someone like him could easily be looked over and forgotten by a target.

"Only thing left for now is sweeping the buildings on Elm for any bugs planted in our absence. There's already a crew securing the area, and another dealing with cleanup. So, it's your lucky day, Todd, you get the bug sweep job."

"I'm already on assignment, Sir." Todd replied.

"What fucking assignment?" I demanded. "I'm the one handing out jobs and this is the only one I've given you."

"Uh..." Todd went pale, his eyes widening as they bounced between me and Phil, and he took a step back with his hands up.

"He's working for Joey." Phil interjected.

"Todd, go wait over there." I pointed at a stack of crates near the farthest visible wall and then turned on Joey. "Why the fuck do you have one of our men on a job only you and Phil seem to know about? One I clearly haven't signed off on!" I demanded.

Joey drew up, squaring his shoulders as he turned toward me. He tilted his head to one side and sneered. "I wasn't aware I needed to ask permission to assign a job that I needed done to one of *our* men."

"It seems like you aren't aware of a lot these days." I shot back. "In case you haven't fucking noticed, our organization is in shambles. We're back at square fucking one, something you weren't there to experience the first time. So, the *only* job right now is getting this organization back on track, rebuilding and recruiting, not whatever secretive bullshit you've got going on."

"You're acting like I'm not aware that we need to be getting our shit back on track! That's what I'm fucking doing, and I don't need your permission to decide how I do that!" He crossed his arms over his chest and lifted his chin in defiance. "I *might* have been around to help with building and recruiting in the beginning, but between you and my brother I was relegated to *proving myself* for most of that! You can't sideline me and then use it against me!"

"You never proved yourself! If Rich hadn't brought you in, you'd be dead." I snapped.

"Oooh shiiit!"

"Shut it, Leighton!" I barked out just as the sound of Phil's palm cracking against Leighton's skull rang out in the warehouse. Turning my attention back to Joey, I stepped into his space. "What you did was get yourself in too fucking deep and on the wrong side of the Golden Devils for slinging dope in their territory. If Rich hadn't claimed you as one of us, they would have put you down for the slight. All because you were too much of a fucking child to take your brother's 'no' for an answer."

Joey's arms dropped to his sides, his fists clenched and his jaw tense as he stepped toward me so we were chest to chest. "You fucking liar." He leaned back enough to shove at my shoulder, his face screwing up when it didn't have the effect he wanted. "I know I screwed up as a kid, but don't make it worse than it fucking was. I caught some charges, and the Horsemen had to bail me out. I worked off that debt, and Rich said I worked off my debt. He put me where he did so I could use my skills for everyone's benefit. I know you always wanted his spot, but don't you put words in his fucking mouth now that he's gone!"

I crowded back into his space so that we were nearly nose to nose and dropped my voice to a dangerous whisper. "No, you got caught by cops on the Devil's payroll. Rich sent you to your parent's to hide out while *we* sorted out how to pay the fucking tax on money we never made. You *cost* us, little brother. But it was a cost we gladly agreed to pay to keep you breathing. If you don't believe me, ask Craig. If you don't believe him... Well, Helen will be here in a week with our delivery, you can ask her just how close you were to a nine between the eyes."

I moved back just enough to shoulder-check him hard as I stepped around him and toward the exit. The need to hit something was riding me hard after Joey's insinuations. He wasn't in a place to reckon with his misconceptions, but if he didn't get his head out of his ass soon, he was in for one hell of a shock.

CHAPTER SIXTEEN

Joey

"Joey..." Craig's voice came through the speakers of the laptop Phil had set up for him to join the meeting via conference call.

"Save it, Craig." I bit out, stomping over and slamming the laptop closed.

My eyes skimmed the almost empty warehouse, briefly landing on Leighton and Phil tearing into a tin can of popcorn before finding Todd where he'd been ordered to wait. I stomped to Todd, causing the man to blanche as my shadow fell across him under the harsh fluorescent lights.

"Keys," I ordered, holding out my hand. "You and me are going on a little drive."

Todd gulped, his hand visibly shaking as he struggled to retrieve his keys from his hoodie pocket. The overloaded keyring jangled loudly, echoing across the space as he placed them in my hand.

"Should..." his voice trembled almost as severely as his hands. "Should I let my ol' lady know I won't be coming back, boss?"

"Fuck's sake, Todd. I'm not taking you out back to shoot you. I have something I need to do and I'm not particularly in the mood to ride bitch on Leighton's bike."

Todd visibly relaxed and stood from his seat, motioning me to follow him out of the exit opposite where Az had left. He led me through the empty parking lot to a travesty of a fucking car. It looked like he drove it straight off a 'Fast and Furious' set and set out to make it even *more* obnoxious. With an irritated sigh, I climbed into the driver's seat and waited for Todd to get in and buckle his seatbelt.

"Do you have any experience taking out security equipment?" I asked as I pulled onto the road and drove away from the warehouse.

"Some. I mean, I'm no Craig, but if it's not too complex I can knock it out for maybe fifteen with my homemade emp if I get close enough."

"Shit. Fine. That will have to do." I said, more to myself than Todd.

He shot me a puzzled glance that I didn't bother providing further explanation for. The last thing I needed was for him to narc me out to Phil, who would then narc me out to Az... again. At least not before I found the evidence I needed to prove that Victoria Bristol was a fucking snake and that Az was wrong about how I earned my place.

Glancing at my watch as we drew closer to my destination, I silently cursed Todd's vehicle choice again. There were plenty of hours left til daylight, but the fucking hunk of fiberglass he called a ride was going to stick out like a sore thumb in Hugo Bristol's neighborhood.

"Todd," I said abruptly. "You need to ditch this piece of shit and find something nondescript if you want to stay away from the end of my gun. No way in hell you're tailing Theodore Abrams in this fucking thing and going unnoticed."

His hands went up in surrender. "This is my personal ride, boss. I have a minivan I use for work, swear."

"You better fucking hope so because we're parking here and hoofing it the rest of the way. This hoodie is all I got against the fucking cold and it's making my trigger finger real, real itchy. This god damned car is completely to blame." I snarled as I pulled off the road and parked behind the community entrance sign. "Come on, let's get this over with."

Todd scrambled from the passenger seat and raced to the trunk of his car, calling for me to pop it as he moved. I moved to the front and waited, tapping my foot impatiently for the few minutes it took him to make his way to me, holding what I assumed was his homemade EMP up with a grin. Pulling the hood of my sweatshirt up, I took off at a brisk pace in the direction of Hugo's mansion. Todd was shockingly adept at following me without making any sound as we wove through the oversized neighborhood, avoiding the obvious cameras. Hugo Bristol's home came into sight and I slowed my pace, allowing Todd to fall into step beside me.

"That one just over there," I nodded toward the gaudy gate with the ridiculously ornate 'B,' "I need to get in there without any footage to show it ever happened. Think you can manage that?"

Todd's eyes narrowed on the gate, flitting around to tops and sides, only pausing when he spotted a camera.

"Yeah, they don't look nearly as top of the line as the stuff we use. I should be able to knock them out, just have to walk by and press the button. No way I can do it and stay out of range myself, but I'll make sure I look like I'm out for a casual stroll."

"Good, get it done, and then keep an eye out for any incoming."

Todd nodded and started in the direction of the house. "Wish this was planned so I could have stolen a dog or something, make it more realistic," he mumbled under his breath as he strolled away.

I pinch my lips against the urge to snap back over his comment. He wasn't exactly wrong, but my gut was telling me that time was of the essence getting into the Bristol mansion now that Victoria knew I was onto her. My eyes tracked Todd, but even watching him as closely as I was, I didn't catch the moment he enabled his device. If it weren't for the fact that he turned back toward me, scanning the cameras to ensure the light signaling they were in operation was out, I'd have never known he'd done his job.

My feet tore across the concrete, and I practically flung myself at the gate, using that stupid fucking 'B' to help lift myself up and over it. Balancing briefly on the narrow poles at the top, I jumped down, letting my body move into a roll so I wouldn't break a leg, righted myself, and raced to the main house.

I almost laughed out loud when I realized how fucking arrogant Hugo Bristol was. He thought his little cameras and precious gate were enough to keep him safe. So much so that the front door was unlocked, an invitation to let myself in if I'd ever seen one. Stifling the urge to laugh, I crept through the mansion, following the same path I'd memorized in our only meeting in Hugo's office. The bastard hadn't even bothered to lock *that* door. If I were a superstitious man, I'd be worried about how easy it had been to access the place I wanted to be.

Easing the door open, I slipped inside and closed it behind me, turning on the flashlight on my phone as I took a look around. I quickly perused the bookshelves, looking for anything that stood out, but it was all boring first editions and legal guides. My fingers itched to move them, in case Hugo was more intelligent than his unlocked doors led me to believe, but there wasn't enough time to get through all of them. I turned to the tidy desk and decided to start there. If I didn't find anything, I could always come back and search his books.

The top few drawers in the desk were a bust. They held a variety of legal pads, pens, and an assortment of other office supplies. Even the legal pads appeared mostly untouched; the top pad was the only one with impressions on the pages like the one before it had been written on and ripped away. I couldn't help moving a few of Hugo's bits and bobbles between drawers just to make the man feel as crazy as his vicious daughter made me feel.

Satisfied that my small intrusion would drive him up a wall, I shifted my attention to the largest drawer at the bottom of the desk. It was the only one with a lock, and I was shocked to find it was actually in use. Pulling open the drawer above it, I snagged a handful of paper clips and created a makeshift lockpick. Once I was satisfied with what I'd crafted, I pulled a credit card from the wallet in my back pocket and set to work with the two items.

"How the fuck does this man put away so many criminals with such shitty security?" I mused when the lock gave way and the drawer opened. "All these files, and nothing but some cameras and a gate to impede the unwashed masses. Fucking hell."

I thumbed through the files, not paying much mind to which criminal he was prosecuting, though a few names were vaguely familiar. There wasn't anything in any of them to help me prove to the guys that Victoria was out to cause us harm. I sat back on my heels, studying the desk as I tried to figure out where to start next with what little time I had left. I refused to accept my impromptu mission had been a fucking bust.

Something about the drawer drew my eye back to it, and I leaned forward to study it more closely. Maybe it was the shadows and lack of light, but the drawer definitely looked deeper on the outside than it did when looking at the files. I started pulling them out of the drawer, stacking them in a haphazard pile and nearly shouted when I shined the light inside the empty drawer. Barely noticeable against the back was a strange slotted hole that could only mean one thing. The drawer had a false bottom. I snagged the letter opener I'd seen earlier and used it to wrench the false bottom away.

"Fucking, *jackpot!*" I hissed as I spotted a thick file folder with Victoria's name and birthdate written on it. The first thing I saw when I opened the folder was a DNA test declaring Hugo Bristol *'not the father.'* "Holy shit." I breathed.

The file was far too hefty for me to examine thoroughly under my current time crunch, but a quick look showed what appeared to be documents from a private investigator and a handful of other DNA tests. I shoved the folder under my hoodie to keep it out of the way as I returned his case files to the drawer. Ensuring everything was how I found it, aside from my intentional meddling, I pulled the folder out from under my hoodie and held it securely to my chest as I switched off my phone's flashlight. No way was I going to lose what could be the fucking motherload now that I had it.

I practically floated with how pleased I was as I crept back to the front door. Except, it wasn't unlocked anymore. I frowned, considering my options when I heard voices in a room just off the foyer, but coming closer.

"Window it is, I guess." I huffed quietly, moving to the closest room with a door before someone found me.

I wasn't sure what room in the mansion I was in since the curtains over the windows were drawn, blocking out the light. I didn't want to risk drawing any attention with my flashlight, so I carefully approached them in the dark. Shadows moved against the curtains just as another set of voices outside the window spoke, followed by the flare of a cigarette.

"What the fuck." I hissed to myself through gritted teeth.

Whatever luck I'd had getting into the mansion had apparently run out. I spent the next half hour or so creeping around, trying to find a way out as I dodged the help and the security team I'd clearly fucking missed on my way in. It seemed like every potential exit was blocked by one or another, and that was even *with* me debating how reasonable it would be to throw myself out of a fucking window just to get out of the fucking house. It was out of sheer desperation that I texted Todd.

Create a distraction. I need an out.

CHAPTER SEVENTEEN

Craig

After Joey disconnected me from the conference call, I attempted to call Az to no avail. Leighton was the only one who answered, and he was more interested in giving an animated, overly exaggerated play-by-play of the argument between the other two. I hung up on him and climbed into bed with Victoria, sleeping until shortly after noon.

Groaning, I forced myself to get out of bed and hunt down something for my pain. The wounds left by Mel's sycophant of an apprentice were healing, but they still hurt like a bitch. Especially when I first woke, stiff from sleep. Wandering through the house, I found myself in the kitchen. Dawn had a cabinet beside the fridge with a variety of medications and vitamins. If I was going to find a pain reliever, it would be there. I'd just opened it to sift through when Az strolled in, his lip split, one eye swollen halfway shut, and his knuckles bloody.

"What the fuck happened to you?" I asked as he jerked open the freezer and grabbed some ice.

"A stupid god damned decision, that's what." He sniped.

"Did you and Joey get physical? Should I be preparing myself to dress little brother's injuries?"

"It wasn't Joey, though he would have deserved it." Az sighed, wrapping the ice in a paper towel and pressing it to his eye. "I made the dumb fuck decision to find myself a Jackal.

Bastard was a scrapy son of a bitch and got in a few good licks, but I'm here and he's…" Az shrugged.

"Alright, Leighton…" I said, raising my brow. "You know, Joey's temper isn't the only one here that needs some cooling off."

"I deserved that," Az replied, tipping his head in acknowledgment. "What's that therapist shit Phil's been preaching at us lately? I had a minor backslide, and I'm aware of it. It was stupid. I can't promise it won't happen again, but I'm trying. Fuck, my face hurts."

I shook my head sympathetically. They weren't the only ones who battled with anger, so I knew how easy it was to slide into solving problems with violence. I turned back to the cabinet, locating the Tylenol. Grabbing the bottle, I shook out four, tossed two back, and handed the others to Az. He moved to the sink, filled a coffee cup with water, and took the pills.

"It will happen again, it always does. It'll take time before that isn't your first instinct… or at least until you stop acting on it when you get pushed too far."

"Joey's just so god damned infuriating these days," Az grumbled, sitting the cup on the counter harder than necessary. "He's acting like he did when he wouldn't take Rich's no for an answer and it's going to get one of us killed this time."

I crossed my arms over my chest and tilted my head as I regarded my friend. "Oh, so you mean he's hell bent on proving his point despite the rest of us telling him that he's obviously wrong. *That* doesn't sound like anyone else I know."

"Really?" Az drawled, arching his uninjured brow at me just as Leighton strolled into the kitchen.

"Oh, harem meeting! This is a harem meeting, right?" Leighton laughed as he moved to the fridge and grabbed a bottle of apple juice.

"Yes, really—"

"Sweet! Point of order, I am the only boyfriend. I would like that added to the record!" Leighton grinned.

I paused for a moment, collecting myself. "No, Leighton.

Yes, Az, really. You seem to have forgotten how you acted not long ago. Nothing anyone said could convince you that Victoria wasn't somehow the head of the Jackals or pulling some kind of strings."

"Yeah, bu—" Az started.

"Respectfully, Az, listen. When you got out of jail and we started down this path, you were so hard headed that none of the evidence mattered to you. No matter how many times someone tried to kidnap her, or she was involved in some kind of shoot out, or that the movements the Jackals were making didn't make *any* fucking sense if she was in charge of anything, you didn't budge. You started fights with us, you were downright *cruel* to Victoria, and you chased that thread down until there was nowhere else to go." I paused for a moment, a painful twinge in my side forcing me to take a breath. "It wasn't until Joey beat the information out of a man with a golf club, and then slit his throat that you allowed yourself to realize you were wrong and she was as much a victim in the situation as anyone else. And you managed to do all of that *without* having lost someone so near to your heart as one of us. So, maybe, you need to take a step back and realize that browbeating Joey isn't going to do anything but make him dig his heels in further."

I leaned back against the counter. I was on the mend, but damn I still hurt, and I was still tired.

"Yeah, Az," Leighton piped in with a look of mock sternness. "Do you wanna be the pot or the kettle in this situation?"

"And *you*," I said, shifting my gaze to where Leighton stood. "Do you really think that turning every instance of grief and conflict into a fucking joke is helping anyone? It's not easing the tension, it's not making things lighter. It makes you look like an inconsiderate asshole, considering that the entire family is both grieving and tearing itself apart."

Leighton's hands went up, the apple juice dangling from his fingers. "Hey! I *am* an inconsiderate asshole, and excuse me for trying to keep from stabbing everyone in sight. Maybe I make everything a joke because it's the only sliver of sanity I can find. Ever consider that Mister-Fucking-Emotionally-Stable." he snapped before dropping his voice to whisper to himself. "Recognized a coping mechanism, check. Maybe that book Phil slipped me is onto something after all."

"Shut it, Leighton." Az snapped before turning his attention back to me. "I'm doing my damnedest to give Joey grace, but *fuck*, Craig. Everything is falling apart around us and I don't have time to coddle him, not even in his grief. Yes, I was a stubborn idiot, and I nearly ruined the best damned thing that ever happened to me before it had a chance to start, but I wasn't setting a match to our *already* burning empire. I'm doing the best I can and if that makes me the bad guy here, well..."

"You're not the bad guy... no more than the rest of us are." I shook my head with a sigh. "I get that you've got a lot on your plate, and no one is asking you to handle Joey with kid gloves. But for fuck's sake, Az, think. Do you think, in his current mental state, telling Joey what happened, throwing his mistakes in his face, and painting him out to be a burden to the family is going to do *anything* to put out the fire? You're just throwing on gas."

Az's hands went to his hair, and he tugged the strands hard enough I was sure he'd pulled a few out. Curling in on himself, he let them slide free, scrubbing over his face as a ragged breath left him.

"This wasn't supposed to be my job." His voice cracked, the words sounded choked as if he said them with a suppressed sob. "Rich was supposed to be here. I'm barely holding my shit together and Joey has completely spiraled out." He abruptly straightened, turned, and planted his hands on the edge of the sink, letting his head hang low as his shoulders began to shake.

"I think you broke him," Leighton murmured, moving close enough to Az to run his hand across the other man's face. "Shit, Craig. These are tears," he said, panic lacing his tone as he held up his hand while Az continued to hang his head. "You fucking broke, Az."

"Shut up, Leighton. If you want to step out, you can." I said, moving closer to Az and touching his shoulder. He jerked as if he was going to move away from me, but I stayed in his space. "Az. I know that you're doing the best you can with the situation you're in. Rich was always supposed to be the boss. Every one of us would have followed him to hell and back if that's what was needed. And now, we follow you. But... you don't have to handle everything burning like the only one holding an extinguisher."

While I spoke, Leighton sat his juice bottle down and moved to Az's other side so that he was sandwiched between us. Leaning around him just enough to catch my gaze, Leighton mouthed silently, *'I'm not leaving just because you broke him.'*

"Someone has to be at the head of this shit." Az said, not meeting my eyes as he blinked rapidly in an attempt to stop the dam from breaking. "But... how the fuck is anyone supposed to handle all this shit? We buried Rich, you and Victoria were kidnapped, you were tortured, Leighton was held hostage by his own family, and Joey's self destructing... I... I can't... I don't know how Rich handled everything all the time. My shoulders aren't... strong enough." Az's voice became more broken and strangled as he spoke, the effort it took to keep himself from breaking down obviously becoming more difficult with every word.

"You can take my family shit off that pile," Leighton offered, awkwardly patting Az on the back. "I had it all under control anyway, nothing at all to worry about. Promise."

Az snorted. "Not the point, L." He heaved a sigh and wiped his eyes with the back of his hand. "Fuck. I don't have time for the breakdown I need right now."

"Bottling this up isn't going to help you, Az. It's going to eat at you and make it more difficult to function. We've always found a way to make time for family." I offered, hoping he wouldn't continue trying to hold the dam up with his bare hands.

"I'll make sure to add it to my schedule, right between scheduling the jaws of life to pull Joey's head out of his ass and taking out whoever is behind all this shit." He huffed with a slight shake of his head. "I just need to focus on something I can actually do something about right now, so if you have anything like that up your sleeve after the meeting, I'm all ears."

I considered his words for a moment, running my hand over my scalp while I tried to offer something productive. "Not... really. I mean, I did notice during the verbal reports that there's been a suspiciously low amount of skirmishes with, well, pretty much anyone. We're in a prime position for anyone to make a play for us, and no one is. And to make things even stranger, while we were on the call I checked the boards, and everything about us, about Victoria, about the free for all, all of it is gone from the message boards. It's been scrubbed, not just deleted. It's like... suddenly, we have no enemies. It makes no fucking sense."

CHAPTER EIGHTEEN

Victoria

I must have read the email a dozen times, but I couldn't stop myself as I sat with the laptop I'd borrowed from Craig on the Innocenti's couch.

Victoria,

I appreciate your concern for the center, but given your current circumstances, it's probably best that you don't return in any capacity for the foreseeable future. As you know, this place is meant to be a safe haven for South Sacona's youth. Unfortunately, your connection to us has caused trouble to boil over here. I won't go into details as I've handled it, but keeping your distance will help prevent more issues.

I am genuinely sorry to have to insist you stay away. You know that I've always adored and thought highly of you. You may not have been a kid from Southside, but you are still one of mine. Stay safe, child, and when this storm finally blows over, you give me a call.

With love,
Blithe McMillan

I couldn't help but feel like the last good thing I had was just ripped from my hands in a single email. A feeling that only made me feel worse because I still had my men. I swatted at a tear that leaked over my lower eyelid just as Joey strolled into the room.

He looked exhausted. His hair was disheveled, and deep dark circles rimmed his eyes. He was even sporting the start of a beard, leaving me wondering when he'd shaved last. I let my eyes drink him in, noting the thick file folder he was clinging to as if it held the answer to all his woes. My fingers gripped the laptop screen as I fought the urge to go to him and try to erase the haunted look on his face. I never knew which version of Joey I would get these days. In rare instances, he was the man I'd fallen in love with. In the others, he was spiteful and cruel.

"Hey," he said softly, his voice raw and scratchy.

"Hey," my voice was barely above a whisper, afraid I'd startle him back into spewing venom.

Joey didn't move, his gaze raking over me as he clutched the file tighter. I cautiously closed the laptop, set it on the coffee table in front of me, and stood. My eyes never left him, watching for any signs he was about to flee or turn hateful toward me. As if reading my thoughts, the side of his mouth quirked up and he shrugged one shoulder slightly.

"I'm so sorry, Joey," I said finally as I stood rooted in place, unsure where else to start. "I wish I could fix this. I wish I could bring him back."

Something I couldn't decipher flashed in his eyes, and he cocked his head to the side, studying me. "You can't *fix* this, Victoria." The pain in his voice stole the breath from my lungs. "I lost my brother, my family is cracking at the seams, and all I have left is a gaping fucking wound that can't heal."

"Joey," my lip trembled and tears pooled in my eyes. "I know... I feel it too."

"No!" He shouted, causing me to flinch. "You're not fucking getting it. I don't feel *anything* except this gaping fucking hole where my brother is supposed to be. I'm drowning and all I want is to feel something, anything other than this."

"I wish I knew how to help."

"You want to help, Victoria? You want to make *this* better?" He snarled.

"Yes, whatever you need, Joey. I'm here." I replied softly.

"Then make me feel something. Drop to your fucking knees and crawl to me and make me *feel*."

"I don't think–"

"Don't ask me what I need and then tell me I'm wrong." Joey scoffed.

I raised my hands to placate him. "If this is what you need, I will do it for you, but I'm not sure this is the sort of thing you want to risk your parents walking in on." I said.

"They're not here. Neither are the guys, except Craig, who was passed out in his room last I checked." Joey replied a challenge in his eyes.

"Are you sure this is what you want?" I asked, still unsure which version of the man I was dealing with stood before me.

"I'm sure," He answered, his voice slipping into the same tone he'd used when he chased me through the woods. "Crawl to me."

My body responded before my brain had a chance to catch up. I stepped around the coffee table and dropped to my hands and knees, lifting my gaze to catch his. Joey widened his stance, facing me fully, a satisfied smirk creeping across his face. I crawled slowly toward him, giving him ample time to change his mind before I leaned back on my heels by his feet. I reached for the button of his pants just as he reached down and grabbed my chin, forcing me to look up at him.

His smirk was gone, a sneer in its place as malice danced across his features. "So fucking desperate for any scrap of attention." his fingers dug painfully into my chin before he shoved me backward hard enough for me to topple over. "Anything you think will keep you in our good graces so you can tear us apart from the inside."

"Joey, I–" tears welled in my eyes and threatened to spill over as I sat on the ground trying to catch up with the mental whiplash he was causing me.

"*Joey, I.*" He mocked. "I told you already, Victoria, I'm not falling for your bullshit anymore. I've seen the fucking light, and I'm not addicted to your fucking poison anymore. You. Are. Nothing." He spat, squatting down to place the file he held in my lap before patting my cheek roughly. "You're not even a fucking Bristol."

He rose to his full height and strolled from the living room. I sat there, dumbstruck, for several more minutes before I remembered he'd left the file in my lap. I couldn't make sense of his parting words, but I had a feeling the second I opened the manila folder, I would. I just wasn't so sure I should believe whatever I found.

I forced myself off the floor and stumbled to the couch, collapsing onto it as I clutched the folder. My hands trembled as I situated it in my lap and flipped it open. The first thing I saw was a report that looked like it was written on a typewriter and had been dated for just shy of three months after I was born. I read it and then reread it.

"No, no, no, no, no. This... this can't be right." I said before flipping through the remaining documents in the file.

There were three DNA tests, the final one dated around my fifth birthday, all stating that Hugo Bristol was not my father. There were another two that stated the same for Uncle Theo. And there were pictures... Pictures that showed my mother clearly involved in a romantic relationship with Theo. The angles made it clear my father had his suspicions and hired a private investigator to follow my mother. I couldn't tell from them whether the photos were before or after I was born. The fact that my father had Theo tested for my paternity led me to believe the affair must have started before I was conceived.

The longer I looked at everything, the more things made sense. My father stopped acting like he gave a damn about me after my mom died. I hadn't seen him more than twice between her funeral and the Gala fire. I'd told myself the reason Theo had fought to keep Az locked up for my attempted kidnapping was because my father was too injured to be in court, but that didn't explain how he'd so easily placed me in their care after Az's release.

I mentally started tallying the number of times I'd seen or heard from him since. There was the one dinner at his house and a handful of voicemails after the manor was blown up, but there had been nothing since. Panic coiled low in my belly, and my breathing grew erratic as pieces I'd ignored seemed to fall perfectly in place. I shook my head hard, trying to dislodge them. My father was a well respected prosecutor. He was *the* best in Sacona. And yet…

The sound of someone walking into the living room tore my attention away from the papers in my hand and lap. Jerking my head up, I caught sight of Craig as he made his way into the room, clutching his bandaged abdomen with his face twisted in a pained grimace. The moment he noticed me, worry flashed across his face.

"What's wrong, Bunny?" He asked, making his way to my side at a pace that was clearly causing him more pain.

I held the papers up as if they were a smoking gun. "I think… I think my father is the one behind everything."

CHAPTER NINETEEN

Leighton

"Could you please stop drumming on the dashboard?" Az growled from the driver's seat.

We'd been driving around our territory in Southside in a rusted-out Toyota all morning. It wasn't my fault that the streets were quiet, and I didn't have another outlet for the energy pumping through my veins. Shit was too quiet, and it was making me nervous, like we were about to walk blindly into a trap at any second.

"This shit is eerie, man." I sighed. "It's like the Jackals got raptured or something. They should be crawling all over the place to claim what's ours. It's not like they don't know we *aren't* dead, when they're the ones who had us and they just walked the fuck off."

"I know." Az replied, one hand moving to tug at his hair. I was seriously tempted to find Dawn when we got back to the Innocenti's and tell her she owed me for the bet she set and then canceled. And they called *me* the cheater for that one. "Have you noticed they don't even have girls on the street? I've seen the freelancers, but not a single one of theirs."

"You think the Devils sent them packing?" I asked, trying to come up with anything to explain what was happening.

"Highly unlikely. Helen is handing over Candy day after tomorrow so we can add that to our little interrogation, but based on what Craig relayed, the bitch was undercover. Even if she found something big enough to make Helen put out the order, they wouldn't have had time to wipe out an entire organization. And as far as the Jackals are concerned, Helen has no reason to intervene on our behalf."

As my mind worked, I drummed out another mish-mashed beat on the dashboard, earning a glare from Az. "Fucking let me out, then." I snapped. "You know I think better when I move. It's this or you let me hit the pavement like I wanted to in the first place, *Dad.*"

Surprisingly, he didn't snap back at my comment, instead easing the sedan up to the curb. Putting the car in park, he turned to face me.

"Fine." He sounded so fucking defeated I almost hugged him. "I want check-ins every half hour. If you miss one, I'm going to assume you're in trouble, and by God, Leighton, you better fucking *hope* you are in that case."

"You gonna take the belt to my ass if not, Pops?" I snickered.

"No. I'm going to make sure you're restrained and can't get loose and then leave you there, fucker."

"Woah man, that's harsh." I replied, putting my hands up in surrender. I did *not* enjoy being left alone with my thoughts and unable to move. I'd rather have bamboo shoots stuck under my fingernails, and Az knew that. "I'll check in. Scouts honor."

"You were never a boy scout, L." Az shook his head.

"Fine, I swear it on *Ma Petit's* perfect pussy. You know I worship at that altar like my life depends on it." I chuckled.

Az slapped the back of my head before leaning over me and opening my door. "Get the fuck out, Leighton. Before I change my mind."

"Alright!" I shouted, unbuckling my seatbelt and moving to get out of the car. "I'm going, I'm going. I'll talk to you in thirty snookums." I blew Az a kiss as I shut the door behind me. He rolled his eyes and slowly pulled back onto the road.

I pulled my hood up and stuffed my hands in my pockets as I strolled down the street. Even on foot, it was still too damn quiet for my tastes, and every street I turned down made me a little more unsettled. I didn't see any of the usual players that worked these streets; there were no branded or marked sellers, muscle, or sex workers that littered the corners. There were freelancers, small-timers, and street rats who flew no colors and wore no brands.

"No way Southside's roach problem just *vanished*," I muttered as I turned down another street. I stopped, stepping off the sidewalk and into the shadow of a house, as I spotted a pair of sex workers that I recognized as freelancers talking to another pair of women I didn't recognize.

They weren't streetwalkers or dealers, and I spotted the tell-tale sign of holsters under their arms. I narrowed my eyes, moving closer. I had to move up several houses before I spotted the Golden Devils tattoo on one of their arms—Helen's muscle and recruiters. I crept close enough to eavesdrop without drawing attention to myself as I leaned back against a brick wall.

"Things may be flush right now, what with the Jackals up and taking off, but unless you know something we don't about why, I can guarantee they'll be back." One of the Devils said, pulling out a business card and holding it out to the sex workers. "If you change your mind, or wind up in trouble over using their corner, you give me a call, yeah?"

It was evident under the doublespeak that the Devils had been ordered to suss out what was happening with the Jackals' disappearance. They might have been doing it under the guise of offering protection, but they were digging like us. I missed whatever the worker responded before the Devils moved away, heading further down the block.

I waited until the Golden Devils were well out of eyeshot before I stepped out of the shadows. I rolled my shoulders and plastered a grin on my face as I approached the women.

"Pam, baby!" I started.

"Don't you come over here 'baby'-ing me, Leighton," She said, dramatically tossing her dark hair over her shoulder as she turned away. "You don't come and see me for, what's it been, some months now. I know I wasn't one of *your girls*, but you ain't even been around to ask questions about the goings on." She turned to face me, pointing one long, manicured nail toward me. "You know I got babies to feed. None of us out here can lose a reliable John."

"Pam, I ain't your John." I said, quirking a brow.

"It don't make no difference to me how you use your hour, you pay for it. That makes you a John. You think you're the only one who pays me just to talk?"

"Who the fuck are you giving information to besides me Pam?" I snarled.

"Psh. It ain't *that* kind of talking, dummy." Pam rolled her eyes at me. "But since you wanna go there, I done missed out on a decent amount of money holding out for you. Which is exactly why you ain't gonna come over here all 'baby'-ing me and shit. The only thing I want from you is what's in your wallet." Pam thrust her hand out palm up, curling her fingers so her nails clacked against her palm in demand before reaching in her tiny purse for a stick of gum and popping it in her mouth.

I looked between her face and her palm for a moment before shrugging. "Fair enough." I pulled my wallet out of my back pocket and opened it. I thumbed through it and sighed before handing it over, earning me a raised eyebrow and a frustrated look.

"Leighton, what the fuck is this?" She demanded, popping her gum loudly to punctuate the question.

"Look, I wasn't expecting to come buy information, this is just what I have on me. I can get you more in a little bit. You know I'm good for it."

"Well you fucking better be. Because I know about that girl you been shacking up with, and I bet *she'd* be interested in the information I have about *you*. Especially how you left that last girl." She snapped, folding up the money and putting it in her bra. I snorted a laugh and shrugged.

"Want me to call her for you so you can tell her? She already knows what I'm like. Oh!" I grinned, pulling up my shirt. "Look, she did this herself! It's a little shaky, but it's the thought that counts! And it's all because I found out I *got feelings!*"

Pam stared at me for a while, just blinking, before she shook her head. "Guess it takes all kinds."

"Anyway, what does $400 buy me?" I said, pulling my shirt back down.

"So, the Jackals ain't been seen on these streets in... How long has it been Janny?" Pam turned to her corner partner.

"I couldn't tell you the date, but I remember the last time I saw anyone with their tattoo was when I had that virgin that had to be like... in his 50s. That was a couple weeks back." She shook her head, lighting a cigarette. "It was kinda sad, he needed Vitamin V to even get it up and it was his first time."

"I remember that. Anyway, it's been since then that we've seen any of those little corner hogs. I heard a rumor they've all moved on to different pastures, but that's all I got for $400." Pam said, just as a silver van pulled up on the opposite corner and flashed its lights. "Now, if you'll excuse me, I've got some actual money to make." She brushed past me with Janny on her heels, sauntering to the van with a grin.

"Well, that wasn't very enlightening," I muttered, shoving my hands into my hoodie pocket and starting back down the sidewalk.

The longer I walked around the streets of Southside, the more the hairs on the back of my neck stood up. Pam said the Jackals had moved, but I knew how much they pulled from the corners in the area, and it was too much for them to leave on the table for anyone to take. That thought played over in my mind, leaving me with the sinking feeling that I was definitely about to walk into a trap at any moment.

"Stop acting like such a little bitch," I scolded myself,

rubbing a hand over my face trying to shake my growing paranoia.

A tug on the back of my hoodie caused me to jump. The hand I still had in my pocket jerked free, pulling along the pocket knife I always carried on me as I whirled to face whoever was stupid enough to try and attack me from behind. I had the blade at their throat at the same moment I recognized them, and my breath whooshed out of me as I dropped my hand.

"Fucking hell, Sarah. Are you trying to get yourself killed?" I practically shouted.

My old friend from the Urchins smirked. "I did call your name a few times first. It's not my fault you were lost in whatever is going on in that pretty head of yours."

"Try getting in front of me next time or else I might not realize it's you before it's too late."

"Yeah, yeah. Anyway, I'm glad I spotted you. I was actually about to call you with something I think you want to see." Sarah glanced around the street as if searching out any spying eyes. "Come back with me to our spot and I'll fill you in."

I motioned for Sarah to lead the way before following her through the familiar alleys and twists and turns I'd learned in the time I spent with the Urchins. It seemed she'd added a few extras in the years since I'd been with the Horsemen. That or she was extra paranoid about someone following us back to the rundown warehouse the Urchins called home.

Sarah didn't relax until we were inside the building, her people standing guard by the doors. Raising her hand to signal me to wait, she cupped the other around her mouth.

"Yo, Twist! Get your ass down here!"

Footsteps pounded on the metal flooring above us, echoing through the warehouse as a boy who couldn't have been older than fourteen appeared at the top of the steps. He held a stack of papers in his hand as he made his way down the steps, moving to join us. I ran my eyes over him again, noting how young he was.

"L, this is my Second, Twist. Twist, this is L."

"Let me guess, your real name is Oliver." I snorted.

"Yeah, so what of it?" His voice was deeper than I expected, causing me to take a closer look at him.

"Wait a minute. I know you... You tried to get into Temptat!on last year and caused a scene when our doorman confiscated your fake ID."

Sarah snickered, a sly smile forming on her lips.

"I'm twenty-three asshole, and your man stole my fucking license. You owe me forty bucks. I still haven't replaced the thing after that shit."

"No way you're twenty-three." I shot back, causing Sarah to bust into a full belly laugh.

Twist looked between us with a scowl before thrusting the stack of papers toward me. "Fuck both of you. I'm a grown ass man, not a fucking child."

"You do realize I'm a fucking Horseman and you just told me to fuck off, right? I could have your head for that." I drawled, crossing my arms in front of my chest instead of taking the papers from him.

"Yeah, well double fuck you, man. You *still* owe me a license." He shot back, handing off the stack to Sarah instead.

The kid had balls, and instead of pissing me off like it should have, I was impressed. "How about a job instead of a license, Twist?" I grinned, causing Sarah to punch me in the gut.

"He has a job already, Leighton. Now do you want this intel or not? I'm happy to send it to your man that put word out y'all were looking for anything suspicious around Theodore Abrams if you'd prefer."

"Give it to me." I replied, rubbing a hand over my abdomen where she'd hit me.

Sarah handed over the stack of pictures printed off on regular paper. I had half a mind to complain about the printing medium, but the photos were at least in color. Good ol' Uncle Theo was meeting on a street corner with a shady-looking guy I didn't recognize. There were several snapshots of him handing over something small to the guy, but I couldn't determine what it was.

"How does this help me?" I asked Sarah, flipping through the pages again.

She sighed and rolled her eyes, moving to my side and jabbing her pointer at the shady guy in the picture. "That guy right there is working with the Russians. He's not a made man by any means as far as we can tell, but he's still on their payroll. Now, what mister prosecutor here is doing with a Russian mobster is anyone's guess, but it sure is suspicious."

My eyebrows shot up, nearly touching my hairline. I couldn't help but wonder if this guy was connected to the same family my dearly departed parents had tried to marry me into. As far as I knew, the Russians didn't have any other business in Sacona, let alone business that required a clandestine meeting with a prosecutor.

"Fuck, that *is* suspicious." I hissed through my teeth before glancing up at Sarah. "What do you want for this intel?"

"For you? Nothing. You may have moved on from the Urchins a long time ago, Leighton, but you're still family and family looks out for each other."

CHAPTER TWENTY

Craig

"Bunny, we cleared your father when we started digging into everything." I said, settling onto the couch and pulling Victoria along with me.

She thrust a handful of papers into my face, the rest spilling onto the floor from her lap. "I'm not his daughter, Craig. It explains so much." She choked back a sob, swiping a hand across her face to clear the tears away. "He basically vanished on me after my mom died and after the Gala, when I thought... When you guys were the ones I thought... He didn't put up any sort of fight to keep me safe from you. He just threatened to pull his donation from the center if I didn't go along with you all as my bodyguards. Aside from a few voicemails immediately after my house blew up, I haven't heard anything from him. What kind of father does that?"

I put my arm around her and tucked her into my side as carefully as possible. "We intimidated the hell out of him to get ourselves into position as your bodyguards. We've come far enough for both of us to admit we were all wrong about each other. I can't tell you why he hasn't tried finding you since the manor, Bunny, but I promise, he was clean when we checked him out. Nothing at all to indicate he's behind the whole mess."

I could see in her tear-filled eyes she wanted to argue the point, but Leighton stormed into the living room before she could utter a word.

"I have good news and bad news!" He grinned, waving a small stack of papers in his hand. The grin dropped the moment he noticed Victoria's state. "What happened?" his tone turned dark. "I swear to God, if Joey's done something else, I'm going to fucking end him."

"No," Victoria sniffled, shaking her head. "I mean, he's the one that gave me these, but it's not his fault."

Leighton's gaze flicked to me as he closed the distance to the couch, shoving the coffee table out of the way so he could drop to his knees in front of Victoria. "Explain."

"I'm not my father's daughter after all." Victoria let out a pained laugh and added the papers in her hand to Leighton's stack.

Leighton scanned them quickly before returning his gaze to Victoria. "You think these mean he's the one that set us all up." Victoria shrugged one shoulder and toyed with her empty hands in her lap. "I'm sure Craig has already explained in detail how we cleared Daddy-O already, but these," he shuffled the papers around so the ones he'd brought were on top, "should erase any doubts about it from that pretty head of yours."

Victoria took the papers and scanned the printed-out pictures. Her brow furrowed in confusion as she studied each one. "What are these, Leighton?"

"Well, remember how I said I had good news and bad news? The good news is, *this* is a lead. That guy right there," he pointed at the man Theodore was speaking to in the photos, "he's Russian mafia. Which means the bad news is dear ol' Uncle Theo is our lead." Leighton cringed and ducked back as if he expected her to hit him.

"This... no, this can't be right." She muttered. "Uncle Theo is a prosecutor, he wouldn't work with mobsters unless they were a witness."

I gingerly took the papers from her as she muttered to herself that the evidence in black and white wasn't real. I scanned the photos of Theodore meeting with the shady character, and if Leighton's intel was that this guy was Bratva, then it was good. I rubbed her shoulders and smoothed down her hair in an attempt to comfort her. These were heavy bombs to drop, but her denial of what was in front of us wouldn't be good for her either.

"Bunny... A heavy prosecutor might meet an informant that's a witness, but not," I paused to consider my words for a moment before continuing, "not like this. People that work for the state that do this kind of meet up aren't lawyers. This is a hand-off of some kind."

"You don't know why he was there or what he's doing. This doesn't prove anything." She pulled away from me, the look on her face turning hard as the idea this was all some kind of mix-up took root in her mind. "Matter of fact, give me a phone. I can call him and clear this up right now."

Leighton shot me a questioning look as he slipped his hand into his pocket and retrieved his phone. I ran through a mental list of the pros and cons of letting her call Theodore and decided that whatever comfort or information she could glean right now was worth more than the downsides. When I nodded to Leighton, he handed her his phone. Victoria dialed Theodore's number and put it on speaker so Leighton and I could listen.

"Theodore Abrams speaking."

"Uncle Theo, it's me, Tory."

We could hear his breath whoosh from his lungs over the line. "Jellybean?" his voice was shaky, almost like he was stunned to hear from her. "Where are you? Are you okay? Your father has been going out of his mind with worry, his doctor had to sedate him."

She shot us both a look as if to say, 'Told ya so' before turning her attention back to the call. "I'm safe. I can't say where I am right now, but I promise I'm safe. Actually... I have a question I wanted to ask you; I think it might be related to everything going on. It could be what finally lets me get back to my life."

"Of course, Jellybean. Anything I can do to help, just say the word."

"Do you happen to have any cases going on right now dealing with the Russian mob?"

"What does that have to do with your situation?" Theo asked, his tone hesitant.

"Please, Uncle Theo. I just need you to trust me and answer the question."

The call went silent for longer than should have been necessary. It was as if Theodore was working overtime to choose his words carefully. Leighton and I exchanged a knowing glance. If things with Theodore were as above board as Victoria believed, he would have answered already.

"I had to check my files, but I'm not currently on any cases with bratva." He answered finally before dropping his voice to nearly a whisper. "What makes you think they're involved, Victoria? Has something *else* happened?"

"Bunny..." I started before Leighton took the phone and hung it up.

"What the fuck, Leighton?" Victoria protested.

"There's no way you're getting into that conversation with your dear old Unc in a way that's not going to lead to him knowing more than he should, *Ma Petit*." Leighton said with a shrug, pocketing his phone again.

"Bunny, he just lied to you," I said, and she started to protest again, but I shook my head. "Best case scenario, he lied about the cases he's working on. Worst case scenario, these pictures are *exactly* what they look like."

I could see her turning that over in her mind as my words sunk in, her brows furrowing as she processed everything.

"He could be a good guy, *the* bad guy, or a bad guy on your side, like nationwide for bad guys." Leighton snorted, "But we need to find out for sure."

"Okay... well... Maybe he's not in a position to be able to tell me what's going on. I mean, we all have our secrets right now. Doesn't mean he's behind all the bullshit." Victoria said, her stubborn streak still a mile long.

Leighton let out a long-suffering sigh. "You could have at least laughed a little at my joke before taking a trip to denial. Now, do you wanna find out for sure or not cuz I need Craig to get this shit done."

"How's this, Bunny. We need more information, that I agree with, so we're going to go find it. We'll start with his office. I'll plant some bugs, we'll go through his stuff, set up a tracer program on his computer. You can come with us, and whatever we find we'll bring it to you." I said, standing slowly while holding my side.

"Fine, when do we leave?" She asked, her tone making it obvious she felt like it was a waste of time.

Leighton licked his lips and tilted his head down toward her lap. "Do we have time for a snack first?"

"Leighton... maybe after, but not right now." I said, shaking my head with a smirk.

Victoria playfully swatted him away before pushing him back so she could stand from the couch. "Bad, Leighton."

Shortly after eleven p.m., we pulled into the parking garage across from Hugo and Theo's office. Victoria still wasn't any happier about our hunch, but she hadn't complained. We climbed from the car; Leighton grabbed the plastic sack with the bugs and motioned for Victoria to lead the way. I was glad she'd decided to tag along, it meant less work to get into and out of the building. All she had to do was put in the code for the front door, and we were in the lobby.

"There a night guard?" Leighton asked, glancing around the open space.

"He's probably in the bathroom. My father thought he was helping the community by hiring the oldest man he could find. The man is sweet as pie, but he's not guarding much other than a urinal these days." Victoria snarked.

"I don't know if that's a yes or a no..." Leighton said with a shake of his head.

"Just… come on, let's get this over with." Victoria sighed, stomping toward the elevators.

We let her lead the way to Theodore's office. Unlike the outer doors, his office had a standard lock that Leighton had to pick. Once inside, I shut the door behind us and took the bag from Leighton.

"You two can start searching the place. I'll handle the bugs, and then I'll handle the laptop." I said, turning to take in the room while I figured out the best places to place them. The city lights filtered through the blinds, casting slats of light across his desk and the wall of law books behind it. The room had a quiet that settled into the bones of a place after being built over decades. The room seemed to reflect the man I'd met, a touch of Southern charm wrapped in old-world elegance. The furniture was worn but comfortable and sturdy, the kind of wood that darkened and softened with time and upholstered in rich, caramel-colored leather. It invited more than just business; the room suggested long conversations, maybe even a whiskey or two poured in the late hours.

But what stood out most were the photographs.

They lined the walls, perched on bookshelves, tucked into the diplomas and legal awards frames. All of them of Victoria. From her earliest years—toddler curls and a gap-toothed grin—to her polished, poised adulthood. There was one of her as a teen in a bright yellow sundress, and her feet kicked up on Theodore's desk like she owned the place. Another of her at what looked like some college event, shaking hands with someone who looked important. Her college graduation, Uncle Theo standing beside her, pride written across his face plain as day. Hugo was also in the picture, standing slightly from his 'daughter.'

It felt like looking at Victoria through a father's eyes. I glanced at her; she was standing in the center of the room, taking it in as well. There was something on her face I couldn't quite put my finger on. It was something like nostalgia but heavier with the weight of why we were here.

I set my bag down on his desk and set to work. I pulled out a handful of RF transmitters, an optical transmitter, the wiretap device, wire strippers, and a voice-activated recorder. It was easy enough to find the line from the desk phone and follow it down through the desk, pop open the plastic cover on the floor below the desk to find the nest of organized cables that powered everything. It would have been better to tap somewhere on the line outside his office, but we didn't have the time to figure out which of the lines was his wherever they came out, so this would have to do. I unplugged the phone line and cut the modular plug to expose the wires inside. Attaching the wires to the access point for the tap was simple enough; I disabled the tap's microphone, wired in the voice-activated recorder, and plugged it all back in. It wasn't hard, but it was much more tedious than setting up a wireless tap, but those were harder to come by for a landline phone.

"Did you two find anything yet?" I asked as I picked up the handful of RF transmitters, turned them on, tested them, and began placing them through the room in hidden places. Behind picture frames on the wall, in the far corner of his desk, another in an empty vase, and even on top of one of his bookshelves just in case.

"There's nothing here but law books, case files, and client information. And none of that looks out of the ordinary for the types of cases he handles. The only records he has of mobsters are in case files, no personal or professional meetings, no out of place notes." Victoria said, rifling through one of his file cabinets.

"I found our Az-hole!" Leighton said with a laugh, holding up a file from another cabinet. "His case was pretty open and shut with *Ma Petit*'s testimony being the only real evidence and no conviction, so there isn't much here either, we didn't know already. The man did some serious digging into Az to find his criminal behavior, that's for sure."

"Interesting… Wonder how he went about that. Az's

record is clean after he graduated." I said absently, looking up at the smoke detector. The stretch to get that down made my side ache just thinking about it.

"You're right. Too bad I can't help you with that." Leighton said, returning the file to the cabinet.

"No, but you can help me with this. Come get this smoke detector down." I said, motioning up at it. Leighton snickered but didn't say anything as he retrieved it. I took it from him and popped it open to place the optical bug inside. There was already a convenient opening, and the camera fit in snugly. It was simple enough and paired with the audio transmitters; we could pull whatever we needed from his office and off the receivers. I handed it back, and Leighton returned it to its base on the wall.

"We done here?" Leighton asked, apparently getting antsy from the anti-climactic trip into the lawyer's office.

"Just gotta do his computer, and then we're good," I said, moving to the desk and starting up his PC. I scrunched my nose as it booted up, the horror of Windows Vista coming into view. "Oh, good lord. Why?"

"Uncle Theo doesn't really do *change*. He's old fashioned." Victoria said, a small smile on her face as she took in my discomfort with what I was seeing.

"This isn't old-fashioned. This is... You know what, never mind. I'm just gonna take a deep breath and do my job. I can work with this." I said, actually needing to take a deep breath. I didn't know who would keep subjecting themselves to this, but it wasn't my computer, so it didn't matter. "Would you have an idea of the password, cause I didn't bring John the Ripper with me." I hadn't brought my laptop to use my brute force program.

"It's Jellybean. Capital J, and the 'E's are 3's. Been the same password ever since I got a jellybean stuck in his keyboard as a kid because he was letting me play on Paint." Victoria giggled. And sure enough, it worked.

"It's more than a little concerning that one of the top

prosecutors' computer is so… insecure." I said, plugging in my flash drive, and after a few keystrokes, I had the tracer and monitor programs loading onto his computer. I'd coded them to be discreet, run in the background to capture everything he did and monitor and analyze the flow of data packets within the system so I could watch his network behavior. Once they were up and I made sure they were working, I shut everything back down and gathered my tools and bag. "I'm done if you two are."

"Do you… have anymore of those bugs left?" Victoria asked hesitantly.

"A couple, yeah. Why?" I raised a brow at her question.

"My father's office is just down the hall, and I thought…" She trailed off.

"That's a great idea, Bunny. Yeah, we can set those up quick." I grinned, patting her head and messing her hair as I approached the door. She shot me a dirty look, but she couldn't stop the smile on her face. That was all I cared about.

We locked Theodore's office behind us and moved down the hall toward Hugo's. Leighton picked the lock easily; this office really needed to look at its security in so many ways. Opening the door, the contrast between Hugo and Theodore's office was jarring, to say the least. Hugo's office was ostentatious and a blatant show of power and wealth. It had all the markings of a high-end interior designer, but there was no warmth or personal touches that said an actual person was ever there. The most significant difference was the *lack* of photographs of his family. A single photo of Hugo, Prudence, and a toddler Victoria was hanging on the wall. One of those stuffy family photos that no one ever wants to take and no one ever looks happy in. The only other photo was a small 5x6 of the same college graduation photo that hung in Theodore's office.

"Oof…" Leighton said quietly. "Based on these rooms, there's no way people aren't mistaking Theo for the father."

"The paternity test says otherwise… but I see your

point," I said, setting my bag down, pulling out the few remaining bugs, and placing them around the room. We'd already cleared Hugo, but information was always valuable. Turning back around, I saw Victoria looking around the office, taking in the same view we had. It looked like she was considering the differences for the first time.

"I guess now it makes sense. I always thought he just wasn't big on photos..." She said, her voice soft and sad in a way that made me want to wrap her up and take away all the things she'd had to learn. And I had a feeling it wouldn't get any better from here.

"Well... at least this should help put any of your concerns about Hugo's involvement to rest. And we'll see what we can find out about what Theo's doing, once way or another." I offered, putting my arm around her shoulder as we left his office and locked back up. "It's always better to know." She looked up at me; her brow furrowed again in the way that said she was turning the information over in her mind. Her voice was soft and questioning when she answered.

"Is it? Cause it feels like the more I learn, the more things fall apart."

CHAPTER TWENTY ONE

Az

"Helen is heading to the warehouse with our guests." I spoke, glancing at where Leighton and Craig sat in Ian's office.

I'd spent the last several days hitting the streets with Leighton while Craig listened to the audio from the bugs he'd placed in Theo's office. He'd said all of three sentences to fill me in on that situation, but I had more significant issues to worry about. There were still no signs of Jackals anywhere in our territory, and reclaiming them had been suspiciously easy. I didn't have the mental capacity to worry about whatever they were planning *and* trying to sort out what Theodore Abrams was up to. Craig was perfectly capable of parsing out anything relevant he uncovered.

"Joey should be with us for this." Craig said, glancing up from whatever he'd been reading on his laptop.

"Well, if anyone knows where he's disappeared to, you're welcome to ask him to join us," I replied, my hand tugging at my hair of its own volition. I was a little annoyed that not only had I developed the tick, Leighton noticed it and smirked every single time I did it.

"Last I saw, he was updating his conspiracy wall." Leighton supplied with a laugh.

"His what now?" I asked.

"You know, his conspiracy wall." Leighton answered, causing me to motion for him to continue. He sighed and

CHAPTER TWENTY ONE | 157

rolled his eyes like I was the problem for not knowing what the hell he was talking about. "He's got a whole wall in his room that looks like some kind of detective work, but it's all about how *Ma Petit* is the big bad evil guy. It's very paranoid conspiracy theorist."

"And you didn't think I should know about this until now because?"

"I figured the little guy would tucker himself out and come to his senses." Leighton shrugged. "It's not like he has any information the rest of us don't have."

My hand tugged at my hair again, and I groaned. "Can someone please go get him so we can head out? Jesus Christ, conspiracy wall." The last part I muttered to myself, trying to figure out why Leighton seemed to think it was a good idea to leave Joey to draw whatever incorrect and outlandish conclusions he was coming to.

"You grab the little tot, I'll grab *Ma Petit.*" Leighton said to Craig as he stood from his seat. "She should be there too."

"You're right, she should. Appreciate you giving yourself the better job, shithead." Craig said with a lighthearted grimace as he moved past Leighton.

"When you pay attention, you get dibs." Leighton laughed, following Craig from the office.

I took a deep breath to prepare myself for Joey and Victoria being in the same space. He'd been so antagonistic toward her lately that there was bound to be an argument on the way to the warehouse we'd secured for taking Candy and her second into custody. I stood from my seat behind the desk and quickly called Phil to ensure we had everything we needed for their stay. Then, I made my way to the minivan we'd secured for transportation.

Leighton and Victoria were there waiting for me. It looked like he hadn't given her any time to dress. She was wearing a pair of black yoga pants and... was that my hoodie? My lips quirked up into a smile as I realized it was before my eyes flitted to her curly hair pulled into a messy bun. Leighton kneeled by her feet, tying her sneakers as she grumbled at him.

"I can do it myself, damn it," She snapped, swatting her hands at him to try and get him to move out of the way.

"So?" He shrugged, dodging her hands as he quickly tied up the remaining shoe. "All done!"

I reached her side just as Leighton stood up. I jerked my chin toward the vehicle, indicating for him to get in, and then leaned down to whisper into Victoria's ear.

"The next time I catch you in that hoodie, I'm taking it off with my teeth."

Her mouth dropped open on a squeak, and her cheeks flushed red. Stepping around her, I shot her a wink and moved to the driver's side door, climbing into the van. Victoria was still standing outside the sliding door when I settled into my seat, and I couldn't help but smirk at her.

"Fucking Az-hole." She murmured as she scrambled inside and settled next to Leighton in the far back row.

I was so busy watching her that I'd missed Craig and Joey arriving. Joey's head popped into the sliding door, and the confusion on his face made it clear he'd caught what Victoria had said.

"What did he do now?" He asked as he climbed into the middle row and closed the door.

"What did who do?" Craig asked as he claimed the front passenger seat.

"I told her that she looked good in my hoodie, is all." I said with a shrug and started the van.

"Oh, so you're speaking to me now?" Victoria demanded, one brow raised at Joey.

Joey ducked his head a bit, wincing slightly at her tone. It felt like the entire vehicle was waiting to see what happened next, but he just sat there momentarily wringing his hands. Knowing we were on a time crunch, I pulled out of the driveway and started down the road, keeping one eye on things in the rearview.

"Listen, I…" He started and then trailed off. "I know that

I've been..."

"A fucking child?" Leighton supplied.

"Off your fucking rocker?" Craig added at the same time.

"A whole ass problem?" I called over my shoulder.

"That's... all fair." Joey said, cringing again as he turned to face Victoria. "Yes. All of that. I haven't been handling, well, at all. I know you didn't mean to get anyone in the mess we ended up in, and I'm... I'm sorry for the way I've been acting around everyone."

My gaze shot to the rearview to gauge Victoria's expression. Her lips pursed, and she took a deep breath before blowing it out slowly.

"Okay," She said. "I can forgive the way you've been acting because I know first hand how grief can mess a person up. It makes you act in ways you'd never act otherwise. Just... no more, okay? We can work through this together."

"Yeah..." He said slowly, turning away from her and looking out the window falling back into silence.

Something about the entire exchange didn't sit right with me. Joey's apology sounded genuine, but it was... off. And the easy way, Victoria let it all go. I made a mental note to speak with her about it when we had time. Joey had been a big enough dickhead she should have been making him grovel. Her easy forgiveness caused my mind to slip to Benson, and I couldn't help but wonder how far she'd let Joey push her.

The rest of the drive went by in silence that continued as we stepped out of the van into the gravel parking lot of the warehouse. Phil was waiting just by the entrance for us, but Helen hadn't arrived yet.

"Got everything you asked for, Boss." Phil said as we made our way inside. "I've got snipers on the top floor in case–"

"It's Helen, Phil. You really think she's going to double cross us? Even if she felt like it, she's not bringing soldiers, she can't kill all five of us by herself."

"And I'm the Queen of England," Phil scoffed. "You

may not think we need em, but I wanted every contingency prepared for. Helen ain't your problem. Candy is; that crazy bitch. How Craig stuck his dick in that woman for two years before he got tired of her particular brand of insanity is beyond me."

"Yeah, I don't know what I was thinking either. Maybe I was fucking drunk the whole time and missed it." Craig said with a shrug just as a large black SUV with fully blacked out windows, towing a small trailer behind it, pulled up before us.

"Look alive," I said, and we fell into position around Victoria as naturally as breathing while we waited. The engine cut as Helen opened the passenger door and stepped out, with Mel climbing out of the driver's seat. I spotted someone in the backseat, but they didn't make a move to get out of the SUV.

"Gentlemen, and Victoria. It's good to see you all well." Helen said, her tone polite but not overly friendly.

"Helen, always a pleasure. I hope these few weeks have been less... eventful for you." Victoria said smoothly, holding her head up. I raised a brow but let it go.

"Our guests I take it?" I asked, motioning toward the trailer.

"Sedated." Mel chimed in, motioning for Joey and Leighton to follow her as she moved to the trailer. The pair followed Mel as she opened the door, which burst open with force. Candy launched herself from the trailer and straight at Joey as the door knocked Mel backward. Joey and Candy fell to the ground as she shrieked something unintelligible. Joey worked to protect his head as she pummeled him from above.

"I thought you said she was sedated!" Leighton bellowed as he rushed forward and snatched Candy's hair, jerking her hard enough to pull her off Joey. Candy twisted in his grasp and flung a fist out blindly toward him. "Not today, wildcat." he snapped as he slapped her across the face hard enough for the sound to echo through the parking lot.

Candy hissed and spit, her arms flailing like she didn't care what she hit as long as she hit something. Whatever they'd sedated her with wasn't adequate, but it seemed they were prepared. Mel got her feet under her and raced to the driver's side door, flinging it open and reaching inside before emerging with a hypodermic needle in hand.

"Hold the crazy bitch still, Leighton." Mel snapped as she tried to get close.

"What the fuck do you think I'm trying to do?" He yelled back as he worked to wrap his free arm around Candy's neck, pulling her into a headlock, his other hand still fisted in her hair. "Any day now, Mel. Fuck! The bitch *bit me!*"

Mel darted forward and jabbed the needle into Candy's thigh before darting away. Leighton's face turned murderous as Candy continued to snap her jaws, biting him a few more times before slowly succumbing to the sedative. The moment he was sure she was completely out, he dropped her unceremoniously to the ground.

"I think I need a rabies shot. Fucking hell. Someone else can carry her ass inside." Leighton grumbled. "Only one person gets to bite me and it ain't that fucking lunatic."

As Leighton was complaining, the back passenger door opened, and for a moment, we all tensed until we saw the shock of blonde hair and flashy, brightly colored clothes.

"Well, well, well. If it isn't Bitch Barbie." Leighton drawled.

"What is she doing here?" Victoria asked.

"I felt it was appropriate that she learned first hand what her mistakes cost." Helen replied calmly.

Joey was moving before anyone could even react. He moved up behind her, grabbed her by the shoulders, and spun her to face him. His face was twisted in a snarl as he backhanded her so hard it sent her sprawling back into the SUV.

"Since you started all this, maybe we'll start with you and you can really learn what meddling can cost." He growled.

"Joey, stop." I called out, moving to pull him away from Tiffany. "She wasn't part of the deal."

"Fuck this bullshit deal!" Joey bellowed. "She deserves to die."

"Do we have a problem, gentlemen?" Helen asked coolly.

"Get your shit together, Joey. Unless you want the rest of us taken out in a fight with the Golden Devils." I hissed, grabbing him by his shirt and giving him a rough shake.

"Fine." He snarled, grabbing my hands and shoving me away. He stepped past me toward the warehouse before he stopped and turned back, pinning his gaze on Tiffany and pointing at her for good measure. "You live today, but the next time I catch you out without protection, you're mine. Helen can't keep you safe forever."

CHAPTER TWENTY TWO

Victoria

Az grabbed Joey by the back of his neck and steered him toward the warehouse, following Mel and Leighton as they packed Candy inside. I could just make out Leighton complaining about having to carry her after she bit him, but against my better judgment, I was more concerned with Tiffany. Joey had hit her hard enough for her head to bounce off the SUV. I may have hated her at the moment, but I wasn't heartless.

"You good?" I asked, not wanting her to read further into the question.

"Yeah… I'm okay," Tiffany replied, her hand sliding from her face to the back of her head.

"Good." I turned to start toward the warehouse when she called out to me.

"Can we talk? Please?" something in her tone caused me to stop and turn back around, even though the last thing I wanted to do was listen to whatever she had to say. "I can't begin to tell you how sorry I am. I fucked up, big time."

"You didn't just fuck up, Tiffany, you got one of the men I love killed. That's.." I shook my head, unable to finish.

"I know," She said, her eyes dropping to her feet. "If I knew how it would play out I never would have passed on the information I had. She wasn't *supposed* to hurt any of you. She was just supposed to extract you from the horsemen and bring you to us so you'd be safe."

"You let a fucking psychopath loose, what the hell did you think would happen?" I screamed, my hands fisting at my sides.

Tiffany winced. "That part wasn't my call. No, it doesn't change what happened or the role I did play, but you have to believe me. I really thought you were in trouble. I've spent the last several years in this world and you haven't. I had no way of knowing that you'd be able to get away if what I thought was happening had actually been happening."

"So, we're dropping the ditzy rich bitch pretense now, huh? Just gonna pretend like you've been a gangster this whole time and never said a word and I'm just supposed to what? Believe that?"

"Because it's true. Helen will tell you as much if you want to ask her."

"How the fuck did you even get mixed up in all this shit, Tiffany? What the hell went so wrong in your life you couldn't tell me, your supposed best friend, instead of joining a God damned criminal organization and ultimately ruining my fucking life in the process? I think I at least deserve to know that since you've decided to take me down with you."

Tiffany's eyes flicked up to mine, and she let out a heavy breath as she held my gaze. "Do you remember that party on Iverson's boat?"

"That eurotrash you hooked up with a few summers ago? Yeah, I remember." I scoffed. "You've always had terrible taste in men. He wasn't an exception."

"Yeah, well, I didn't tell you what happened *after* the party ended. Why he up and went back home the very next day. He wasn't interested in me for the arm candy or my personality. He was looking for a mule. He had enough coke in one of the cabins that everyone on that boat that night could have OD many times over. I like to party as much as the next girl, but I wasn't interested in smuggling his drugs, not knowing who my older sister's mother is. We fought and he locked me in a closet. He was too stupid to take my phone, so I called Helen."

"You know, if you had told me any of this when it happened, I might have actually felt sorry for you, but after everything you did, I don't think I can." I interjected.

"You don't fucking know what it means to owe someone like Helen." Tiffany snapped. "Yeah, she treats me like another daughter, I get a little more leeway than the average soldier because of it, but she's a fucking mobster Tory. If I told her no when she said I owed her for her help that night, she would have put a bullet in my head and tossed me over the side of the yacht. Part of staying alive meant keeping my silence. The *only* good I thought came out of the whole mess was being able to save you when *every goddamned thing I found* said you needed saving."

My head reared back like she'd slapped me. Her words seemed to almost echo what Craig had said when he refused to take her as payment for Rich's death. I could feel my grip on the hatred I'd nursed for her starting to slip away as I started to understand, for probably the first time, everything that had led to the choices she made.

"I don't know if I can forgive you." I spoke finally. "I'm so angry at you for all of it. I just… Give me some time and space. I'm not going to promise we will ever be friends again, but I will think about what you just told me and maybe, when things aren't so raw, *maybe* I can consider forgiving you."

"That's the best I can hope for, I suppose." She replied with a half-hearted smile. "For what it's worth, I never stopped being your friend, even if you've stopped being mine. Helen doesn't know this, but I heard your boys are looking into Theo. Word on the street is he's secretly meeting with the Russians. I had Georgialynn do a little digging, quietly, and, well… here." She stuck her hand in her pocket and pulled out a small flash drive, holding it out to me. "There's not much to find on the Russian he's meeting with, but what is there, you and your boys will want to see."

I took the device from her hand and stuck it in my pocket without a word. There was nothing else for either of us to say. Tiffany could apologize all she wanted, but I needed time if I was ever going to get over her causing Rich's death. She may have thought she was extending an olive branch with whatever information she'd just handed me, but the branch wasn't hers to extend.

"Fucking hell, we still gotta carry the other one in there." Leighton's voice rang out, giving me an excuse to walk away from Tiffany without a word. "This one better still be knocked out, Mel or I swear to God!"

Turning toward the warehouse, I spotted Craig following behind Leighton and Mel as they made their way back to the trailer. He must have noticed the discomfort left over from my conversation with Tiffany on my face because he motioned me toward him and tucked me into his side as soon as I reached him.

"You alright, Bunny?" He murmured in my ear, not wanting to draw attention to us.

"Are any of us alright?" I snorted, shaking my head as I gently patted his chest. "I'll fill you all in later, I don't want to have to rehash it four times. Suffice it to say, Tiffany thinks she's given me a peace offering. I haven't decided if I want it to *be* a peace offering."

"We don't have to stay if you're not up for it." Craig offered. "Things are going to get pretty intense in there once the Golden Devils leave."

"*That* I want to deal with." I replied. "I need to see the woman who took him from us suffer with my own eyes. Maybe even inflict some of the pain she's caused us onto her with my own fucking hands."

Leighton and Mel neared with the second Devil just in time for Leighton to hear the last part of what I'd said.

"That's my vicious girlfriend. I'll help you get your hands as dirty as you want *ma petit.* Like the only boyfriend in this harem should!" I couldn't help but laugh at his antics. "I'll even share if the others want in."

I couldn't help but laugh at his antics, though I had the brief thought that something had fundamentally changed in me for me to find them as funny as I did these days. "It's adorable that you're willing to share, but you are *not* the only boyfriend, Leighton." I shot back, causing him to poke his lower lip out in a pout.

"You couldn't have told me that *privately*? Now what am I supposed to hold over the other guys?" He winked before shifting the weight of the sedated woman he was helping carry inside with a grunt.

It was that wink that did me in. I doubled over in laughter at how ridiculous the whole... just everything was. I was standing outside of a warehouse with one of my *four* boyfriends after a conversation with my ex-best friend about her role in getting my fifth boyfriend killed, and about to watch the woman who pulled the trigger and her second in command be tortured for it. If someone had told me I'd end up here back before the Gala, I'd have thought they lost their mind. Now, all I wanted was to help gut Candy and then go home and curl up with my men.

CHAPTER TWENTY THREE

Joey

I grabbed one of the folding chairs, turning it so that I could sit in it backward. Leighton and Mel had tied Candy to a chair after she'd been re-sedated and carried into the warehouse. After the show she put on outside, I wished there was an anchor point on the floor to secure her to, but we hadn't had time to find a better location for our interrogation.

Time seemed to crawl by while I waited for her second to be secured to a chair and for one of them to wake up from the sedation. There wasn't a clock in the building, but I could almost swear I heard the slow tick... tick... tick of the seconds dragging by. The others had pulled out their own chairs and sat around me, waiting. I stole a glance at Victoria, who was seated between Az and Craig. Her presence made my stomach sour, and bile rise in my throat over the show I'd put on in the van apologizing. I hadn't meant a damned word I said to her. There was just something about lulling her into a false sense of security only to crush her later that soothed the beast inside me in ways the little jabs and hateful words alone hadn't been able to.

A groan sounded from Candy's second-in-command. My eyes flicked to the woman, taking in her every moment as she rolled her head and fought to open her eyes.

"Water," she croaked.

Az reached into the cooler on the floor beside him and

pulled out a bottle of water, cracking it open as he strolled toward the woman. He carefully put it to her lips and helped her take a few sips.

"Shiiit." She slurred, her head jerking up as she tried to take in the space with unfocused eyes. "Sssomebody get me soome coffee."

"Why would we do anything for you?" I snapped, causing Az to glare at me over his shoulder.

Her hands jerked in an attempt to raise, and she grunted again, letting her head loll back on her shoulders. "Tell you everything... Jusss... need coffee. Clear..." she grunted. "Clear the fog."

The sound of a chair scraping on the concrete floor behind me had me looking over my shoulder. Leighton had left his seat and moved to grab some kind of coffee drink from the cooler. I gritted my teeth and rolled my eyes. We weren't supposed to be kind to either of the women we held. They were payment for Rich's life. They both deserved to suffer.

Leighton handed the drink to Az, who helped the woman drink it. After a few deep gulps, she blinked as if her vision were clearing a little.

"I'm not gonna run." She sighed. "You can untie one of my hands and I can hold the drink myself."

Az nodded, leaning down and undoing the binding on one of her wrists.

"What the fuck?" I demanded. "We letting prisoners dictate how they're kept now?"

"Joey," Craig warned from beside me. "She's only here because she's Candy's second. She's not the one that pulled the trigger."

"Yeah, Joey," The woman drawled, her head rolling in my direction as she squinted her eyes at me. "I already know I'm not leaving here alive, a little mercy ain't gonna change that." she grabbed the drink from Az and took a deep swig. "Fucking Candy. I knew that bitch was gonna get me killed some day."

She downed the rest of the drink and motioned for

another. Az complied, and the rest of us waited silently as she drank it, letting it wipe out the lingering grogginess from the sedation. When she'd finished the second bottle, Az finally broke the silence.

"What happened, Jen? How did we end up here?"

Her shoulders slumped forward, and she puffed out a heavy breath. "Me and Candy went undercover with the Jackals about a month before your arrest. There'd been some evidence they were encroaching on our territory, but nothing solid to prove it, so Helen sent us in to find out for sure. Candy did whatever needed to be done for us to climb the ranks, but we never got farther than her running her own crew. The Golden Devils run a tight ship, but it's nothing like what the Jackals got going on. Moving around in the ranks is near impossible, and nobody but a select few at the very top even know who's running the show. How they manage to stay so locked down without the right hand knowing what the left is doing is anybody's guess. However you swing it, we weren't getting anywhere with figuring out how they were getting product into our turf without it linking back to them because nobody was talking outside of their own crews. Then word came down that the big boss wanted your girl." She nodded her head toward Victoria.

"We've been aware of that for a while. It doesn't explain what happened."

"It was every crew for themselves. Word came down that whoever snagged your girl would be rewarded with a special assignment. Nobody ever said for certain, but it was heavily implied that the assignment was where we needed to be to figure out how they were slinging on our streets. Another crew got to you first in that cabin. We figured that meant our chance at finding what we were after was shot and started making plans for extraction. But then Craig killed the hacker."

"It would be nice if you would just get to the fucking point already." I snapped, earning a nasty look from Az.

Jen lifted her chin in defiance and stared me in the eyes.

"Or what? You'll kill me? I'm already a dead woman, it won't hurt you to hear me out."

"Enough." Az interjected. "Finish talking."

"Where was I... Oh, right, Craig killed the hacker. There must have been something you took from her house when you snuffed her because upper management lost their shit. The order came down that we were throwing everything at you boys. The big boss wanted your entire empire wiped out. Had a couple meetings between the crew leads with targets and a date for a coordinated strike. That's about the time Helen contacted us. She said the game had changed. She wanted us to get the girl and one of you for questioning and leave the rest as a distraction for the Jackals while we fortified our streets.

"Candy called in every contact she had. Mercs, independents, you name it, she called them. The plan was for them to get to you first and corral you to where we would be waiting so we could follow Helen's orders and then stage a car accident for our extraction. We took her Jackals crew to the location we'd been assigned, waited for the fighting to break out and then slipped away in the chaos. The plan worked perfectly. You boys went right where we wanted, as far away from the actual fighting as we could manage, all while thinking the Jackals were on your ass. I don't know why Candy decided to disobey orders to leave all of you alive. Take one and leave the rest alive, that's what Helen told us. It's why we used contacts we could call off as soon as we were clear instead of bringing along the Jackals."

"So, you got Craig and Victoria in the vehicle, and then what? Called everyone off as soon as you were clear?" Az asked.

"That's about the gist of it, yeah. Helen knew you'd think the Jackals were behind the abduction and that the four left behind would be hellbent on taking them out. You'd either manage it or get yourselves killed in the process, either way was a win for us. Knowing Helen, though, the minute she realized you weren't really a threat to your girl, she'd have sent you an offer of assistance. We'll never know for sure since

Candy fucked it all up killing Rich."

"Are we done now?" I scoffed. "None of this fucking matters. What matters is Rich is dead and we're owed her goddamned life for it."

Jen cringed instinctively before looking down at her lap. "Look, there's one last thing, and then I ask that you have a little mercy and make it quick. I overheard Candy on the phone with someone when we got back to Devils' territory. I didn't catch much, but what I heard sounded like she was planning on handing your girl over to the Jackals the second Helen turned her back. Your girl there put a wrench in those plans when she lost her shit over Craig." Az stepped forward, pulling the pistol he had stowed under his jacket from its holster. "Wait! Shit, please." Jen pleaded.

Az cocked his head to the side and studied her as she used her free hand and her mouth to unclasp a chain around her neck that had been hidden by her shirt. She carefully held it together with her freed hand and offered it to him.

"You can do whatever tests you think are necessary, but afterward, can you please get this to Helen to give to my sister? It's the only way she will believe I'm not coming back alive."

"Yeah. We can do that." Az answered, motioning Craig forward and handing him the necklace. "Anything else before we..."

Jen pressed her lips and started to shake her head slightly. "Just make that stupid cunt suffer. I shouldn't be here; we all know it, so make her suffer for it."

"Fuck's sake," I huffed, drawing my weapon and stalking forward. "No more of this bullshit. We're not dragging it out anymore." I placed the muzzle of my gun against Jen's forehead as soon as I was close enough. "Bye, Jen," I said, pulling the trigger.

Victoria's alarmed yelp echoed around the warehouse with the sound of the gunshot. I had to bite the inside of my cheek to keep from sneering at her. She didn't belong here.

"Is there any way to wake this bitch up, or are we going

to be sitting around here waiting again?" I snapped.

"Actually, I think I have some Naloxone in a bag in the SUV." Craig answered.

"And you're just telling us now?" I asked incredulously.

"Nobody fucking asked, and I am, y'know, a little bit out of sorts from the pain medication for all of my injuries. You don't have to be a dick about it." He said over his shoulder as he slowly returned to the SUV. A few minutes later, he was back, shuffling toward the chair that Candy was tied to.

I snatched the applicator from his hand and administered the naloxone. Craig glared at me over my impatience, but no way in hell were we letting him get close enough to administer it in his state. I tapped my foot impatiently, waiting for it to kick in, barely holding my tongue when Candy's eyes blinked open.

Her head jerked upright, and she blinked rapidly as she took in her surroundings. "Fuck."

"Good morning... What's the opposite of sunshine? Something really insulting since she *fucking bit me?*" Leighton laughed.

"Not my finest moment," Candy said, her voice still hoarse and sleepy. "You tasted like shit. Anyone got a toothbrush?"

"Whether or not you'll have any teeth left to brush after this is going to be entirely up to you," I clipped, pulling her head back so I could look her in the face.

"You know why you're here, Candy," Az said behind me.

"I almost sent flowers to the funeral. I heard it was a lovely service, but it's too bad his woman missed it." Candy said, looking me in the eye. I sneered, bringing my fist down on her overly calm face. I let her go as blood trickled from her nose. Victoria made a sound behind me. I suppose it was meant to be a snarl, but it gave me the impression of a kitten trying to be intimidating. Candy's head lolled to one side momentarily before she started laughing.

"Starting with head strikes? How am I ever supposed to

keep a clear head for your questions, boys?" The humor in her voice made me want to take her head off, and I drew back for another blow.

Az's hand gripped my shoulder and pulled me back just far enough for him to step between us. He kept his eyes pinned on her as he rolled up the sleeves of his button-down shirt. "We need her conscious if we're going to find out anything. I've got this."

"That's right. Be a good little boy and let the boss play," Candy laughed. "We all know *Daddy* is in charge, let him show us what a big dick he has."

I started to lunge forward just as Leighton wrapped his arms around my waist and jerked me back. I saw Victoria stepping forward at the same moment, her face twisted into a snarl. It was downright unjust how they let her get involved while holding me back from the justice I deserved.

"He's not *Daddy*." Victoria hissed, her voice so low I almost missed it. "You fucking killed him."

Candy tossed her head back and let out a full belly laugh as if Victoria had told the most hilarious joke. When she was finally done laughing, she took a few wheezing breaths as if she'd start up again at any second. Then, she smiled broadly at Victoria.

"The things I've heard, I'm a little surprised you're such a daddy's girl. Though, I suppose when you don't know who daddy really is, you'll beg for just about anybody."

"Enough!" Az's voice boomed out.

"Why did you kill him?" Victoria demanded at the same time.

Candy cocked her head to the side and studied Victoria closely before licking her teeth like a predator. The smile that split her face was manic and starkly contrasted with the saccharine tone from her mouth. "Because he begged so prettily for you to choose anyone but him. I couldn't let such a perfect declaration of devotion go to waste. When she–"

Candy's words were cut off as Victoria launched herself

at the small table next to her, snagging a knife and slamming it viciously into her thigh. A pained howl ripped from Candy's lips, and her body attempted to flee the pain, jerking back so hard the chair rocked beneath her weight.

Victoria's face was twisted in righteous fury as she stood, blood on the hand that had held the knife. For a moment, she didn't look like a kitten playing at being scary. She looked like a lioness staring down at her wounded prey. I hated how it made my cock twitch and my body respond. Every cell lit up, wanting to chase her. I wanted to catch her, to see what it would be like to have this savage side of her fight back while I claimed her again. I felt like an addict fighting the urge not to relapse as I worked to remind myself this version was the real her. The vicious woman she hid under all her spoiled naivety.

"You fucking bitch!" Candy shrieked. "And to think, I gave you a choice. I should have just killed all of them!"

Victoria lunged forward again, grabbing hold of the knife in Candy's thigh and jerking it free. I knew the moment the first spurt of blood shot from Candy's leg that Victoria hadn't made a novice's mistake. Time seemed to slow, Az reaching out to grab Victoria as she shrieked like an enraged banshee, Leighton scrambling to find anything to stop Candy's femoral artery bleed. A pained hiss was all I needed to tell me Craig was trying to remove his belt. But all of it, every single movement we made, was for nothing. The damage to her thigh and the amount of blood with each spurt meant we had maybe minutes.

"Who the fuck is behind this, Candy?" I shouted, knowing she wouldn't answer but hoping she had time to say something. "Who the fuck ordered my brother's death? You can't tell me someone didn't order it."

Candy's head started to sag from blood loss, but she rallied long enough to tilt it back and smile at me. "Wouldn't... you... like to... know."

I was so caught in tunnel vision that I didn't notice Craig

had reached her with his belt in hand. He struggled to lift her injured leg as she lost consciousness, intent on using it as a tourniquet.

"Fucking, Leighton give me a hand damn it." He yelled.

Candy's breathing rapidly grew shallow, her chest barely moving as Leighton rushed to help Craig. In the few seconds it took him to reach them, her chest had stilled on a strange rattling breath. It was a death rattle. I'd heard it many times before, but *it was never* until we'd finished our questioning.

"Fuck!" I bellowed, storming toward the warehouse door and pausing long enough to slam my fist into the wall beside it. "FUCK!"

CHAPTER TWENTY FOUR

Az

My hand went to my hair and I tugged it, growling at myself over the action. Victoria stood with her mouth gaping open in shock in front of Candy, still holding the bloody knife. Angry wasn't the right word to begin describing how I felt about how everything went down.

"Leighton, get a hold of Phil and sort this mess out." I barked, my tone causing Victoria to flinch.

"Yep. On it." He replied, more subdued than I could ever remember him being as he strolled from the warehouse, pulling his phone out as he went.

My eyes moved from Victoria to Craig. He still stood over Candy's body, his belt hanging useless and bloody from his hands. I moved without a thought, closing the distance between us in a few long strides.

"I didn't mean–" Victoria started.

"Stop." I bit out, turning my attention back to Craig. "I told you, I fucking told you not to give her more god damned ammo. That I'd reconcile this shit when the time came, but it wasn't supposed to be today!" I yelled. Craig opened his mouth to respond, but I cut him off. "Fucking hell, I'm not actually saying it's your fault, but I *am* yelling at you for it! She shouldn't have fucking been here, but I knew, I fucking knew, if I tried to stop her you'd just talk me out of it. And you," I whirled on Victoria, and her eyes widened. "All you had to do was be our peace, but you just couldn't do that. You keep inserting yourself where you don't have the skills to be, so fuck. Fucking, *fuck it!* Starting tomorrow, you train like a fucking grunt. I don't want to hear a single god damned complaint out of you over it, either. We could have learned something today, but instead, you let your emotions run you, and you killed our only lead. That will *never* happen again."

"I know you're pissed," Craig started slowly. "But we *did* get information today from Jen. And knowing Candy the way I do, we were never going to get anything from her that we didn't already have."

"Jen's info didn't do anything except clarify what *already* went down. Yeah, you *knew* Candy, but that doesn't mean we wouldn't have gotten anything else out of her. The bitch loved to fucking slip bits of information out to taunt you the whole goddamned time you were fucking her!" I bellowed, throwing my hands up.

"Az, you have every right to be angry, but you know as well as I do she wasn't going to give us anything because we *wanted* her to. She'd rather have died. I know we don't *know* that for certain, but we do."

"Again. Angry, yelling. *You* just happen to be here!" I snapped.

A sniffle near us drew our attention, and I turned my head to see Victoria wiping tears from her eyes, leaving a blood smear across her cheek as she curled in on herself.

"I... I didn't mean to. I just... I was so angry. I don't —" Victoria's voice quivered, and my mind warred between wanting to comfort her and throttle her.

"Well the fuck aware." I snarked, barely able to rein in my anger enough not to rip into her completely.

"Bunny, that's the problem. We don't kill people without intention..." Craig trailed off, thinking, "Well, occasionally Leighton does. But *even then*, it's never when it's important. Everyone we end has a purpose."

"What about me?" Leighton called out, walking back

into the warehouse.

I rolled my eyes at him and returned my attention to Victoria. "Tomorrow, when Ian leaves for work, you start training. No more going easy on you. No running to Craig when you feel like it's too much. When one of us says jump, and we will say jump, you start jumping. We'll tell you when you've jumped high enough. No sass, no backtalk, you take your orders and follow through, just like any other boots on the fucking ground for the Horsemen. Do I make myself clear?"

"Yes, Sir." Victoria said, looking at her hands as she fidgeted with her fingers.

"Don't either of you go easy on her either. She's in this for real now, no backing out and no pulling punches. She wasn't built for this life, but she's here and we're going to make sure she fucking survives it. Where the fuck is Joey?" I asked, effectively ending the conversation about Victoria's training.

"What?" Joey's clipped response had me turning in his direction, where he stood just inside the warehouse door.

"Starting tomorrow, you're back to training her with the rest of us. She's following in your fucking footsteps, and since she won't take 'no' for a fucking answer, we're going to make sure she's not a danger or a liability." I snapped back.

"The fuck? I get training her to keep her safe, but since when are we *bringing her in*? That's *never* been the plan!" He started storming toward us, a heavy glower on his face.

"Since she keeps killing people, that's when. She has a body count of two, do you really want her racking up more on *accident*?"

"She killed Rinaldo on purpose." Leighton remarked.

"Not what I meant smartass, and you fucking know it." I growled, reaching out to smack him in the back of the head. "This was an accident, otherwise she'd never have landed another body on my watch."

Phil walked in with a small crew following behind him, acknowledged us with a two-finger salute, and started directing the clean-up operations. I gave everyone a harsh look, moved outside to the SUV without looking back, climbed in the driver's seat, and slammed the door.

I had to remind myself to slow down when we got closer to Dawn and Ian's house; it wouldn't do for us to get pulled over for speeding while we had two people covered in blood in the car. My hands hurt from how hard I gripped the steering wheel as I pulled in, cut the engine, and climbed out. I slammed the door behind myself and stormed up to the house.

Fuck, I wanted to hit something. Or to smash things up like I had in my room at the manor, which felt like a lifetime ago. I couldn't do either here, and I had to remind myself not to jerk the front door off the hinges as I stepped inside. Dawn noticed something was off the second I stepped inside.

"Come with me." She ordered. Standing from the couch and moving toward the kitchen.

I followed her in silence as she led me through the door in the kitchen and into her greenhouse. She paused near a set of shelves, opening them and reaching high enough that she had to stand on her tiptoes. Before I could ask if she wanted help, she'd pulled down a whiskey bottle and returned for two glasses.

"When Rich would call me, I'd always come out here." She started, pouring both of us two fingers before handing me a glass. "I didn't drink every time, but the times when it was bad… When the things he was telling me made me sure I was going to bury one of my boys, I'd have a drink to calm my nerves." She took a sip from her glass and then let out a huff. "Who'd have figured it wouldn't be any of those calls that cost me one of you." She shook her head and then pinned her gaze on me. "You wanna tell me what's going on? What's got you all in a tizzy?"

"I don't think you want to know, Dawn." I sighed before taking a sip of my whiskey.

"Well, the way I figure it, you can tell me, or I can just guess until I get it right. Either way, I think you need to let it out before it eats you up inside."

I set my glass down on the long table where she had plants in the process of being repotted and studied her. Rich called her when there was a problem he couldn't solve, but, as far as I knew, he never told her more than he needed to work shit out. My chest twinged with the reminder that I wasn't him. I didn't know what lines I couldn't cross when talking to his mother. I knew I was starting to crumble under the pressure of his absence.

"Alright. I'll start guessing." Dawn nodded, taking my silence as an answer while I was still wondering if I *could* talk to her about what happened at the warehouse. "Your interrogation didn't go too well. If I had to wager, based on the glimpse I got of the rest of them getting out of the SUV when we stepped back here, somebody got a little trigger-happy before you could get your answers."

My head whipped back in shock. "How–"

"My son may not have wanted to tell me everything, but I'm not stupid. I raised two mobsters, so I know enough. It didn't take a genius to know he moved us all the way out here away from Sacona so we couldn't be used against you boys. And you definitely don't have to be the brightest to put two and two together when your child is telling you about a problem and a few days later there's missing gangsters or bodies in the paper." She reached out and patted me on the shoulder. "So, who messed up? My money is on Leighton. That boy has had impulse control issues as long as we've known him. I still have nightmares about Collin confetti."

"Victoria, actually," I answered, unsure I wanted to know what Collin confetti was about.

"Can't say I saw that one coming." She huffed, taking another sip of her drink. "Can't say I'm mad about it either, though. You boys need a woman who has your back just the same as you have each other's. She's got the will, so tell me, Az, you gonna give her the way?"

I raked a hand through my hair with a groan. "Rich

didn't want this for her. *I* don't want this for her, but she's not leaving me any choice." I started pacing along the length of the table, my hand on the back of my neck. "I told her, I fucking *told* her that we didn't need her to be a sword for us, we could do that. We need her to be our peace! But she won't listen!" I could feel my chest tighten as my mind started flashing with all the ways this could go wrong.

Dawn sipped her whiskey, watching me with a patient look as I paced, but didn't say anything. I picked up my glass, downing the contents and relishing the burn on the way down.

"I keep feeling like if he were here, he'd know what to do or, or what to say. She fought him, yeah, but it was... it felt different. He would have known how to handle her. Fuck, how to handle all of this!" I set the glass down before I threw it. My chest was tight, my head hurt, and my eyes burned. "I wasn't meant for this role! I was his right hand, his back up. I wasn't meant to lead, and everything is falling apart around me and I don't... I... I can't make it stop."

My words were starting to jumble in my head; the world was going blurry as tears filled my eyes despite my attempts to stop it.

"He said the same thing to me once," Dawn's voice was soft as she set her glass down, "After Richie and Victoria got into their little spat because of his stubbornness, he called me. He was heartbroken and ashamed of himself. But he believed he was doing the best thing for her. I remember how he sounded when he said he felt like everything was falling apart, slipping through his fingers, and he didn't know how to catch it all. He was fighting with Joey, scared to death for all of you." She sounded so distant as she recalled their conversation, and something inside me started to crack. "His shoulders weren't made of steel, but he tried to carry it all anyway. I kept trying to tell him, that's what God and your momma's for." She cleared her throat, looking at me. "The point is, don't try to create an image in your mind that he would have had all the answers. He was only human, too, and he struggled. It's okay to feel like you don't know what to do next, struggle, or even be afraid."

"I still *need* him here." I croaked out. "It's not the same with the other guys. I don't know how to explain it, but it's just not. Without him, I don't have the one person I could go to when I needed my head sorted out. He had you, and I just... without him, I've got nothing." I sobbed.

"Listen to me, Az Casadei." Dawn said sternly, gripping my chin in her hand. "I know I ain't your momma, God rest her soul, but you're my son as much as the rest of them. I know you looked up to Rich and he helped you through some pretty dark days. You two were close, and he loved you too. It's okay to grieve that. You *need* to grieve that. But don't you ever for a second think you've got nobody in your corner because, boy, I've been cheering you on since the first time your momma showed me them baby blues."

I was trembling from how hard I was trying to hold on to my composure, and it felt like I was pushing a boulder up a hill. Dawn let go of my chin and wrapped her arms around me, pulling me down so my head was tucked under her chin like a small child. She patted my back with one hand when she positioned me how she wanted. "Now, you let it all out, honey. I ain't going anywhere."

I wrapped my arms around her and buried my face as well as I could in the side of her neck. The scent of baked goods, a soft floral perfume, freshly turned dirt, and the hint of whiskey wrapped around me like an extension of the hug she gave me. And the part of me that was cracking finally broke. Sobs wracked me, and it took everything to keep standing as I held on to the petite woman. She shushed me and rubbed her hand up and down my back as I cried.

I don't know how long we stood there before the well ran dry. Dawn's steady comfort and the back pats felt like they were piecing my mind back together, one shushing sound at a time.

CHAPTER TWENTY FIVE

Victoria

I woke to warmth, a glance at the clock showed it was still the middle of the night.

Craig's arms were still around me, his breath slow and steady against the back of my neck. For a moment, I let myself pretend everything was fine—like the afternoon hadn't happened, like I wasn't still wearing the weight of Candy's blood under my skin. But the second I shifted, just enough to stretch, Craig stirred.

His hold tightened slightly. "You okay, Bunny?" His voice was rough with sleep, and somehow, that made it feel safer to answer honestly.

"I don't know."

I felt him press a kiss to my shoulder, the scruff of his jaw grazing my skin. "Talk to me."

I turned in his arms, facing him. His eyes were already open, watching me in that quiet way of his that always made it feel like nothing I said would ever be too much.

"I don't think Az is done being mad at me," I admitted. "He hasn't even looked at me since we got back."

Craig's thumb brushed against my hip under the blanket. "He was pissed, yeah. Scared too. You know how he gets when he's scared."

"Yeah," I whispered. "Loud."

He gave a small, grim smile. "Very."

I bit the inside of my cheek. "And Joey... he was just starting to come around again. Just starting to be Joey again, and now he's furious that I'm gonna start training for real. Like I've betrayed him just by trying to belong."

Craig sighed, pulling me close enough for my forehead to rest against his. "Joey's working through his own mess. Doesn't mean you don't get to take up space in this."

"What if taking up space means losing him?" My voice cracked a little at the end. I hated that it did.

He kissed me.

It was soft, his lips brushing mine like he was trying to soothe something deeper than my skin. But then he kissed me again—firmer this time, more certain—and I felt his fingers slide up along my spine.

One kiss melted into the next until I wasn't sure when I'd moved, only that I was suddenly straddling his hips, the blanket slipping low on my back, his hands resting at my waist like he didn't want to spook me—but wanted me all the same.

His mouth lingered at the corner of mine. "I can't speak for everyone, but I know you're not losing me."

And when he kissed me again, it was anything but soft.

Craig's hands slid up under the hem of the shirt I was wearing—his shirt, soft and worn thin, the fabric brushing my thighs as I shifted in his lap. His thumbs traced the curve of my waist like he was memorizing the shape of me all over again.

I kissed him harder.

I didn't want soft, not anymore. Not with the storm still churning inside me. I wanted the way his mouth opened under mine, the way he groaned low in his throat when I rolled my hips, the way he gripped my thighs like he was barely holding himself back.

"Fuck, Bunny," he breathed, lips against my jaw now, down my neck. "You're gonna kill me."

"You started it," I whispered, tugging at the hem of his shirt. He lifted his arms without hesitation, and I pulled it off, tossing it somewhere I'd pretend to find later. His skin was warm beneath my palms, solid. Familiar.

Craig pulled my shirt off me, slow and deliberate. The air was cool against my bare chest, but his hands were already there, rough palms cupping my breasts like they were his to worship.

He pulled me down to him, his mouth on my collarbone, teeth dragging over my skin, and I felt myself arch into him. My hips rocked again, and this time he groaned into my chest, letting one hand trail down between us, slipping under the band of my underwear.

"God, you're soaked," he murmured, voice low and reverent like a prayer. "You want this?"

"I *need* this," I said, fingers digging into his shoulders.

His name left my mouth in a gasp as he touched me, fingers slipping through slick heat, teasing me until I was grinding shamelessly against his hand. I could feel him hard beneath me, his cock straining against his boxers, and I wanted all of him—right *now*.

"Take these off," I said, tugging at the waistband of his underwear, breathless and hungry.

"You first," he said with a wicked grin, and I didn't need telling twice.

I shifted back just enough to peel mine down, and Craig kicked his off in the same motion.

I buried my face in his neck as his hand slid between us, fingers brushing exactly where I was aching, and I couldn't hold in the whimper that broke from my lips.

"You're killing me," I breathed against his throat.

"You're the one riding me like that, Bunny," he said with a ragged laugh, voice rough and reverent all at once. "You think I'm gonna stop you?"

Skin to skin now, nothing between us, his hands on my thighs, guiding me back over him like he couldn't bear the space.

I reached for him, wrapping my fingers around the length of him, and he cursed under his breath, hips jerking slightly.

I sank down onto him, his head falling back against the pillows, both of us gasping as I rocked slowly onto him.

"Victoria, I—" Az's voice cut through the haze of breath and heat and moaned half-words. I lifted my head at the sound. His eyes locked on me—bare, flushed, grinding on Craig like I was trying to drown the past in pleasure, and I froze.

Almost.

Craig didn't. His hands tightened at my hips, pulling me down harder against him. "Don't stop now," he murmured loud enough for all three of us to hear.

Az's expression changed.

That sharp intake of breath, the way his jaw clenched. Anger wasn't what moved through him now. It was something darker, hungrier.

His gaze roamed over me like a man starved, then cut to Craig, then back to me. "I came to apologize," he said, voice low, controlled, but slightly frayed at the edges. "I shouldn't have yelled. You didn't deserve that." Az took another step inside. "But I stand by what I said about your training. You need it. What happened can't happen again." His eyes dropped to where Craig's hands still gripped my hips, the sweat-slick line of my spine. "Though clearly, you're... recovering well."

There was a bite in his voice but no jealousy. Just heat. Interest. Something dangerous that made my stomach flip. His eyes were dark, sharp with restraint, but his expression was all hunger. That calculated kind that didn't just want to take—it wanted to *own*. His broad shoulders filled the doorway, tension running through every line of him like a thread pulled tight. He looked like he'd been trying to talk himself out of crossing that threshold ever since he opened the damn door.

"You gonna keep watching, or...?" Craig said, smirking now like he already knew the answer. Az's gaze dragged up my body again, and I felt it like a touch. He stepped inside and shut the door behind him with a quiet click. The sound made the air in the room shift, heavier with expectation.

"Like hell I'm just gonna watch when she looks like *that*."

My breath caught.

Az stepped forward, slow but deliberate, his eyes locked on mine as if daring me to look away. His shirt was already unbuttoned—when had that happened?—his chest bare, inked, all sharp muscle and intent. The way he looked at me wasn't soft, wasn't sweet. It was hunger. It was possession.

He stopped at the edge of the bed, staring down at me like he wanted to devour every inch. His tongue flicked across his bottom lip as his fingers went to his belt—not with care, but with frustration like the leather was in his way. The metal buckle clinked, rough and fast, and then he shoved his pants down in one impatient motion, not bothering with finesse.

He looked like he was stalking me, every movement calculated but coiled tight with restraint, as if the act of undressing was just a necessary delay before he pounced. I could see the tension in his jaw and how his hands twitched like he wanted to tear away the rest of the space between us. His gaze never left mine, and I felt it like a physical touch, dragging down my skin with every breathless second. He was already hard, cock flushed and heavy as it sprang free. When he stroked himself once, slowly, and it was almost enough to make me come on the spot.

"Beautiful," he murmured, not even to me directly—more like to himself, like he was confirming something he'd known all along. He moved to the bed with slow, deliberate steps, one hand trailing over the back of my thigh, up the curve of my ass. I shivered beneath his touch. He didn't kiss me. He didn't ask. He just leaned in behind me, palm dragging down my spine until my body arched, offering more without even thinking.

"She's perfect like this," Craig said, voice rough, proud. His hands stayed locked on my hips, holding me in place as I rolled against him. "You want her?"

Az's chuckle was low and wicked as he leaned closer, mouth at my ear. "What do you think?"

Craig grinned and reached behind the nightstand, pulling out a neatly coiled length of soft rope. He held it up without ceremony.

"Knew you had some," Az said with a smirk.

Craig handed it over. "She loves it. Don't you, Bunny?"

I nodded, already breathless. Az wasted no time. His fingers were sure and fast, binding my wrists behind my back with practiced ease. The tie was simple, tight, and secure but never painful. His grip was commanding even in something as simple as tying rope. My shoulders pulled back, chest arching forward, fully exposed between them now, entirely at their mercy.

"Color?" Az asked, low and close.

"Green," I whispered. No hesitation.

"So good when you surrender," he murmured, his hand curved around the back of my neck as he pressed his body to mine, hips aligning behind me.

I trembled, already dizzy from Craig still beneath me, his cock still buried inside me, hard and aching with restraint.

"She's been making the prettiest sounds," Craig said, sliding his hands up my thighs again.

"I heard," Az said.

Craig's hands moved up to cup my breasts, thumbs brushing over my nipples. "You're gonna take both of us, Bunny," he said, voice thick. "You're gonna be such a good girl for us, yeah?"

"Yes," I breathed, and then I felt him. His hand between my cheeks, slick fingers spreading lube I hadn't seen him grab, but somehow, he always came prepared. He worked it in with expert care. Slow, steady, coaxing me open with one finger, then two, never rushing. My body rocked between them, overwhelmed and trembling.

Az lined up behind me and pushed forward, slow but deliberate. The stretch stole the air from my lungs, delicious and sharp. My bound hands clenched in the rope as my body adjusted, filled entirely from both sides now.

"*Fuck*," I cried, already overwhelmed by the feeling of both of them inside me.

Craig kissed me, slow and messy, his hands guiding me to move again. Az growled behind me, holding my hips tight as he began to thrust deep and steady, driving me down harder onto Craig with every movement.

They took control of me like they'd done it a thousand times before. My body wasn't mine anymore—it was theirs. Used, shared, worshiped in the dirtiest, most intoxicating way.

Az leaned down, lips brushing my ear. "You look so fucking good like this, Love. Tied up. Full. *Obedient*."

Craig's hands gripped my waist as he looked up at me through hooded eyes. "Come for us, Bunny."

Then they *slammed* me into it.

Az's hands locked down on my hips, pulling me back against him as he drove forward, deep and unrelenting, every thrust perfectly timed with the snap of Craig's hips beneath me. Their rhythm was merciless, with Az controlling the pace and Craig grinding up to meet it. I was just caught in between, wrecked and helpless to do anything but feel.

My cry broke free, high and desperate, but Az clamped his hand over my mouth before the sound could fill the room.

"Take it," he growled into my ear, voice pure sin. "You take all of it, Love. Every fucking inch."

Craig's grip on my thighs turned bruising, fingers digging into my skin as he thrust upward, hard and deep, chasing his own high while I unraveled between them. My back arched, a tremor ripping through me as the orgasm hit like a live wire—sudden and violent, too much and not enough all at once. I shattered.

A thousand sharp pieces of myself splintered apart, and all I could do was feel—the stretch, the burn, the fullness of being taken by them both at once. My muffled screams poured against Az's palm as my body seized in wave after wave of pleasure, my cunt fluttering around Craig, my ass tightening around Az as they both kept moving, fucking me through it like they wanted to see me break.

Az bit down on my shoulder, hard enough to leave a mark, and the pain only pulled me deeper, sending sparks of lightning across every nerve ending. Craig's head dropped back against the pillow, his mouth falling open on a ragged groan as his thrusts grew erratic.

"*Fuck*, Bunny... I'm gonna..."

Az grunted behind me, that final snarl in his throat the only warning before he slammed in deep and held me there, buried to the hilt.

They came almost together. I felt all of it. The heat, the stretch, the overwhelming sensation of being completely and utterly claimed. Their hands, their breath, the way they held me so tightly it felt like they were stitching me back together even as they tore me apart.

And in that brutal, beautiful moment, I gave in completely. There was no guilt. No fear. Just surrender.

Euphoria.

Their movements slowed, breath-catching and syncing as the last waves of release passed through us like the tail end of a storm. Az's hand loosened over my mouth, his fingers dragging slowly along my cheek before sliding down to cradle my jaw. He kissed the side of my neck, soft now, reverent, and rested his forehead against the curve of my shoulder, breath warm against sweat-slick skin.

Craig let out a long, low exhale beneath me, his hands easing their grip on my thighs, gliding up and down in long, soothing strokes. His lips brushed over my chest, my collarbone, whatever skin he could reach as if to say I've got you without needing the words.

I stayed still for a moment, completely boneless, my body humming with the aftershock. I couldn't think, couldn't move. I could only feel.

Az was the first to move, pulling back carefully, making sure not to jolt or jar me. I whimpered at the loss, my muscles twitching with the sudden emptiness, and he ran both hands down my arms, slow and grounding.

"I've got you, Love," he murmured. "Breathe for me."

Craig helped guide me forward gently until I curled against his chest, and Az moved behind me again. He knelt on the bed behind me, reached for my wrists, and carefully untied the rope. His fingers were gentle as they worked the knots free, not rushing, his touch brushing lightly over the faint red impressions the bindings had left on my skin.

"There we go," he whispered, pressing a kiss to the inside of each wrist as he freed them. "So fucking good for us."

Craig pulled the blanket around us as we moved onto our sides, tucking it over my shoulders as I settled between them, skin flushed and still tingling. His hand found my waist, rubbing lazy circles there, while Az gathered me in from behind, wrapping his arms around my middle and pulling me close until his chest was to my back, his breath slow and even near my ear.

I melted into them with one arm slung over Craig's chest, my back curved to Az's warmth. Their hands didn't stop moving—small, instinctive touches. Comfort layered on top of carnality. Az's thumb traced soft lines along my ribs. Craig's fingers played with my hair.

No one spoke for a while; we didn't need to. I closed my eyes and let them hold me, letting their presence soothe the ache and buzz under my skin.

"I'm sorry, Love," Az broke the silence, his voice low and careful against my ear. "For how I handled things earlier. I was angry. Scared. But I shouldn't have yelled."

My eyes opened slowly. I didn't speak, just nodded, letting my fingers tighten around Craig's side.

"But I meant what I said," Az continued. "You need to train. No more accidents. We can't afford it."

"I know," I whispered. My voice was raw but sure. "I want to. I want to be better."

Craig leaned in and kissed my forehead. "We'll be with you every step of the way, Bunny."

That promise wrapped around me just as tightly as their bodies did.

CHAPTER TWENTY SIX

Victoria

"Rise and shine," Az's voice held a bite of command.

Noticing the lack of warm bodies beside me, my hand snaked out and gripped the blanket, tucking it under my chin. Cracking open one eye, I noted the time on the clock read five a.m.

"Go away, it's too early." I grumbled, snuggling further into the bed.

"Not happening, Love." Az replied just before I felt a sharp tug ripping the blanket away.

I flopped onto my back, arms and legs spread, resembling a starfish, as my eyes popped open wide in shock. Craig's chuckle drew my attention to him first. He stood near the dresser, wearing a pair of basketball shorts with a T-shirt in his hand.

"Move it, Princess." Az barked, dragging my attention to him. He was dressed similarly to Craig and clearly ready for a workout.

"Fuck off, Az-hole. We barely went back to sleep an hour ago after you two wore me out." I snarked, sitting up and reaching a hand out to try and snatch the blanket back.

Az jerked the blanket further from my reach before tossing it toward the bedroom door. "I told you, you're training to be one of us starting today. You can get your ass up and dressed, or I'll be left to assume that you'd prefer to sit at home when we conduct business. And just so we are crystal clear, *if* you aren't dressed and ready in ten, this is done. No more going with us on interrogations, no training beyond your basic self defense, you will, for all intents and purposes, be a mob girlfriend and nothing more."

The urge to needle him died under his intense stare, and I found myself climbing from the bed instead. Craig offered me a sheepish smile and a kiss on the cheek before bending down to grab his sneakers and strolling from the room.

"Ten minutes, Victoria. Be out front in ten minutes or we leave without you." Az said, following Craig from the room.

I hurried to throw on undergarments, yoga pants, and a t-shirt, making a mental note that I would have to educate Az on how much time a woman actually needed to get ready. Grabbing a pair of socks, almost as an afterthought, I rushed to the bathroom. It was like I could *feel* the time counting down as I brushed my teeth and fought to get a brush through my curls. Stomping my foot as the brush caught on a particularly rough snarl, I tossed it down and used my hands to gather my now poofy hair into a messy bun on top of my head.

"Ten minutes, fucking hell," I grumbled to myself as I headed to the living room to put on my socks and shoes. "I need ten minutes to deal with my hair alone."

I made it outside just in time, based on how Az scowled when he looked up from his watch and saw me exiting the front door. Shooting him a self-satisfied smile, I strolled toward the SUV we'd taken to the warehouse the day before.

"Uh-uh, Love. We're not driving." Az chuckled darkly.

"What do you mean? I thought we were supposed to be hiding out. Walking out in the open doesn't make a whole lot of sense if we don't want to be seen." I shot back.

"We're fairly safe here, Bunny." Craig interjected. "We're a little more than an hour outside of Sacona, and when Rich bought this place, I did a deep dive on all the residents. No gang connections, no felons, just good, wholesome people. Between that and all the work I did to keep the deed from ever being connected to us, we can safely wander around town."

"Oh really?" I asked, with a brow arched in his direction.

"Yes, really," Craig laughed. "Just take a burner with you to be safe if you decide to go exploring. There's a stash of them in the top right drawer of my dresser."

"All this time and I could have taken a fucking walk." I muttered.

"Enough chit-chat." Az barked. "Let's get moving. We'll run to the diner, stop there for breakfast and then head over to the boxing club to work on some refreshers, they have an MMA setup that's perfect for takedowns."

Everything he said sounded miserable, and we were only halfway to the diner, by Craig's estimation, when the misery started to set in. I'd never been a distance runner, even my treadmill workouts were focused more on bursts of speed and high inclines. It didn't help that the concrete under my shoes wasn't nearly as forgiving on my joints as the moving belt.

The boys might as well have been out for a routine morning jog through the park, the way they chatted while eating up the pavement ahead of me. Craig's gait was easy and fluid, even with the fresh white bandage peeking out beneath the hem of his shirt where the fabric had ridden up. Az kept pace beside him, perfectly upright, the bastard, barely even sweating.

Meanwhile, every step I took sent a dull throb up through my ankles and into my knees like I was being punished for some long-forgotten crime. My lungs burned. My mouth tasted like pennies. And the early morning chill had nothing on the heat radiating off my skin.

"You're doing great, Bunny!" Craig called over his shoulder, turning to jog backward for a few paces to flash me that annoyingly sincere smile. I knew he was trying to be helpful, but I hoped he'd trip. Az reached out and whacked him in his shoulder, which caused him to stumble a little, and I almost felt vindicated until Az opened his big mouth.

"That's *not* treating her like every other initiate, dude."

Az called out loud enough to know I heard him.

Craig grinned at Az, then held up his middle finger like he was doing all this for fun.

"Fuck off," I panted, more breath than voice. Craig might have been lying, but it was a nice lie.

Craig and Az both chuckled as Craig turned back to face forward. I could have sworn they picked up the pace as the road curved into a slow incline. My feet started to feel like lead, and my pace began to slow as my stomach revolted. I managed to pull a mocking face at Az's back and flip him off with both hands just before my stomach forced me to stop and dry heave on the side of the road. This was it, this was how I died. Not a kidnapping, not a fire, not some random gangster taking me out. No. This fucking run that Az insisted I go on to learn the ropes. The only ropes I was learning were the ones that lined the staircase to fucking hell because this definitely was *not* heaven.

"I'm dying." I whimpered just as another dry heave wracked my body. "I'm just gonna lay down here and die."

"You're not going to die," Craig's voice came from behind me before I felt his hand on my back rubbing in comforting circles. "You've already done the hard part. You just have to keep your feet moving."

"I can't," I whimpered, debating whether my stomach was done trying to turn inside out. "Just leave me, let the vultures have me."

"That's not very gangster of you, Love." Az snickered.

"When I throw up, it'll be on you, Az-hole." I lifted my hand and flipped him off without looking at him. "You're lucky I like your dick because I am pretty fucking convinced I hate the rest of you right now. I should just," I straightened up, curled my hands into claws in his direction, and twisted my face into an irritated snarl.

"Alright, Love, you've had your little bitching session. Time to keep moving. For the record, you don't have to keep pace with us, you just have to keep moving." He crossed his arms over his chest and tilted his head, watching me sternly.

"And how exactly am I supposed to know where to go when you two disappear off into the sunrise, fucking speed demons?"

Craig chuckled and shook his head. "Well, for one, we'd never actually let you out of eyeshot, and two, it's literally just straight down this road. You can't miss it."

"Now, move it." Az snapped, slapping my ass hard.

I managed a middle finger for both of them before starting again at a slow pace. Both of them laughed as they passed me, looking fresh as fucking daisies. I decided right then and there that I wasn't going to put out for *either* of them if they kept this torture up during my 'training' period. When the diner finally came into sight, I had thoroughly murdered both of them in multiple ways in my imagination. I may have even buried them alongside the hellish path they'd taken us on. To my dismay, they both appeared to have barely broken a sweat, Craig slightly more than Az, while my feet were attempting to refuse to even walk the last few yards to the diner door. They went from sluggish to cement-heavy and then to full-on mutiny as I slowed to a stop outside the diner. I bent forward, my hands on my legs, trying to breathe through the burning in my lungs and the nausea clawing up my throat.

"I hate both of you." I muttered between gasps of air as I all but limped by them through the door, collapsing into the first empty booth I saw.

Az shook his head, sliding into the booth across from me and waving down a waitress. He didn't bother giving anyone a chance to look at the menu, rattling off an order that sounded meant to feed a football team. Fortunately for his safety, he ordered me a coffee. I suppose the evil glare I was giving him was enough for him to know I would commit murder intentionally if I didn't get my caffeine in my preferred method.

"Nope," He said, snatching the sugar and cream out of reach as soon as my coffee arrived. "Unless you want to actually vomit, you're going to need to take it black."

"You are ruining any scrap of enjoyment I have left." I hissed before letting my eyes slide to where Craig sat next to him. "And you're just letting it happen. Fuckers."

Craig shook his head and laughed. Az started droning on about the plan once we got to the gym, but I tuned him out. After the run, his voice made me want to dump my hot coffee over his perfectly styled blond hair. He became a chorus of wa-wa-wah-wa's until he *finally* shut up when two waitresses appeared at our table with trays of food. A plate of eggs, bacon, and pancakes was set before me, and a second, along with a glass of orange juice, was slid in my direction before I'd even taken the first bite.

"Eat as much of that as you can. You need the fuel to get through the rest of the morning." Az ordered.

I waved my hand over the plates in dismay. "I can't eat all of this. I know I'm a big girl, but fucking hell, that doesn't mean I eat like a damned linebacker!"

"Just eat what you can, Bunny." Craig said. "Az is just overcompensating for being so hard on you. But make sure you drink the juice."

Az growled something at Craig I didn't care to pay attention to, but otherwise didn't correct him. I tried to take my time eating, hoping that if I just took long enough, Az would call it a day and we could go back to the Innocenti's. My plan seemed to backfire when Az lifted the glass of juice to my mouth and demanded I take a drink before reaching for my fork.

"Do it and I will stab you with it." I snapped, but I got the hint and finished what I could of my food.

"I'll pay the bill, you two head on over to the club. I'm sure Leighton is wondering where we are." Az said when I'd finally eaten all I could.

The boxing club was caddy corner from the diner, which was both a relief to my feet and a death sentence to any hope of dragging out my reprieve. I followed Craig inside and spotted

Leighton almost instantly. He was facing our direction in the ring that took up the center position of the club, squaring off bare-knuckled against someone I couldn't make out through all the padding they were wearing. I wasn't the least bit surprised by the grin on his face as he sparred. It wasn't nearly as feral as the fight he'd taken me to as an apology or the way he dove into the firefights we'd lived through, but it was one hundred percent *him.*

"There you are!" He called out, hopping from foot to foot as he spotted us entering the club. He made a hand signal to the person in the ring with him and practically sprang over the ropes, landing on the floor next to the ring. "I was starting to think you murdered Az and ran away for good."

"I was very tempted." I huffed. "Still might."

"That's my girl," Leighton smirked, leaning forward and planting a chaste kiss on my lips. "Az tell you the plan here?"

"If her face was anything to go by, she completely tuned out everything he told her out of spite," Craig chuckled, causing me to scowl at him for being right.

"Well, quick run down time. We're gonna work on takedowns, breaking holds, and hitting. If you do *really* well, I'll even hold Az in place so you can use him for real world punching experience." Leighton grinned, waggling his eyebrows. "I reserved this ring for the next couple of hours for us."

My eyes went to the ring farthest away, and I felt a pang of longing for that one. I didn't particularly want to have my ineptitude on display for everyone to see, and the ring Leighton picked felt like it was under a blinding spotlight with its positioning.

"Let's go, *Ma Petit,*" Leighton said with a clap.

I begrudgingly followed him to the ring and let him help me into it. It didn't take long for my embarrassment to fade into the background as I worked to focus on not letting him put me on my ass. Just when I thought I had the hang of it, he turned me to where Az and Craig stood waiting behind us in the ring. The three of them put me through my paces, making me do the moves repeatedly until I got them right. I was fairly certain I would be sporting a myriad of bruises by the time we exited the ring and got to work at the punching bags.

"That's enough." Az said finally when my arms felt like they were going to fall off. "You're heading back with Leighton to work on spotting. Expect this to be your routine for the next little bit with some weight lifting mixed in."

"I thought you said you'd hold him so I could get real world practice." I pouted at Leighton.

"I said if you did really well." He winked. "Come on before he decides to make you lift weights *today*."

"All three of you better sleep with one eye open, I swear to God." I huffed, drawing a laugh from them before Leighton led me from the gym.

CHAPTER TWENTY SEVEN

Victoria

The rest of the day passed in a blur of sore muscles and feet. Leighton insisted I needed to keep moving to minimize the soreness, and Dawn was happy to help me stay busy in the greenhouse. I listened to her talk about her plants and the job Ian picked up when he found he didn't particularly care for the idleness of retirement, offering the occasional response when needed. Lunch was practically an on-the-go meal. Dawn and I ate sandwiches as we repotted plants. I nearly wept in relief when dinner time came because I could finally sit still. I fell on my food like a wild animal, all the extra activity heightening my appetite. I was so focused on my meal that I didn't even notice Leighton had slipped away before anyone else was finished.

"Come on, *Ma Petit*," Leighton said, appearing at my side as Dawn cleared the empty dinner dishes. "I've got something for you."

"If it's your dick, I don't want it. Return to sender, recipient no longer at this address."

Leighton threw his head back with a laugh before reaching a hand out to help me from my chair. "It's not my dick... At least not right now."

"It better not be," I muttered, taking his hand and letting him pull me from my seat.

To my surprise, he led me into the bathroom, where

a steaming bath was already drawn. The scent of lavender floated up on the steam, and there was the slight fizz of the last bits of a bath bomb in the water.

"I put epsom salt in there, it's good for muscle aches. Thought after today, you could use a little pampering." Leighton beamed. "I thought of this all by myself too."

"This... this is so sweet," I was *not* going to cry over a fucking bath, and yet my eyes burned. Traitors.

"Are you gonna get in?" He asked, his expression shifting into uncertainty.

"I mean, yeah, but I didn't realize I was going to have an audience." I replied.

"Oh, that's because there's more when you get in the tub and I promise it's *still* not my dick." He grinned.

I narrowed my eyes at him briefly, gauging his sincerity before stripping out of my clothes and easing myself into the hot water. A groan of relieved satisfaction slipped from my lips as I settled in, the heat soothing my aching muscles. The pop of a cap sounded from beside the tub, and I turned my head to find Leighton squirting body wash onto a washcloth.

He hadn't been joking when he said he would pamper me. Not a single innuendo or sexually charged joke left his mouth as he washed, first my body and then my hair. He remained laser-focused on following my instructions when I walked him through properly washing my curls, and it was enough to make me practically melt into the bottom of the tub. When finished, he settled on the toilet and let me soak in silence until the water turned tepid.

"There's just one more thing," He said as he held out a fluffy white towel when I finally climbed from the bathtub.

"If it's your dick, *now* I'm receiving packages." I winked.

"Okay, *two* more things." He laughed, making sure the towel was tucked around me tightly and then pulling me along toward his room. As soon as we were inside, he shut the door behind us and moved to light a candle on his dresser. "Lay face down on the bed so I can massage your muscles. Can't have you getting a cramp when the package arrives." He smirked.

"It was funny when I made it an innuendo, now it's just cheesy," I laughed.

I positioned myself on the bed so that I could lie on my stomach with my head turned toward Leighton. He opened the top drawer of his dresser and pulled out a bottle of massage oil before moving onto the bed beside me. Wordlessly, he set to work kneading the oil into my shoulders and began working his way down my body at an agonizingly slow pace. Each press of his hands had me melting further into the mattress until I was sure I would be nothing but a puddle by the time he was done. He'd just reached the arch of my second foot when there was a knock on his bedroom door. I was too relaxed to yell at whoever had the audacity to interrupt.

"We don't want any!" Leighton called out.

I heard Craig's laugh outside the door before it opened. "Have you seen—Ah, yes you have. There's my Bunny."

"I knew I should have locked that damned door, what do you want? I was just about to deliver a package, if you catch my drift, and you're mucking up my mojo." Leighton replied.

"Double deliveries? Is it my birthday?" I mumbled with a slight giggle.

"Delivery drivers *do* sometimes work in pairs." Craig said with a deep chuckle.

"Threesome? Alright, shut the fucking door, *lock it*, and grab the actual lube out of my dresser. I've got an idea." Leighton said, his tone bright enough to cause me to roll over onto my back.

"That sounds concerning..." I laughed.

"I don't know how to make this a package metaphor." Leighton frowned. "So, let's just go with two car garage."

I heard the door shut and lock, Craig's voice taking on a husky tone. "I've enjoyed double stuffed snacks before."

Leighton's head whipped toward Craig, and he let out a dramatic gasp as he clutched his chest. "You *bitch*, how did I not know this?"

"Blame your hetero life mate for not sharing the tea, I don't kiss and tell."

"That fucking cheater! I was supposed to be his first double peter! And he kept telling me no. Mother fucker."

"Uh, guys... Are we gonna... y'know? Or are you just going to keep bantering?" I asked, not quite sure I was even going to be able to take them the way they wanted. "It would be nice if someone could start by explaining just how exactly you think you're both going to fit in there."

"We'll go slow and make sure you're prepped for it, Bunny," Craig assured me as he strolled toward the bed with a bulk-sized bottle of lube.

"You're gonna love it, *Ma Petit*. And once we prove that to you, you'll be able to take all four of us without needing hands." Leighton smirked as he unceremoniously stripped out of his clothing. I didn't miss how his gaze fell to the 'V' we'd carved into his chest or how his fingers softly caressed the letter.

"Let's not put carts before horses," Craig said, removing his clothes just as eagerly but without the same rush.

"Eh, no take-backs." Leighton shrugged before belly-flopping onto the bed between my legs.

"What the actual fuck, dude?" I shrieked as I bounced slightly off the bed.

"Shhhh.... I got you," Leighton murmured, grabbing my legs and placing them on his shoulders. "Snack time."

"Shut–" My words cut off with the first swipe of his tongue through my folds.

Leighton lapped at me like a man starved, bolts of electricity sliding through my veins when his tongue circled my clit with just the right amount of pressure. My hands went to his hair, gripping it tightly and holding him in place as I began riding his face. My breath came in short pants as I worked to keep quiet, and that only made him work harder, sliding two fingers into me and curling them as his tongue worked me perfectly. My back bowed off the bed, and my hand flew from his hair to my mouth as an unexpected orgasm tore through me. I bit my palm nearly hard enough to break the skin, trying to stifle the sounds escaping my mouth as Leighton worked me through it with his skilled tongue and fingers.

"Your turn," he smirked at Craig, sitting up and back on his heels. "I say she needs at least one more before we start working her up to both of us. There's toys in the bottom drawer if you need assistance."

Craig moved to the dresser and opened the bottom drawer, rifling through it for a moment before a grin spread across his face. Leighton moved to cradle my head, his hands still roaming my body as Craig took his place between my thighs. I tried to see what he had, but Leighton wouldn't let me sit up enough to look.

"What do you have, Craig?" I asked impatiently.

"Hush or I'll give you something to do with that mouth, *Ma Petit.*" Leighton rasped, moving one hand to grip his cock.

"You'll see," Craig smirked up at me, pushing my legs further apart, and any further insisting I might have done went blank in my mind when he pushed inside me with one quick thrust. My back arched, and I tried to reach for Craig as he started to move slowly.

"Ah ah, you didn't ask," Leighton said, grabbing my arms, holding them above my head, and nodding to Craig. I heard the sound of the toy clicking on just a moment before I felt the intense sensation of it on my already sensitive clit. I yelped, my eyes rolling back while he moved inside me, the toys insistent pulsing and vibrating making everything feel ten times more potent.

I was hurtling toward another orgasm in what felt like seconds as Leighton held me down and Craig pumped into me. The room filled with the sounds of my whimpering as my body jerked, electric pleasure streaking through my system in a way that had my mind blanking of anything and everything.

"Fuck... fuck... Oh! Fuck!" My eyes rolled back as I

careened toward the edge. "Please, please don't stop!"

Craig and Leighton chuckled in unison as Craig used his free hand to push one of my legs up, making every stroke hit the sweet spot, and I could feel the tension in my spine tighten to a breaking point.

"I'm... Fuck! I'm gonna..." I started to say, and before I could get anything else out, Craig grabbed my hips, rolling us so that I was impaled on top of him, the toy still pulsing against my clit as I sank down on him.

It happened so fast that I didn't realize Leighton had moved until I felt the pressure of his finger join Craig's cock buried inside of me. He curled his finger toward the spot inside me that caused my entire body to lock up with the strength of my orgasm. My vision went black, and my hearing faded briefly.

"That's right, *Ma Petit*, squirt all over his cock." Leighton whispered in my ear as he pressed a second finger against my entrance, slowly easing it into me with each of Craig's thrusts.

"So... full..." I whimpered. "I can't..."

"Shhh, you can do it, Bunny. Focus on me." Craig cooed, his hands skimming up my sides in a gentle caress as his hips slowed to allow me time to adjust to the new sensations.

After a few moments, my body began to move of its own accord, my hips rolling as I mindlessly tried to take them both deeper and faster. A dark, dangerous chuckle was all the warning I got before Leighton worked a third finger into me alongside Craig's dick.

"That's right, *Ma Petit*, take everything we give you like the greedy girl you are." he breathed against my ear. The tone of his voice was nearly enough to throw me over the edge again, but the cold touch of lube along his fingers stopped me from falling over.

"One more, Bunny." Craig groaned, clicking the toy up a setting.

It was exactly what I needed, my entire body shattering under the weight of my orgasm. I collapsed forward on Craig's chest, and he and Leighton continued to work me over as if I weren't a boneless, mindless puddle already. Leighton's free hand slid from the base of my neck down my back and over my ass until he reached where they were stretching me wide.

"Fuck, this is hotter than I imagined." Leighton murmured. "Are you ready for me, *Ma Petit?*" I could only moan in response.

He pulled his fingers free of my body, and I let out a bereft whimper. Craig's chest rumbled beneath me in a silent laugh as his hands went to my hips to force me to remain still. My body instinctively tensed when I felt the tip of Leighton's cock against my opening.

"Relax, Bunny. We've got you." Craig said, moving one hand to my back to rub soothing circles. "Relax and breathe."

Leighton slowly pressed forward, a slight pinching sensation accompanying his movements as he inched his way into my core alongside Craig. Craig focused on keeping me relaxed and breathing while Leighton worked to seat himself fully inside me at a torturously slow pace that allowed me time to adjust to the overwhelming and slightly uncomfortable sensation of fullness.

"Fuuuuck," Leighton groaned, stilling completely when his hips were finally pressed against my ass.

"Holy... shit..." Craig's moan was deep and guttural as his eyes rolled back in his head. "Those... fucking piercings..."

Leighton chuckled knowingly, and I attempted to roll my hips, wanting to pull that sound out of Craig again. He swatted my ass instead, causing me to still.

"Give us a minute, *Ma Petit.*" Leighton panted. "It's a tight fit, we all need to adjust so we don't blow too soon."

I don't know how long we stayed like that, me stuffed full of both of them, none of us moving, before Leighton *finally* rolled his hips experimentally. Craig and I both moaned at the same time, Craig muttering something nearly unintelligible about Leighton's piercings again.

"Ride him," Leighton ordered, reaching around to pull

my back to his chest.

I rolled my hips without hesitation, the pressure and discomfort giving way to a depth of pleasure I'd never felt before. Leighton moved his hips so that he was thrusting in tandem with my movements on Craig's cock, both of them making wild and feral sounds that mingled with my primal moans. When Craig started moving, my body stilled between them, unable to function with their alternating strokes. My eyes rolled back in my head before falling shut, and I was lost in pure sensation. Their hands were everywhere, and the toy was still pulsing and vibrating on my clit. One of them pinched my nipples, causing my entire soul to shatter as one long, seemingly never-ending orgasm rolled over me. I was awash in pleasure, lost to the tides of it, and completely swept away, certain that I'd died and this was what heaven felt like. I barely felt the sting of teeth in my shoulder or heard the groans as their hips stuttered to a stop, the heat of their release only dragging out my own until it took me completely under into unconsciousness.

When I finally came too, Craig was cleaning me up with a warm washcloth, and Leighton was finishing securing a fresh sheet. My mouth fell open in shock at the implication they had knocked me out so thoroughly they could change it without disturbing me.

"Welcome back," Leighton grinned, climbing into the bed beside me as Craig moved to do the same on the other side. "I want to ask how you're feeling, but I have to tell you something first."

He looked so nervous I couldn't help but worry. "What? Oh God, did you guys rip me?"

"No, no, no," He rushed out, reaching an arm back to rub his neck. "I, uh, I bit you hard enough to break the skin and I didn't ask if it was okay first. Craig cleaned it up and put antibiotic ointment on it, but uh... yeah... I shouldn't have done that."

"L, I'm proud of you. I think that's the first time I've ever heard you being worried about it before." Craig said, but there wasn't any humor in his voice. It was sincere praise for his friend.

"I'm not an idiot. I always get consent. Usually in writing so they can't sue me." Leighton scoffed.

"I think I'd prefer to be asked in the future, but given the circumstances and the fact I was barely aware of anything at that point... I can see how it got away from you. It's fine." I said, reaching up to smooth the worry lines from his forehead with a small, tired smile. I could see him physically relax as he snuggled back in against me. "Besides, if this is the reward I get after being tortured by Az all morning, I gotta know when our next run is."

CHAPTER TWENTY EIGHT

Joey

Az stirred his coffee like it owed him something. The spoon clinked against the side of the mug in a rhythm that was starting to grate on my nerves. Or maybe it wasn't the spoon. Maybe it was the fact I wasn't sleeping for shit lately. Maybe it was just Az. Sitting there with his elbows on my mother's worn oak table like he owned the goddamn place.

He didn't, obviously. But Rich did. And now Rich was dead. So.

I pushed the last of my toast around the plate, not hungry anymore, not that I really had been in the first place. Mom had gone all out like she always did—eggs, bacon, fresh biscuits, everything—but it all tasted like ashes in my mouth. Resentment will do that.

Az, on the other hand, looked like he'd just walked off a magazine shoot. Fresh white button-down, hair like he'd styled it with a goddamn ruler. And the way he kept stealing glances at me over his mug? Yeah. He was watching. Clocking me. Like he thought he could catch me slipping.

"You're taking her this morning," he said finally, like it was just a normal Tuesday. Just a thing we do. Go shoot guns. Breathe air. Train the woman I think might've gotten my brother killed.

I took a slow sip of coffee to buy myself a second. It burned going down. "Yeah?"

"She's gonna need the basics again," he said, eyes on his cup. "Care, handling, muscle memory. All of it."

"Already gave her the rundown."

"How long ago was that?" he asked. "Before she was expected to maybe actually use any of it. It was just a precaution." I didn't say anything. Just tapped my thumb against the side of my mug. Once. Twice. Harder than necessary. Az looked at me now. Full-on. Calm, but I could see the tension under it. That thread of suspicion he was trying so hard to bury. "You good with that?"

"Sure," I said. I even made it sound like I meant it. "She's not gonna learn anything useful if she keeps holding the damn thing like it's gonna bite her."

"Exactly." Az's gaze lingered like he was trying to decide whether I was playing nice or playing games. Then he gave a tight nod and went back to his coffee. Right on cue, the door creaked open behind me. Soft steps on hardwood, slower than usual. I didn't turn because I didn't have to. I could feel her.

She moved like someone who'd been thoroughly ruined the night before. Which, from the sounds I'd ignored behind a closed door upstairs, she had been. When I did glance at her, I noticed a deep mark on her shoulder peeking out from the collar of her shirt, and I *hated* how my body responded to it.

"Morning," she said, a little rough. There was that edge she always tried to hide behind sarcasm when she was unsure.

Az gave her a warm, polite nod. "Morning. Sit, eat."

She eased into the chair next to mine with a quiet wince. Sore. Good. She was quiet for a beat, then: "Thought I might get the morning off after yesterday."

Az smiled into his coffee. "You thought wrong."

She gave him a narrow-eyed look, half challenge, half pout. "You're going to make me hate you through all this, aren't you?"

"Absolutely," Az said. I smirked into my mug. I couldn't help it. There was something satisfying about being the person to rob her of her wish of a relaxing morning after getting worked over in Az's routine and then railed out by the other two. It took the edge off of the knowledge that meant I had to spend actual time in her presence.

"Joey's taking you to the range," Az added, standing. "You'll need to go over safety first. Again. Don't skip it. Then target practice."

Victoria glanced at me, then back at Az. "I know I need to get miles better with guns but—"

Az looked pointedly at her, then at me, then back at her. "That's why we're training."

She held up her hands in mock surrender. "Yes, Sir."

Az clapped me on the shoulder as he passed. It didn't feel friendly. "Don't be an asshole."

"Wouldn't dream of it," I said, sweet as poison. Silence fell like a dropped blade when the door shut behind Az, and I let it hang. Let her stew in the quiet for a minute while I rinsed out my mug and set it in the sink like I didn't want to launch it through a window. Then I turned. She was watching me. Wide-eyed. Hopeful, like maybe we'd bonded or some shit over shared bullets and bacon.

"You sore?" I asked, voice flat.

Her lips parted, surprised. "Uh… yeah. Little bit."

"Good," I said, grabbing my jacket from the back of the chair.

Her face tightened, that softness she'd walked in with hardening in real-time. "I thought we were past this."

I gave her a cold smile. "You thought wrong. You've got ten minutes," I said, already turning away. "Wear something that won't get you laughed off the range."

I didn't wait for her response. Just headed for the stairs two at a time, needing distance before I said something that'd get me slapped again—or worse, looked at like she pitied me.

My room smelled like oil and powder and cedar cleaner. Comforting. Familiar. The safe was already open from last night—I hadn't been able to sleep and ended up cycling through gun parts and old memories at three in the damn morning like a lunatic. I pulled a couple of pistols from the foam slots, clean and familiar, like muscle memory. Then grabbed a heavier one just for the hell of it. Not for her. For me. Then I shoved a couple spare mags into my jacket. I didn't need them. She did. She'd probably drop one, jam the slide, or forget to check the chamber. Again.

The thought of her with a weapon in her hands again made something twist low in my gut. I didn't trust her. Not with a gun. Not with my friends. And sure as shit, not with my dead brother's legacy.

I locked everything back up, double-checked the weight of what I was carrying, and stood still for a second. Long enough to breathe. Long enough to think.

If she was gonna be around, I might as well use this. If she *was* working with the Jackals, sooner or later, she'd fuck up. Show her hand. Maybe not today, maybe not tomorrow. But no one could fake it forever—not with the pressure we lived under. The Jackals weren't subtle. She'd trip. They always did.

And if she didn't? Then maybe I'd finally push her far enough to leave. Either way, I win.

When I came back downstairs, she was waiting by the front door in leggings and a jacket I knew wasn't hers. It was Craig's. The sleeves were too long, the hood too big. She looked ridiculous in it, as if she was trying to be taken seriously.

"Cute," I muttered, pushing past her and heading for the car.

She followed, silent until we were halfway down the block. The silence was heavy but not the kind that soothed. It scratched at the inside of my skull.

"You used to like when I wore your clothes," she said, like we were reminiscing. Like we were us.

I scoffed, eyes on the road. "Yeah, well. I also used to like anchovies. We all make mistakes." That shut her up.

For about twenty seconds.

"I meant what I said, you know," she tried again, quiet. "I was glad you apologized. I've missed—"

"Don't," I cut her off. My voice was low, but it hit like a slap. "Don't talk to me like we're friends. Like you *know* me."

"I *do* know you."

"No," I snapped, eyes narrowing. "You knew *him*. The guy who gave a shit. The one who sat by your bedroom door when Az went on a rampage and Leighton was too rough with you and played nice so nobody scared you off. He's dead, Victoria. You buried him with my brother."

Her breath caught in her throat. I didn't look at her. I didn't want to see whatever expression was crawling across her face right now—hurt, guilt, hope—any of it. I didn't want it. She went quiet again, but I could feel her watching me. Probably still searching for pieces of the man I'd been. Pathetic. She might as well have been looking for a ghost.

We were two stoplights away from the range when she finally spoke again, soft and hesitant.

"I don't understand why you hate me so much."

I barked a humorless laugh. "You don't? That's rich. You roll into our lives, start sleeping with everyone like you've got some God-given right, and then shit starts going sideways and people start dying. You think that's a coincidence? 'Cause I don't."

Her jaw clenched, but she didn't say anything. Smart girl. When we pulled into the lot, I shifted the car into park but didn't move. Just let the engine tick while I stared straight ahead.

"You're not gonna go runnin' back to Leighton or Craig or Az, tattling that I wasn't sunshine and flowers today, right?" I said, voice like glass on asphalt. "Because I promise you, if you so much as breathe a word that I've been anything but polite, I'll make sure you *feel* it."

She blinked, startled. "Joey—"

"I *will* make you regret it," I repeated, slow and steady. "So you keep your mouth shut and play the good little trainee, or I'll stop pretending altogether." Her face went pale. Not scared, just shocked. Like she hadn't realized how far gone I was. Good. Let her see it. Let her finally stop trying to dig through the ashes for a man who wasn't ever coming back. "Let's go," I said, getting out of the car and slamming the door shut behind me. "Lesson one. Keep your fucking finger *off* the trigger unless you plan to shoot."

She followed me into the lobby like a kicked dog. Head down, steps soft, silence loud. It should've satisfied me. Should've felt like a win. Instead, it pissed me off.

I could feel her behind me like a shadow, like a weight, like a lie waiting to be exposed. It wasn't guilt. I didn't feel guilty. Not for putting her in her place. Not for reminding her where she stood. This was something else. Something twisted. Like I was being baited. Everything about her was just another performance—designed to pull sympathy and make people trust her. So they wouldn't see the knife until it was in their back.

The girl at the front desk, mid-twenties, with glossy lip balm and the kind of smile that had probably gotten her a lot of tips, looked up when we came in.

"Morning!" she chirped. "You booked lane four, right?" I gave her a curt nod. She glanced between us, smile widening, like this was a fucking date. "We've got a couple's discount running right now—"

"No," I said before Victoria could open her mouth. My voice was smooth. Friendly, even. "That's not necessary."

The girl blinked. "It's free ammo for—"

"Still no," I said, giving her the kind of look that made people stop asking questions.

I didn't look at Victoria, but I felt her flinch. A little twitch beside me, like that'd actually landed somewhere soft.

Good.

We got our lane. Back corner, mostly soundproofed. I dumped the gear bag on the bench and opened it without a word. Victoria stood awkwardly off to the side until I tossed her a set of ear protection and a pair of safety glasses. She caught them, barely.

"You remember how to hold it, or are we starting from scratch?" I asked, pulling one of the pistols from the bag and checking the chamber out of habit. She didn't answer, just stepped closer, hesitant, and reached for the gun like it might bite her. I grabbed her wrist before she could touch it. Not hard, just enough pressure to make a point.

"Wrong," I said, tone clipped. "You don't just reach for it like it's a damn soda can. Respect the weapon. Always. Got it?"

Her eyes flicked up to mine. "Got it." I handed it to her this time, grip-first. She took it. Her fingers curled around it almost right. Almost.

"Better," I said. "You're pinching the grip. It's a gun, not a wine glass, *Princess.*" I moved around behind her and adjusted her stance with the same cold precision I'd use on a street guy who needed a refresher. Hands on her hips. Tap to her shoulder. A tug on her elbow to keep the line clean.

Her scent hit me then. Something floral. Leftover shampoo from Craig's shower, maybe. I stepped back quickly, jaw tight.

"Safety?" I asked. She blinked, then fumbled for it. She clicked it on, but her grip shifted. I saw the mistake before it even happened.

"If that were loaded, you'd have just flagged your foot," I snapped. "Try again. Grip first. Then safety." She swallowed whatever she'd been about to say and did it over. Then I made her do it again. And again. Until her knuckles were red and her arms were trembling. Next, I pulled out the field strip mat and laid it down.

"You're cleaning this before we fire it," I said, placing the disassembled pistol parts in front of her. "And putting it back together after. You remember how?" She gave a slight nod, and I just stared until she sat down and started the process. It went okay at first. Hands steady. Movements tentative, but close to right. Until she got to the firing pin. She froze, and I waited. "Where's the pin?" I asked, voice flat.

Her lips parted. "I—I thought I—"

"Not doing that very well today, are we?" She looked up, eyes flashing with something close to frustration. I leaned against the table and crossed my arms. "You think you're ready for any of this? You can't even clean the damn weapon right. Forget pulling a trigger—what're you gonna do when someone's trying to kill you and your gun jams because you forgot a part?"

She stared at the pieces in front of her, blinking fast. "You don't have to be this cruel," she muttered.

I barked a dry laugh. "Yeah? You want things to be how they were before? Maybe if you figure out how to get my brother out of the hole in the ground, we can work on that." Her head snapped up, and I saw it—pain. Guilt. A flash of something twisted in my chest before I shoved it down again. "You think if you train hard enough, learn enough, suck up to the right people, you'll finally belong?" I sneered. "That's not how this works. This isn't Girl Scouts. This is blood. This is fire. And if you don't get it perfect, someone *dies*." I stepped closer, crowding into her space just enough to make her look up at me. "So get it *right*," I said. "Or get the fuck *out*."

She said nothing. Just turned back to the weapon and picked up the pin with shaking fingers. Put it in place. But that didn't mean I stopped watching her hands like they might suddenly turn into claws. She finished the reassembly, slower this time. Careful. Like she knew if she slipped again, I'd pounce.

And I would.

Because if she was going to show me who she really was, it'd happen here. Under pressure. In the grind. And if she didn't? Then I'd keep turning the screws until she cracked. Because sooner or later, everyone does.

CHAPTER TWENTY NINE

Victoria

By the time we pulled into the driveway, my arms were trembling, and my head felt stuffed with cotton. I was so tired —the kind of tiredness that had weight, like it was dragging my bones down inch by inch. I couldn't remember the last time I'd felt this wrecked.

Joey slammed the car door like punctuation and stalked up the porch steps without waiting for me. He didn't speak. Not when we got out. Not when we stepped into the house that still smelled like breakfast and wood polish and something that was starting to feel like grief soaked into the wallpaper.

But the moment the door shut behind us, he changed. He straightened and rolled his shoulders back. When Dawn stepped out from the kitchen, drying her hands on a dish towel, he even managed a small, convincing smile.

"Hey, Mom."

"You're back early." Her brows lifted, eyes flicking between us. "How was it?"

"Good," Joey said easily. "She's got solid potential." I stared at the floor. My fingers curled into the hem of Craig's jacket, like maybe if I held on tight enough, I could shrink into the background. Invisible.

"Glad to hear it," Dawn said, but her voice gentled when she looked at me. "You alright, sweetheart?"

"She's just worn out," Joey answered before I could. "It

was a lot. I pushed her."

No shit.

"I'm gonna shower and then I have to head back out," he added, already heading toward the stairs. "Dinner smells good, save me a plate?" And just like that, he was gone. The silence he left behind was too big.

Dawn tilted her head slightly like she was reading between the lines. She always did that, looked at people the way a gardener looked at leaves. Not for what they were but for what they were supposed to be.

"You're shaking," she said quietly.

"I'm fine." My voice was thin. Brittle. I blinked hard, trying to keep the tears where they belonged, buried deep, hidden behind sore shoulders and a jaw that wouldn't unclench.

"Take a walk with me." The words landed softly. Familiar. Like a lullaby she didn't even have to sing anymore. I nodded once and followed her out the back door.

The greenhouse door creaked open with the same softness Dawn always carried, like even the wind wouldn't dare disturb this place. The warm, green-sweet air wrapped around me like a memory I hadn't earned. Alive in a way that made something in my chest twist. Everything here was growing. Breathing. *Healing.* It smelled like earth, like water and memory. Like Rich.

I didn't belong here.

Dawn moved through the space like she was part of it. Brushed her fingers across leaves, She checked the soil with the back of her hand. It gave the illusion of giving her plants attention, but I knew better. She was watching me.

I stood in the doorway long enough to feel the ache creeping up my legs, arms trembling from fatigue and tension. I'd spent the day bracing—against recoil, against words, against the threat of something worse. My chest was tight like I'd been holding in a scream since the range and forgot how to stop.

"You're not fine," she said after a long moment. Quiet. Not accusing, just... certain. "You've got that look. Like you're trying not to bleed on the carpet."

I huffed a laugh that didn't sound like one. "I'm just tired."

She turned to face me, soft and unwavering. "Then rest. But if there's more, you don't have to carry it alone."

I shook my head. "I can't."

"You can," she said simply. "You're safe here." My jaw clenched. I wanted to believe her. God, I *wanted* to believe her.

My voice came out small. "I don't want to make things harder."

"For who?" she asked gently. I didn't answer. She snipped another leaf. "It's okay if you're not ready. But when you are, I'm here." I stared at the floor. Dirt and scattered petals and the edge of a cracked ceramic pot. I could still hear his voice—"*If you so much as breathe a word. I'll make you regret it.*"

"I don't know what's wrong with him," I whispered, and even that felt like too much.

Dawn didn't look surprised. Just still. "Joey?" I nodded. She finally turned toward me, one hand braced on the edge of her potting table. "Tell me."

The dam cracked. Just a little. "He... he was awful at the range, but it wasn't just that. He's been like this since... since Rich—" My voice broke on his name. "He says things. Mean, cruel things. He says I'm pretending to grieve. That I didn't even *love* Rich. That I'm using them."

"He called me a whore," I said, and the word made me flinch as it left my mouth. "Said I jumped between brothers like it was a game. That I'm the reason Rich is dead. If I hadn't put them in this situation, his brother wouldn't be in a coffin. That the wrong person died that day..." There was a ringing in my ears. I couldn't stop now. It all poured out, fast and messy. "He apologized in front of the guys. But that was for them, not for me. He didn't mean it. And now... he waits until we're alone. Acts normal in front of everyone else. But then it's like he wants to *break* me. Like he's punishing me just for being here."

That's when it started. Not a flood. Not yet. Just the first cracks in the dam. "I tried to talk to him in the car. He shut me down. Told me I didn't know him anymore. Said the version of him who cared... that guy died with Rich." I blinked hard. My voice got smaller. "He said I was a mistake."

Dawn stopped what she was doing. Set the shears down very gently.

I laughed, but it was hollow. "He said I was to blame," I whispered. "That I slept with all of them like it was some fucking game and that Rich died because of me. That people start dying when I show up." Her breath caught, almost too soft to hear. I swallowed hard. "At the range he... he grabbed my wrist. Not hard, just enough to let me know he could. Told me I didn't belong. Corrected my grip like he was training a stranger off the street, not like he cared if I shot myself by accident."

I turned away. I couldn't look at her when I said the next part. "Joey said if I told anyone how he treated me today, if I even *breathed* a word, he'd make me regret it." The greenhouse went still. Even the air seemed to hold its breath. And then it all rushed out of me too fast, too raw to control.

"I'm trying to keep up. I tried to be what he needed. What *any* of them needed. I thought if I learned fast enough, if I proved I could be useful, maybe I could... But nothing's good enough. I messed up the reassembly on the gun and he just *ripped* into me. Said I'd get someone else killed. Said this isn't Girl Scouts, this is blood and fire." I blinked hard. The tears weren't coming—too deep for that. What I felt was *worse*. That hollow, bone-deep fatigue. Like the pain had burned out and left nothing but smoke behind.

"I keep thinking the old Joey's in there somewhere. The one who stayed by my bedroom door when I was scared, talked to me softly and wanted to keep me safe, the one who called me 'Sweetheart'. But I'm starting to think maybe he really did die with Rich. And this thing that's left—" I shook my head. "It hates me. *He* hates me."

Silence. Then Dawn sank onto a nearby chair by the window, her hands folded in her lap like they were holding something precious or fragile.

"I lost Rich," she said. "But with Joey... it feels like I'm still losing him. One piece at a time." I looked at her then, and for the first time I saw it, not just the grief of a mother who buried her son. But the profound, slower grief of a mother watching her surviving son turn into someone unrecognizable. "I thought he was angry. Angry at the world. At you. At the loss. And maybe he is. But if he's hurting you—if he's *threatening* you—then that's not just grief. That's something else. It's not the man we raised..."

Dawn's words hung in the air, weighty and filled with that same quiet desperation that tugged at me, too. I didn't know how to answer her or make sense of the growing distance between Joey and me.

But then, something in her posture softened, like she was pulling away from the sharp edges of grief. Dawn exhaled, slow and careful, like she was setting something heavy down between us. Her gaze drifted toward the glass panes, where condensation clung like ghosts.

"You know," she said softly, "when Rich was about twelve, he used to stand in Joey's doorway at night. Wouldn't go to bed until his little brother was asleep. Said Joey had nightmares, and he wanted to be there in case he woke up scared." A small, wistful smile tugged at her mouth. "He was just a kid himself, but he acted like it was his job to carry the weight of the whole house." She looked back at me, her voice lowering. "Rich always needed to be the one holding it together. For Joey. For us. For everyone. If he could be in control of the mess, he believed it couldn't swallow him."

I swallowed hard. Dawn stood again, slow and steady, like she was reclaiming some piece of herself.

"Rich loved you, Victoria. Not the easy kind of love. The kind that roots deep and grows slow and painful. I saw it. Even when he tried to hide it behind all that responsibility he thought he had to carry." She came closer, fingers brushing a curl back behind my ear with the kind of quiet tenderness that cracked something open in my chest. "Joey's hurting. And grief makes monsters out of all of us, if we let it. But I won't let him make one out of you. You hear me?"

I nodded, but barely. My throat felt too tight.

"If you were any of the things he said... Rich would have known. And he wouldn't have let you within a hundred miles of this family, let alone his heart." Her voice didn't waver, not once. "My son may have been stubborn. May have been too careful with the pieces of himself he gave away. But he was not a fool." I bit my lip, holding in the sob rising behind my teeth. "You loved him just the same. In that slow stubborn way that becomes part of your bones," she said. "I think he knew it too." Then she braced herself. "You need to tell the boys what Joey's been doing. They deserve to know. And you deserve to be safe."

"But he's your son—"

"And I'll handle him." Her voice was soft but decisive like a gate swinging shut. "That's my job. Not yours."

"He'll hate me," I whispered. Silence settled between us, soft as dusk. Then Dawn reached out and took my hand in hers. It was warm, worn from soil and life and loss.

"He already thinks he does," she replied, steady as bedrock. "But hating you won't bring Rich back. It won't fix what's broken in him, and it sure as hell won't break you. He doesn't get to do that. Not here. Not in this house. Not under my roof."

Her words settled around me like a blanket I couldn't quite feel. They made sense. They even sounded like the truth. But the air still smelled like *him*. Like earth, and water, and memory. Everything around me was growing. Breathing.

Healing.

And maybe that was the cruelest part. Because whatever part of me knew how to grow, how to breathe, how to be anything but a wound... I think it died with him.

Or maybe... it was never there to begin with.

CHAPTER THIRTY

Joey

It was late when I returned to my parents'. I'd spent the evening and nearly half the night checking in with my crew and hunting Jackals. I wanted to find someone to take out every ounce of frustration left behind from dealing with Victoria all day, and the thoughts that seemed to trail along with me no matter how hard I shut them down. My mind kept latching on to how inept she was with the gun, and it wanted to believe that nobody could pretend to be that bad *that* well. Whenever the thoughts popped up, I pummeled them back, but it was starting to feel like playing whack-a-mole with my mind.

The house was dark when I slipped inside, everything quiet enough for me to know the others had all gone to bed for the evening. Taking the stairs two at a time, I headed toward my room, ready to crash for the night. Light illuminating the hallway around my door was the first indication I got that something was off. Creeping carefully to the door, I peeked inside. On my desk was a plate of food, and standing in front of the wall opposite the desk was my mother. Her hands were clasped to her mouth in horror as she took in the wall where I'd been slowly compiling all the evidence I had against Victoria.

"Mom?" I said softly, trying not to startle her.

She flinched and turned to face me, her eyes filled with worry. "What is this, Joseph?" She asked, motioning toward the wall.

"Evidence." I shrugged, moving further into my room.

Her eyes turned back to the wall, and she shook her head. "Of what, Joey? Because from where I stand it looks like... I don't know, obsession? Misdirected anger? Something worse?"

"It's proof Victoria is behind everything, that's it." I huffed, stomping over to the wall. I jabbed a finger at one of the court filings I'd pinned there. "This shows her so-called uncle had details about Az that nobody should have. This," I pointed at the paternity test results I'd found, "show Victoria isn't who she says she is. And I strongly suspect that this," I moved to Theo's paternity results, "was falsified. The map there lays out all of the attacks with dates. Every one of them happened after she either took off or contacted someone."

My mother moved toward me and placed her hands on my face. "Honey, this is insanity. You know as well as I do that girl had nothing to do with this."

I jerked my head from her hold, rearing back like she'd slapped me. "You don't know that!" I hissed. "You weren't there, mom, but if you just *look* at what I have here, you'll see."

"I am looking, Joey." My mother spoke softly as if she were coaxing a wild animal. "I've been looking at this wall for hours trying to figure out what in the hell is going on with my son. None of this adds up to what you want it to. If any of these pieces connected that way Rich would have known and handled it."

"How can you take her side?" I bellowed, too hurt and angry to care that I was probably waking the rest of the house. "Rich is dead because of her, and you're still falling for her innocent princess act. She's not the fucking victim, mom."

"Joseph Dario Innocenti, don't you dare raise your voice to me." She snapped, narrowing her eyes. "I'm not choosing anyone's side. There aren't any sides in this. You're letting your grief twist you into something you won't be able to come back from if you don't straighten up soon. I may not be a gangster, but I'm no fool. You're tearing that poor girl to pieces, hoping it'll put you back together, but it won't, son. You're going to destroy both of you if you keep this up."

"Poor girl? Poor girl?! Are you serious? Rich knew she was the one behind it all when we decided to get our revenge for Az. It wasn't until she started bed hopping between everyone that he changed his mind. Even then, it took awhile for her to sink her hooks into him and make him look the other way while she broke us down from the inside. She made us want her so all of us, even Rich, would be too busy thinking with our dicks to see the blows coming."

My mother's palm cracked across my cheek hard enough to whip my head to the side. "Don't you dare disgrace your brother's memory that way." She hissed. "He didn't stop blaming her for Az being locked up because he wanted to sleep with her. He stopped believing it because the deeper you boys dug, the clearer it became that that girl was just as much a pawn as the rest of you. He spent hours on the phone with me talking over everything just to find the right way forward for all of you, including her."

"What the fuck, mom?" I shouted, holding my face where she'd slapped me.

"That's enough, boy." My father's voice boomed from my bedroom door.

My eyes moved to him, catching sight of the others crowded in the hallway behind him. My father strolled into the room, moving to my mother's side and wrapping an arm around her shoulder. With him no longer blocking the doorway, Az, Craig, Leighton, and Victoria could see my evidence wall. When I heard Victoria gasp, I knew they'd figured out what I'd collected there.

"Is... is this what you think of me?" She murmured, hovering just inside the door.

"I don't have to think when I can see it plain as day." I spat. "You may have killed my brother, but I'll be damned if I don't figure out your end game before you take out the rest of us."

"I–" her voice caught on a sob and I ignored the way my parents were both glaring daggers at me.

Az stepped around her, gently pushing her back into Craig's arms. Leighton stepped forward at the same moment, his face twisted in a snarl. Placing a hand on his chest, Az shook his head at Leighton, something unspoken passing between them before Leighton rolled his shoulders and stepped back.

"Last. Fucking. Warning." Leighton bit out, pointing at me before disappearing down the darkened hallway. Craig tucked Victoria under his arm, and they followed behind him.

Az ran a hand roughly over his face before sliding it into his hair and tugging. Heaving out a heavy sigh, he pinned his eyes on me. "You're done, Joey. I have half a mind to sideline you until you get your head on straight."

"Sideline me? Are you fucking serious right now?" I demanded lurching forward. My father's arm shot out and stopped me in my tracks.

"I'm not. Not yet, anyway. Leighton is right, though, Joey. This is your last warning. Stay away from Victoria, drop whatever this insane vendetta is against her, or else you're done. If you don't, I'll pull your crews, all your access, everything. You won't be a Horseman if you keep this shit up."

"Fuck you, Az." I snarled.

"Go," My mother spoke, jerking her head toward the door for Az to leave. "We got him. You go take care of Victoria."

"You go on to bed, Darlin'." My father spoke, gripping the back of my neck once Az was gone. "I'll deal with him."

"Alright," she replied, patting my father's chest and kissing his cheek before turning to me. "This isn't the man we raised you to be, Joseph. You need to find *that* man and come back to us. I don't think I can bear to lose two sons."

My father held me in place as my mother left the room. We stood silently for several minutes as he studied my wall, never letting go of my neck. Finally, he let out a hmph sound and steered me from the room. He used his grip on me to direct me from the house, past my mother's greenhouse, and into the shed just beyond. Once inside, he pointed to an empty stool next to the counter, where he'd do minor repairs before grabbing a second stool for himself.

His eyes raked over me slowly from head to toe, and I could almost feel their weight. It was like he was trying to find whatever he thought was broken inside me so he could decide how to fix it. I fought to keep still, the feeling that he was peeling me back layer by layer, making me want to squirm on the stool.

"What do you need, son?" He asked finally.

My mouth opened and shut, and I blinked at him. "What?"

"I'm asking you how we fix this." He rubbed his palms roughly down the material of his flannel pajama pants. "Do you need someone to listen to everything you think you know and point out the flaws in your argument? Do you need to hit something like you used to when you were younger? Tell me how to help you, Joseph."

"I need my brother back and the bitch that got him killed six feet under." I snapped.

My father straightened his back and looked at me. "Well, as much as I want him back too, that ain't gonna happen."

"I can still get rid of *her*." I insisted.

He sighed and shook his head. "I understand wanting revenge. Believe me, son, I've been there, but blaming her because you don't know who's truly to blame ain't bringing him back." I opened my mouth to protest and shut it immediately when he glared at me. "I saw that mess you call evidence. Now, your brother didn't call me to talk things over like he did with your mother, but your mother tells me things. Everything on your bedroom wall is something Rich talked over with your mother, except them paternity tests. Those may be new, but they don't magically make the rest fit your conclusion."

"They prove she lied about who she is. And if she lied about that, she's lied about everything else." I insisted.

"Did she know about them? Before you shoved them in her face and shamed her for it?" My father asked. "Don't lie to yourself or me now, son."

"Why does it even matter if she knew?" I demanded. "None of this would have happened if she'd never come into our lives. Rich would still be here if she had never–"

"That's the crux of it, huh?" My father interrupted. "It ain't that you think she's the culprit. You're looking at the past trying to find any path that doesn't lead here. Why not go further back? If I hadn't left the rodeo for the factory so me and your mom could put down roots, you boys would have grown up on the circuit instead of Southside. We probably still would have had our money troubles, but Rich wouldn't have got it in his head that the way you boys are living now was the only way out of there. He wouldn't have ended up murdered because he'd never have been in that life. So, why not blame us?"

"That... that's a massive leap, Dad." I sputtered. "We still could have ended up here even if you'd never left the circuit."

"That's my point, son." He replied, looking me over again. "I can see you ain't ready to really hear what I'm saying, so I'm not gonna keep harping on. You think on what I said, now. Really think on it. I doubt you'll be jumping to the same conclusions about that girl once you do."

"Unlikely." I muttered.

He stood from his stool with a disappointed shake of his head before clapping his hand on my shoulder and squeezing it. "One last thing before I head on back to bed. You ever speak to your mother the way you did tonight and we won't be having a discussion with words. Nobody, not even you, speaks to my wife that way without taking the beating they deserve for it."

CHAPTER THIRTY ONE

Victoria

The couch cushion dipped beside me, and before I could even blink, Craig's arm was around my shoulders, tugging me into his chest like he'd been waiting for me to fall apart the second we were alone.

Maybe I had.

The silence between us was soft, not stifling. His hand ran slow circles against my upper arm, grounding me as I stared at the blank television screen. Neither of us had turned on a light, The glow from the streetlamp outside spilled in through the window, striping the hardwood floor in pale yellow lines.

"I didn't know he hated me that much," I finally whispered, the words catching on a breath I didn't realize I'd been holding. "That wall? That's not grief. That's—" My voice cracked, and I shook my head, eyes burning. "That's hate. That's twisted."

Craig didn't answer right away. He just pulled me closer, his hand coming up to cradle the back of my head, pressing a kiss into my hair.

"You didn't deserve any of it," he murmured. "What Joey's doing… it's not your fault. Grief warps people. Especially when you don't know how to carry it."

"I miss him," I said, voice tight. "Rich. God, I miss him. And I miss Joey too. I miss who he used to be. Now he looks at me like he's waiting for me to snap my fingers and destroy his world."

"You didn't destroy anything," Craig said firmly. "You're not the villain in this, Bunny. You're the one still standing after everything fell apart."

The ache in my chest felt like something carved into bone. Like the kind of pain you didn't just cry out, you bled out. I must've stayed tucked under his arm longer than I realized because the next time I blinked, I felt the energy in the room shift. My eyes flicked toward the hallway, and Az was standing there.

He was barefoot, his clothes sleep-wrinkled and disheveled. Tension wound tight beneath his skin, and he looked like he was one wrong word away from breaking something. Craig's arm loosened from around me, his gaze cutting toward Az before he pressed another kiss to my temple.

"I got her," Az said quietly. Craig nodded once, like they'd said everything they needed to without speaking, then stood. He paused before leaving, brushing a strand of hair behind my ear.

"You good?" Craig asked me softly, brushing his thumb one last time before standing.

I nodded, even if I wasn't.

He kissed my forehead warmly and said, "I'm right down the hall if you need me."

Az didn't move until Craig was gone. Then he exhaled hard, like holding it in too long had started to hurt.

"Come here," he said, voice low and rough.

I stood and crossed the room slowly. His arms came around me when I was within reach, tight and anchoring, everything I didn't know I'd been craving. His hand slid up the back of my neck and held me there, his lips pressing against my hair like he could pour everything he couldn't say directly into me.

"I'm sorry," I breathed against his chest. "I didn't want to make things worse. I didn't want—"

He pulled back, eyes locked on mine. "Stop. You didn't do this."

"But I—"

"I said stop." That edge in his voice, commanding but not cruel, made my knees want to buckle. He saw it, felt it maybe, because his gaze softened by half a degree.

"You're coming with me," he said, threading his fingers through mine. "I've let this go too long."

"Az..."

"No arguments, Victoria." I swallowed hard. There was something final in his voice that had my pulse fluttering.

The walk upstairs to his room was quiet. Our fingers laced together the whole time in a way that reminded me that he *had* me. Az didn't bother with the lamp when we stepped inside. The door clicked shut behind us, and the soft wash of moonlight spilled across the floor, catching the sharp lines of his jaw and the heat in his eyes.

"Sit," he said, nodding toward the edge of his bed; I couldn't do anything but obey.

He stood in front of me, arms crossed over his chest like he was holding himself back from touching me. Again. His eyes dragged over me slowly—taking in every bit of the wreck I knew I looked like. Still in Craig's hoodie, eyes rimmed red, hair a mess from the night's unraveling.

"I hate seeing you like this," he said quietly.

I blinked up at him. "Like what?"

"Small. Shaken. Like you don't know who the fuck you are." His voice was sharp, but it didn't sting. It settled deep instead, curling around something tight in my chest.

"You're mine," he said. "You're *ours*. You forget that?"

"No," I whispered. "I just—sometimes I don't know how to hold it all."

Az stepped between my knees, dropping his hands to either side of my face.

"You're not supposed to hold it all," he said. "Not alone. That's what we're for."

I swallowed, throat tight.

"You think I haven't been carrying it too?" he went on, his voice roughening. "Grief. Guilt. Rage. All of it. I've been walking around ready to burn this whole fucking city down, but I keep my hands steady for *you*. I do my best to stay calm for *you*. And you think I can't see that you're doing the same thing for *us*?"

My lip trembled. Az didn't flinch.

"You don't have to be strong right now, Victoria. You don't have to be anything but mine." He leaned in, mouth brushing my forehead, my temple, my cheek. The touch was gentle, like he was kissing away every brick of the wall I'd built up inside.

"I know you want control back," he murmured against my skin. "But you don't need it here. Not with me. You don't have to worry. You don't have to explain. You don't even have to *think* unless I tell you to."

My breath hitched.

"You want that?" he asked. "You want me to take it all?"

I looked up at him, and something inside me folded like fresh laundry. Because *yes*. Yes, I wanted that. I nodded. His eyes darkened, and his thumb dragged slowly along my jaw.

"Use your words, Love."

"Yes," I breathed. "Please."

Something shifted. No, *snapped*. Whatever restraint Az had been clinging to unraveled between one heartbeat and the next. His gaze hardened, jaw locking into place, and when he stepped back and looked down at me it wasn't with concern or gentleness. It was with *ownership*.

"Stand up," he ordered. I did immediately. His hands were on me in the next second, not rushing, but with a surety that left no room for hesitation. He stripped the hoodie and tank top from my body, dragging the fabric up and over my head, baring me to him inch by inch. My shorts followed. Then my panties. His touch wasn't rough, but it was decisive, like every inch of skin he exposed belonged to him, and he was reclaiming it. When I reached for the hem of his shirt without thinking, his hand closed around my wrist.

"I didn't say you could touch." I froze, breath caught halfway out of my lungs. He leaned in, voice like heat against my throat. "You don't get to lead here. You *follow*."

"Yes, Sir," I whispered, the words spilling out without thought. He released me and stepped back, eyes raking over every part of me, a slight tilt to his head like he was committing the view to memory.

"Now, take off my clothes. Slowly." My fingers shook as I reached for his shirt, pulling it over his head and revealing the taut, decorated muscle underneath. His body was tension and control, fire coiled under skin, but he didn't move a single inch. He just watched me like he was silently directing every move. And perhaps he was.

I undid the waistband of his joggers and eased them down, along with his briefs. His cock sprang free, thick, hard, already leaking at the tip. But I didn't let my eyes linger. Not until he gave me permission. When I'd finished, he took a step closer, his voice low and commanding.

"On your knees." The rug was rough on my skin as I dropped. "Look at me." I lifted my gaze slowly, my heart thundering. "Open your mouth."

I parted my lips slightly, breath catching in my throat. Az gripped my chin, tilting my face higher, forcing my eyes to meet his fully.

"Wider." My jaw stretched under the weight of the order, lips parting further. He didn't move, didn't speak. He just looked at me. His chest rose with a deep inhale, slow and steady like he was trying to memorize everything about the sight before him.

"You have no idea," Az said, voice rough with want, "how fucking beautiful you are like this." Heat bloomed low in my belly. "This," he said, stepping forward and brushing his fingers down my cheek, "is how I want to see you after every bad day. After every fight. Every time the world tries to take a piece of you." He slid his thumb into my mouth, pressing down on my tongue. "You are *ours*. And I'll remind you as many times as it takes."

He slid his thumb deeper, pressing down until I whimpered, until my eyes fluttered closed from the pressure of his dominance, his *claim*. Then he withdrew it.

"Show me," he said, his voice like honey on steel. "Start slow." I didn't hesitate. My hands curled around the backs of his thighs, and I leaned in, my lips parting wider to take the tip of his cock into my mouth. He was already hot, already leaking, and the salty tang of him coated my tongue as I sucked gently, teasing him just a little. A low groan vibrated from deep in his chest.

"That's it," he murmured, hand sliding through my hair. "Just like that." I sank down farther, letting him fill my mouth inch by inch, the stretch of him making my jaw ache in the best way. He didn't push. Not yet. He let me set the pace, and I took my time lapping at the base, swallowing him deeper, hollowing my cheeks as I sucked.

I *loved* this. Loved the sounds he made, the way his fingers tightened in my hair, the soft curse under his breath when I pulled back to swirl my tongue around the tip.

"God, baby," Az hissed. "You're such a good little cock whore." I moaned in response, the vibration making his cock twitch. His tone dropped, dangerous now. "No thinking. No worrying. Just this." His grip in my hair shifted, tightening. "Relax your throat," he ordered. "Take me deeper."

I breathed in through my nose, easing farther down until the head of his cock nudged the back of my throat. My eyes watered, but I didn't stop. I couldn't, not when he groaned like that. Not when his hand flexed in my hair and his abs tensed like he was barely holding himself together.

"That's it," he growled. "You feel that? That's mine. That tight throat, those pretty lips. You were made for this." Tears spilled from the corners of my eyes as I pushed further, letting him use my mouth, giving over completely. It was overwhelming in the most perfect way. I felt powerful and small all at once. But as I felt his thighs tense, his breath hitch, his grip in my hair so hard it was painful, I knew he was close. I wanted to taste it. To take *everything*. To please him so deeply, he forgot every damn thing that had ever hurt.

"Victoria." His voice was sharp. Warning. "Stop." I tried to hold him in, just a few more seconds—

His hand wrenched my head back with a brutal yank, my mouth slipping off his cock with a wet pop as I gasped, coughing around the sudden loss.

"What the fuck did I just say?" His voice was a snarl now, eyes burning as he gripped my jaw, forcing me to look at him.

"I-I'm sorry, Sir—" His fingers tightened.

"When I speak, you listen. Your desire doesn't tell you what to do, Love. *I do*." Shame and desire warred inside me, burning through my veins in equal measure.

"Yes, Sir," I whispered, lips swollen, throat raw, tears streaking my cheeks. His gaze dragged over me, drinking in the wreck he'd made.

"Good girl," he murmured darkly. "Now get on the bed. On your back. Legs open. I'm not done teaching you how to listen."

I scrambled onto the bed, heart racing, limbs shaking. The sheets were cool beneath my back as I spread my legs for him, my body aching to be filled, to be used. Az didn't rush. He grabbed a condom from the nightstand, tore it open, and rolled it on with smooth, practiced ease. His eyes never once left me.

"You wanted to keep going?" he muttered, voice low and lethal as he climbed between my legs. "Wanted your mouth full of me while I came down your throat, didn't you?" I whimpered, nodding before I could stop myself. "That's because you're so eager to be used. So fucking desperate to please. Even when it means you'll disobey to do it," he growled, gripping my thighs and yanking me down the bed until our hips collided.

"Yes, Sir," I gasped, my whole body bowstring tight,

needing. And then he slammed into me. I cried out, stars exploding behind my eyes as he drove himself to the hilt, not giving me a second to adjust. He set a brutal rhythm from the start. His hips snapped against mine, his hand fisted in my hair as he bent over me, his mouth right at my ear.

"Right now, this body is mine. Say it."

"It's yours," I gasped.

"Louder."

"It's yours, Sir. All yours!"

"Good girl." He reached down and grabbed my throat, not squeezing, just holding, like a reminder. "You think about anyone else when I'm inside you like this?"

"N-no," I whimpered.

"Damn right you don't. You don't think at all, do you, baby? Not when I've got your perfect little pussy gripping me like this." I shook my head, breath caught in my chest, vision blurring as he drove into me again and again, the bed creaking, the headboard knocking against the wall. Neither of us cared. "Fucking made for me," he groaned. "My good little whore. My perfect girl. Look at you... look at you taking it like you were born for it."

Every word sent a fresh bolt of heat through me, pooling low in my belly, building until I couldn't tell where the pain ended and the pleasure began. My legs were shaking, my nails clawing at his back as he fucked me into oblivion.

"Sir—I—please—"

"Don't hold back," he snarled, slamming into me harder. "Give it to me. Let me feel it." The dam broke. My entire body arched up off the mattress as I shattered beneath him, crying out his name like a prayer. My vision went white. My limbs trembled. I couldn't think. Couldn't breathe. I was nothing but sensation and surrender and his.

Az didn't stop.

Not when I came. Not when I cried out his name like a prayer. He didn't slow down—he owned me. And when the tremors started to fade, he shifted. His hands slid under my knees, folding me open, deeper, fuller than before. His thrusts slowed, but they didn't soften. His hand slid between us, finding my clit, rubbing slow, maddening circles that had my body twitching from the aftershocks.

"I could stay buried in you forever," he murmured, gaze locked on mine. "You're so fucking good for me." I whimpered, too raw to speak, too full to think.

"You think I'm done?" he asked, voice rough but reverent. "Not even close." he said, dragging himself almost all the way out before thrusting back in, slow and deliberate. "You're perfect like this. A wrecked fucking mess." He kissed the corner of my mouth. "You make me fucking insane."

He kissed me then, deep and claiming, his tongue sweeping into my mouth like he was devouring me from the inside out. His fingers on my clit, rubbing tight circles, had pressure building in my spine that was driving me crazy.

"You gonna give me another?" he asked. "Gonna let me fuck you until you scream again?"

"Yes, Sir," I whispered, legs trembling in his hold. My second orgasm built slower, like fire crawling up my spine, coiling tighter and tighter around every nerve. I felt every inch of him, every breath, every ragged moan he pulled from my lips.

"That's it, Love," he said. "Come for me again. Let me see you fall apart."

I shattered again with his name on my tongue, a wreck beneath him, drowning in the way he moved, the way he *loved* me. Because it was love, in the way Az gave it. Brutal. Beautiful. Unrelenting. My body clenched around him, my nails digging into his back again as I sobbed through the pleasure. Az growled something low and unintelligible before slamming into me one final time.

And then his release tore through him like a storm, his whole body going taut, his groan punched out of his chest as he poured himself into the condom, hips grinding through the aftershocks.

"My good girl," he murmured.

Az didn't move for a long moment. He just stayed there, buried deep, his forehead resting against mine, our breaths mingling as we came down together. His hand was still on my throat, but now it was gentle, almost absent-minded, the barest brush of his thumb along my jaw like he wasn't ready to let go of the connection.

"My good girl," he murmured again, quieter this time. I swallowed, blinking up at him, body boneless beneath him. Every inch of me ached in the best possible way. Wrecked, yes, but treasured.

His eyes were on mine, fierce and dark and heavy with something unspoken. Then he shifted, slowly, carefully pulling out and slipping away to dispose of the condom. I whimpered at the loss, at the chill of air hitting my skin, but he was already back and tugging the covers down, sliding his arms beneath me to lift me into them like I weighed nothing at all.

"You okay?" he asked, voice low but steady, his lips ghosting the crown of my head as he pulled the blankets around us. His chest was warm against my back, his hand splayed wide across my stomach, grounding me.

I nodded, curling into him. "Yeah. Just... floaty."

His arms tightened, and I could hear the smile in his voice. "Good."

He didn't say much after that; he never did in moments like these. But I could feel it in the way he held me. In the way his nose skimmed the back of my neck. In the way his thumb drew lazy circles on my skin, over and over like a heartbeat.

"I missed you," I whispered into the silence. "I know Craig and Leighton took care of me, and I'm grateful for them. But I missed *you*."

He exhaled hard, burying his face against the side of my throat. "I know. I hated being away from you. Hated not having the time. Not having the fucking *space* to be with you like this."

"I understand," I murmured, fingers curling over his

forearm where it wrapped around me. "You've had the weight of everything on your shoulders since..." His arms tensed briefly before he softened again, pulling me tighter.

"I'm trying to carry it," he said after a long pause. "But fuck, it gets heavy sometimes. And I forget I don't have to do it alone."

"You don't," I whispered, turning my head just enough to kiss his bicep. "You never do."

He didn't answer, not with words. He wrapped his arms around me tighter, his whole body curved around mine like a fortress. I felt the tension bleed from him bit by bit, replaced by something quieter and safe. I reached for his hand beneath the covers and threaded my fingers through his.

"Sleep," he said. "Just for a little while. We're okay."

This time, I didn't fight it. Az tucked his face into the curve of my neck, his breath warm and steady against my skin. Together, we drifted off, tangled in each other, anchored in the quiet. The storm settled, and for a little while, we had peace.

CHAPTER THIRTY TWO

Leighton

We fell into a routine over the next few weeks. Az and I would start Victoria's day with a run and then time working on breaking holds, attacking, and takedowns at the gym. Afterward, we'd have lunch, and Craig would take her to the range before dropping her with me to continue practicing spotting targets without being noticed. When we weren't training her, one of us ran interference to keep Joey away. I was still debating whether or not to beat him into oblivion whenever I wasn't with *Ma Petit.* So far, I'd managed to keep my hands to myself.

"Would you sit down, Leighton?" Az snapped as I bounced around Ian's office.

"*Fine.*" I sighed dramatically, flopping down next to Victoria.

"After the last few weeks, I've come to the conclusion that Victoria is ready to go out on a hunt. Craig got word that some low level Jackals are hanging around just shy of Uptown."

"That's near Golden Devil's territory." I mock whispered to Victoria, earning a scowl from Az.

"Tiffany of all people sent over photos to Craig. They aren't *in* Devils' territory so they're not stepping in, but they are close enough they thought we might like the heads up."

"Tiffany?" Victoria asked, clearly surprised.

"She's been surprisingly helpful, Bunny. Between the

flash drive she gave you and the intel she's been sending over about this Jackals crew. It's obvious she has an ulterior motive, but I suspect that motive is getting back in your good graces."

"That's a lot of words to say she's sucking your dick to win back our girl." I laughed. Victoria elbowed me in the side, and I frowned at her. "What? I didn't mean *literally* sucking his dick. Obviously she's not doing that."

"Can we focus please." Az groaned. "If you can't pay attention, Leighton, then I'll be taking Victoria out to deal with this crew."

I mimed zipping my lips and tossing away the key. Victoria's first hunting trip was mine, and there was no way in hell I was letting Az take over.

"What exactly *is* a hunt?" Victoria asked. "Because it kind of sounds like I should dress in camo, take a shotgun and shoot these guys on sight before taking some cheesy ass picture with their bodies."

"Eh, not far off." I chuckled. "We scope them out, kill as many as it takes to get at least one subdued and back to J– er that fucknugget's torture chamber."

"Craig will be doing the interrogation," Az said. "I know Victoria has witnessed two of our interrogations at this point, but this time will be a *hands-off* learning experience." Az's gaze flitted to Victoria. "You won't be anywhere near the tools until I'm sure you can control your impulse to stab first, question later."

"Yeah, *Ma Petit. That's* my job." I mimed, stabbing the air with a grin.

"It happened once." She pouted.

"And look at where it got you. Running several miles before dawn and getting your ass kicked on the mats." Az smirked.

She raised her hand and slowly flipped him off. "I managed to take Craig down this morning."

'To be fair, Bunny, I'm only about eighty percent." Craig replied.

"Oh, fuck you too, Craig." She huffed, her lips poking out in a pout as she crossed her arms over her chest.

"I am currently the favorite aren't I?" I chuckled.

She raised a hand and tapped her index finger against her chin as if she were thinking it over. "Hmm. I'm gonna go with... yes." she answered, one side of her mouth tilting up in a smile.

"I am gonna show you all my tricks, *Ma Petit*. You're gonna be the best at snatching mobsters off the street in no time. I'll even let you play with my grenades just for saying I'm the favorite."

"No!" Az and Craig hollered in unison.

"Fucking hell, Leighton. This needs to be done as quietly as possible, no god damned grenades." Az snapped. "Now, if you're done trying to raise my blood pressure, we have other things we need to discuss."

I gave him my cheesiest grin and stuck both thumbs up near my face. Az rolled his eyes and gave his attention to Craig, motioning for him to speak.

"There was some decent intel on the flash drive Tiffany handed over. Not only did it have the intel on this group of Jackals Leighton and Victoria will be hunting this evening, there was some intel on Theo." Craig paused, his eyes flitting to Victoria as if to ask whether or not to continue. She slid to the edge of her seat, her hands dropping to her lap, fingers laced together as she held them tightly, and nodded. "There were over two dozen photos and a handful of video surveillance clips of Theo meeting with a member of the Bratva. He's been smart and hasn't been handling any of that business in his office so the bugs we planted haven't given us anything. These, though... He's been meeting with Sergei Kumarin. He showed up about six years ago in the Petrov ranks, and worked his way up pretty quickly. Last known information on him was that he was a soldier working directly for Alexi Petrov, Capo and third son of the current Pakhan."

I let out a whistle. "Sounds like Theo is in deep." I

cringed, realizing I'd said that out loud. "Sorry, *Ma Petit.*"

"Anyway..." Craig interjected. "Each video shows an exchange. There's nothing about what's being exchanged, but we can safely assume he's getting money in return for whatever he's handing over."

"I really can't believe Uncle Theo would be mixed up with mobsters." Victoria murmured with a slight shake of her head. "There has to be something else going on that you're not seeing."

"I wish that was the case, Bunny. I really do." Craig replied.

"You don't get mixed up with someone like Kumarin by accident. The only way you meet with someone at his level is with illegal dealings." Az added.

"I just can't accept that." Victoria sighed.

"Well, if it's any consolation, there was information on your ex, Benson on the drive as well. Looks like the little worm has holed up with some Jackals. Given his family connections to them, I'd wager he's joined up for some protection."

"Protection from what?" Victoria scoffed. "His daddy's money can buy him out of any trouble he finds himself in."

"Protection from you, *Ma Petit.*" I smirked. "In case you decide you want to send us after him. No way he didn't figure out who we were after everything that went down. A smart man would know all it would take is one word from your pretty mouth and we'll gut him."

"It wouldn't even require a smart man to know that." Az added.

"Anyone with half a brain and shoddy observation skills would have figured it out." Craig said.

"Death threats should not be so sweet." She laughed with a shake of her head.

"Um... Yes they should." I retorted.

"Anything else?" Az asked Craig, steering the conversation back on track.

"That's it. If what we learned from Jen holds true, we

won't get anything out of the Jackals Leighton and Victoria bring in. I wish I could say we had something that made this all tie together, but..." Craig shrugged one shoulder. "At least Bunny will get the practice she needs."

"I mean... We can catch a Petrov Brat if you want." I offered.

"Absolutely not, Leighton. Stay the fuck away from the Russians. We don't need them coming at us right now. *If* they're involved then we will have to go the negotiations route and pray to every god there ever was that they're feeling generous." Az replied.

"Uh... My almost dead wife was Bratva. I feel like I should probably mention that. I can... I can't believe I'm saying this, fuck me, I can make a phone call. No clue if the Sidorov's have dealings with the Petrov's but it might be worth the agony of talking to my sister to find out."

"You couldn't mention this, I don't know, at any point since we found out Theo is talking to the Russians?" Az drawled.

"And have to deal with my sister? You know how Lacey is. Why the hell would I call her when it's *not* a last resort?" I snapped.

"Fine. Just make the fucking call, *after* you deal with these Jackals." Az sighed. "If there's nothing else, then we're done. We'll meet back tomorrow and debrief."

"Aye aye, captain!" I chuckled with a mock salute as I stood from my seat and pulled Victoria along with me.

A couple hours later, Victoria and I were creeping toward Uptown in the dark. We'd dressed in dark clothing, and she looked kind of adorable in her dark hoodie with her hair pulled back. I had to keep reminding myself we were on a hunt, and I couldn't pin her up against the side of a building. It surprised me how distracting having her along was, considering hunting was among my top three favorite things to do. I slapped myself a few times to regain my focus before going over the plan with her.

Using the information that Craig had gotten from Bitch Barbie, we crept our way toward Uptown. We were a few blocks away, the dark of night still covering us, when I spotted our intended targets ahead. A streetlight in front of a brick townhouse illuminated the five of them. Two of them were seated on the concrete steps, and the other three were standing in a loose semi-circle in front of them on the sidewalk. The sounds of laughter and chatting carried to us, but they weren't quite loud enough for me to make out what they were saying.

"Remember our plan, *Ma Petit?*" I asked, nodding toward the group.

"Yep." She replied, reaching for the bottle wrapped in a brown paper bag.

She took it from my hand and walked ahead of me, swaying slightly as if she'd been drinking. I stayed back, watching as she pretended to take a drink from the empty bottle, and stumbled just a few steps away from the Jackals. It was enough to get their notice, just as we'd planned, but when the nearest man to her reached out to help steady her, I had to bite back a growl and shove away the urge to charge in and gut them all on the spot.

"Hey there sweetness." He said as his hands touched *my* woman.

"Thhanks." Her fake slur was so realistic I almost believed she was drunk. She swatted his hands away before straightening up and taking a few weaving steps forward.

"Where ya going, baby?" He called after her, signaling his friends.

Victoria grunted and swayed on her feet, pretending to take another sip from the empty bottle. "Home."

"Ah, don't be like that. You look like someone who's looking for a good time. Why don't you let us show you what we got and we have a little fun, huh sweetness?"

All five of them were on their feet, slowly closing in around her. None of them were paying attention to the direction she'd come from, giving me the perfect opportunity to get close unnoticed. I slipped a knife from my pocket into one hand and freed my blackjack with the other. I caught her eye just as I brought my blackjack down on the back of the nearest man's head, hard enough to knock him unconscious. Victoria didn't hesitate, shifting her grip on the bottle to its neck and slamming it into another man's head.

The Jackals we were up against were clearly new and poorly trained. It took next to no effort for me to dispatch four of the five. Victoria stood proudly over the fifth with her booted foot on his back as I pulled zip ties out of my hoodie pocket and secured our catch. When I stepped up beside her to deal with her man, I noticed the blood from her split lip. A snarl ripped from my throat, and before I knew what I was doing, I had my gun out and aimed at his head, pulling the trigger with the next breath.

"Leighton!" Victoria shouted, half in shock. "What the hell?"

"He hurt you." I shrugged. "He had to die. Besides, we only really need one of these guys. Two at most. I figure we go ahead and take two so we can show Az and Craig how well you did."

"Leighton…" She started, but my hand moved to brush my thumb over her busted lip, interrupting whatever she was about to say.

"Go get the car so we can load them up. I'll deal with the rest of them." I said softly, my hand squeezing the grip of my gun.

"I think we should take them all, Leighton. One may know something the others don't,"

"Car, *Ma Petit*. I am barely holding my shit together and I need you to go get the fucking car before I go completely feral and rip these bastards limb from limb."

"It's just a split lip. I'm sure you've had worse on a hunt, Leighton." She sighed.

"Car." I bit out, my tone nearing a growl. "That's an

order."

She pinched her lips together, clearly unhappy with me. I wasn't exactly pleased about it either, but it was the only thing I could think of to get her to go before she saw the worst parts of me. She stared into my eyes a few more moments before stomping her foot with a huff and turning back in the direction we'd come from to retrieve the car. As soon as I was sure she was far enough away, I turned back to the four men tied up on the sidewalk.

"Lucky fucking day you pieces of shit. I don't have time to give you what you really deserve for hurting my girl." I knew they were still out cold, which only made them luckier in my opinion. It didn't stop me from needing to voice it aloud just before I put bullets in two of their heads and then settled onto the steps to wait for Victoria to return with the car to take the others to Craig.

CHAPTER THIRTY THREE

Victoria

"You're still pouting."

"I'm not pouting," I snapped, arms crossed tight over my chest as I followed Leighton to the back of the car. "I'm irritated."

"Same difference, *Ma Petit*." He grinned, entirely too pleased with himself as he popped the trunk. "You're cute when you're mad, though. Like a bitey kitten. Fierce and fuzzy."

"You're being ridiculous. It's a *split lip*."

"Exactly," he said, as if that somehow helped his case. "You got hit. That means I didn't keep you safe."

"Or maybe I just didn't duck fast enough," I muttered, but he was already reaching into the trunk and hauling out the first of the unconscious bodies like he was dragging a gym bag, not a grown man with a potentially fractured skull.

The warehouse loomed ahead, all concrete silence and yawning shadows. The door creaked open under Leighton's boot, and the scent hit me immediately—faint traces of gunpowder, oil, and something metallic beneath it all, which I refused to identify too closely. This place had memories. Candy's laugh still echoed sometimes when I wasn't careful.

I drew up short. Craig was already there.

He stood in the center of the room like he belonged to it, sleeves rolled up, black button-down molding to his chest like it'd been tailored for the sole purpose of ruining me. He was calm, relaxed even.

My heart did something stupid in my chest.

"You're hurt," he said quietly when I got close enough. Not a question. Not an accusation. Just a statement, spoken in that warm, even voice that always made me want to confess things I hadn't even done yet.

"Not really," I muttered. Craig's brow lifted as he looked from me to Leighton.

"Leighton," he said, voice still soft but edged with steel. "What happened?"

"She took a hit to the face," Leighton said, unrepentant. "Good thing we only planned on bringing a couple. I lost my temper. Shot three. Left two for you. Figured that was generous, but she's all mad about it."

"I'm mad you were *dramatic* about it."

He looked over his shoulder at me with a grin. "Dramatic is my middle name, *Ma Petit*. That, or bloodthirsty. You pick."

Craig didn't say anything; he just met my eyes across the space as Leighton manhandled the last body into position. He held my gaze as he moved, shackling wrists to the chairs that had been bolted to the floor since we'd last used them. They used to slide around the floor when someone fought too hard. Not anymore. I shifted on my feet, suddenly not as steady as I'd felt a few minutes ago.

Craig must've noticed. Of course he did. He always did. His voice came softer when he finally spoke again, still busy tightening the restraints.

"You're observing today. That's it. No hands-on until Az clears it. We need you sharp, not shaken."

"I'm not shaken." His gaze flicked up to me again. He didn't argue. He didn't have to.

Leighton finished securing the second man and cracked his knuckles like he was getting ready for a game instead of torture. "You want me to stick around, or...?"

Craig shook his head. "I've got it from here. Go clean up. You got a phone call to make. We'll debrief later."

"Sweet. Text me if you need a shovel." He whistled a little tune as he strolled out, like he hadn't just delivered two half-dead men into a murder room with the casual flair of a pizza delivery driver. Then it was just me, Craig, and the faint hum of overhead fluorescents that buzzed like they were keeping secrets. He turned toward me fully, wiping his hands on a dark rag he pulled from his back pocket. His eyes were unreadable, and something in him was different. Like he was hovering between the Craig I knew and the Underboss I'd never seen him be before.

"You okay?" he asked. I wanted to say yes. I wanted to meet his steady gaze and be a girl unfazed by what came next. Instead, I looked at the bruises already blooming on one of the Jackals' faces. The blood crusting his temple. The memories that tugged at the edges of my mind.

"I don't know." Craig didn't push. He just stepped close enough for his presence to wrap around me like heat from a fire and gently brushed his fingers along the edge of my jaw, his thumb ghosting over the swelling of my lip.

"I hated seeing that."

"It's nothing."

"To me?" His voice dropped an octave. "It's not nothing." I swallowed hard. He stepped back slowly, giving me space but not letting go of the weight of his gaze. "Stay to the side. Watch everything. The way I move. The pressure I use. Where I cut. Where I don't. This isn't just about getting answers. It's about discipline, and controlling the situation." I nodded once, sharper than I meant to. He gave me the faintest smile. "Good. Let's begin."

He pulled on a pair of black nitrile gloves, flexing his fingers as he walked toward the table near the wall. The tools were already laid out in a perfect row—scalpels, pliers, clamps, things I didn't know the name for but had seen used before. There was a surgical method to the madness.

When Craig turned back toward the first Jackal, his entire demeanor shifted. His shoulders squared. His face went still. And just like that, the man I shared a bed with sometimes, who held me after nightmares, who wrapped rope around me like I was something precious, was gone. In his place was the Underboss of the Horsemen.

I should have been watching the Jackals.

Should've been cataloging their micro-reactions, their tells, their words, what little they said between grunts of pain and strangled silences. But I wasn't.

I was watching *him*.

Craig moved with the slow, precise rhythm of someone who knew exactly what he was doing and exactly how much of it he could live with later. He approached the first Jackal with a stillness like he'd already made peace with what he was about to do and didn't see the need for drama or cruelty.

Each question is punctuated by a calculated action. A shallow cut along a tendon. A slow twist of pressure on a dislocated finger. Nothing sloppy. Nothing cruel for the sake of cruelty. Craig didn't flinch when blood hit his gloves. He didn't pause when the man screamed or when the second one started to panic against his restraints. He just adjusted the chair's angle slightly, like he was rearranging furniture, and continued to ask his questions in that same steady voice.

I didn't flinch. I should have, maybe. But I couldn't take my eyes off him. His hands moved with complete control. Like he'd studied every vein, every nerve ending and knew exactly how deep to go to hurt without killing, how long to hold before the body broke and the mind gave in.

There was something terrifyingly beautiful about it. Not because of the violence. But because of the *restraint*. There was something almost reverent in the way he worked. The way he cleaned the scalpel between each pass and spoke directly to the man in the chair like he mattered, even when he was tearing answers out of him an inch of flesh at a time. I wasn't prepared for that.

The second Jackal started talking before the first was finished bleeding. Gave names. Locations. Schedules.

Rambling whatever information he thought might save him. Craig nodded occasionally, like a professor satisfied with a correct answer. He barely glanced at the Jackal, making mental notes without saying a word. The power in the room shifted entirely around him. He wasn't big or loud, but he owned it.

And me? I was barely breathing.

The smell of blood was thick in the air now, metallic and sharp, but I barely registered it. I could only see Craig's strong, capable hands moving with calm authority. One of the Jackals whimpered, but Craig didn't respond; he'd gotten what he was after.

"Thank you," he said quietly, not looking at either man as he walked to the table and swapped out the scalpel for a pistol. "That's all I needed."

And before I could blink, he raised the gun and put a bullet clean through the first Jackal's temple without ceremony or flourish. Just... over. The second one tried to scream, but it came out wet and gurgled. Craig turned, adjusted his grip, and fired again.

Silence.

There was no movement except for the blood slowly leaking across the concrete. Craig stood still for a second longer, just breathing. Then he peeled off the gloves, pulled out his phone, and dialed a number I'd seen him call a dozen times before.

"Phil," he said. "We've got two at the warehouse. No rush, but bring the van." A pause. "No, they're done." Another pause. "Yeah. The back entrance should still be clear." He ended the call and looked at the gloves before folding them once and sliding them into his back pocket like they were just another part of his macabre uniform.

Then he looked at me.

The mask didn't fall away all at once. It slipped slowly, just enough for the warmth in his eyes to return, tempered by that razor-thin edge of who he'd just been. The man and the monster were balancing.

"You alright?" he asked again, softer this time.

I nodded, but my voice didn't work. My mouth was dry, my skin hot. I was hyper-aware of everything. Every drop of sweat trailing down my back, every slow inhale that tasted like iron, every inch of space between us that felt charged. Craig took a step toward me, and my breath caught. His gaze dropped to my mouth, then to my throat.

"You're not afraid of me." Not a question. Another one of those damn statements he always got right.

"No," I whispered. "I'm not." His hand lifted again, brushing my cheekbone, trailing heat down to the curve of my jaw.

"You should be," he murmured. "Really, you should be afraid of all of us." But there was no real warning in it—just truth.

"I'm not," I said again, firmer this time. Craig's smile was slow, crooked, just a little dangerous. And God help me, I wanted to taste it.

Craig stepped closer until I could feel his warmth, the solid heat of his body, and the subtle scent of sweat, steel, and blood that somehow didn't repulse me. I knew that smell would stick to me if I let him touch me here. In this room. With two corpses cooling behind us.

"Victoria." My name in his mouth wasn't soft. "You need to get out of here."

"I don't want to."

"You need to." He was trying to be good. Better. Trying to do the right thing and draw that invisible line neither of us had crossed in a room like this before. But the part of me that had watched him work with rapt fascination, the part that *wanted* him, she stepped forward.

"I want to stay."

He stared at me like he was trying to read between the lines. Then, very quietly, he said, "Not here. Later. When I've washed them off my skin."

And somehow, that turned me on more.

The drive back was a blur. I couldn't focus on the road or the dull hum of the tires against asphalt. My thoughts were too tangled in the memory of Craig's hands, his voice, and the cold efficiency with which he'd delivered death. It felt like he could tear me apart with the same precision.

Whenever his fingers flexed on the steering wheel, I had to bite my lip to stop myself from making a sound. I could barely control the heat building between my legs. There was an urgent need to climb into his lap, crawl across the seat, and kiss him until I couldn't breathe, think, or remember where he ended and I began.

When the car finally rolled into the driveway, I was a live wire, strung so tight I thought I might snap in half. Craig didn't make me wait. He was already out of the car before I could even open the door, and I followed him, my feet barely touching the ground as he pulled me behind him toward the house.

Az was already at the door to the office when we entered, arms crossed, eyes narrowed expectantly. He opened his mouth as if he was about to say something but froze when he saw the way Craig was pulling me along behind him. Az stopped mid-sentence.

"I'll debrief later," Craig muttered, cutting him off before Az could finish his thought. "Tomorrow. I don't care." Az blinked, clearly annoyed but not willing to argue. He probably had a thousand questions, but it didn't matter. Craig had spoken.

From somewhere inside the office, I heard Leighton's loud and playful voice. "It's not fair, you know. I take her out hunting, and you get to reap the benefits. What kind of deal is that?" I felt my cheeks flush, though I wasn't sure why, maybe because the words made everything feel more real.

Craig didn't respond; he just pulled me along with him, his fingers curling around mine as he led me upstairs to the bathroom. The soft thud of our boots on the stairs seemed deafening in the otherwise quiet house. My skin was still humming, my body aching in a way I didn't want to ignore.

Craig didn't even look at me as he yanked his shirt over his head, tossing it aside like it was nothing. His chest was smooth and sculpted, decorated in intricate tattoos now marred with the thick scars left behind by the hack job done on him while under the care of Mel's apprentice. But it wasn't the lines or the muscle that made him so goddamn irresistible. It was how he held himself, how he made everything feel purposeful.

He yanked at the button of his pants, and I was still too stunned to move until he was pulling me toward him, hands impatient. Everything felt raw, urgent.

"Craig," I whispered, feeling the tremor in my voice, the need lacing through me.

He didn't answer. Instead, he kissed me hard, his lips crashing into mine like he couldn't wait a second longer. His tongue tangled with mine, deep and demanding, and my hands fumbled to get his pants off as quickly as I could. He pulled me closer, pushing me up against the sink, his hips pressing into me with a need that mirrored mine.

He wasn't patient this time. His hands were everywhere, grabbing at me, pulling me in tight like he couldn't get enough. He tore away my clothes with the same urgency like they were a barrier between us that didn't even exist. The water in the shower was running—when had that happened?—steam billowing in thick clouds as he all but dragged me into the stall with him.

His mouth never left mine as he pressed me against the wall, the heat from his body seeping into me. The water hit our skin like a violent, scorching wave, but neither of us cared. It paled in comparison to the heat between us. The sensation of his lips on mine sent a shock of electricity straight through my chest and down my spine.

I couldn't think anymore. My body had already given in to the chaos, the fire he sparked in me every single time he touched me. But it wasn't enough, not yet. I needed more. His hands moved lower, sweeping across the curve of my hips, pulling me flush against him. His cock was hard and thick as it pressed against my stomach, and I knew there was no turning back. Craig was here *now*, and I wasn't going to pretend I didn't want this.

His lips left mine only to move down my throat, kissing, biting, marking me with something primal, something that said I was his. He wanted me, needed me in a way that left me dizzy with desire. I didn't care anymore if he was the monster in that warehouse or the man I'd fallen for. At that moment, there was no distance. No control. Just the wild, searing thing between us that had been building all night.

One of his hands gripped my thigh, lifting it until my leg wrapped around his waist, and then the other followed. He held me up easily, which must have been from adrenaline since he wasn't all the way healed, but it still made my breath catch. His cock nudged at my entrance, thick and demanding. Then he drove into me in one powerful thrust. My gasp broke into a cry, swallowed quickly as his hand came up and clamped over my mouth.

"Shh," he breathed, voice hot and ragged against my ear. "You'll wake the whole house, Bunny."

I couldn't help it. The feel of Craig inside me, stretching me, claiming me... it was almost too much. I bit down on the edge of his palm, not hard, just enough to ground myself while he started to move, every thrust hitting so deep I saw stars.

The rhythm was brutal at first, fast and relentless, like he was chasing away everything that had built between us. The warehouse. The blood. The silence in the car. Each thrust drove us further from it, replaced with something just as raw and *alive*.

I held onto his shoulders, nails digging into the muscle there, my back scraping slightly against the tile with every thrust. The water poured over us, hot enough to sting, but it didn't matter. Nothing mattered but the man in front of me, inside me.

And then... he slowed. The change was subtle.

Intentional. His pace shifted, deep and deliberate, hips rolling into mine with a devastating precision that made my toes curl. His hand slid from my mouth to cradle the back of my head, pulling my forehead to his, our breaths mingling.

"That's it," he murmured. "Take it, baby. Just like that. You feel so fucking good..."

A sound slipped from my throat, needy and broken. He kissed me, slow and deep, all tongue and heat. His words wrapped around me, warm and possessive, as he rocked into me again and again.

"So beautiful," he whispered. "I love the way you fall apart for me. The way you take what I give you. Every fucking inch."

His hand moved between us, thumb finding my clit, rubbing slow, tight circles that sent sparks bursting behind my eyes. I was unraveling, the pressure in my core coiling tighter with every stroke, every thrust. He kissed the corner of my mouth, then my jaw, then dragged his tongue along the shell of my ear.

"I love you, Victoria," he said, voice raw now, the words catching. "All of you. Even the sharp, broken pieces. Especially those."

That was it. My body snapped like a bowstring, my climax crashing into me so hard it stole the breath from my lungs. I cried out Craig's name, hands clutching at him like I might fall apart entirely if I let go. My legs trembled around him, my entire body shaking as the pleasure rolled over me in wave after relentless wave.

But Craig didn't stop. His rhythm picked up again, harder now, chasing his release as he buried his face in my neck. I could feel him losing control, his breath hot and ragged, fingers bruising into my hips as he drove into me one last time and stilled, buried deep.

He groaned my name like a prayer, his whole body going taut before shuddering with his release. For a long, suspended moment, we clung to each other—his weight pressed against me, the water still pounding down, our hearts trying to slow down. He didn't pull away right away. He just held me there, his forehead against mine, eyes closed. Like I was the only thing anchoring him.

Eventually, his breathing slowed, his body relaxing just enough for the tension to bleed out of his shoulders. Then he eased back with a soft, reluctant sound, and I felt the slow, careful drag of him pulling out before he finally set me down. My legs wobbled when they touched the floor, and his hands held me steady as he chuckled low in his throat.

"Jesus," I muttered, blinking up at him as I tried to catch my breath.

That earned a full grin, and for the first time since the warehouse, I saw *him* again. Not the mobster or the torturer. Just Craig. The man who knew how to put me back together no matter what had me shattering apart.

"Stay still," he said, voice softer now, almost fond. "Tilt your head back."

I did, closing my eyes as his fingers threaded into my hair, gentle now as he reached for the shampoo. There was something sacred in the way he touched me then, like he was washing away the violence, the blood, the part of himself he never wanted me to carry when I left his arms. Warm water cascaded over my scalp, his fingertips massaging slowly, lovingly.

"You're not allowed to be this good at this," I whispered.

Craig leaned close, lips brushing my temple. "Too late, Bunny."

CHAPTER THIRTY FOUR

Joey

I'd been doing my best to avoid my parent's house since the night I found my mother in my room. With all the extra time I was putting in with my crew, we'd managed to secure a new warehouse and setup for the operations I typically carried out. In between, we were hitting the streets looking for Jackals near our territory and coming up empty. I was starting to grow restless, and I didn't have anything to keep my mind busy since Craig had revoked my access to our data backups. No papers to pour through, no guns to sell, no Jackals on the streets to take out. I decided it was time to move rather than wait for the next attack.

"We're going on the offensive tonight, boys," I told my crew, who stood in a loose semi-circle around me on the warehouse floor. "We'll be moving in on the Jackals posted on Twelfth and Poppy. I want to see it all burned to the ground, no prisoners, you got me?"

"I'm not sure this is a good idea, Sir. Did Az sign off on this?" Terry, one of the older members of my crew, spoke as he stepped forward from the crowd.

"Am I or am I not the Boss here, Terry?" I demand. My crew didn't need to know that I was barely on speaking terms with the other guys. They'd effectively shut me out the second they closed ranks around that fucking viper, Victoria.

"You're the boss, sir," he replied.

"That's what I fucking thought. I don't need Az to sign off on my movements. There's only one person who makes the calls for this crew and that's me and me alone. If you have a problem with that then maybe you aren't cut out to work for me."

Terry dipped his head in respect and lifted his hands in surrender. "I'm good, boss. Whatever you say, we'll get it done."

"That's what I thought. I want to move in an hour. Get yourselves armed and ready to roll out. Anyone not on time will face consequences." I barked before heading toward the space I'd claimed as my office.

I had an hour to kill, and then I'd finally be doing something productive. Settling in at the desk Phil had procured for me, I switched on the desktop computer and reviewed the intel my crew had gathered a couple weeks back on the territory we were going to hit. It appeared to be a standard residential area to anyone not in the know. There were two blocks of townhouses with a handful of single-family homes interspersed, each housing a Jackal foot soldier who had worked on Candy's crew. They were under new management, but their new Capo was a freshly made man with barely enough experience to keep from losing control of his people. He hadn't even established a perimeter patrol around his territory, practically inviting me to waltz right in and snatch it from his grasp.

Reviewing the intel barely took ten minutes, and I was left to deal with my warring thoughts. The harder I tried to steer my mind away from the viper, the more it turned toward her. My father's words played on repeat. Telling me over and over again to go back farther if I wanted to find someone to blame. That small piece of me that still wanted Victoria to be the pure, loving soul I'd thought she was latched onto it. The stronger it got, the more pissed off I became. Why couldn't they see I was right, and why the hell couldn't I snuff out that stupid voice that whispered I was wrong?

My internal struggle had settled into anger simmering

just beneath my skin by the time the hour was up. Snatching my weapons from my desk, I secured them to my body and stalked out of my office. My entire crew was there waiting for me.

"Glad to see you all understand who runs the show." I smirked. "You've all had time to review the layout of the two blocks we'll be hitting tonight. Tonight we make those mother fucking Jackals pay for coming for us. No more sitting back and waiting for them to take from us again and again. I want the streets to run red with their blood and when they stand there in the reflection of the flames of their burning homes, I want them to know, the Horsemen always hit back."

Cheers broke out among my men, and I let them revel in our pending revenge for just a moment. With a sharp whistle, I called them back to attention and motioned for them to load into the SUVs that waited outside. We drove toward our destination in the rapidly darkening streets, pulling off into a parking garage a few blocks away just as dark fully settled in.

We made it to the first set of townhouses without issue. I couldn't help the satisfied smile that split my face as they went up in flames, the Jackals inside each sporting a bullet to the head. Things were going exactly as I planned until the first bullet whizzed by my head.

"Take cover!" I shouted to my crew as I raced to the nearest house that wasn't burning.

The flash of a muzzle had me dropping to the ground to slide behind it. Getting my feet back under me, I peeked around the corner and fired back, taking out a Jackal on the front lines. The intel I had made it seem like this would be an easy hit. None of the Jackals were supposed to be on guard and prepared for an attack, but the rapid firing of guns back and forth told me they'd been prepared.

"We should retreat, boss." Terry called out as his back hit the wall of the house I was hiding behind.

"No." I barked. "We take them out like we planned."

I mentally marked my next hiding spot and tore out

from behind the house, opening fire as I raced to my new vantage point across the street. I felt heat singe my arm as a bullet tore through my shirt, just missing hitting my bicep. I blindly fired back, pleased when I heard a body drop. At least I was until I turned my head to check on my crew and realized the body that dropped was one of mine. Worse, as I squinted against the flames from the house we set fire to, I noticed a group of Jackals moving to take position behind us.

"Fuck," I hissed before sticking my fingers between my lips and letting out a loud whistle. "Retreat!"

I heard the voice of my crew echo the order as we scrambled to disengage from the firefight. Trusting them to find their own way out, I zigzagged my way through the homes, taking side streets and alleys where I could. My lungs were burning with strain, and my breaths came in short pants, but I kept running until I was certain I was clear. Eventually, I made it back to the parking garage without anyone tailing me.

Nobody spoke on the drive back to the warehouse. The plan had gone to shit, and we all knew it. Sure, we'd managed to take out a handful of Jackals, but it wasn't enough. It wasn't the scorched earth I'd been chomping at the bit to dish out. We parked our convoy of SUVs behind the warehouse and stalked inside, feeling defeated. I'd just stepped toward my office when Terry grabbed me by the arm and forced me to stop and face him.

"We can't do this again, boss." He said solemnly. "We're all hurting over the big boss, but you gotta get it together, man. No more of these half-cocked fucking missions."

I jerked my arm free of his grasp and scowled. "You really want to do this right now? Did you forget the repercussions from the last time someone questioned me?" I snarled.

"If telling you that you're not acting like yourself is enough to get me shot, then go ahead and do it. But we lost four good people today because you were fucking reckless."

"Reckless? I was reckless? We moved based off of intel,

how the fuck is that reckless."

"You got that intel two weeks ago, boss. Did you send anyone to verify it hadn't changed? I already know you didn't because I'm the mother fucker doling out jobs in your absence. Shit clearly changed. Shit we should have known about and would have if you weren't so lost in your head. I held my tongue long enough and it cost us four lives. How many more do you need before you start acting like you know what the fuck you're doing again?"

I reared back, wishing I could put Terry in his place, but I couldn't. He was right. I'd been so busy salivating over the thought of revenge while waging a war within myself over Victoria that I hadn't followed up on the intel. A snarl ripped from my throat at the realization the viper was fucking up my ability to run my crew properly. Terry shook his head in disappointment, as if he thought the sound were directed at him.

"The whole crew can see you falling apart. If you can't get it together soon, I can't say they won't ask to be reassigned. After tonight, I can't say I blame them."

Terry watched me for a moment, making sure I wasn't going to shoot him. I couldn't help the snort that left me as I waved him away. He was right, but I didn't have the first goddamned clue what to do about it.

CHAPTER THIRTY FIVE

Leighton

Az and Craig were in the living room when I came down the next morning. Their eyes were focused on the TV, and the tight set of Az's jaw told me something was wrong. He lifted the remote and muted it the moment he spotted me.

"Where's Joey?" He asked.

"Fuck if I know," I shrugged. "I haven't exactly seen him since that night in his room. From what my guys have told me, he's been holed up in that warehouse of his getting things back up and running."

"Someone made a move last night. Three homes set on fire and a dozen bodies. Craig already hacked the coroner's office and confirmed most of them are Jackals, but four of them were ours."

"Fuck." I hissed. "Where?"

"Not anywhere near the locations the ones you brought me last night gave up. They didn't have anything beyond the rest of their own crew to give me. We already knew that from Jen though, so that wasn't a surprise."

"Someone slipped him intel he didn't bother sharing with the rest of us." Az bit out. "That's the only thing that makes sense. Fucking hell, I knew after that fucking wall of his that he'd gotten secretive, but I didn't expect this." Az tugged at his hair in frustration. "We had a plan. Take advantage of the Jackals going ghost as long as we could to prepare, dig up everything we could find, then take them on. What the hell was he thinking?"

Craig leaned forward, resting his elbows on his knees. "How did we let him get this far gone? No way the Jackals don't retaliate for this and we've got no way of getting intel without getting one of ours killed because Joey decided to go rogue."

"I might be able to do something about intel." I offered. "But you two will have to deal with Joey if you want him to keep breathing."

"Fuck!" Az shouted, tugging at his hair again before giving me his attention. "Find out what you can. I'll send someone to hunt down Joey and we'll deal with him later."

"On it," I replied, stepping back and heading upstairs to my bedroom.

I took the stairs two at a time in my hurry, practically running once my feet hit the second-floor landing. The second I reached my room, I made a beeline for my nightstand, where my phone was still plugged into the charger. Dialing a number I knew by heart, I put the phone to my ear and waited.

"Leighton?" Sarah answered on the third ring. "Quite a show you boys put on over on Twelfth and Poppy."

"Wasn't an authorized hit." I replied.

"Shit. What do you need?"

"Anything the Urchins can find. One of ours went rogue and decided to get revenge on their terms instead of ours. We need to prepare for the backlash, but we can't put boots on the ground to get what we need." For some reason, my mouth had decided to protect Joey instead of naming him as the idiot who went rogue.

"Whatever you need, Leighton. You know the Urchins have your back. Always."

"Thanks, Sarah. Call me when you have something and we'll set the meeting."

"Sure thing, Leighton. Keep your ass alive in the meantime. You may be a Horseman now, but you will always be family. Don't make us attend your funeral." She ended the call without saying goodbye.

Az. Craig and I all holed up in Ian's office for the rest of the morning. Craig worked on his laptop, doing whatever it was he did with the thing to gather information, while Az put out calls to our men to find Joey. None of Joey's crew answered their phones, and I could tell it was ratcheting up Az's temper with each man who sent him to voicemail. Just when I was sure he was about to explode, my cell phone rang in my pocket.

"Sarah, you got something for me?" I asked, not bothering with a greeting.

"I think so. Where do you want to meet?"

I rattled off the address of a safe house we'd recently secured and told her we'd meet her there in about an hour. The tension from Az's growing temper seemed to evaporate as I set the meeting, and by the time I ended the call, he was looking at me with something akin to hope.

"Craig and I will go with. Once we have the intel from your contact, we'll head over to Joey's new warehouse and see if he's still there while you hunt down his crew and see if you can't get some fucking answers out of them. Where's Victoria? She's going to be pissed, but I want her to stay here. This isn't like the hunt you took her on, the Jackals are most assuredly looking for us and will shoot first if they spot us. She's not ready for that kind of heat."

"She was still asleep when I came downstairs." Craig said. "If she hasn't made her way in here to find us, I'm guessing she's not up yet. It *was* a long ass night."

"Make sure. If she is, leave her a note so she knows we're out. She can be pissed about it later when we get back." Az replied.

Craig met us at the front door ten minutes later, confirming that Victoria was still sleeping and he'd left a note. We loaded into the SUV and drove to the safe house in silence. Something that seemed suspiciously like anxiety coiled in my chest as we made the nearly hour drive, warring with the need to protect my woman and family. I was so wound up that

I didn't wait for Az to put the vehicle in park before I was climbing out of the door when we pulled into the driveway of the small cottage we'd secured as a safe house.

The front door was unlocked, but that wasn't a surprise. Sarah would have beat us here. When I stepped inside and didn't immediately spot her in the living room, I went to the small kitchen, expecting to find her making a cup of tea. That had always been her go-to when dealing with heavy shit, and she'd consider war between the Horsemen and Jackals to be heavy. I stopped in my tracks just inside the kitchen.

"No, no, no, no, no." The word tumbled from my lips over and over.

Sarah was splayed out on the dining table, her hands stretched out and pinned down to the table with large knives. Blood was everywhere, dripping off the finished wood and making a soft pattering sound as it hit the linoleum flooring. I stumbled toward her, something inside me twisting in a way that made me sick to my stomach.

"No. Fuck. Come on, Sarah, breathe." I commanded as I reached the table, my hands falling to her chest and starting some semblance of compressions.

On some level, I knew it was pointless. Sarah's throat had been slashed, and the cuts along her body were all deep. Her jaw was slack, allowing her mouth to hang open just enough to see that someone had cut out her tongue. Still, I couldn't stop. Incoherent words spilled from my lips as I desperately tried to bring her back to life.

"Leighton," Craig's voice was soft as his hand landed on my shoulder. "She's gone. You gotta stop man, she's not coming back from this."

I ignored him, continuing to do compressions even as I felt her ribs snap under my hands. I was vaguely aware of my name being spoken again before a hand jerked my shoulder, pulling me away and turning me from Sarah's lifeless form.

"NO!" I roared, violently shrugging out of Az's hand and turning back to the table. "I can't let this happen. Not *this.* Not again!"

There was a wetness down my face I didn't quite understand, and I swiped it away with my hand, smearing Sarah's blood across my cheeks. My eyes burned and blurred, but the wetness still came. Az tugged at me again, hard enough to spin me around before he wrapped his arms around me in a tight hold that almost resembled a hug.

"She's gone, Leighton." He murmured, and something inside me cracked open wide.

Everything I had refused to feel came surging forward. Feelings I didn't even know I was capable of crashed over me, threatening to drag me under.

"It's my fault. It's my fucking fault." I cried out, my voice cracking on a sob. "I shouldn't have asked her to get intel. I got her killed. She's gone, just like Rich. I can't.. I can't..."

I felt Craig move in, adding his arms to the hold Az had me in and I wanted to rage against them. I didn't deserve their comfort.

"This isn't on you, Leighton." Az said.

"Yes, it is." I insisted. "Just like Rich. If I had prepared more, stashed more weapons... Thought shit through like he always told me I needed to do, neither of them would be dead. He would still be here and I wouldn't have had a reason to ask Sarah to dig up information."

"There's nothing any of us could have done differently." Craig replied in a tone meant to be soothing.

His words hit something inside me that streaked blinding pain through my entire body, and I fought to break out of their hold. They only closed in tighter, forcing me to bear the weight of their bodies as their arms tightened to keep me from breaking free.

"This isn't your fault, Leighton." Az insisted again.

I wanted to shove him away, but I couldn't. He and Craig were holding me too tightly between them for me to do much more than squirm.

"I knew we were at war and I didn't prepare. I was too

busy having fun. Too busy not thinking things through and just revelling in the hunt. I should…" Tears streamed down my face, and I realized I'd been crying the whole time, something I'd never actually done in all the time I could remember. "I should have…"

"No." Craig's voice was hard enough to break through the guilt drowning me alive. "All of us can say we should have done something different. That doesn't make it our fault. That doesn't make it your fault either, Leighton."

"Hindsight is a bitch," Az added. "But we couldn't have done anything differently than we did. You did everything you should have done, Leighton. *You* are the reason the rest of us are standing here. Candy's men were going to put a bullet in each of our heads after she took off with Craig. You stopped them. *You*. Not me, not Joey. You."

"But–"

"No but's man. You know I'm right." Az cut me off.

"Why does it hurt so badly, then? I'm not the guy that feels things, but I… fuck, it hurts."

"You've always felt things, L. You just didn't acknowledge it or know how to process it." Craig replied. "It's okay to hurt. We're all hurting over Rich."

"I wish he were still here," I whispered.

Craig and Az squeezed me tighter in response, letting me take as much time as I needed to find my way through the tidal wave of unfamiliar emotions that had burst free. I couldn't say how long we stood there in some strange three-person bear hug, but eventually, I found my way back to the surface.

"Are you gonna be alright for now?" Az asked gently as they released me from their hold.

"Yes…no… fuck I have no idea." I replied with a shake of my head.

"That's normal." Craig offered with a sad smile.

"Yay." I drawled sarcastically, rolling my eyes. "Look at me feeling things and shit."

Az snorted, and Craig shook his head. "Yeah, you're

gonna be just fine if you're back to cracking jokes." Az said. "I'm gonna call Phil to deal with this. Craig, you stay in Leighton's place to look for anything she might have brought for us. Leighton, you can come with me or you can head back to the Innocenti's. Your call."

Swiping my face with the back of my arm, I took a second to consider his offer. "I'll go with you. I need to hear for myself what the fuck Joey was thinking. He has to answer for his fuck up."

CHAPTER THIRTY SIX

Victoria

My body froze the moment I heard the front door open. My breath caught halfway to my lungs. I stayed still, listening. Slow, heavy footsteps. Not Az—his stride was sharper, more purposeful. Not Craig or Leighton, either. I knew this one. I knew it in the pit of my gut the same way you know when someone's staring at you in the dark.

Joey.

The footsteps stopped in the doorway. I didn't look up at first. I couldn't. Not until I felt his eyes on me, sweeping the room like a searchlight.

He stepped into the kitchen, shutting the door behind him more forcefully than necessary. "Didn't think anyone would be here with the news that came through." He looked around, eyes landing on the empty chairs. "Where are they?"

"Out," I said, watching him carefully. "Didn't say where."

He nodded slowly, jaw tightening, then loosening again like he was working through something in his head. "Saw what happened on Twelfth and Poppy," he said after a beat, voice low. "Didn't hear about it 'til I was already on my way back. Four of ours, gone. Just like that."

I flinched. I hadn't heard about it yet. The coffee in my stomach turned bitter.

"Jackals?" I asked, swallowing hard.

"That's the theory." He moved to the counter and leaned

against it, crossing his arms. "Starting to feel like they're ramping up again. Retaliation, maybe. Or something worse."

I didn't say anything. My brain was still catching up, still trying to untangle the knot of fear, grief, and anger that always seemed to come with Joey's presence now. Something about his tone was...off. It wasn't cold, exactly, but not kind either.

It was measured, like he was trying something on.

"I've been thinking," he said, and I tensed automatically. "My parents... they said some things. Things I didn't want to hear, but..." He exhaled through his nose, dragging a hand over his jaw. "But maybe I needed to. I don't know what to believe right now," he continued. "Everything in my head's a mess. I keep turning over the same shit, and none of it makes sense anymore. I just know I keep waking up angry, and I don't even know what I'm mad at. Or who."

I looked at him. He was paler than usual, as if he hadn't been sleeping. His eyes were bloodshot. And there was something in them I hadn't seen in a long time. Was this just another trick?

"I'm not saying things are better," he said before I could speak. "They're not. And I'm not... healed, or whatever bullshit word you wanna use. But I'm trying. I'm trying to figure out what's real. What matters." I was still clutching my mug too tight. My fingers ached. "And what matters," he said, his gaze fixed on me now, sharp and unreadable, "is that if the Jackals are coming for you again, you need to be ready."

My stomach dropped. "I've been training with the guys."

Joey nodded. "Yeah, but you and I both know that's not enough. If things escalate, you can't rely on someone else always being there to throw themselves in front of you. And I'm the best for the job of training you on a weapon." His voice darkened.

I flinched again, but he didn't apologize or soften.

"The range we went to before, they keep a private lane open for me. I was thinking..." He hesitated, then offered a weak, almost convincing shrug. "We could go. Just you and me.

I'll run you through some drills. Nothing crazy. Just... get your hands steadier. Make sure you know what you're doing if it comes down to it."

I stared at him, heart thudding hard against my ribs. Every instinct screamed at me to say no. To get up and walk away. To remember every venomous thing he'd thrown at me, every accusation, every time he'd looked at me like he wanted me dead. But he wasn't looking at me like that now. And damn it, the logic made sense. It always did with him. That was the worst part.

I swallowed. "You're serious?"

"I wouldn't offer if I wasn't." His tone was calm. Convincing. He looked a little tired and worn down, but like this might be the first step back to something. Not forgiveness. Not trust. But maybe conversation. I looked down at my coffee. Cold again. My fingers were still trembling, just barely.

"You'll let me drive?" I asked quietly.

Joey cracked a ghost of a smile. "Not a chance."

I forced a breath past the lump in my throat, set the mug down, and stood. "Fine. But if you so much as twitch the wrong way..."

"You'll shoot me?" he asked, still smiling. "That's the spirit."

I brushed past him and went upstairs quietly, changed into leggings and Craig's old hoodie, pulled my hair into a loose ponytail, and slid my worn sneakers on like this was just another errand. I stared at myself in the mirror for a long moment before heading back down, trying to find the part of me that still believed he wouldn't hurt me. They still remembered who he used to be. It wasn't easy.

Joey was already at the door when I came down, jingling keys in one hand and holding a thermos in the other. He didn't look at me; he just handed me the thermos with a grunt.

"Figured your coffee probably went cold."

I blinked. "Thanks." He didn't say anything; he just pushed the door open and started walking. I followed.

The late winter afternoon was cool but not cold. The cloud cover cast the world in a dreary light that made everything feel muted. The only sound was our footsteps, his heavier, more purposeful, mine careful and trailing just a half beat behind. Like always now.

His car was parked a few houses down. One of the black sedans that all the guys drove, windows tinted deep enough to make it look abandoned. He opened the passenger door for me without comment, then rounded to the driver's side and got in.

We drove in silence for a while, the only sound the faint hum of the engine and the distant rush of cars on the freeway.

After a few minutes, I tried. "So… what exactly happened on Twelfth and Poppy?"

Joey's jaw flexed. "Don't know all the details. Just heard there was an ambush. Four down. Jackals probably."

"That's all you know?"

"Yeah." His tone made it clear he wasn't inviting follow-ups, but something about how his fingers tightened on the steering wheel said otherwise. His shoulders were hunched, more tense than the situation called for. He didn't look like someone who'd heard about a disaster. He looked like someone who'd *survived* one.

Still, I nodded like I believed him. "Okay." We didn't speak after that. I sipped the coffee. It was sweet. He always remembered how I took it.

When we pulled up outside the range, I frowned. The place looked deserted. No cars in the lot, lights off in the main lobby, steel roll-up gate halfway down over the storefront. Definitely not open. Joey didn't comment. Just pulled around to the side lot, killed the engine, and got out.

I followed him as he led us around the side of the building toward a narrow, shadowed alcove where an unmarked door sat half-sunken into the wall. It didn't have a keypad or a handle I could see; just a slim keyhole above a rust-stained doorknob.

"Are you sure this is okay?" I asked, hugging my arms

against myself.

He nodded. "They know me. I've done this before." Then he crouched a little, shifting his body just enough to block my view of what his hands were doing. I heard the faint snick of metal; and then the door eased open with a creak. He stepped aside and motioned me in.

I hesitated, just for a second. Something cold spidered up my spine, whispering you don't know what he's really doing. But I shoved it down and stepped past him into the dim hallway beyond. He followed, shutting the door quietly behind us. The lock clicked.

The range was cold. Not physically, though the air conditioning was cranked too high in here. It was the kind of cold that settled under your skin and stayed there, even if you didn't feel it at first. The soundproofing on the walls swallowed up everything but the softest echoes of our footsteps—a dead kind of quiet.

Joey led us past the front line and down to one of the private lanes in the back. I trailed behind him, each step sending a quiet tap tap tap across the polished concrete floor. He dropped a black duffel bag on the little table in the lane and unzipped it with quick, practiced motions. A few boxes of ammo, two handguns, and safety gear. His movements were clean and methodical, like muscle memory was doing the work for him while his mind was somewhere else entirely.

I watched him from a few feet away, hands stuffed into the front pocket of my hoodie. "You okay?" He didn't answer right away.

His jaw ticked, eyes locked on the bullets he was lining up with too much precision. "Fine."

"You don't look fine." He stopped, knuckles whitening around the casing in his hand. For a second, I thought he'd ignore me, maybe snap. But then he exhaled sharply, set it down, and turned to face me.

"I've got so much shit in my head. Rage. Grief. Worry. Frustration. You name it, it's in there, fighting for space. And

I..." he dragged a hand down his face, eyes bloodshot, "I can't think straight half the time. I don't know what's real, I don't know who I trust, and I don't know how to fix any of it. I just..." His gaze flicked up to mine, and for a heartbeat, he looked wrecked. "I just need to find a way to work things out."

My chest tightened. That familiar ache returned, the one that whispered he was still in there. That there was a version of Joey I loved, who loved me, buried under all this pain and fury.

I took a step closer. "Tell me what to do. How I can help. I'll do whatever it takes." Something in his expression shifted. The grief was still there, but it twisted suddenly, bitter and cruel, curling into the corner of his mouth like a cracked smile.

"Why am I not surprised that's your offer?" he said quietly, almost to himself.

"What?"

He tilted his head, eyes narrowing. "You think getting on your back again is gonna get you back in my good graces? That how it works for you, *Sweetheart*? Keep our balls empty and we'll look past everything you've done?"

The words hit like a slap. I blinked, the air stolen from my lungs. "Fuck you," I breathed, taking a step back, turning to go.

But his hand snapped out and caught mine. Fast. Firm. I barely had time to react before he twisted me back around and pushed until my front hit the cold concrete wall of the lane so hard it made my teeth clatter. My palms pressed against the surface roughly enough to feel the scrape against my skin. His body was behind mine now, close enough to feel the heat of him. My pulse was a frantic drumbeat in my throat.

"I didn't say I wouldn't *do* it," he murmured in my ear. "I said it wouldn't get you anywhere this time."

My breath hitched. This wasn't like last time. Joey wasn't wielding his anger like a weapon. He was quieter now, focused, and somehow that made it worse.

"Tell me no," he said, voice low, almost gentle. "Tell me no if you still don't want me. If you don't miss how my teeth feel on your skin. If you don't think you deserve to be fucked like the little whore you turned into for us."

My fingers curled slightly against the wall, muscles tight with confusion, fear, and heat. I hated the way my body betrayed me, how my breath came faster, how my thighs ached with memory. Because I *did* miss him. I *did* want. Even now.

He took the silence as his permission, as though the lack of words meant I was just waiting for him to decide. He pulled me harder into him; his chest pressed against my back, his breath hot and heavy against my ear. The motion was deliberate and controlling. I could feel his lips curve into something that wasn't quite a smile but a grimace of satisfaction. His hands slid around my waist, pulling me flush against him, his fingers splaying wide, almost possessive.

A sick rush of heat pooled low in my belly, and I hated it. I hated that the simple proximity of him made me feel dizzy and wanting. *Hungry.* I should've stopped him. I should've pushed him away. But my body couldn't keep up with my mind.

"Don't fucking pretend you don't want this, *Princess*," Joey muttered into my ear, his voice hoarse and raw. His fingers slid under the fabric, brushing against my skin, drawing out a shudder I couldn't hide.

I hated that he could still pull that from me. That my body remembered him and reacted even now, even like this. I bit my lip, but he noticed. He always noticed.

"Yeah," he breathed, almost to himself. "That's what I thought."

His hand gripped my hip, pulling me back against him, making it impossible to ignore how hard he already was. I felt my knees weaken, hands trying to support me as the concrete bit into the skin. His other hand tugged at the waistband of my leggings, dragging them down just enough. Not with care, never that anymore, but with urgency and frustration. His anger hadn't left him. It had just shifted shape.

And I let him. I let him because I wanted to believe this

meant something. That maybe if I gave him this and showed him I wasn't scared, he'd remember how things used to be. That part of him would come back to me.

The heat of him pressed against me, the rough drag of fabric shifting as he freed himself. A breath caught in my throat as he slid in, burying himself deep in one hard thrust. The wall scraped my palms. My eyes shut tight.

Joey's breath was jagged against the side of my neck, a low growl vibrating from his chest as he pulled back, then slammed forward again. Hard. Unforgiving. His fingers dug into my hip like he was holding onto something just to keep from unraveling.

"You want to be useful?" he muttered, teeth grazing my skin. "Then *take* it." I did. I braced myself and took every brutal thrust. My mouth fell open on a sound I didn't mean to make. Heat flooded my core and climbed my spine, twisting through me in sharp, humiliating waves of pleasure I wasn't supposed to feel. Not like this. Not with him like this. But my body didn't care. It remembered him, remembered this, even if the version of him pressed against me now was something jagged and monstrous.

He slammed into me again, faster now, his pace unrelenting. Like he hated me. Like he needed me.

"You always make it so easy," he hissed. "Always so fucking ready to bend over, aren't you?" I flinched, but it wasn't enough to stop him. "I could *destroy* you," he breathed, palm flat against my lower back, pinning me harder to the wall. "Break you apart until there's nothing left but a shell. And you'd *still* beg for more, wouldn't you?"

My breath hitched, but not from fear. Because I would, I would let him ruin me if it meant I could have even a piece of the man he used to be.

"Say it," he snarled.

"Yes," I whispered, the words shameful and real. Joey's rhythm faltered for just a moment, just long enough for him to snarl something unintelligible under his breath and slam back into me even harder, like he was punishing me for saying yes.

His hand slid higher beneath my hoodie, nails dragging across the skin of my back, leaving red-hot lines in their wake. My cheek pressed hard against the wall, and I braced myself with both hands, the sting of rough concrete biting into my palms.

Every thrust knocked the breath from my lungs and made my knees quake. My thoughts blurred. Faded. All I could feel was his fury, his heat, his weight behind every movement. I shouldn't have let this happen. But now I couldn't stop... wouldn't stop.

He growled behind me, one hand twisting in my hair and yanking my head back so he could hiss into my ear, "You want to come for me? Want to scream for the man who hates you?" I whimpered, teeth catching my bottom lip as pleasure knotted low in my belly, coiling tight and sharp like a wire pulled to the brink. "Do it," he spat. "Fucking come on my cock like the good little slut you are."

That was it.

My body broke, convulsing around him with a cry that cracked something open inside me. I screamed his name, loud and raw, all of it too much: the pain, the need, the twisted agony of still loving him.

I felt him snarl against my skin, his rhythm turning erratic, desperate. His grip bruised my hips as he slammed into me one final time and came with a grunt, hips jerking as he spilled into me. His teeth clamped down on the curve of my neck, biting hard, so hard I cried out again, breath catching from the sudden flare of pain. He didn't let up. Not until I felt warmth bloom under the bite. I knew he'd broken skin, and it would bruise deep.

He stayed there for a moment, chest heaving, his weight pressing into me like gravity had doubled. And then, slowly, he let me go.

Joey stepped back from me, his hands pulling away, leaving me cold in the empty space between us. His breath was ragged, but he didn't meet my eyes. Instead, he looked around, almost like he was pulling himself together before he could even think about looking at me.

He adjusted himself, tugging his clothes back into place with mechanical precision, like this was just another thing to check off on some to-do list. His movements were sharp and dismissive, as though he didn't want to linger on the mess he'd created. "Fix yourself," he muttered, his voice raw but still carrying that edge. It was the command of someone who wanted to get this over with. He wasn't even looking at me when he spoke. Just like always, always *away* from me.

I stayed frozen, my mind still reeling, my body trembling with the aftermath.

He grabbed the duffel bag off the floor, slinging it over his shoulder with a practiced motion, then turned toward the door.

"I'll meet you outside," he said, his tone flat. No warmth. No remorse. Nothing.

I stood there, barely holding myself up, as the silence between us thickened. Joey was already halfway to the door before I could even blink, his back to me. Just like that, he was gone.

I could almost see it. A flicker of regret in his eyes. Maybe? Or maybe it was just the weight of what he'd done settling in. Or perhaps I was just *still* seeing what I wanted to see. But the moment passed before I could confirm it. He didn't stay long enough for me to know if it was real or just the reflection of a man who'd gone too far and didn't know how to fix what was broken between us.

I didn't wait. I couldn't. I forced myself to start pulling my clothes back together. My hands were shaking so badly it felt like the smallest tasks were too much for me. The fabric felt wrong against my skin. Everything about me felt wrong.

My palms ached from the burn of the concrete wall. My cheek was raw and scraped, the evidence of his force still marked across me. My knees were also sore and bruising, and they were already starting to swell under the fabric. I knew it would hurt tomorrow. Hell, it would hurt for days.

But none of that mattered. Not really. I was numb. I was just trying to breathe and make sense of the mess inside me, but there was nothing to latch onto. Everything I wanted and thought I needed had crumbled the moment Joey touched me.

I wanted to scream. I wanted to demand answers. To make him see how much this hurt. But I knew he wouldn't hear me. He hadn't heard me all along.

My throat closed up as I swallowed back the tears, the deep, ugly truth that had started to sink in. I didn't know if I'd ever get back to what we were. And I didn't know if I wanted to. But I also couldn't stop hoping, couldn't stop wanting him. Even though what he'd become was nothing like the man I loved.

I took a deep breath, but it only made the ache inside me worse. I wiped the wetness from my eyes, steadying myself as best as I could. I couldn't let him see me like this.

The door to the gun range felt miles away as I slowly made my way out. Each step felt heavy, like the weight of what had just happened was pressing me down and holding me in place. I was so small in this moment. And the more I tried to move forward, the more I realized I was walking toward nothing.

I didn't want to be here but didn't know how to leave.

By the time I stepped outside, I was already feeling the hollow ache deep in my chest, the one that would likely stay with me for days, for weeks. The ache that reminded me that I chose to stay. Joey was already in the car, his hands gripping the wheel, his face hidden in the shadows, making it impossible for me to read him. I slid into the seat, breathing through the hollow space inside me that had once been filled with hope. With love. With the sound of Joey laughing against my neck and telling me I was the only good thing in his world.

That version of him felt a million miles away. And I didn't know if I'd ever see him again.

CHAPTER THIRTY SEVEN

Craig

Joey was holed up in his room when I got back from dealing with the body at the safe house. I made a quick call to let Az and Leighton know before searching for Victoria. After everything he'd done, my skin itched at the idea she'd had to spend any time alone with him. I hoped for all our sakes she hadn't.

I found her coming in through the back door; her brows furrowed as she held one of the prepaid smartphones from my nightstand up to her ear. My eyes raked over her, checking for signs that she'd had to deal with Joey. She was curled in on herself, but I couldn't tell if that was due to whoever she was speaking to. I noticed some discoloration in her cheek and jaw, scrapes we hadn't seen before. I touched my fingers to her chin, taking stock of her injuries. I hadn't remembered bruising from the fight with the Jackals, but I had been pretty focused on my work at the time.

"Are these from the other night?" I whispered, raising a brow.

"I'm fine," She mouthed in response, patting my hand and waving me off as she shuffled closer to the counter. She had a fairly distinct limp that I *knew* I hadn't clocked before. I eyed her as she moved, wondering when that had started. If it was from the fight, I felt like I would have noticed either at the warehouse or during the night following. I'd been rough with her, but I didn't think I'd gotten *that* rough. Maybe she needed a break...

"Wait, Tiff. I'm going to put you on speaker so you can relay all this to Craig." She said into the phone.

I arched a brow in another silent question. The last I knew, Victoria was still too angry with Tiffany to have called her, but she also desperately needed someone who wasn't us to talk to about everything going on. Part of me hoped that her reaching out to the girl meant she was forgiving her for making the same call any one of us would have made in her shoes. The day had been strange enough that her accepting Tiffany's olive branch wasn't making it any weirder.

"I'll tell you later." Victoria whispered, putting the phone on speaker and moving to lay it face up on the nearby counter. "Okay, you're on speaker."

"Well, as I was saying before, your Uncle Theo cornered me at the event dad was hosting. You know how he likes to shove his money in people's faces and rub elbows with the elite."

"Why did Theo corner you?" I asked in an attempt to redirect her to whatever it was Victoria thought I needed to hear.

"He doesn't know about my connection with the Golden Devils. As far as anyone on the outside is aware, I'm just an airheaded party girl, but. I'm also Tory's bestie. He thought I could get a message to you and since I'm such an *idiot*, he wasn't too worried about me knowing all kinds of details."

"Fuck's sake, Tiff, spit it out already. We get it, you're not as dumb as you let everyone think you are." Victoria huffed.

"Right. Sorry. So, it looks like Hugo is mixed up in some serious shit with the Bratva."

"Hugh? As in Victoria's father?" I asked, not sure she wanted Tiffany to know that Hugo wasn't actually her father.

"The one and only. Seems he was working on a federal case that should have been a slam dunk. Theo said the feds handed over a casefile that would have made any prosecutor's career. It ended up with a hung jury and nobody knows why, even the defense team seemed shocked their guy didn't go down. I couldn't say it to Theo, but from the sounds of it, he was an acceptable loss as a fall guy, but your dad screwed something up and he walked."

"Can you make any sense out of this with the info she gave us about Theo meeting the Russians?" Victoria asked me.

"Either Theo's lying or it's not something that makes sense, Bunny." I replied.

Tiffany snorted on the other end of the phone. "Bunny, that's cute. But no, Theo isn't lying about the case. That shit is public record; I don't need to be a hacker to google a court case and confirm what Theo said." She paused as the sound of background voices came over the phone. "Look, all I know is what Theo and Google told me, and that he wants to set up a meeting with Tory. He's probably banking on your curiosity and crazy intense sense of justice to get you to the meet."

"When and where?" Victoria asked immediately.

"No, Bunny. We need to discuss this with the others before we make any decisions about meeting Theo." I interjected.

She narrowed her eyes at me with a scowl. "If Theo was the fucking problem he wouldn't have gone to Tiffany to reach out. Candy didn't exactly seem the type to keep names to herself if it got her what she wanted, and Tiffany being a god damned gangster would have come up if Theo was the boogeyman here. Candy would have told him."

"I'm not saying we aren't going to take the meeting, Bunny. I'm saying we need to discuss it as a group. We need to think about the possibility that he is just pretending not to know about Tiffany's involvement with the Golden Devils. You have to admit it's weird as hell that he told her as much as he did about your father's Bratva case. He could have just said your dad was in some trouble and he wanted to meet so you could discuss it. That's all I would have said even *if* I thought Tiffany was just a dumbass ditz."

"Hey!" Tiffany sounded offended on the other end of the call before taking a breath. "He's right though, Tory. He didn't have any reason to tell me that stuff."

"I thought you wanted to be my friend again, Tiff. You're supposed to side with me on this shit." Victoria snapped.

"I *am* on your side, babe. The side that keeps your ass alive." Tiffany retorted. "If you weren't too trusting for your own damned good, you would have figured me out the second I got myself into the mess with Helen. If you'd questioned me even a little, I'd have cracked in a second. We wouldn't be *here* because you would have known and I'd have made sure you had the tools to keep yourself safe long before your harem of horny horsemen arrived on the scene. No offense, baldie, still love your cooking babes."

"Well, if we don't end up having to take you out too, I'm happy to do a brunch when all of this is over." I chuckled, shaking my head.

"Yaasss, bitch. We need brunch and mimosas." Tiffany cheered. "Listen, I've got to go. Talk to your harem about this meeting. Seriously, Tory. Don't just up and run off to meet Theo. If they decide it's worth the risk, you can call Theo for the deets."

"That sounds like Bitch Barbie," Leighton called as he strolled into the room. "Are we friends with her again?"

"Yes," Tiffany said.

"No." Victoria snarked at the same moment. "She's not agreeing with me so fuck that bitch."

"Aaaanyway, love you too bitch. Crazy Eyes, Baldie, Az-hole if you're there too. Seriously, gotta run. Tootles!" Tiffany's voice pitched high on the last word before the call disconnected.

"Ok, but for real, are we friends with her again?" Leighton asked, his brows dipped in confusion as he looked at Victoria for an answer.

"Maybe? I don't know. I'm still so fucking mad at her, but it was nice to just talk to my friend for a little while."

"About that…" I turned and motioned for everyone to move to the dining table and take a seat. "Theo wants a meeting with Victoria."

When Victoria sat, I turned her chair and knelt to push the leg of her pants up above her knee. I gave them a quick recap of the phone call as I inspected her knee, finding it swollen and with the same discoloring on her cheek and jaw.

"What's wrong?" Az said, leaning over as he took his seat, Leighton mimicking his motion from the other side of the table.

"She's got a limp, and bruising I don't remember seeing before so I wanted to check her out." I said, testing her range of motion and pressing gently on the swelling.

"It's about the right time frame for bruises to really start showing up after her and Leighton's hunt," Az replied, rubbing his chin thoughtfully before turning to Leighton. "You didn't mention her taking a tumble or anything to injure the knee, though."

"Because she didn't. Not when she was with me at least." Leighton replied, his eyes narrowed on Victoria as if he could pluck out all her secrets that way.

"Well…" She dragged out the word, shifting uncomfortably in her seat. "I mean, between Az and Craig, the Jackals weren't the only people who've been man-handling me recently. So…"

"I feel left out. This is so unfair." Leighton whined, tilting his head back dramatically. "I want to man-handle you, *Ma Petit*. I deserve it after today. I was a *good boy* and *felt feelings*." His eyes widened dramatically. "*Feelings, Ma Petit!*"

"Leighton… you do realize that when you're protective, or angry, or happily getting on everyone's nerves, that those *are* feelings, right?" I said, rolling my eyes with a grin.

"My *eyes leaked*, Craig! Stop trying to steal my damned thunder!" Leighton raised his voice, pointing his finger at me.

"See, that right there, that's an *emotion*." Az chuckling.

"Fucking traitors!" Leighton yelled, moving around the

table and scooping Victoria up and over his shoulder before I could stop him. "Let's show these assholes how they *should* have responded to my emotional growth, *Ma Petit!*"

He took off, bounding from the kitchen toward the stairs, Victoria's laughter trailing after him.

"Should we interfere or let him be?" Az smirked.

"I mean... we should at least make sure her leg is supported properly, right?" I grinned. "It's the only responsible thing to do, really."

"Right. Responsible." Az chuckled, standing from his chair. "Gotta be responsible. Though, I guess we'll have to see who gets there first to decide who gets that job."

I rubbed the back of my neck and hobbled around the side of the table. "I mean, I'm still pretty uncomfortable from having to squat down like that."

"That's fair—" Az started before I pushed him back into his chair and sped out of the kitchen as fast as I could put distance between us. "Oh, you mother *fucker!*" Az shouted, laughter in his voice.

I can't say I'd ever imagined racing Az to a foursome, but it felt right in the moment. After everything we'd been through recently, we all needed the moment of levity it brought. I just wished Joey would get his head straight before it was too late.

CHAPTER THIRTY EIGHT

Victoria

"I feel the need to say again that I don't like this." Az said, his hands gripping the steering wheel of the SUV so hard his knuckles were white.

"We talked about this," I sighed from where I sat in the back seat beside Leighton. Craig was silent in the passenger seat in front of me. "This is a public place, upscale enough we shouldn't see any Jackals, busy enough for the privacy we need for whatever Uncle Theo has to say. All three of you will be sitting in the hotel restaurant where you can see me and you've got men watching the exits. This could be our only chance to end all of this and stop running."

"I still don't have to like it," he muttered under his breath as he turned into the hotel's parking garage.

Easing to a stop for the valet, the guys quickly checked their weapons before Az unlocked the doors, and we slid out. Moving to my side, he slipped my arm through his and turned us toward the door that led from the garage into the hotel lobby. Craig fell into step behind us, and Leighton kissed my cheek before slipping into the shadows, intent on locating where the valet was parking the car. The guys had all agreed the vehicle would need to be checked over for explosives or other boobie traps before we left, and that required knowing where it was parked.

Once inside, I freed my arm from Az's hold and smoothed my hands over my dress. It was the same one I wore when the Golden Devils dropped Craig and me off at Rich's funeral, and the wave of sadness that washed over me when I put it on clung to me. I shoved it down, raising my head as I squared my shoulders and started toward the hotel restaurant. Craig and Az followed behind at a distance, just far enough not to draw attention to the fact I hadn't come alone. Uncle Theo had insisted they could come when we called him on one of the burners for the details of the meet, but the guys hadn't wanted to risk it being a trap to snatch all of us at once. Ultimately, they'd decided I would appear to come alone while they stayed close enough to intervene if I needed it.

"Welcome to Nova. Do you have a reservation?" The petite blond behind the hostess stand asked as soon as I pushed through the restaurant's glass doors.

"It's under Abrams." I smiled back.

She tapped something into the tablet in her hand and then smiled brightly. "Chantelle will take you to your table, Miss, you're the first to arrive."

Another petite blond stepped forward and motioned for me to follow her. My eyes scanned the place, taking in the sleek design and chic tables full of obviously wealthy patrons. The soft hum of conversation mixed with the clink of champagne glasses followed us to the table, where a dark-haired man in the restaurant uniform pulled out a chair for me before disappearing into the crowd.

"Can I start you with something to drink while you wait for your companion?" The waitress asked.

"Water is fine, thank you," I replied, shifting to watch Az and Craig be escorted to their own table by yet *another* petite blond. I started to think it was a requirement for front-end employees.

My waitress said something I missed, but I waved her away, adopting behaviors I had witnessed my entire life. My father hadn't been a bad man before my mother died, but he did have that arrogant way of ignoring and dismissing the help that seemed to be part and parcel of the upper class. My mother had always scolded him for it while insisting that I always be kind and gracious instead. I was too busy watching my men be escorted to a table that required me to shift my body away from the entrance to see them while *their* waitress giggled and pawed at them to give a damn about the lessons my mother had taught me. When Craig smiled back at the woman, I nearly snatched the knife from the prettily wrapped linen and marched over to stab her in the fucking eyeball. The sudden violent urge caused my head to rock back in shock, and I forced myself to turn back to sit in my chair properly and stare at the table while I waited for Theo.

My waitress appeared with my glass of water and I moved a hand from my lap to play with the stem of the crystal glass it was in. I refused to move my eyes from the table in case seeing the guy's waitress caused me to lose my shit. The sound of the chair across from me scooting back across the carpeted floor allowed me to let out a relieved breath. A hand grabbed mine off the stem of my water glass just as I looked up from the table.

"What are you doing here, Benson?" I demanded, narrowing my eyes at my ex.

He wore a tailored black suit, his dark hair slicked back in a pompadour. His lips were turned down in a sneer, and his hand tightened on mine.

"That's no way to speak to your fiance." He scoffed. "I'm here to take you home, where you belong. I've let you play house with those thugs so you could get that little rebellious streak out of your system, but I'm done waiting."

"I'm not going anywhere with you, Benson." I hissed, attempting to jerk my hand away from his.

His other hand shifted under the table, causing the tablecloth to sway and drawing my attention. "You will or I will use the gun I have in my hand here," he glanced down at the table to indicate his hidden hand, "to deal with your little boytoys. It's bad enough I had to go underground and pay for protection when they put out a hit on me, but we're in *my* territory now and I will not be cowed."

His hold on my hand tightened painfully, and I turned my head, my eyes instinctively seeking out my men for help. Leighton had arrived at some point, but there were also four strange men I didn't recognize sitting around the table with them. My guys looked completely enraged to the point I could swear I saw Az's jaw muscles ticking from where I sat.

Turning back to Benson, my eyes widened as I spotted Theo stepping up behind him. Benson mistook my surprise for shock over the men at the other table, and his lips quirked up in a slimy grin.

"We're going to leave now. If you go without a struggle I'll make sure your playthings don't suffer."

"I think you'll find she won't be going anywhere with you,"

Theo spoke, his hand clapping onto Benson's shoulder, causing him to startle enough that his hidden hand moved out from beneath the table and revealed he'd been lying about having a gun. "You, however, will be coming with us."

Benson's face grew red and mottled with anger. I could practically see the steam pouring out of his ears, and the mental image caused me to smirk before I remembered he had men holding my guys hostage at their table.

"Those aren't his men, Jellybean. They're mine. They spotted Benson entering the hotel and heading toward the restaurant with his little entourage and intercepted his men before they could get to your men. Turns out, they prefer guaranteed cash to a questionable check." Theo moved to stand at the side of the table, his hand still gripping Benson's shoulder as he used the other to casually flip open one side of his suit jacket, flashing a real gun in the process. "Now, I believe it's best we move this somewhere more private. If you two will be so kind as to come with me."

He hauled Benson from his chair, positioning himself to walk beside him as his free hand slipped the pistol free and pressed it into Benson's side. I turned to look for my guys; they were still seated at their table, anger clear as day on their faces as they watched me.

"Your men will be along behind us, Jellybean." Theo said. "Come along now."

Not sure what else to do, I stood and followed as Theo led us from the restaurant to an elevator in the main lobby. He shoved Benson against the back wall as soon as the doors slid closed, keeping the gun aimed at him as he pulled out a key card and swiped it to take us to the penthouse. None of us spoke until we stepped out of the elevator into the chic living room area the doors had opened into.

"Have a seat, both of you." Theo ordered. "Would you like something to drink, Jellybean?"

"No." I replied, shaking my head as I eased around him toward the closest couch. "I want you to tell me what the hell is going on."

"As do I." Benson snapped.

"You aren't owed anything except a bullet between the eyes, Benson." Theo spat before turning to me with a softer expression. "You, however, deserve answers and I will give them to you just as soon as your men arrive."

As if on cue, the elevator doors slid open, and Craig, Leighton, and Az stepped into the penthouse with wary expressions on their faces. Unable to stop, I shot off the couch and launched myself into Az's arms.

"You're alright, Love. We've got you." He murmured, his hands rubbing soothing patterns across my back.

"I didn't know what else to do when I saw the men at your table, so I came with him when he told me too."

"It's okay, you did the right thing." Az assured me before giving his attention to Theo. "Would you like to explain to me why you had five men hold us at our table with guns before they shoved us into the elevator and sent us up here to you?"

"This is absolutely ludicrous!" Benson shouted, lurching from his chair and starting toward where I stood in Az's arms. "Not only have you threatened me with a gun, you've brought the same men that put a price on my head straight to me, and now they're pawing all over my woman–"

The sound of a single shot caused me to jump and left my ears ringing momentarily. I blinked up at Az in confusion and then turned around in his arms to find Benson clutching his chest, his mouth gaping open in horror.

"I would apologize for not being a good enough shot to make this quick, but after what you did to my daughter, you deserve to suffer." Theo said calmly as he stalked toward Benson with the gun still in his outstretched hand.

Theo fired another shot, causing Benson to jolt backward before falling to his knees. Benson's free hand went to his abdomen, where blood was slowly blooming through his white button-down shirt. Another loud pop and Benson's shoulder jerked backward, another and he fell completely over. Theo moved until he stood directly over Benson. Then he squatted down, pressing the gun to Benson's temple. My eyes squeezed shut at the same time as Theo's finger squeezed the trigger.

"As much as I enjoyed seeing that fucker get what he deserved, I believe you have some explaining to do." Az said, handing me off to Craig behind him.

"Yes, well, why don't we adjourn to the kitchen so we don't

have to stare at the mess while I explain? I'm sure we could all use a drink after that anyway." Theo replied.

I kept my eyes squeezed shut, allowing Craig to lead me from the living room. I didn't open them until he whispered in my ear that we were in the kitchen, just as he settled me on a barstool at the island counter.

"Where would you like me to start?" Theo asked, pouring himself a glass of what appeared to be scotch.

"I know you had an affair with my mother and that my father isn't my father." The words were out of my mouth before I could stop them.

Theo froze momentarily before sitting the crystal bottle of liquor beside his glass and pinning me with his gaze. "I did, and he isn't. I'm your father."

"Bullshit. I saw the paternity tests. Neither of you are my father."

Theo sighed heavily. "Your mother paid to have the results falsified. Hugo had already found out about the affair and she was afraid of what he would do if he knew the truth. I think she was afraid of what *I* would do if I had known."

"I–" Theo held up a hand, silencing me before he slipped from the kitchen. I looked at the guys, who all looked just as flabbergasted as I did.

"Here," Theo spoke when he returned a few minutes later. Striding to the island, he laid a file folder before me. "This should be enough to prove I'm telling the truth."

I opened the folder and carefully looked over the information inside. There was a paternity test from a different company with an address well outside Sacona. It was dated prior to the one that Joey had given me, and it stated without a doubt that Theo was my father. Flipping to the next page, I found a bank statement, with a large deposit highlighted, from just a few days before the date on the results from my father's house. Making a note of the name on the bank statement, I flipped to the next page and found the answer to the question I hadn't yet asked. There was an employment record for the same name as the bank statement from the testing facility.

"All I had to do was follow the money." Theo spoke, flipping to the last page in the folder. "This is a bank account that belonged to your mother. The highlighted line is a transfer out of the account for the same amount as was deposited to the technician."

"You've known my entire life?" I asked.

"Yes," Theo answered.

"So, why work with the Russians, why try to kill me? I don't understand." Nothing made any sense, and I was left feeling off-kilter as I tried to wrap my mind around Theo being my father *and* trying to harm me.

Theo's head reared back as if I'd slapped him. "Allow me to disabuse you of this notion that I've tried to kill you. I would *never* do anything to harm you. That's why I never spoke up about who I really am to you. It's why I worked so hard to maintain a friendship and working partnership with Hugo, so I could stay close to you in case you ever needed me. I am absolutely *not* working with the Russians."

"How do you explain the intel we found that says you are?" Az interjected, reaching into his suit jacket and producing a photo of Theo and the Russian mobster.

I forced myself to shove everything I was feeling aside to focus on the moment at hand. I couldn't let the news of my paternity derail us from the reason we were here. We needed answers; there would be time for me to freak out later when we were back at the Innocenti's.

"That is Misha Antonov," Theo replied, tapping the photo. "He's FBI and my contact for passing information about Hugo's dealings with the Petrov family."

"We looked into this man and his name is Sergei Kumarin, not Misha Antonov." Craig spoke, causing Theo to look at him and frown.

"He most assuredly is not." Theo retorted. "I don't know all the details, but I do know that he has been undercover with the Petrov's for quite some time now. When Hugo got mixed up with them, he contacted me under the guise of wanting to bring me onboard as well. Instead, I've been feeding him everything I can get my hands on from Hugo's interactions with the Petrov's. I'll give you his card before you leave and you can call him yourself."

"Let's say for argument's sake, that we believe you. How do you explain your emails with Rinaldo Marino? You were offering him some sort of gift." Az asked.

Theo frowned, his brows drawing down in a way I was familiar with. His hand moved to rub his chin, the final sign that he was sorting through his memory for the name. After a moment, his eyes widened. "Oh! I don't know how I didn't make the connection when his name was released after the situation at the manor. He had made quite a large donation to the youth center in exchange for a meeting with Victoria. Fairly standard stuff. He and about twenty others received the same, along with a Rolex as a thank you."

"Oh, oh shit! That's right! We did send out Rolexes the last fundraising round." I said. "I can't believe I didn't recall that at the time."

"Not your fault, *Ma Petit.* You were under a lot of stress at the time." Leighton piped in. He'd been so silent the entire time I'd nearly forgotten he was there.

"What about the men downstairs?" Az asked. I could tell from the look on his face he was trying to process all the information Theo had thrown at us.

"Private security. While I trust the feds to do their job, I wanted to take extra precautions. The last bit of information I handed over gave me the impression that the Russians are working with the Jackals. Hugo had notes about them asking him to take on a case for one of them and they wanted the guy to walk."

"Why use Tiffany to get to me? Why not call one of the guys?" I asked, unsure what to make of anything he'd said.

"Would any of you have answered if I had?" Theo sounded defeated.

"You didn't have to tell her anything about Hugo's involvement with the Russians when you asked her to have Victoria meet with you." Az drawled.

Theo moved around the island, stepping between me and an empty barstool. "Do you know what Tiffany is involved in?"

"What?" I asked, my gaze shooting to meet his.

"I needed to know she was still loyal to you. She's been working for Helen for three years now, I *had* to be sure. If she hadn't told you everything I said, I'd be telling you not to trust her."

"What do you know?" Az asked as I studied Theo's face for any signs of deceit.

"Helen is my estranged sister. We haven't spoken since she decided to step into her grandmother's role, but I've kept tabs on her movements and I knew within weeks that Tiffany had gotten involved with Helen's gang."

"Why didn't that come up when I looked into you?" Craig demanded.

"Helen is my half sister. My father never formally acknowledged her, not even to sign her birth certificate. I only knew about her because my mother told me." Theo shrugged. "There wouldn't be anything to find connecting us."

The trill of a cell phone rang out, and Leighton startled, reaching into his pocket to retrieve his phone. His eyes narrowed at what he saw on the screen before he signaled that he was stepping from the room, answering the call just as he strolled out of the kitchen.

"This is all... a lot to process." I muttered.

Theo reached out and took my hand gently in his. "I know it's probably a shock to find out that I'm your father, but I promise you, Jellybean, I'd never do anything to hurt you. Everything I've done has been to try and keep you safe. If you don't believe anything else I've told you, believe that."

"I..." the words cut off in my throat. I didn't know what to think, let alone how to respond.

"We'll look into everything you've told us. If we can confirm it, then we'll leave it up to Victoria to decide how to proceed. If not..." Az shrugged, letting his words trail off to leave their implications hanging in the air.

"We need to leave. Now." Leighton barked from the kitchen doorway, his face twisted into an enraged scowl.

"What about the body?" Craig asked.

"Don't worry about it. I'll call Misha to help me handle it." Theo answered, pulling a card from the pocket inside his suit jacket and holding it out to Az. "This is his card. He'll confirm everything I've told you."

Theo pulled me to my feet and wrapped me in a hug before Craig pulled me away. The guys fell into position around me in a way that kept me from seeing Benson's body as they hustled us back to the penthouse elevator. Leighton checked the car over quickly once the valet brought it to us before rushing us into it.

"What the hell is your problem, Leighton?" Az snapped from the driver's seat as he pulled into traffic.

"Just get us the fuck back to the Innocenti's." Leighton snapped before clenching his jaw so tightly I was sure his teeth were going to crack. "I've got a promise to keep."

CHAPTER THIRTY NINE

Joey

I paced the living room floor, waiting for the guys to return. They'd left with Victoria a few hours before, not even bothering to tell me where they were headed. I'd decided in the time they'd been gone that I would force them to deal with me. To explain to me why I was being cut out of my own damned organization. It was time they chose me or that fucking viper who'd sank her fangs in them. The front door opened with a bang, causing my head to snap in that direction. My eyes narrowed on Leighton as he stalked inside, chest heaving like he was half a second away from losing his shit.

"What the fuck, dude?" I demanded. "Have some fucking respect for my parent's house."

"You!" He bellowed, pointing his finger at me as he stormed closer. "I fucking told you the next time you fucked with her, I was going to fucking kill you."

"What the hell are you talking about? What did that fucking viper say to you?" I shouted back.

Leighton moved in close, grabbing fistfuls of my shirt and pulling me closer so that we were practically nose to nose. "*She* didn't tell me shit. Tiffany called me while we were dealing with Theo and filled me in on your little trip to the gun range. I know all about how you assaulted my. Fucking. Woman."

"Is that what she said?" I shot back, shoving him backward a step, but not far enough for him to lose his grip on my shirt. "She wanted it. She practically begged me for it."

Leighton removed one hand from my shirt and hit me in the mouth. My head jerked back under the impact, and I tasted blood.

In the time it took me to straighten back up, he'd tightened his grip on my shirt and was forcing me backward through the living room toward the back door.

"Get the fuck off me, Leighton." I snapped, shoving at him. I barely noticed the others following after him as I struggled to keep my balance and break free of his hold.

"Leighton." Az called after us.

Leighton snarled and forced me backward faster. I stumbled over my feet as the kitchen whizzed by in a blur. With a final hard shove, my back slammed against the wooden door, my head making a loud thunk as it connected with the wood. Leighton let go of me long enough to reach down and turn the handle. I took the opening to swing a fist at him, but the fucker ducked just in time. His shoulder slammed into my abdomen, and suddenly, we were falling. We landed in a heap on the grass, the air forced out of me under his weight.

"I don't want to fight you, Leighton." I yelled, wrapping my legs and one arm around him as I used the other to try and roll us over. "Not over *her*. She's not fucking worth it."

Leighton reared back, animalistic snarls and growls spilling from his lips as he slammed his head forward into mine. Pain bloomed in my face, whiting out my vision for just a moment following the sickening crack of my nose breaking. Leighton pulled back again, and I unwrapped my legs from his body, planting them on the ground to help me throw him off with my hips.

I scrambled to my feet, holding one hand out as he circled me. The other moved to my back, checking that my gun was still tucked in my jeans. It wasn't loaded, but it might act as a deterrent if Leighton couldn't get control of himself on his own.

"He'd be ashamed of you." Leighton snarled, circling around me as he looked for an opening to attack again.

That felt worse than the throbbing in my nose. Everyone seemed so sure that if I were right, Rich would have already known that. He would have already dealt with it, but he loved her instead. I wanted to stop and demand he explain his logic to me so I had something solid to argue against. Some way to silence that little voice in the back of my head that kept screaming I'd been an idiot and ruined the best thing that ever happened to me.

Instead, I turned with him, keeping him in my line of sight. I'd seen Leighton at his worst, but in all the time I'd known him, I'd never seen him look so rabid. Blood dripped from his forehead; whether it was his or mine, I couldn't say. His eyes looked black from how wide his pupils had blown; he snapped his bared teeth at me, a clear threat.

"Leighton, stop it!" I heard *her* call out. It was enough to distract me as I looked over my shoulder toward the house to glare at her.

It felt like a freight train ran straight through my middle as Leighton slammed into my stomach. The world shifted, and I flung out my fists, aiming for his arms in the hopes of making him drop me. Leighton didn't flinch as they made contact, ignoring blow after blow until he slammed me into the ground on my back. He dove on top of me, and I brought my hands up to protect my face as he threw a flurry of punches. I could hear Az and Craig calling out, their voices getting closer before one of them pulled Leighton back just enough for me to go on the attack.

As we fought and rolled across the backyard, we became a dizzying ball of fists, elbows, and feet. I'd managed to split Leighton's eye and land a punishing blow to his ribs, but he was so far gone to his rage that he didn't seem to feel any of it. I, on the other hand, felt it all. Every split of my skin, every creak of bone as he tried to break me apart with his bare hands. He kept me on my back, making it impossible to get to my gun, or else I'd have pulled it to get him to stop.

"That's enough!" Az's voice boomed out over the yard.

Leighton's bloodied face was jerked away from my field of vision, and I scrambled upright. Both Craig and Az were struggling to hold him back, their arms straining around his body as he fought to get to me again. Az's eyebrow was split open, and I could only assume Leighton had managed to hit him during our tussle.

"Go inside, Joey." Az called, not taking his eyes off Leighton. "Ice your injuries and then lock yourself in your room so we can get him calm."

I managed to get myself to my feet, wrapping an arm around my ribs as I spit a glob of blood on the ground. There were streaks of blood all across my parents' green grass. Swaying slightly, I made my way inside, using the walls to hold myself up once I'd made it through the door. My vision blurred as I lurched toward the fridge to grab some ice from the freezer.

"Here, let me help." I jumped at the sound of her voice, sending a wave of nausea through me.

"Go the fuck away, Victoria."

"Please, Joey, you're hurt. Just let me help."

I scoffed, easing myself over to grab some paper towels from the counter before digging into the freezer for the ice.

"Will you at least tell me what happened? Why did Leighton go after you like that?" She asked, moving to lean on the counter beside me.

I wrapped a handful of ice in the paper towels and then pressed them to my nose before looking at her. To anyone else, she would appear the picture of concern. Her brows were dipped in manufactured worry, and her wide eyes shone with unshed tears.

"You know exactly what set him off, Viper." I scoffed before wincing at the pain it sent lancing through my head.

"Please, Joey. Just talk to me. Don't shut me out like this."

Jerking the ice away from my face, I glared at her. "Stop, Victoria. Just fucking stop. Stop trying to fix things for us, stop following me like a wounded animal. Stop trying to make it better. You *can't* make it better! Richard is *dead*, and it's your fucking fault. None of this would have happened if not for you. He even tried to warn us. If what just happened with Leighton is any indication, you've already cost me the rest of my brothers. I'm not going to let you suck me back in just so you can put the rest of us six feet under. Maybe the kindest thing for all of us is to kill you before you get the fucking chance!" My hand slipped to my back, pulling the unloaded gun from my waistband before I pressed the muzzle against her forehead.

Victoria went so still I could barely tell she was still breathing. Her jaw tensed, and then determination filled her eyes. "If you can, then do it. But I don't think you will, because I know that *my* Joey is still in there."

Pain shot through my jaw, and my head rocked to the side; Victoria gasped in horror just as my father's hands went under my arms to keep me upright. The gun that had been in my hand fell to the floor and skittered across the linoleum.

"Go get some air, little lady. I'll handle my *son*." My father ordered, anger and disappointment painting his features.

My father and I stared at each other as we listened to Victoria's footsteps retreat. I barely caught Craig's voice telling her to take a burner and then the ring of his phone before he answered.

"You hit me." I said quietly.

"You held a gun to an innocent young woman's head and threatened to kill her. A single punch is the least of what you deserve for that." My father replied.

"She's—"

"Rich used his *dying* breath to tell that woman he loved her. What do you think he'd do if he found out you were treating the woman he loved this way over something she had *no* control over?" My father demanded. "You're damned lucky your mother isn't here to witness any of this. It would kill her to know what you've done. You need to get yourself straight and crawl on your knees and beg that girl's forgiveness."

"I'm not begging her for *shit!*" I hissed.

My father shook me hard one time. "This damned vendetta you've got is done. If I have to have you locked up so you can get yourself straight, I will. We tried giving you space to work this out on your own, but you're letting your grief twist you into a man I don't recognize. Right now, you're *not* my son."

"I—" I started, but as soon as I opened my mouth, it was like my words wouldn't come out. "I'm just trying to keep you all safe. Victoria—" I whimpered, tears burning my eyes as they fought to break free over my father's words.

My father let out a heavy sigh and let his head hang between us as he continued to hold me under the arms. "You're wrong, son. I don't know why you refuse to see it, but you're wrong. I know somewhere under all that anger you're still you. I just don't know how to help you dig your way back to us."

I gently pulled free of my father's hold as my lips turned down in a sad smile. "This is who I am without him, Pop."

My father's face crumpled in a way I hadn't seen since Rich's funeral, but before either of us could say anything else, the door slammed open so hard it bounced off the wall.

"We need to go, now!" Craig nearly shouted, panic written all over his face.

"What? Why? Did you assholes not get Leighton calmed down or something?" I frowned.

"No. Victoria is walking to the diner, I've been on video call with her the whole time. There's a black van with tinted windows. It's been behind her, slow enough to be suspicious." He said in a rush, and my heart punched my ribs as he shoved the phone at me. Victoria's face filled the screen, her expression filled with fear that she was barely masking. I could see her trying to control her breathing despite the image jolting and shaky as she walked.

"They're following me..." She said in a low voice.

A scream ripped from her throat so sharp it sliced straight through my chest. Then the phone hit the ground with a crack, giving us a tilted, broken view of the sidewalk and a pair of scuffling feet. Victoria's stance told us she was trying to defend herself, but more boots entered the picture.

"Quit fucking around Victoria. Whatever this ploy is, you can drop it now," I snapped, refusing to believe this was anything other than a setup.

She didn't answer. Craig rushed around me, presumably to grab the others, as I watched six men that I could see surround her. She dropped into a defensive stance before striking out, only to take a hit to her jaw so hard her head rocked back. My chest tightened at the sight. I knew just how bad that hit would have hurt. The voice in my head was screaming at me that this was *real*. She took another hit to her ribs and doubled over with a pained cry.

"Oh fuck, no, no, no." the words tumbled out. "This isn't... it can't be.. She's supposed to be the bad guy. Fuck! Fuck! No. VICTORIA! FIGHT BACK!"

I watched, horror slowly washing over me as she struggled to use everything the others had taught her, only to be met with a flurry of fists. I couldn't deny it any longer, not with the beating she was taking; this was real. I'd been wrong. So fucking wrong, and she was being hurt while I could only watch. All because I'd been so damned determined to be wrong.

Another set of boots moved closer to the screen as her attackers wrestled her off her feet. I could barely hear their murmured words over her screams before a foot came rushing forward, stomping her phone and causing the screen to go black.

"Victoria!" I shouted, shaking the phone as if somehow I could get the image to come back. "Answer me!" Nothing. "Victoria! Answer me, god damn it!" Nothing happened, no response—just a dead, black screen and silence.

The walls of the room seemed to collapse inward, the air draining from my lungs, my body locking up with a cold, sick fear I had never felt before. This wasn't staged; this wasn't a bit or performance. This was *real*. It repeated in my head like a sick chant. I'd just watched the woman I loved, the woman my brother had loved, get beaten and kidnapped. And it was real. She was gone. And the last thing I'd done—

Oh god, the last thing I'd done was threaten her with a fucking *gun* and tell her she was better off dead. It might have been unloaded, but that didn't change what it would have been in her eyes. It was a threat. I'd hurt her, belittled her, made her cry... I'd *assaulted* her.

I crumpled forward, choking on a sound I couldn't control, the ground giving way beneath me as I hit my knees. What if the last thing she thought of me was that I hated her? I deserved everything Leighton had done. Worse, even. I should let him finish the job.

But... they'd need guns to get her back. They'd need someone behind a trigger to make them pay for every bruise they put on her skin, every pained or fearful whimper that left her lips. I was a monster, but I'm still *her* monster even if I had been lost and blind for a while. I was going to do whatever it took to get her back, and once she was home and I knew she was safe, I'd let her decide how to punish me. Even if it meant letting Leighton finish the job.

CHAPTER FORTY

Victoria

The cold from the hard concrete seeped through my jeans, causing me to shiver. The only warmth wherever I was came from my breath in the burlap sack over my head. My chest and shoulders felt strained, and my wrists burned from the rope that held them behind my back. Everything ached.

I'd used everything the guys had taught me to try and get away from the men who'd ambushed me on my way to the diner. The blacked-out van finally pulled up behind me in the curve. It had been creeping along behind me for several minutes before that, but the six men launching themselves out of the sliding door at me without the van ever stopping took me by surprise.

I just barely managed to dodge being taken to the ground when they leaped at me, but I didn't hesitate, letting the phone drop to the ground so I could defend myself. I fought back with everything I had, all the training the guys had put me through coming to me like second nature. My attackers hadn't seemed to care about whether or not they injured me, their fists landing blows that left my ribs feeling bruised, my lip busted open again, and one eye swollen shut. They'd muscled me into the back of the van, using their fists to try and subdue me as I continued to fight back. One of them landed a blow to my head that knocked me unconscious just as the van peeled away. When I woke up, I was here—kneeling on cold, hard concrete, a sack over my head, and silence aside from a steady drip of water somewhere behind me.

It felt like I'd been here for hours when the sound of multiple footsteps reached my ears. The rattle of a metal door sliding open followed, and I could tell by the way the air moved that at least two people had moved to stand behind me. My head jerked back as the burlap sack was pulled away, scratching my face. Overhead lights blinded me, and I blinked against the sudden brightness, trying to adjust.

The sound of a throat clearing snapped my attention to the person standing before me. I let my eyes move from their polished boots, up their body, and settling on their face. Shock and recognition warred for dominance inside me, and I said the only thing I could as I looked into the face of the person who'd been after me all along.

"You."

To be continued...

AFTERWORD

Wow, that was heavy. We knew we were going to go to some dark places dealing with the grief that Victoria and each of the guys were dealing with over the loss of Rich, but as the author in our duo who is typically gleeful about breaking your hearts, I was surprised at just how stripped raw pieces of this left me. Each of the character's breakdowns was an ode to our own losses and grief, but Joey's spiral is really what tore me wide open. It took me several days after completing the draft to recover from the emotional wreck his journey left me.

Grief can twist a person into someone they wouldn't recognize. It can drive them to a place that seems like insanity to others as they struggle to find anything to help them cope. That was the journey we planned for Joey. We wanted to push him to the brink of unforgivable, but I wasn't prepared for how devastating it was to do that. Sure, I expected C.M. to cry, and rage, and give me hell for the plan I convinced her to follow for him. If you've followed us on socials or talked to us, you know that's a given just as much as my thoroughly non-apologetic attitude toward absolutely breaking your hearts. But this one got to me. Now it's time for me to put a jar of my own tears on the shelf alongside yours and begin the work of redeeming him in the final book.

I won't promise that there won't be parts of J is For Justified that absolutely destroy you. That is, afterall, something I love to do to our readers. I will, however, promise that the last book in this journey won't have the same pain soaked pages as this one did, and you will get to our happily ever after. After all the suffering we've put you through, you deserve a happy ending.

XOXO,
Zoe

WHERE TO FIND US!

Website:
https://www.shatteredsirens.com/

Newsletter:
http://eepurl.com/i7jMas

Instagram:
https://www.instagram.com/shattered_sirens

Facebook:
https://www.facebook.com/groups/1772403106844917

BOOKS IN THIS SERIES

The Horsemen Series

A Is For Arson

L Is For Larceny

C Is For Corruption

J Is For Justified (Pre-Order Available!)

ABOUT THE AUTHOR

Zoe Dunn

Zoe Dunn is an American author who has been passionate about writing since childhood. With a foundation rooted in her love of horror and suspense, Zoe brings a Gothic-inspired edge to her romance novels, blending atmospheric storytelling with compelling character arcs.
Known for her skillful misdirection and unexpected twists, Zoe takes readers on journeys where love blossoms amid shadow and uncertainty. Her work showcases her ability to balance darkness and romance, creating narratives that keep readers eagerly turning the page. Zoe strives to craft intricate, immersive tales where passion, tension, and resilience take center stage, making her stories both unforgettable and deeply engaging.

BOOKS BY THIS AUTHOR

Meddling Memaws

The Wolf's Bite

ABOUT THE AUTHOR

C.m. Bowen

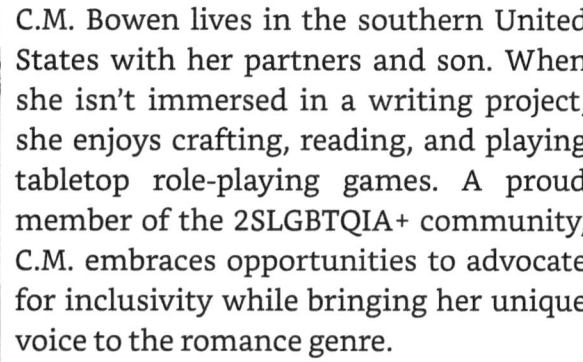 C.M. Bowen lives in the southern United States with her partners and son. When she isn't immersed in a writing project, she enjoys crafting, reading, and playing tabletop role-playing games. A proud member of the 2SLGBTQIA+ community, C.M. embraces opportunities to advocate for inclusivity while bringing her unique voice to the romance genre.

C.M. has been writing since adolescence, drawing inspiration from her early love of fantasy and later transitioning into paranormal romance. After attending university, she chose to pursue writing professionally, finding her place as both a fiction editor and author. C.M. specializes in romance, focusing on emotional depth and spice, always eager to explore new sub-genres and push creative boundaries.

BOOKS BY THIS AUTHOR

The Devil Inside

The Prince's Game

The Prince's Kiss

www.ingramcontent.com/pod-product-compliance
Lightning Source LLC
Chambersburg PA
CBHW061514020726
47502CB00006B/2072